# SHATTERING BOUNDARIES

B.J. KURTZ

Shattering Boundaries
Copyright © 2018 BJ Kurtz
Printed in the United States of America

All rights reserved.
No part of this publication may be reproduced, stored in a retrieval system, or transmitted, in any form or by any means, electronic, mechanical, photocopying, recording, or otherwise, without the written permission of the author.

\* \* \* \* \*

This book is a work of fiction. Places, events, and situations in this book are purely fictional and any resemblance to actual persons, living or dead, is coincidental

\* \* \* \* \*

Cover design by Adam Kurtz

Editing by Rose Ciccarelli & Jeanne Cadeau

Formatted by Debora Lewis arenapublishing.org

*For my students,
who inspire me every day.*

## Acknowledgments

With every book, I am reminded that there are a lot of people who help me along the way. Their love and support for my dream of having a writing career is what keeps me writing. Now, with my sixth book finished, I want to take a moment and thank those who make it all possible.

First, I'd like to thank my parents. You were the first to encourage me, and you have never faltered in your belief that I and my writing have value. You consistently influence my life both in what you say, but also in how you live yours. Your encouragement gets me through the darkest of days and allows me someone who can share in my successes. You are my rock, and I cannot thank you enough.

I want to thank my brother, Adam, whose talent always amazes me. This is my dream, and yet you have devoted your skill to help me continue. I could not do this without you and I am forever grateful that you continue to support me with your art, your visions, and your love.

I'd like to thank my beta readers, including Angela Garcia and my mother. Yours are the first eyes to ever see my novels. You provide me with validation when I need it. You catch my haunting homophones and strange word choices. You push me to be better while not tearing me down. Most of all, you are honest with me when there is something that needs tweaking. You help me grow while still being dedicated fans, and I cannot thank you enough for all you do.

I'd like to thank Kristy Reynolds and Casi Ruffo. I could not have built a character like Chloe without you. The hours you spent with me discussing the darkest aspects of child upbringing helped me to create characters that I am so proud of. You helped me to tell a story of people who can overcome a world that defines us by our flaws. I could not have written this story without you. I thank you both for your wisdom as well as your service to countless kids growing up with dark lives. It is a tough job, but you both do it with grace and love.

I'd like to thank my editors Rose Ciccarelli and Jeanne Cadeau. I am lucky to have found such gems as you. You bring quality to my work. I have grown as a writer because of you both. With your help, I am able to produce something that I am proud to share with the world. Thank you to my formatter Debora Lewis for turning my words into something I can publish and share. Thank you to my website guru, Valerie Lancaster. All of you make this dream of independent publishing possible. I would not be able to do this without you all.

Thank you to Erica for your poem to open the novel. It is perfect. You are a bright star and I was blessed to get to know you in my classroom. It is a privilege to see you blossom into a beautiful person. Keep writing and pursuing your dream!

I'd like to end by thanking my fans. I love sharing these worlds with you, and seeing the joy in your eyes when a new book comes out. It really makes the whole experience of writing come alive for me. I truly feel my purpose is to share these ideas to both entertain, but hopefully also to inspire you all. Please continue to share in this experience with me, to share your joy and your support. You keep me writing, and I will do so as long as you let me.

Finally, to the students I see every day. Life deals some of us unfair cards, but I have watched children overcome so many obstacles to achieve such great things. You inspire me. I am proud of you all, and blessed to say I shared a small chapter in your world. May you continue to battle against the darkness that tries to take our happiness. And may you always know that—even if others say you are flawed—you have value here in this world.

## DARKNESS

It's inside all of us—threatening to overtake.
Even the brightest of smile, shown on the outside,
may not be real.
May not come from within.

He dwells in the past,
using our memories, actions we'd like to forget
to haunt us.
To remind us of our mistakes.

She uses the labels others throw at us,
to do more damage than anything,
we could do to ourselves.
Steering her ship, more than our own.

They sustain their stereotypes,
their ideas of in or out,
of what is or isn't acceptable
with or without our permission.

Will we have what it takes?
To tear this veil of darkness to the ground?
To rise up, as individuals, as humans, as one?
To let the light break through?

To overcome?

~ Erica Zaborac

# One

The tips of her hair practically glowed in the sun's rays creeping through the window. The hairstylist called it lime-green. It certainly wasn't a color one could buy in the store. Two-inch tips, that's all her aunt would agree to. She counted herself lucky to get that, but did push the boundaries and dyed her bangs as well. It's not like the green was too much of a shock. There was more drama when she dyed her blond hair black in the fall. She twirled a strand of hair around between her fingers, watching the color shimmer in the sunlight.

"A-hem," a feminine voice cut through her examination. "Ms. Parker?"

Chloe knew refusing to look up would confirm what her aunt believed... that there was a problem. *Houston, we have a problem.* Chloe almost laughed at the movie reference. They had watched *Apollo 13* in her American History class. It was pretty good, at least on the academic-movie scale. Chloe sighed, letting the strand of hair go. It drifted back to her chest.

She looked up. The office was meant to look like a living room. Well, maybe more like the living room of a very nerdy family without a TV. Who would live without a TV? Some kid with a worse childhood than hers. Okay, maybe lacking a TV wasn't as bad as her childhood. Yet no amount of fluffy pillow, houseplant, and floral print could hide the stale atmosphere of an office.

A boxy desk stood in the corner, surrounded by degrees and awards hanging on the wall. Large bookshelves lined the wall filled with the brightest ideas in academia. Most titles were along the lines of "diagnosing child disorders" or "the adolescent personality." Disorder, condition, mental illness. As a child, these words had jumped out at her… as they did again. Words of judgment. Words that confirmed there was something wrong with her.

The psychologist had aged over the years, silver sparkling in the brown hair just brushing her shoulders. She had new glasses. Got them just two years ago. That was what happened when adults turned a certain age. They got glasses and their eyes wrinkled. Dr. Lewis had those wrinkles around her eyes, along with frown lines cutting against her face. She really shouldn't frown so much.

Dr. Lewis placed her notepad on her lap and leaned forward. "Chloe, you seem distant today."

Distant. That was a good word. Not too critical, but certainly indicating there was a problem.

"I think you'd feel better if you'd tell me about the accident."

Brakes screeching, metal smashing, glass shattering. All these sounds plagued her ears. Much too loud for a memory—but, then again, her memories always were. "Nothing to tell," Chloe said with a shrug. "A minor fender-bender. No big deal."

Dr. Lewis had this look during these sessions. It reminded Chloe of superheroes who could shoot lasers from their eyes. Her lasers were not visible red lines across the room. They were hidden. And instead of cutting through objects, they cut into stories, exposing the lies underneath.

Dr. Lewis adjusted her glasses and sat back. She glanced at her notes for only a moment, but it made Chloe want to sink further into the soft cushions. That was Dr. Lewis' first weapon in this room. The comfy couch designed to make her drop her guard.

How much was written in that file? Chloe Parker. Age 16. Or maybe it had the age when she had started coming. Five. Then there were the diagnoses. Eating disorder. Ten percent PTSD, now at a ten percent disability rating. Slight case of reactive attachment, especially as a child. How many years were in the binder? How many memories and disorders?

She had gotten better. Did they purge the file hoping she was cured? Did they summarize her history and begin again today? That's what this was about: determining if she had relapsed. Determining if Dr. Lewis needed to add classifications to her disorders and increase the number of visits.

"Your aunt tells me your grades have dropped."

"They only dropped to C's," she refuted before Dr. Lewis finished her sentence. "You know how she is. Always worrying. But, there's a quiz this week and a project still. My grades will go back up. Besides, I thought C's were good."

Dr. Lewis nodded. "And Algebra Two?"

Chloe couldn't help but cringe. Her one D. The whole reason she was sitting in this stupid office. She wanted to say Mr. Barnes was an egotistical jerk who didn't understand there was more to life than x's and graph analysis. She wanted to say no one should be expected to listen to his voice drone on and on about asymptotes and parabolas for an entire hour. It was torture. His refusal to take her late assignment on Monday was what caused this. And she'd bet her allowance he added that zero in faster than any other grade this semester. But no adult wanted to hear this. They were *excuses*. Like that was a bad thing. And with her, any little change meant catastrophe. She couldn't blame them. Not really. Not with what she did as a child those first few years with her aunt.

So, instead of unleashing a perfectly good explanation, Chloe settled on, "It was one grade. I can go to tutoring. And my friend, Abby, she's really good at math." *Just don't check her grades.*

"And the nightmares? How are they?"

Chloe tried not to glare at her. Dr. Lewis knew too many secrets. That's what adults did. They listened to small children too stupid to realize everyone had an agenda. They listened, took in every revealed secret, and never forgot. Chloe let the clock behind her tick against the silence.

What was she supposed to say to that? She could lie. She could deny the dark figure from her childhood was back, standing in the shadow of every dream. His features were darkened except for the masquerade mask. Orange and red beads plastered around the eyes, a long beak arching in front. Sharply tipped. The mask glowed in the darkness. That's how she knew he was there. That, and the smell. Most would call it pleasant. Most did not know what he was like.

If Chloe denied his return, any other spin would fall apart. She couldn't lie. Not on this. Dr. Lewis never asked a question she didn't already know the answer to. It took Chloe years to figure that out. But once she did, she realized these lovely little talks were not about sharing and opening up. They were about judging responses and actions. Dr. Lewis evaluated them and then stood in a room with other adults to develop a proper course of action. No, adults talked. Above all else, this was the most valuable information any child could learn. Adults always talked, so stories must be developed to compensate.

Chloe sighed. So a little truth with a spin. But what was the spin? "Okay," Chloe said. She tried to relax her straight back. Appear less defensive: that was the key to this working. "I'm not going to lie. The accident was—*screeching, crunching, a shadowed man*—upsetting. I mean, it was my first time driving with my license. Kaitlin was in the car with me. It was really more embarrassing than anything else, you know?" Chloe shrugged, willing the images down, refusing to let them surface. *That's enough truth for today.* "That's what the dreams are. But it's nothing like before." She played her best smile. "I would tell you if it was."

Dr. Lewis studied her. If this were the movies, there'd be an electric sound accompanied by lasers... maybe blue lasers since her look didn't kill. Finally, Dr.

Lewis sighed. She looked over Chloe's shoulder at the clock ticking on the wall. "It seems our time is up."

Chloe listened to muffled voices from her straight-backed seat. This room did not pretend to be anything other than a waiting room. Chloe smiled when her aunt emerged from behind closed doors. From the look on the adult's face she knew... the comfy seat had failed today.

## Two

The grey pebbles covering this flatland might look like sand, but they felt more like rock pushing against Tess' ankle-high boots. The land glowed dimly against the black sky, reflecting the swirl of galaxies glowing above her head. Some yellow, some blue, but most were deep purple specks clustered in a rotation. She couldn't see them moving, but they were. All galaxies revolved around a central point. If most people knew that point belonged to a black hole, slowly cycling existence into its grasp... well, they might feel differently about life priorities. Maybe that was a fate the human race deserved... death in a black hole of nothingness.

Every ten feet stood a door closed against a frame. No wall, no corridor. Just the frame against empty space. The doors didn't even pretend to be part of a hallway; they were scattered like the toys of some toddler god. Some doors were wood, some were painted, and some looked like entries into carnivals or horror houses. Some were Victorian and huge; others she'd have to crawl through. Each door was as unique as the subconscious they represented. She passed a wet, rotting door with vines growing through the cracks in the frame. Something about that door did not signal the subconscious of a stable person.

The pebbles crunched beneath her feet as she wandered through the flat space. Such a soft sound against the void soothed her. There was something hypnotic about a place without smell or sound. Tess stood alone with choices about what world to jump into, what reality to exist within. Reality—she had spent so long fighting to stay in hers and yet longing for it to change. There were no doors back then for her to jump out of her life and enter a better one. Then again, she had been stupid before. She probably wouldn't have taken the door if someone had offered. She thought she could "overcome" anything. Right. Such an idiot. She wouldn't make those mistakes again. Not now.

She knew her soul had drawn the short straw when life destinies were handed out. Life had rarely treated her with dignity. Death had a funny way of showing her an outside perspective, to truly see how absolutely horrid life could be. At least her existence now was better. She was better. And she could overcome anything, even when everyone else fought against her.

Tess adjusted her black leather jacket, making sure the new insignia pin was clearly visible below her right shoulder—the constellation Lyra. She didn't think anything about wearing her typical jeans, black tank top, and black jacket. After all, it was her lucky outfit. She had survived many battles in it. But that was before she was promoted. That was before she had to stand in a position of authority, to play the political games that came with such a position.

As Tess approached her destination, she stuffed the feeling down. That was the weakness talking. No one, she thought, will question her worth.

As she rounded a white door with a brass handle, she found the man she was looking for. A black robe covered most of his body—the assigned uniform for any shadow lurker. His face was smooth, shimmering like glass. No defining features. He was built to blend in. That is except for a small birthmark behind his ear. It was the only identifying mark on a shadow lurker's body. Someone had to be looking for the birthmark to notice it, allowing the species to stay true to its purpose of blending in.

His eyes were translucent, indicating he hadn't adapted to his costume yet. He turned to face her, his black pupils looking like pinpricks against his eyes. His right hand clutched some sort of face covering. He nodded at her as she approached. "I have yet to congratulate you on the promotion to Chief Guardian." The pitch in his voice was deep, but with the harshness of unoiled gears grinding together.

Tess squared her shoulders, standing with arms folded behind her back. "Argumas, I hear you are busy these days."

From this distance, Tess felt Argumas' height. He was close to seven feet tall, although he typically slouched to six-eight. She tried not to tilt her head upward. No need to feel too much like a child in his shadow.

Argumas shrugged. "Four children and three adults. Most of us handle five forms, so it's not too costly."

"I'm sure the extra power you receive is worth it," Tess said, raising a brow.

Argumas just grunted.

"And you have a returned soul? Someone from seven years ago?"

His nod rocked his shoulders as well. He glanced down at the object in his hand. From here, all she could see was the cardboard backing and eye holes.

Tess reached inside a pocket of her jacket, removing a small charm. Tinkerbell hung from a golden pedestal by fishing line. "The Governess of the North-Eastern Hemisphere asked me to give this to you." The Governess had no idea about the trinket, let alone where she was. But he had no reason to doubt her, so Tess tried to keep a straight face.

After a moment, Argumas gripped the trinket between two puffy fingers. Even with his face scrunched with concern, there were very few lines. He delicately lifted the charm up to examine the flying fairy with outstretched wand.

"It has meaning. We would like you to place it somewhere to be noticed." Tess added quickly, "Without intending to tell you how to complete your task."

Argumas nodded, gently placing it in a robe pocket. Tess tried not to show her pleasure.

An old aroma drifted to her, one that brought back memories of her life. Tess leaned back. "Is that... *Old Spice*?"

"It's part of the character." He straightened. "Would you like to watch?"

Tess hesitated. It was an intriguing question. Visiting someone's subconscious was always interesting. She could see their deepest inner secrets. Such information could be useful, especially with this particular door. But such action was beyond her scope as guardian. It wasn't wise to draw too much attention at this stage. "That doesn't seem like proper protocol."

"What benefit is there to being a spirit if you don't interact with living beings every now and again? You need to stay relevant, you know. You have been guardian, what? Fifteen years? That's a long time."

He had a point. Guardians didn't typically last more than two decades. They became too outdated. And once outdated, the effectiveness of the job suffered, signaling it was time to move on. She had too much to accomplish. Her promotion was a surprise, but it left her in optimum position to take down her enemies... if she was careful.

Yet why would he help her? There was no benefit for him. What if it was a trap to ensure she failed? She could be ousted from the position before she even got settled. No. She couldn't afford to be clumsy. Not when the cost was so high.

"Besides..." Argumas' gaze drifted to her neck.

Tess straightened. She'd have to wear a turtleneck to hide the tips of silver scars reaching up from her collar. Most of her scars cut along her arms and torso, but there was a thick one that reached up behind her ear. Even in this world, the sight of them created a certain amount of ogling she never particularly cared for.

"You would indubitably assist in my task for today." Argumas twirled the mask into position. "Oh, but lose the jacket. It lessens the effect."

Tess locked her jaw, feeling a warm flood against her skin. Argumas gave a smug smile before resting the mask over his eyes. With his already featureless face, the mask was his only defining characteristic. It was thin, rounding over his now brown eyes and across his cheekbones. The mask moved on its own, adjusting to the edges of his face until it practically became part of his skin. The orange and red beads glowing in the darkness were almost pretty, the enchanting swirled pattern calling for her to lose herself. But then there was the long, arched beak in front with the sole purpose of digging out her gut.

Argumas turned, clasping onto an old, rusty doorknob. The battered, rusty metal door squeaked open, revealing blackness. Cool air rushed out, bringing with it the smell of jasmine. It brought her back to childhood, before her mother died.

Argumas raised a finger in the air. "Don't forget the jacket," he said as he stepped inside.

Tess grumbled. If she was going to use this girl, she really needed to see into the girl's subconscious. And even better, it was by his invitation. Nothing that happened as a result could be entirely blamed on her. Tolerating him was part of the deal. She pulled out of the jacket and threw it on the ground. She didn't have to make herself a spectacle. She'd let the cuts encompassing her body stay silver against pale skin. No need to electrify them.

Tess took a breath at the threshold. She hadn't left the comfort of this side in a long time. Why would she? She hated anything resembling reality. But who could say how close this dream would be to any reality she knew? It could be filled with fairies and woodland creatures for all she knew.

With this thought she stepped through, almost running immediately into the trunk of a tree. Tess hesitated. Moonlight glowed through the glass window, its rays bouncing against her skin. There were trees in this bedroom. She shook her head. She shouldn't have worried. The dream realm had its own version of "reality".

Argumas stepped into the middle of the room, his mask glowing. As if on signal, the room's light unnaturally turned from white to red. The hairs on her arm rose. The window shook against his presence, walls falling away like cardboard scenery in a cheap high-school play. The sound was deafening, like the collapsing of a skyscraper.

When the sound dissipated, only the woods and the twin bed remained. Tess heard a muffled sound coming from the corner. Turning, she could make out a closet with wooden slats running horizontally along the door. Green eyes peered at her through the slats, but didn't acknowledge her presence. They were focused on Argumas.

Tess caught her breath. She was expecting a child. But the eyes that stared at her were certainly older. Teenager? The girl trembled, her breath unnaturally audible. The ground shook and the closet doors crashed down as Argumas faced the girl.

The bright green color tipping the teenager's hair practically glowed against Argumas' radiating mask. She was much too thin for someone with a proper relationship with food. The girl screamed, placing trembling hands against her ears. She started counting. Wait, not counting. Chanting. But what?

Leaves crunched against the carpet as Tess moved closer. The girl's voice was soft, but definite.

"This is not real, this is not real."

A subconscious that chanted such things was trained to track reality. The girl was a little more disturbed than Tess had thought. But she could still serve a purpose.

Movement caught Tess' eye. The trinket dangled from a tree limb, Tinkerbell capturing only the white light of the moon in a spotlight. With the girl's eyes closed, she'd never see it. Tess grumbled, looking around her.

Argumas stood in the center of the room, palm open wide. She could see the power rushing into him from the dream. The girl must be terrified because the visible energy waves rushed into him like heat rising from the desert asphalt. He didn't care about the trinket. He didn't understand its power.

Tess slowly gazed down at her arms. Her scars pulsed against the energy flowing in the room. The girl gasped, pushing harder against the back of the closet. With the gasp, Tess' scars flickered white. She didn't have much time before the girl woke up. She could feel it.

Sighing, Tess gripped her hands so tight her nails dug into her palms. She breathed in the air tainted with jasmine mixed with Old Spice. She exhaled through her mouth, forcing out the air in a gust. Raising her arms before her, Tess gripped the pain radiating in the center of her body. She unwound the tightly wrapped emotion and pushed. Everything burst with energy that sent lightning crackling along the scars on her body like a power cord. It sizzled against the night and she noticed Argumas lower his arms slightly.

Before he could stop her, Tess locked her jaw, pointing her arms to the closet. In an instant, she sent one bolt soaring out of her outstretched arms from the tip of the scars on her arm. The lightning burst struck a few feet in front of the teenager. The girl screamed at the sound, her arms falling from her ears and her eyes opening to view the smoldering ground.

A reflection of white crossed her face and the girl finally looked up. Tess smiled as Tinkerbell rotated on the branch. The world stilled for a moment, the girl's audible breath filling the void as if on speaker. Tears glistened against the green eyes locked on the trinket. Tess bit her lower lip. This had to work. She had lost so much. It *had* to work.

The entire room shook in one big jerk, throwing Tess to the ground. When she regained her surroundings, she giggled. Moonlight slipped past the blinds in the window, leaving only a fraction of the room visible, but she could clearly see the forest had disappeared. She stood in the middle of a rather small room with a twin bed and dresser. The light only illuminated two of the numerous posters thumbtacked to the wall. One poster had an attractive couple posing with creepy trees behind them. Some TV show, more than likely. Another had a white mask and a rose against a black canvas. Phantom of the Opera? Both posters reeked of reality. *It worked.* Others had tried and failed for so long, but she had figured out how to do it when no one else had.

Tess stood. An unseen, sheer curtain pushed against her skin. She was right up against the veil to reality. All she had to do was push. And Argumas was here too! It actually worked.

The girl jumped from the twin bed, breathing heavily. She wore black cotton pants and a black shirt with some sort of band logo on the front. Her black hair with green tips was matted and hung just past her shoulders. Her eyes were open, but she clearly still saw some blend between dream and reality. When she saw Argumas—who stood frozen in the center of the room—the girl let out a deafening scream, clawed at the bedroom door until it opened, and raced down the hallway.

The long beak pointed at Tess for a second before Argumas marched over to her. When he touched her shoulder, the world shook once more. White light blinded her until they stepped back through the rusty door. Argumas slammed it shut, removing the mask. His eyes might normally have pinpoint pupils, but they somehow reflected his rage.

His body shook as he threw the mask to the ground. "What did you do?"

Tess shrugged. "It was your dream. Very strange how it ended. Does that happen often?"

Argumas' nose wrinkled in a snarl. "What did you *do*?"

Tess had to be careful here. There was only so much a shadow lurker would take before they tossed aside proper protocol and remembered their more violent nature as a feeder of energy. And there was only so much she could justify when her actions were called into question. "You are the one who invited *me*. How was I to know my presence would do that?"

"No. It was the trinket." Argumas moved closer, standing at his full seven feet. "I am not in the business of night terrors. They are too unstable. And no Governess would wish to meddle in that practice. I'm only going to ask you this once. Who gave you that trinket?"

Tess held his gaze for a long moment. Then she adjusted her shirt, crouched, and retrieved her jacket. She felt Argumas' examination as she eased the leather back over her scars, which had returned to normal. She smiled at him, which she knew was a mistake the moment she did it. But she held her stance. "What a luxurious position—unknowing. The Order of Dreams grants you the privilege to feed on states of subconscious. You live a simple existence. But what I am fighting is something greater. I am fighting against a Darkness that threatens everything—even your basic life. So excuse me if I do not shake because you're irritated that things did not move the way you wanted."

Argumas hesitated before reaching inside his pocket. Tinkerbell dangled in front of his translucent eyes for a moment before he said, "When you became

Chief Guardian, many believed it a mistake." Tinkerbell swirled. "They said you were corrupted. They said you were part of this Darkness hovering in the corners of our realm. That you are actually leading the pursuit."

Tinkerbell turned, her wand pointing at Tess.

"I defended you," Argumas added, tilting his head, gaze still locked on the fairy. "I may be a simple being, but the subconscious state holds power beyond this realm. If broken, the power can be both catastrophic and revivifying. You may think little of that, but protecting it holds the foundation of this entire universe." In an instant, Tinkerbell tumbled to the pebbled ground. Argumas' black boot crushed her against the pebble with a crack, grinding her to further his point.

Tess met Argumas' gaze. If he thought the destruction would somehow unnerve her, he was highly mistaken.

The shadow lurker leaned toward her, his voice lowering. "I think others saw what I did not. But I see you now. And the Governess will certainly hear of this."

Argumas marched past her, his head leading his charge past the doors. Tess watched him go. "Make sure that she does," she said to herself. She cast one last glance at the galaxies above then to the rusted door. They were all moving toward a black hole of existence. What was done in the meantime was what truly mattered. Adjusting her jacket, Tess strolled past the doors, the crunch of the pebbles marking her exit.

# Three

Chloe examined the lines in front of her. She closed her eyes, speaking softly to herself, "'Make me a willow cabin at your gate,/ And call upon my soul within the house;/ Write loyal cantons of condemned love/ And sing them loud even in the dead of night...'" Chloe wrinkled her nose, looking for the line. "'Even in the dead of night...'" Sighing, she opened her eyes. *Halloo your name to the reverberate hills.* It wasn't a hard line. Chloe threw down the book and rose from the short ledge. Act One! She was stumbling in Act One! Really?

Chloe passed the empty tile floor of the middle section of three leveled platforms making up the cafeteria. Everything had been cleared for the day, the smell of bleach and cleaner still lingering. After two and a half years of working from beginner's drama to advanced, she finally had a shot at something worth bragging about: the role of Viola in the spring production of *Twelfth Night*. They were in week four with only two more weeks before dress rehearsals. She had her lines down after week one. Everyone was singing her praises. What would they think now that she couldn't even remember Act One?

She wasn't sleeping well. That was it. Just last night she thought she saw.... His glowing mask came to mind, but she pushed the image aside. He was *not* in her room. She was still dreaming. Her scream had awakened the house, and by the time her new uncle had caught up to her, she was on the front lawn with the house alarm blaring. It was embarrassing. What's worse, she told him she thought she saw someone in her room. The new uncle wanted to call the cops—which made her like him slightly better—but her aunt assured him this was not uncommon. Not uncommon?! She hadn't done anything like that since she was seven, but it wasn't uncommon. They had yet another appointment scheduled for tomorrow. It would have been today, but Chloe had cried that she'd miss rehearsals and thereby lose her spot in the play.

And now here she was, forgetting the words so it wouldn't even matter! Shakespeare and his twisted words! No. She was just tired. She needed to relax. That minor crash had her all jumbled. It was stupid. She shouldn't be reacting so much. So what? Someone bumped into her car on her first time driving. Her aunt didn't even get all that upset. Stupid guy behind her was reading an email on his smartphone. It wasn't even her fault. No one was hurt. No one was taken away in an ambulance.

Chloe had cringed against the loud crash and crunch of metal. The sensation of being pushed forward and yet held back by her seatbelt overwhelmed her. She could still feel the strap cutting into her chest. Then the shadow of a man rushing to her door. She had looked up, still unsure what had happened. Then, out of the shadow, his face.

Chloe whipped her head back and forth, fighting the image from her mind. She looked down at her shaking hands. *You have got to get a grip*! Did she want to backslide? Was that it? She had to remember all the sessions: psychologists, psychiatrists, doctors, and social workers. It was a cycle of concerned adults and restrictions. Up until two years ago, her aunt still required her to text every time she went anywhere: what was she doing? How was she feeling?

Did she want that again? "Because you know that's what will happen if you don't stop," Chloe whispered to herself.

She sighed, picking the booklet back up and opening it. She stood straight, shoulders back. After just a glance, she let the booklet fall from view. Staring at the wall as if it were Olivia, she said, "'Make me a willow cabin at your gate,/And call upon my soul within the house./ Write loyal cantons of condemned love/ And sing them loud even in the dead of night/ Halloo your name to the reverberate hills/ And make the babbling gossip of the air/ Cry out 'Olivia!' Oh, you should not rest/ Between the elements of air and earth,/ But you should pity me!'" She ended, her words bouncing up the vaulted ceilings, booklet raised triumphantly in the air.

Clapping brought her back to the school. She turned to find Tyler on the top platform next to the gate. He was dressed for baseball practice, his pants hanging loosely and his school hat perched on his head. His smile brightened his brown eyes. She liked his hair better longer, but he had buzzed it along with the other players. Some sort of unity thing. She was just glad they hadn't decided to bleach it again like they did for basketball playoffs. But putting up with his new look was a small price to pay for dating the team captain.

She smiled, taking an exaggerated bow. Tyler bounced down the three steps and walked over to her. She threw her arms around him, letting his kiss wipe away any visions of accidents and forgotten lines. His arms wrapped tightly around her waist made her feel safe. No masked beak men would come get her here. No businessmen with smartphones could hurt her here. Yet she could still feel her nerves prickle as images of shadows on the floors tried to take her back.

"You'll do great today," Tyler said, stepping back, hands lingering at her waist.

"I keep forgetting my lines."

Tyler pushed a strand of hair behind her ear. "Nah. You've got this."

Chloe smiled at him. "What are you doing here? Aren't you going to be late for practice?"

"Coach sent me in so someone could come unlock the gates. I saw Hannah. She said you were overly quiet today in science."

Hannah. The girl thought she knew everything there was in the world of stage production. She was working the play's sound system. That wasn't any surprise. She was the one to call for any city production. And, while she was good, Chloe doubted she was going to be some big-shot producer like she expected. She'd probably be stuck in this city and continue her work as an adult volunteer. Or become a realtor and take over the successful family business.

Her neediness made the friendship a challenge, but being Hannah's sidekick certainly sent Chloe on a lot of adventures she otherwise couldn't afford. Last summer, Hannah's mom had talked her aunt into letting her travel with them to a fancy San Diego resort. They spent most of their time showing off their bodies at the beach, but it beat being stuck in town and scraping vomit and God knows what else off the floors at the city pool.

"I have to get my grades up so my aunt will get off my back."

Tyler grinned. "So you have to be a dedicated nerd for a while?"

Chloe rolled her eyes. "Something like that."

"Well, I heard your voice and had to come see you." He gave her one last, longing kiss. "Okay, I gotta get back." He bounced back up the steps. He paused at the top to face her, hand resting on the blue rail. "A bunch of us are going to Pizza Hut after practice. You in?"

Chloe shook her head. "I can't fail another math test."

Tyler coughed a laugh. "Nerd looks good on you, babe." He turned and called over his shoulder, "Just don't make it a habit."

She watched him go, feeling the frown that tugged at her lips. He was captain of the baseball team. He had a lot of scouts looking at him for scholarships. Who knew where that could lead? She couldn't blow this. She wasn't going to let some old dude in a BMW ruin everything she had worked toward.

She flipped in the booklet to Act Two, Scene Two. She glanced momentarily at her text then began. "'I left no ring with her. What means this lady?/ Fortune forbid my outside have not charmed her!/ She made good view of me, indeed so much/ That sure methought her eyes has lost her tongue,/ For she did not speak in starts distractedly./ She loves me, sure! The cunning of her... the cunning of her passion... invites me in this... this...'" Chloe threw down her booklet and swore.

"I don't think that's in the play," a female voice said.

Chloe forced a smile, looking up at Sam. She was not as chunky of a girl as her outfit seemed to suggest, but the trendy fabric and jean shorts clung too tight to her rolls. The curls in her naturally black hair hung loosely over her shoulder, looking just as pristine as they had this morning. They probably didn't dare fall out of place for fear of the girl's wrath. That, or Sam spent a whole lot more time in the bathroom than Chloe ever could notice. Even still, she would be a knockout if she could find a better wardrobe.

Sam strolled to her. "Abby said you had a study session with her this afternoon for Mr. Barnes' quiz tomorrow."

"Someone needs to tell that man quizzes aren't the only way to see if students understand."

Sam smiled. "I hear the junior class is organizing T-shirts that say *I survived Barnes*."

"Well," Chloe said as she picked up her booklet, "I wouldn't give him that kind of honor. He's making my life hell."

"My class really irritated him today. As punishment, he gave us the quiz early."

Chloe's ears perked at this.

"Ten multiple choice questions." Sam reached into a front pocket, retrieving a ripped sheet of notebook paper. "I memorized the answers." She held the paper out for Chloe. Chloe looked around the room, searching for any unwanted attention.

When she saw no one, she reached and gently took the paper. "A, B, A, A, C..." Chloe trailed off. "Are you sure it's the same as tomorrow?"

Sam shrugged. "He grabbed from a big stack of copies he had already made. But the first problem asks to graph *y equals log x plus seven.*"

Chloe felt a buzz from her back pocket. She pulled out her phone to find a text from Hannah. *Rehearsal. Where R U???* Chloe quickly punched the letters OMW then stuffed her phone back into her packet. "I gotta go, but thank you! You really are saving me."

As she grabbed her backpack strap and lifted it onto her shoulder, Sam crossed her arms. "I certainly hope you are better at memorizing letters than that play. Because I don't want to hear you got caught trying to write those down somewhere. Mr. Barnes is good. He'll catch you."

Chloe slipped another arm through the second strap, adjusting the bag. "I can memorize it. Thank you."

"Just remember, Mrs. Green has a big poetry project coming up. We need to partner because I have the spring concert choir and don't have time for that boredom."

Chloe nodded. "Agreed." She felt her phone buzz again and cringed. "I really have to go." She leapt up the steps and rushed through the open gate into the hallway. She crossed the floor, trying not to look up at the big clock ticking above her. She didn't want to know how late she was.

She rushed toward the glass front doors, taking a sharp left. As she yanked open the blue door to the auditorium, she felt a smile on her face. She was going to conquer this. She would get her grades up and learn the material later. There was nothing wrong with that. Then her aunt would calm down, the doctor visits would stop, and the lines of the play would come back to her. She wasn't relapsing. Her dreams were just a product of stress. She was going to be fine.

The cool air of the auditorium hit her face, promising a brighter future. She had to believe in that future. She had come so far. She couldn't go back.

## Four

Water of the purest blue lapped against the white-marble path. The path's softness made Tess' boots squeak as she walked. She could hear a sparrow chirping from one of the white columns erupting from the water's surface. She wound through the calm water, the sky glowing pink around her, finally reaching the courtyard. The path opened into a circular platform. White columns wrapped along the edge, blocking the center from outside view. Honeysuckle spiraled up the columns, yellow trumpet flowers dancing in the cool breeze as they perfumed the area in a warm, fruity scent.

Tess ascended five marble steps leading to a red glass throne. The throne itself, folding and wrapping in such elegance, resembled the shape of the honeysuckle flowers. It was hard not to admire it each time she came. But there would be no time for appreciation today. The crowd had already gathered.

Argumas stood in front of the throne, arms crossed. He must have felt it necessary to bring his own support, because next to him stood a fox on hind legs, a baby dressed in rags, an owl, some demon creature with an overbite, and three shadow lurkers. It was a scene from the craziest of dreams on stage before her.

When she caught sight of the other group beside Argumas, Tess hesitated on the last step. Three beings stood together, dressed in grey cloaks of various sizes, hoods hanging down their backs. One of them, as expected, was her boss, Kamahalana, the Deputy of Order—a brilliant blend of panther and human. Her pronounced yellow eyes were her most captivating feature on a blocked face, and a pronounced elongated nose. Her round ears stood alert on top of her head and her hands were a little too round with nails that looked more like claws. But her black skin came from the human half, not the panther. To her right stood the only other Chief Guardian of Order, Thomas Brinkman, in his pinstriped suit and flashy blue tie. While the Department of Order was fifty percent spirit and fifty percent other, it was unusual to have two spirits occupy the position of chief guardian, or so she was told when she was promoted from associate. Thomas' hair was slicked back and his hands clasped behind him. He looked like a toddler ready for church.

On Kamahalan's left was the Deputy of Spirit, Lisa Crowe. Her olive skin testified to the longevity of her life. The grey-haired woman stood straight, folding her hands in front of her. The two males next to her had to be her chief guardians. The Deputy of Dream was next, a reddish-brown horse with charcoal-black mane. Two slits were cut into Nakima's rather large robe for his black wings. Just one of them could wrap all the way around Tess. Nakima stood with his two chief guardians as well—a grey bunny with red specks in its brown eyes, and a green fairy with glitter where normal freckles would be. Both stood as tall as Nakima's shoulders.

Tess took a deep breath, trying to build up her confidence with every step. She focused her attention on the Governess. The woman sat tall on her throne, a purple silk dress hanging loosely around her porcelain skin. Her eyes were more round than a human's, and glistened under the soft light of the courtyard. Golden hair the thickness of Nakima's mane was braided tightly and hung over one shoulder. The hairstyle accented her pointed ears, a loop of pearl beads wrapped around the hole in her lobes. Her arms rested on the sides of the throne, fingers twice as long as most humans' gripped the edge. The first time Tess had laid eyes on the Governess of the North-Eastern Hemisphere, she thought the woman was a perfect blend of alien and elegance. Somehow the Governess captured the beauty of the fairies, the mysticism of the dream creatures, and the humanity of the spirits. Her button nose looked more like a rabbit's and her porcelain skin reflected the smoothness of Argumas' features. She was the perfect blend of everything she ruled, which was probably the best trait for a being in her position.

The Governess smiled, her face radiating compassion. Tess stood at attention in front of her, just off to the side of the entourage of deputies. She would never have been able to see the Governess outside of typical ceremonies. She should thank Argumas for the role he played in leading her here. However, with all the deputies and chief guardians, Tess wondered if her plan was about to backfire. This sure looked a lot more like a hearing to determine if a termination to the realm of Judgement was warranted. If that was the outcome, Tess would have the shortest term of any chief guardian removed from office.

"Hello, Chief Guardian of Order. I welcome your presence."

*Figures.* Tess was the one in trouble and yet pleasantries were being exchanged. This was why the Darkness was ripe to take them all down. "I thank your high Governess for the honor." Tess cast a glance at Thomas, but he looked straight ahead.

The Governess shifted her attention to Argumas. "Now that we are all present, I am ready to hear your complaints, Argumas, creature of Dream."

Argumas, to his credit, stood at his full seven feet. "The Chief Guardian of Order intercepted me before I carried out a routine dream. She asked that I use a trinket. Then she manipulated the situation so that the dreamer noticed her trinket. Such action resulted in a night terror that mimicked reality. Not only was this action reckless, but I believe it was the Chief Guardian's actual intent. I believe she is working on a deeper plot to attack the subconscious state."

Tess tried not to roll her eyes. For a creature of Dream, he certainly didn't know what constituted a night terror. They were a veil away from reality. Did he not recognize that? If not, at least she could keep it a secret.

The Governess hesitated, her nose twitching with breath. "And do you have this trinket?"

Tess stifled her grin as Argumas slouched down to his typical height, looking more like a tired vulture.

"No, Madam," Argumas answered, his gaze dropping to the golden sandals covering the Governess' thin, webbed feet.

"I see." The Governess tapped an index finger; the pink polish on her pointed nail glimmered in the light. "You invited her into the dream, am I informed correctly?"

"Yes, Madam."

"Why do you think the Chief Guardian of Order has ill intentions?"

"She used her spiritual powers to interfere so the dreamer was forced to notice the trinket, a token with more meaning than the Chief Guardian is willing to share. She seemed pleased with the night terror. So either she is ignorant—which I have never heard any being accuse her—or she is naive—which, again, I doubt given her years serving the Order—or it was her plan all along. And if it was her plan, then what motives could there be to create a night terror if not for ill intentions?"

*He was such a simpleton.* The Deputy of Dream must have coached him. Tess held her ground, knowing her turn would come.

The Governess smiled sweetly at Argumas. "I thank you, dear creature, for your presence here today. I thank you for your courage to express such grave concerns against a friend."

*Friend like a sticker in a shoe.*

The Governess shifted her attention to Kamahalan. "Deputy of Order? Can you help us understand the nature of this trinket?"

Kamahalan's yellow eyes made Tess shiver when she glanced over her shoulder. Tess straightened. She had to be strong.

"No, Governess."

The Governess pursed her lips in a thin line. Tess locked her jaw, forcing herself not to interrupt with her defense. Patience was key in these proceedings. After all, patience was viewed as a trait of the innocent, while eagerness the desperation of the guilty.

After a moment, the Governess asked, "Did you not designate the Chief Guardian to deliver this trinket for the shadow lurker's assignment?"

"Your highness!" Argumas interjected. "She said it came from you!"

The Governess smiled at the Deputy of Order. "Deputy?"

Tess breathed a little easier. Argumas should interrupt more. That would only help her cause.

Kamahalan hesitated. "I believe my Chief Guardian thought she was working under my directive."

The Governess shifted in her seat, her head tilting slightly. "And why is that?"

Tess almost tilted her head as well. *Yes, why is that?*

"We have been investigating the abuse within various subconscious states, the subcons. The Order believes a group of creatures is trying to infiltrate and collapse the veil. I cannot speak to the details as it is still an ongoing investigation, but I believe my Chief Guardian was testing a theory we were contemplating. Since she is a spirit, it is easier for her to approach the veil without catastrophic repercussions." Kamahalan cast another judgmental stare Tess' way before adding, "However misguided her actions, I do not believe they were done with ill intent. I apologize to our fellow creature of Dream as well as the Deputy of Dream. The last thing the Department of Order wishes to do is offend those we serve."

Kamahalan turned her head toward Tess. Tess could read her stare. She was supposed to speak up at this moment and extend apologies as well. Tess pretended not to see her and squared her shoulders. It was scary how close Kamahalan had come to the truth behind her actions. She wanted to believe herself to be a little less transparent than she evidently was. But part of the bigger issue here was this overemphasis on proper protocol and public relations. If one more person thanked someone or apologized, Tess didn't know if she could hold in her disgust.

A silence hovered over them. This was the moment of truth. She would either set in motion a plan to take down the Darkness or she would be sent to Judgment to defend her existence.

The Governess turned her attention to Tess. Her nose twitched back and forth in silence. Tess always wondered if she could smell something more than the honeysuckle in the air. Could she smell guilt? Could she smell a lie? For the purpose of today, Tess certainly hoped not.

"Chief Guardian. Why did you bring the trinket to the creature of Dream?"

Tess knew she had to choose her words cautiously. There was so much to say and so much she couldn't say in front of others. If she wasn't careful, they wouldn't proceed with the investigation. And then where would she be? But that twitching nose seemed to scan her, waiting for a lie. Start with a little truth then. "I wanted to see if the dreamer could approach the veil."

There was a gasp and chatter amongst the chief guardians. Argumas stood straight. His featureless face somehow managed to look smug. *Such a simpleton.*

"This particular dreamer goes by the name Chloe Parker. I heard from my fellow Chief Guardian of Order that she could see past the veil when she was a child."

Thomas straightened at this.

"She would be walking down the street and see a creature of Dream or a guardian of Spirit. I would yield to my friend," Tess emphasized the word, but avoided looking in his direction, "to see if these stories are true."

Argumas frowned, his translucent eyes peering at her for the first time. Finally, he met the Governess' inquisitive gaze. "When I first met her, she was five. Trauma heightened her emotions."

The Governess raised a thin brow.

Argumas sighed. "Yes, at times she could see through the veil, though she never crossed it. That action would be horrible!" He threw the accusation toward Tess.

"I agree with my friend." Tess took a step forward. "But I was not trying to cross the veil. I wanted to find out if she could see past it. And she saw my lightning strike. She felt my presence. When we were in the—" Tess chewed on the word for a moment. "—*night terror*," she acknowledged to Argumas. "All of these point to one conclusion. She can still see through the veil." And she could bring them to the veil, added Tess silently. If she could do that, then she could be used to break it. Tess just had to figure out how. But this was not the place for such revelations. Not with this audience of unknown allegiance.

Argumas went to speak, but Tess cut him off. "There are beings on this side who are, as we speak, trying to break the veil." Thomas glanced an accusatory glance at her before maintaining his choirboy stance. "I am not suggesting we get her to cross. I am suggesting a spirit—who as we all know has the divine right to do so—approach the veil and communicate with her. I suggest we gain her assistance to monitor a realm outside of our current reaches. With her help, we can identify possible threats and eliminate them on our side."

"This is ridiculous," Argumas shouted.

"There is no evidence," Nakima assisted in a deep voice, "that such drastic action is necessary given the current state of any perceived threat."

Tess bowed slightly. "If I may, your highness, I request we adapt our proceedings to include only those with the highest clearance."

Argumas stumbled over his words before saying, "She is just trying to manipulate us. Your highness, she knows she overstepped her boundaries as Chief Guardian and is trying to cover it up with tales of the Darkness and threats!"

Tess remained silent at this, maintaining her bowed gaze on the Governess. The Governess tapped an index finger three times, straightened in her throne, and finally focused on Kamahalan. "Do you know what she is about to share?"

Tess refused to look at the yellow eyes she could feel examining her. Kamahalan nodded. "I do. And it is highly sensitive."

The Governess smiled brightly. "I thank you all for joining us. At this time, I excuse all guardians—except for those belonging to the Order—as well as any other beings present."

Argumas hung his jaw as the creatures next to him argued. A heavy wind blew through the courtyard, whipping the deputy robes. It was momentary, but it instantly quieted any objection. Sickening pleasantries aside, the Governess could overpower them all combined. It took only a moment for the courtyard to empty except for the deputies and Thomas. She had hoped the Governess would excuse him as well.

Tess caught the gaze of Argumas as he exited the courtyard. He studied her with his typical blank expression. Tess smiled at him, causing him to snarl. He turned and marched out of the courtyard, his head still leading the way.

When everyone had exited, Tess continued. "Over the course of an Earth year, the Order has uncovered four separate corrupted subcons. One resulted in the momentary possession and the untimely termination of the host."

The Governess straightened at this, her round eyes creasing.

"The Order tried to intercept his spirit, but a guardian of Spirit had escorted him to the Judgment Realm before we could."

The Governess turned to Lisa. She smiled. "My guardians are very thorough. Spirits wandering around on this side of the veil pose a serious threat."

"You witnessed the possession?" the Governess asked Tess.

"No," Kamahalan interjected. "She was an associate to her predecessor at the time. Such information would be beyond her."

"I told her," Thomas spoke for the first time. "I thought I was helping her feel welcome in the new position by sharing my ongoing investigation with her." He refused to look her way when he said, "It seems I should apologize. I did not know she'd become so carried away with the information."

Tess glared at him. He was such a boss-pleaser. She couldn't stand it. She could feel the inquiry coming from the deputies. Not that it bothered her much. She was used to judgmental glances and hateful stares. She had experienced enough in her former life as well as in spirit.

"That is unnecessary," The Governess stated. "Is the threat she speaks of real?"

Kamahalan clasped her hands in front of her. "Yes."

Tess caught sight of a nail digging into her boss' dark skin. She had overlooked the politics involved in being a deputy. This neglect would certainly lead to some sort of punishment later.

The Governess focused back on Tess. "Chief Guardian. I admire your drive and dedication to your position, but there is a system in place. Proper actions must be taken to maintain smooth operations between the departments. Everyone must exist in the same realm while meeting their individual needs. Interference should only occur when conducted through the proper channels."

Tess nodded. "Understood." She waited, trying not to feel too nervous. *This was it. Was she in the clear?*

"I am bothered, however, by the revelation of possession. Such occurrences should never be held secret within the Order."

Kamahalan's chin rose slightly. "Of course."

"I think you would agree, Deputy of Order, that having access to information across the veil can greatly assist in your efforts to rectify the situation... especially since four compromised subcons in an Earth year borders on being an epidemic."

Tess couldn't tell by her stance, but she knew she'd hear of this later. Kamahalan wouldn't appreciate having her leadership called into question. She might be the longest running deputy, but such an honor came with the realization that longevity can lead to ineffectiveness over time. Tess might have inadvertently put her on the defensive. She could see a demotion if Kamahalan became too enraged. Not that she cared about the position. She just wanted to finish what she'd started.

"I agree, your highness. But there has been no precedent for sanctioned ghost hauntings."

Or maybe the retribution would come quicker than expected. To have her idea reduced to that of a common ghost haunting. Again, Tess tried to maintain her patience. This was going her way. She shouldn't hinder that.

The Governess stood, adjusting her dress. "I agree. Deputy of Dream?"

Feathers ruffled as Nakima's wings rose to attention.

"Please assist the guardians of Order. We will make contact within the dreamer. I see no need to change. But, Chief Guardian—"

Tess straightened.

"No more night terrors. A tear in the veil will only hurt us more than assist." She smiled sweetly, adding, "That concludes our session. I thank you all for coming."

As everyone filed out of the room, the Governess added, "Chief Guardian of Order, please stay a moment."

Tess hesitated. She would prefer to encounter Kamahalan's wrath than to be alone with the Governess. Only when everyone had left did the Governess stroll from her throne. Her golden sandals shimmered as her dress waved behind her. When she stopped only a foot away, Tess could smell the sweetness of a desert rain. Her eyes remained big and glistening, but the pupils narrowed into slits, which gave her more of a reptilian appearance.

In the same pleasant voice, the Governess said, "I respect Kamahalan. She has served her position well. But of all the six associates, I do wonder why she chose you to advance—especially given the nature of your mentor. I can guarantee if I begin to question her judgment, your position will be the next in question."

The air instantly turned heavy with humidity. She had experienced summers in the south that were less suffocating.

"Is that understood, Chief Guardian?"

Tess nodded. "Yes. But I assure you, there is no reason to question either."

The Governess' eyes turned back to normal as the air lifted. A pleasant breeze drifted past them, bringing with it the sound of chirping birds in the distance. "Wonderful. I thank you for your presence."

When the Governess turned to stroll back to her throne, Tess allowed herself a single shiver. Before she could find herself in any more trouble, she scurried down the steps of the courtyard. She reached the pathway only to practically run into the sturdy frame of Kamahalan. Her shoes squeaked as she stopped, standing at attention.

Kamahalan's eyes appeared more animal than human, especially when she was irritated. "We have a lot to discuss."

Tess nodded, noticing Thomas standing at attention just behind her boss.

"I know your potential. And I am probably one of the only beings in the Department of Order who believe the Department of Spirit shouldn't have discarded you at the first opportunity."

Tess straightened at that, but said nothing.

"But you are too independent-minded and maybe even hungry for power. I don't typically misjudge people, but perhaps these traits are not your strength but rather your corruption." When Tess didn't say anything to this, Kamahalan motioned toward

Thomas. "You will be working with Thomas from now on. After all, the situation you outlined was so dire I can only expect two chief guardians are warranted."

"I can do this alone," Tess said, casting a glare in Thomas' direction. She couldn't be paired with him. He would hinder her. After all the progress made today, this could not be happening.

Kamahalan leaned closer. Tess could smell iron on her breath when she said, "Who is Deputy of Order?"

Tess tried not to slouch under her gaze. "You are, of course."

"The moment you forget that is the moment you are transferred to Judgment for spiritual placement. And I have a feeling you are not ready to atone for your life quite yet."

Tess could feel the scars on her skin buzz under her jacket. She shoved her tears down.

Kamahalan backed away. "Thomas can fill you in on what you don't know. Out of seniority, Thomas is the lead in this investigation. The two of you can contact the Deputy of Dream and organize an encounter. Because *that* is how these things operate."

Tess nodded, her scars still buzzing. Deep down, she hated them all. She should let the Darkness destroy everything. It is what they deserved. But she couldn't. She had to rectify Mathias' death. That was the only thing she cared about. Beyond that, she just wasn't sure anymore. Maybe everyone had a point. Maybe there was Darkness in her after all.

Kamahalan whipped around, marching down the path, water lapping against the marble.

## Five

Tess stood in a dark auditorium watching Chloe on stage under a blazing spotlight. She was dressed in rags, her long hair now buzzed, but her green highlights still shimmered against the stage lights. It seemed out of costume for the paly, but apparently even the dream couldn't take that personality out of her appearance. Tess could tell the room was blue, but all defining details were faded. That is, except for the unnaturally lit soundboard at the back of the theater where a blond teenager with glasses stood. A crowd sat in the first few rows, but their faces were featureless. They flickered into focus when Chloe addressed them or cast a nervous glance their way, before fading from view.

The stage itself was empty except for Chloe and a young boy dressed like he was about to step into a royal wedding. In fact, he held himself with the same posture she saw in videos of Princess Diana's wedding. Chloe, on the other hand, stood with shoulders sagging. She wrung her hands, looking nothing like her character, but a teenager struggling with stage fright. Her voice was soft, but shaking along with the rest of her body. "'My father had a daughter loved a man, / As it might be, perhaps, were I a woman, / I should your lordship.'"

The boy's voice boomed as if on speaker, "'And what's her history?'"

"'A blank, my lord.'" Chloe's, in comparison, was barely audible. "'She never told her love, but let concealment, like a worm i' the bud, feed on her damask cheek...'" Chloe hesitated, scanning the stage for something to save her. From the sick look on her face and the flickering of the faces, maybe she was searching for the words to jump out at her.

"*Twelfth Night*," Thomas said beside her. "I loved this play."

How was she supposed to do this with him here? He'd want to take over the whole thing. She didn't care what Kamahalan said. She couldn't let him take the lead. Not on something this important. Not when their objectives were so different. He was a complication on an already complicated case.

"'She sat smiling,'" Chloe said, standing straight, "'despite her sadness, pining away. Isn't that true love for sure?'"

Tess frowned. "That doesn't sound like Shakespeare."

Chloe's whole body shook as she scanned the faces in front of her. They momentarily flashed images of teenagers. Some looked like teenagers in the play. But others looked older. Maybe parents or teachers? Whoever they were, they were important to her... and clearly disappointed.

Words appeared on the jumbo screens hanging on the wall. The screens in a normal situation would be facing the audience, like a concert. But these screens faced the stage. White lettering flashed across the dark

screen. Chloe adjusted her rags, puffing out her chest—which Tess noticed was much too flat for a woman. "'We men may say more, swear more, but indeed our shows are more than
will—'"

"You've got to be kidding me!" A short woman with a cane emerged from behind a curtain. Her nose was pointed and her auburn hair was wrapped tightly in a bun. She glared at Chloe over her iron-rimmed glasses. "You don't know your lines? We go on tomorrow!"

Chloe turned to face the woman, shaking her head. "It's okay. I can use the screen. It'll be fine."

"Jessica!" The director's screech echoed off the walls.

A little red-haired girl came skipping up the front steps from the audience. Unlike Chloe, her outfit looked stage-ready. She also had short hair, although it looked more like a wig. Like Chloe, her front was too flat under a puffy white shirt. However, her hunter green blazer matched the quality of cloth currently resting on the boy's shoulders, and her black pants had most definitely been outdated for centuries. This child looked ready to go on tomorrow.

"Take over," the director said, pushing Chloe away in disgust.

Chloe stumbled, falling to the stage. "No," she said. "I can remember them. I'm fine. Really!"

Some kid dressed in a dirty baseball uniform strolled from the darkness and stared down at her. "You're pathetic. I can't believe I ever saw anything in you."

Tess frowned at the statement. She had heard similar phrases much too often in her real life to like them being tossed at someone else—even if it was in a dream.

Chloe screamed, pounding her frustration into the stage. The stage started to crack.

"I hate to do your job," Chloe said to Thomas, "but you might want to intercept her before we transfer dreams."

Thomas hesitated. He faced the girl at the sound system, whose face was slowly blurring. Tess rolled her eyes.

She strolled down the aisle. "I always hated Shakespeare," she announced to the room.

Chloe froze. The auditorium shook for a moment. Her subconscious had identified a foreign object. Spirits could intercept subconscious dreams easier than other creatures, but it was still a risk.

Thomas was at her side in an instant. "What are you doing? If you aren't careful, we'll go into a night terror."

The stage was shoulder height, but Tess hopped up with little effort. She loved the lack of true gravity in dreams! The individuals on the stage had all disappeared. From this viewpoint, the stage stretched as big as an entire room. The black floor met with darkness over the edge. Tess noticed her boots rested on a cover to the orchestra pit. She had to be careful. She didn't feel like falling into the pit should the subconscious think of it.

Chloe eyed Tess up and down. Tess had chosen to wear a black turtleneck under her leather jacket. No use frightening the kid too much. And she certainly didn't need Thomas to instruct her on the clothing options, although he offered his opinion anyway. Her spiked hair had always been a source of spectacle in her real life, especially since she got the cut after her divorce. She had wanted to shave off all trace of the weakling she was before. Like the pieces of her past would fall away like the strands of hair. Like she could reinvent herself at thirty. *Such an idiot*. That decision followed her to the afterlife just to kick her one more time.

"Wh... who are you?"

Tess smiled. This was a lot easier than she thought. Most subcons only acknowledged spirits in dreams if they belonged to long-lost relatives. It was a way of speaking beyond the grave, making atonement for things left behind. Not that Tess had anyone she wished to try it on. The fact that Chloe interacted with her meant she had a strong connection to *any* presence in her dreams. She was so strong. The stretch of her abilities was endless.

Her gaze drifted toward Thomas, who decided to use the steps to the left of the stage. Always the suck-up.

"Do not be alarmed," Thomas said with outstretched palms as he neared.

Tess wanted to chastise him for his cliché response. Why not say "*take me to your leader"* next? She didn't know how much longer she could deal with him.

Chloe eyed him, and much to Tess's dismay, the girl relaxed. Thomas was an act. He always was. She couldn't help it if some people fell for his choirboy appearance and innocent charm. He was as fractured as everyone else. He was just better at hiding his flaws. But Tess had a lot of experience with people who could charm in public but were someone dark in private.

"You look too old to be a student here. Are you a new teacher?" Chloe asked.

Thomas smiled, his eyes kind. "No. I am here because I need your help, Chloe."

"You need *my* help?"

Tess stared at them. It was like she wasn't even here. Why *was* she here if she let Thomas control everything? "Chloe, this is a dream."

The stage shook slightly, although Chloe didn't seem to feel it. Thomas glared at her.

"You are special, Chloe," Tess continued before he could rebuke her. "You can see things others cannot."

Chloe backed away. She scanned the room, looking as if she was sure to find something that haunted her. Was it Argumas she sought? She certainly looked like a victim scanning the crowd for a stalker.

"Chloe," Thomas said in his soft voice. "I cannot imagine what you are thinking. But my partner—while lacking compassion—is correct. We are spirits. We come from a place where dream and afterlife exist."

Chloe was dramatically shaking her head like a toddler refusing to eat mushy peas.

"There are dark forces trying to disrupt our existence. We need your help."

Chloe put her hands to her ears much the same way she had in the closet. "Not real, not real, not real."

Tess swore. "Now look what you've done!" She marched over to the girl and grabbed her arms. When she did, the girl's appearance immediately transformed. Her long hair was back, green tips and bangs glowing in the spotlight. Her rags were replaced with jeans and a black shirt with a Mexican sugar skull in the middle. This time when the room shook, Chloe glanced at the floor.

"I am real, Chloe. I am a spirit, but I am real. He is real. We have a real problem and we need your help."

Chloe's scream echoed in Tess's ears long after her body had disappeared. With the subconscious gone, all other images left the space. The stage was half the size as before, yellow lights marking a path up the theater seating. The lights hanging on the wall illuminated them in a soft glow.

"That was a disaster!" Thomas shouted behind her.

*Oh, no. He wasn't going to blame this on her.* Tess whipped around. "You're the one who sent her into a chant!"

"I knew it was a mistake bringing you. You can't handle any situation with protocol and dignity!"

"I'd like to point out if we had approached the veil and appeared to her, she couldn't vanish from us!" Tess swiped a hand to display the empty theater. "But, protocol."

Thomas marched down the steps on the right side of the stage. "Kamahalan will hear of this in my report."

"I'm shaking at the thought!" she shouted after him. "You know what?" Thomas hesitated halfway up the aisle. "I am tired of everyone threatening me. Agree with me or not. We both know I am right because I am the *only one* who wants progress."

Thomas said nothing. He just turned and left her, vanishing when he reached the back aisle. Tess gripped her hands until her nails dug into her palms. She couldn't let them get to her. She had to find a balance of working with them, even if their protocols were obnoxious. She knew that. She knew Kamahalan would take her off this case if she wasn't careful. She had to learn how to work with Thomas, or at least give the appearance of doing so.

And more than anything, she had to do something at which she had consistently failed since entering the afterlife: convince someone she could be trusted.

## Six

Silverware clinked against plates in the silence around the table. Chloe sat on one of the backed stools around the high-top table. The dining room was really just an empty space between the kitchen and the living room. Normally, the table's main purpose was to gather papers and household items. But her aunt was on some sort of "families should eat together" kick. Chloe couldn't be blamed for the new development. It had started months before the accident. In fact, it had started about six months after the wedding.

Her aunt shoveled mashed potatoes into her mouth, smiling at them all as she chewed and swallowed. If the frowns around the table were any indication, she was the only one enjoying herself. Chloe's aunt was an altered reflection of her mother. In life, her mother had the same bright blue eyes. While her aunt's hair was in a trendy bob, Chloe's mom had always worn it curled just past her shoulder. Both had round cheeks and a soft nose. And both chose to pluck their well-pronounced eyebrows into a defined arch. Her aunt's face was a little wider and she held herself with less confidence, but when the light was dim enough, Chloe could pretend for just a moment that her mother was still alive.

She didn't know what was worse: the child whose parent faded from memory with time, or the child whose access to a reflection never allowed that image to fade. At the moment, with her dreams becoming stronger, she wished the image could fade. But even with that thought crossing her mind, she felt the guilt well up inside along with the feel of her mother's last goodnight kiss on her forehead.

"How was your day, sweet pea?" Her aunt asked with an encouraging nod.

The sigh to Chloe's right was clearly audible. Her ten-year-old cousin, Molly, stabbed a piece of roast with her fork. She hated the nickname. Chloe didn't know why her aunt insisted on using it.

"Fine," she said, managing to keep the annoyance in her voice to a minimum. Molly's blond hair was a shade lighter than her mother's. Currently, half of it was clipped up in a thin ponytail. The clip was hidden by a big blue bow. She still had on the clothes she wore to school this morning: knee-length jeans and a shirt depicting some trendy actress dressed up as Cinderella from yet another movie rendition of the old tale. If Molly ever grew into her long limbs and wide nose—and if she'd focus more on her makeup than her books—she would have the run of the high school in a few years.

"Just *fine*?" her mother pushed sweetly.

Molly shrugged. "School is school." She looked up, thoughtful, "Although Mrs. Williams finally let me read a real chapter book today, not one of the small ones like the others. It was over a hundred pages!

*Shiloh*. It's about a dog. I can't wait for silent reading tomorrow."

Chloe shoved the dry roast into her mouth—totally needed more salt—shaking her head. *Could have the run of the school... but won't*. She'd be one of those girls Chloe saw standing by the teachers' closed doors in the morning discussing the homework assignment. She'd be one of those top students competing for scholarships and speeches at graduation.

"Doesn't that dog die?" Her uncle said. One of his round arms rested on the table as the other shoveled a heap of mashed potatoes and peas into his mouth.

Molly's eyes grew wide, causing her uncle to sit up, fork hovering over his plate.

"Oh, I don't know for sure. It's been so long—I'm probably wrong." His kind brown eyes looked past bushy brows, his brown beard shifting with his smile. "Mixing it up with another book, I'm sure."

Chloe held back her scoff. She couldn't picture him ever reading. He drove a UPS truck for a living. Not that his profession banned him from scholarly activity. What doomed his reading was his complete attention to the latest action movies on television or the current sports playoffs. Chloe frowned at him. One would think a UPS driver would be a little more fit. He had the makings of a nice pot belly and while his arms were wide, it was not from pure muscle. But his smile brightened the room and he made Chloe's aunt happy. And after Chloe had messed up the last marriage with all her issues, she was not going to cause this one to fail.

"What about you, Chloe?"

Chloe froze at her name, pulling her from her thoughts. "What about me what?"

Her aunt signed, fork hovering. "How was your day?"

"It was fine." This resulted in a disgusted eye-roll. Adults should be above such action. *So much for family dinners bringing families together.*

"How did you do on your math test?" her uncle contributed. This earned him an appreciative look from his wife.

"I got a B on the quiz today," Chloe offered.

The sudden applause from her aunt made the cheating she had to do to get that grade worth the stress. Chloe smiled, some of the tension easing out of her shoulders. At least one thing was going in the right direction.

"See," her aunt praised. "A little extra work and you're back on track! You should continue to meet with Abby though," she added with a scoop of peas. "Just so you're ready for the next one."

The next one. That would be trickier. She should probably try to learn the material… or figure out which of her friends had the class period before her. "For sure," Chloe said with a nod, avoiding her aunt's approving stare. *Wasn't it time to move on to some other topic?*

"Don't you have a play or something?" her uncle said after a moment.

Ugh. Not that topic. Chloe shoved more pot roast into her mouth. It needed gravy. "It's okay," she mumbled through the food. Hopefully they found the action so repulsive they'd end this line of inquiry.

Her aunt stared at her. She must have hound in her blood. "Just okay? You were so excited about getting the lead part."

Chloe shrugged. "It's just stressful, is all. We have so little time left and a lot still to do."

"Are you sure that's the only thing bothering you?"

Chloe stabbed her fork into the last piece of roast, the metal scraping her plate. "Yes." She could hear it too. She was too defensive.

The silence scraped against her skin as it always did in times like this. She wished she knew how to stop the direction this conversation was taking, but she never could. Soon she'd have to text her aunt every time she left the house and adhere to a strict curfew. And then there were appointments and strategy sessions. She didn't know if she could tolerate all that restriction again. Her personal life certainly couldn't survive it.

"Molly," her aunt said, "Can you please help me clean up the kitchen?"

Molly grabbed a few dishes from the center of the table then practically jumped down from her seat. She rushed around the breakfast bar and into the kitchen.

"What's the point?" Chloe said, throwing her fork on the table. "She can still hear us."

Her aunt's eyes narrowed. "Why don't you want to talk about the play?"

"Maybe she—" her uncle was cut off by a raised hand.

"Chloe?"

Chloe leaned back in her chair, folding her arms. "Why does something have to be wrong? I feel like you *want* something to be wrong with me." Yes. Use *I feel* statements, just as she was taught to do in countless sessions. Maybe that would stop this.

"I don't want it," her aunt said, sitting back. "But I know you."

Dishes rattled together in the kitchen as water rushed from the faucet. "You know me?"

"Yes. Chloe, we've been through too much for you to push me away."

Chloe could feel the heat rise to her cheeks. "Maybe I wouldn't push you away if you could trust me."

"This isn't about trust."

Her mother's eyes. She hated that she saw her mother's eyes staring at her right now, disapproving and critical. "No, this is about you still living in the past. No matter how many new husbands and family dinners you have—"

"Hey!"

"—you will always live in the past," Chloe shouted over her. She stood from the chair. "But not me! I'm doing fine!"

More dishes clanking in the kitchen.

"So leave me alone!" Chloe clenched her hands into fists as she shouted the words across the table. She wasn't sure who she was yelling at anymore: her aunt, her dead mother, the nightmares that plagued her... or maybe it was the entire world. But everything just needed to back off!

Before another word was spoken, a metal tray collided with tile floor in a high-pitched bang. What Chloe heard instead of a tray dropping was a clear gunshot. Chloe collapsed to the floor, scooting up against the wall as she gripped a piece of wood next to her.

In an instant, her arms were wrapped around her torso, gripping at a stuffed Elmo. The closet was small and dark. She shouldn't be in there. It was past her bedtime. Her mother would be mad. But she had built a fort in here this afternoon when her father left. She wanted to sleep here. It was so safe. She thought she heard him again. Shouting. They were always shouting. Then the sound. Such a loud sound against her ears.

Chloe could hear her small breath against the closet door. The silence prickled against her skin. When her bedroom door creaked, she shivered. She wanted to pee, but her mom would be mad. She had to hold it. But the shivering worsened when she smelled his cologne. She could smell him before she could see him. He strolled into her room, his shadow hesitating at the bed. She wasn't there. What if she had been there? She wanted her mommy.

Moonlight trickled through her curtains, glimmering off the metal in his hand. The gun looked small in his large hands, hands that used to toss her in the air and catch her. Always catch her. Her heartbeat was too loud. Her breath was too loud. He would find her. He couldn't find her. But why not? He always protected her. He might hug her and love her and tell her everything was okay.

Chloe gazed up at him. He towered above her. But as he turned to face the closet, his face shadowed, she froze again. All she could see was his nose. Her mother always said she was glad Chloe hadn't inherited such an arched feature on her face. She always called it a beak. Her dad didn't like that.

Chloe backed further into the shadows. She shut her eyes, placing her hands against her ears. She rocked back and forth... back and forth. Quiet. Be quiet and still. Back and forth. The smell of his cologne left her room. And then there was a second gunshot.

"Chloe!" A hand grabbed her shoulder and Chloe jerked back. Her head smacked against the wall. She was crouched not in a closet but on the floor of her aunt's house. She stared at the bearded face of a man she barely knew and yet found comfort. Her aunt stood behind him clutching Molly, who had tears welling in her eyes.

"Chloe," her uncle soothed. "You're okay, Chloe. No one will hurt you."

Chloe found she was holding her breath. She sucked in air, potatoes, and pot-roast, bringing her further back. Her fingers hurt. She looked to find white fingers gripping the side of the china cabinet. She forced herself to let go, her hand aching in protest. Chloe's eyes teared when she looked back at Molly. "I'm sorry," she said as her uncle helped her stand.

"Are you okay?" he asked. He had never seen her like this. These episodes had been before his time. And Molly... she was so young back then.

"I'm fine. Everything's fine. I swear." Chloe forced a smile and tried to fight back the tears shaking her body. "Can I please be excused?" Chloe didn't wait for an answer. She forced herself to walk down the adjacent hallway. Last door on the right. She could make it before she cried. They couldn't see her cry. How was she going to explain her tears? Stress?

Chloe shoved the door open, flinging herself behind it and pushing it closed. She breathed against the door, her hands still pushing. Pushing against the door. Pushing against the memory. Pushing against her life. Pushing, pushing, pushing—that's all she did. And it was working. It was working until that stupid accident and that stupid man in the BMW with the big stupid nose! Chloe ground her teeth, fighting against the memories that tried to surface.

She focused on her breath. She wasn't there. She wasn't in that closet. She wasn't in that house. Chloe turned suddenly, rushing to the closet. She pulled open the metal doors. Her clothes hung in no particular order in her closet. The bottom was filled with shoes, discarded clothes, and anything else she shoved in there when her aunt told her to clean her room. But she looked past all of that, searching.

Finally she saw it and smiled. She shoved the clothes to one side, hangers scraping against the rod. There, tied neatly around the rod, hung a red ribbon. Most people wouldn't notice it. Chloe ran a hand down the silk ribbon. Her breath immediately eased and her world stopped shaking. The threat of tears left her as did the old emotions that whirled inside.

She pinched the ribbon and closed her eyes. "This is real," she said softly, sighing in relief. Then her eyes opened. *Great.* How was she going to explain *that*? Chloe readjusted her clothes, the ribbon no longer clearly visible. It was time to tell her aunt about the man in the BMW. It was time to tell her how much he looked like a man from her past, a man she had masked in the dreams that plagued her. A little more truth. Just a little more to show them she could handle it. The stress of the play. That would explain the rest. That could even explain her math grade. But everything was fine. She was fine. She'd tell her once Molly went to bed. Chloe's eyes remained fixed on the ribbon. Because this is reality.

# Seven

As Tess marched through the large field, blue cup-shaped flowers swayed along with the grasses of the valley. A stream rushed by her side, foam marking its path through large rocks, while birds danced through the air, resting on top of the many trees lining the edge. It was the picture of a field painted by many an aspiring artist. Dare she say? It was dreamlike. If Tess were Deputy, she'd exist in a tall skyscraper in the city. Lots of lights and people and machines. But using a scene of nature to house a winged horse? That was just too stereotypical.

"I love it here," Thomas said. The few moments she had forgotten his presence had been such bliss. "Don't you?"

Tess held back her disgust. "Sure. Very beautiful."

Nakima stood in the middle of the field. He stretched his wings to full length. Together, they stretched almost double the length of this body. The black feathers shimmered like oil against the rays of an unidentified sun. He pounded his front hooves against the meadow. Again, the picture could have been painted by the best artist, even though it wasn't reality. The whole pleasantness of the scene really did make Tess' stomach turn. In her previous life, she might have appreciated such things. But now? She saw it for what it was: the illusion of perfection.

Nakima folded his wings as they approached, his head held high. "And what brings the two chief guardians of Order to my home?"

Tess looked at Thomas, who motioned for her to begin. Of course. Leave her to deliver bad news. Tess cleared her voice. "We thank you for granting access to Chloe's dream."

Nakima bowed his head in acknowledgement. She had never been good at strategizing, but starting with pleasantries seemed like a good start.

"However, we were unsuccessful in making contact."

Nakima's ears turned. In her experience, that was as close to a frown as he came.

"We did talk with her," Thomas offered. "But she was frightened away." Tess didn't miss his quick glance in her direction. The result was effective because Nakima turned his muzzle on her.

"Look. I am more than happy to take the blame here," Tess began. "Everyone seems more than willing to cast it."

Nakima snorted, turning to walk closer to the stream. "You can have access to her as much as you need," he said, stopping just before the edge. Small lights flickered off the edge of a leaf rolling with the current. "You needn't ask permission every time."

The lights circled upward, almost looking like an elegant version of a tornado. Nakima swished his tail as he waited.

"We thank you for your kindness," Thomas said, placing a hand to his heart.

The lights whirled faster and faster until they became a blur. Thomas looked about ready to leave. Of course. Why would he want to push this further than standard protocol?

"There is one more thing I wish to discuss," Tess added.

Thomas faced her. "No," he insisted, "there isn't. We know you are busy. We will leave you to your work."

Nakima eyed them for a moment. The lights stopped spinning and flattened, holding up a sheet of paper for Nakima to read. The horse swished his black tail before turning away from the lights—which stayed obediently in place. "You two seem to disagree a lot about this case."

Thomas sighed. "You have no idea."

"My partner and I," Tess stopped. Pleasantries. She would get further leading with pleasantries like Thomas did. "Sir, my partner has served his position for many years. He has numerous commendations to his name. Just last year, he helped negotiate an easier protocol for the guardians of Spirit to intercept their assignments." That accommodation was a joke. In actuality, the new protocol made it easier for the Darkness to operate. But she was right to use the example. Nakima looked rather pleased at her ability to praise Thomas.

"Yes," he said. "We are well aware of his worthy reputation. He has worked with my guardians on many cases with positive outcomes."

Tess fought hard not to roll her eyes. She figured she was successful because neither Nakima nor Thomas looked irritated with her. "Yes," she said slowly. "And I am new to my position."

"It is not your newness that upsets people," Thomas added, to which Nakima grinned. He actually grinned! His blocky teeth showed for only a moment before he regained his original expression. So much for pleasantries.

"I have made some mistakes," Tess fought to say. Everything in her body screamed for her to take it back. She wanted to put these people in their place. She wanted to tell them how stupid they were. That so much was being done behind the scenes. They were the topic of jokes and ridicule as subconscious states were under attack. She wanted to tell them they were all going to lose this fight. But they wouldn't listen anyway. One day, she would be standing there with the smug face telling them how their preconceived perceptions had failed them.

Nakima turned to the paper, scanning its contents. The writing looked more like pictures, although they weren't hieroglyphics per se. She was losing his attention.

"However," Tess continued. "As someone new, I bring new ideas. And I believe they are worth consideration."

Nakima finished reading the paper, leaving Tess in silence. He considered for a moment, then nodded at the light. "Please summon my chief guardians to discuss assignments for the guardians of the Unrest Division."

The white lights whirled, the paper disintegrating between them. Then they swirled into the creek, disappearing under the current. Nakima turned to her. "I only have a short time. I have over a million unclassified dreams happening tonight and creatures waiting for their part. Can we please arrive to what you wish to ask of me?"

"It is not important," Thomas interjected. "You have done enough to assist us."

"No," Tess insisted. She wanted to shove his bony body to the ground. Maybe stomp on his head.

Nakima swished his tail, his ears lowering. "I appreciate your respect, Chief Guardian Thomas. But I am afraid this conversation is only prolonged by your objections."

Tess knew the comment was an insult in her direction, but she didn't care. It was a victory against a system stacked against her. "Deputy of Dream, I believe no matter how many times we approach Chloe in dream, we will not make proper contact."

Nakima's eyes narrowed. "Are you saying you wish to give up?"

"No," Tess said quickly. "I think there is another way."

"Please," Thomas interrupted, "don't waste his time with discussions of meeting at the veil. The Governess—"

"I know what she said," Tess said, stomping a foot. "And if you'd stop interrupting me, you'd see that's not what I wanted."

Nakima swished his tail, looking over his shoulder at the meadow. This childish bickering was wasting his time. She knew that. And she also knew in his eyes she was the only one to be blamed here.

"Besides," Tess said with a sigh, "if I wanted to approach the veil, I would be talking with the Deputy of Spirit, wouldn't I?"

Nakima looked pleased at this statement. She knew her order of rank after all. She was sure they were all shocked. Thomas crossed his arms, but remained silent. Finally.

"I respect the Governess' decision. I want to work within protocol, Deputy. That is why I have come here."

Nakima took a deep breath, nostrils flaring when he expelled the air all at once. "And what, dear child, are you asking of me?"

Tess hesitated. This was her chance. She couldn't falter now. "I want to bring Argumas with us."

Nakima turned his head to the side. "All of this to ask permission to bring a creature already assigned to her?"

Tess gathered her courage. She had to make this work. "No. I want Argumas to come so he can remove his mask in front of her."

Tess missed most of Thomas' shouted objections. He had practically lost all choirboy appearances in his shouting about protocol and absurdities and apologies. She remained focused on Nakima. Being a horse, he was harder to read. But the fact that he remained still without pinning his ears and shouting had to be a good sign.

After a moment, Nakima reared up on hind legs, front legs pumping the air. When Nakima rested back on all four hooves, the ground shook. Thomas' objections subsided.

When all had settled and the birds continued chirping, Nakima said, "Such an action would break major protocol in the dream design."

Tess nodded.

"It would effectively remove Argumas from his assignment forever. Not to mention the risk of instability within the subconscious."

"We would have more than four compromised subcons in an Earth year if it were that easy," Tess said, eyes narrowing. "Besides, she can already see the veil. This suggests her subconscious state is more aware of reality than others normally are. I believe she is strong enough to endure."

"I know it sounds easy," Nakima said. "One who does not exist in Dream does not understand the complexities. Argumas can't just go into a dream and do whatever he chooses. He is summoned and driven by the subconscious. If he does this, goes against the subconscious state, he would actually exhaust his power. And, if the subconscious attacks him, it may be a very long time before he can ever participate in *any* dream again."

How long had she known Argumas? He was one of the first beings to greet her with warmth when she became a guardian apprentice. He encouraged her to keep trying to become a true guardian. And, when she had made Chief Guardian, he was the only one to congratulate her. Then she went and messed up his dream. And now what? She was asking to risk his life.

Something so absurd, even Thomas remained silent against it.

"When I forced Chloe to see the trinket," she said after a moment, "I was not harmed. I imagine an uninvited spirit in that circumstance should have received just as much of an attack."

Nakima nodded.

"And when I grabbed her arms and forced her to acknowledge that Thomas and I were real, again she did not retaliate. Most would have collapsed that theater on our heads. Or brought forth a fire-breathing dragon to char us. When attacked, a person fights back. No amount of weakness can change that. When flight isn't an option, they fight or die." Tess paused, gathering her thoughts. She had to say this right. She was convincing him—she could see it. "But she didn't. I believe, for whatever reason, she has a heightened awareness against the things of the veil."

Tess hesitated, casting a glance at Thomas. She wished he wasn't here. She wished she didn't have to say this in front of him. But she didn't have a choice, so she continued. "The Darkness is attacking people's minds. They are trying to break through into possession. They want the subconscious to bring them to the veil and help them cross. So far, their presence remains only whispers and urges."

Thomas stared at her, questioning. She wasn't supposed to know this either.

"Chloe, her mind is different. She can see us. She knows we are there. She knows we are *real*. And it shakes her. What makes her subconscious unstable is not the actions against her, but the images she believes are not real that feel real. Argumas represents a haunting in her life. And the same mind that knows we are real is starting to wonder if he is as well. If we can break down what is real and what is not, if we can show what her mind is already discovering on its own, then maybe… just maybe we have a chance at reaching her."

"Deputy," Thomas said, "my partner is too naive to know what she is asking. She does not understand the human mind like you do. She is maybe a little too ambitious and I apologize for this waste of your time. Please, don't let her rashness alter you from allowing our continued access to Chloe's dream. I will operate within given protocols and accomplish what we need."

Nakima was silent for a long time. The stream rushed next to them, birds chirping in the trees around them. A small breeze brought with it the sweet smell of tree sap and wildflowers. None of it soothed her nerves. Tess couldn't read him. She wished he was a human with the numerous muscles in the face to express his feelings. She didn't know how many face muscles horses had, but however many, they were never enough to read emotion.

Finally, he said, "If her mind is as powerful as you say, doesn't this mean she could possibly be a target if discovered by those in the Darkness?"

Tess hesitated, glancing at Thomas. She had revealed too much. She was trying to dance around that conclusion. It was a working theory of hers when she came across Chloe's case. Under normal circumstances, Chloe would be too high-profile to attack. Not without following proper protocol. She was about to reveal a theory for all sides to see and take the gamble that no one else had similar access. Yet, anything less than the absolute truth here would result in Nakima denying her request, she was sure.

Finally, she nodded. "Yes. I believe a mind like hers can be used to break the veil."

Clouds darkened the sky above them. Nakima was silent as the air turned cold. "One more danger in acting out your plan."

Tess looked up at the clouds accumulating above. She was losing his support. And for what? To reveal what she hadn't wanted? No. She had to make sure this continued. It was the only way to guarantee she stayed in control of everything. "I promise," Tess said as she stared back at Nakima, "if you let Argumas come with us, I will remain silent. I will let Thomas take the lead on this." The words tasted like iron on her tongue. She couldn't believe she was doing this. How many risks was she going to take? First Argumas, now this? Maybe they all had a point. She was too focused on the outcome.

But then again, the accumulating clouds turned white and puffy in the clearing sky. Nakima studied her and she knew she had won before he said anything.

"I will let you test this theory. I don't know how you have acquired so much information, but I think the risk is strong enough to warrant drastic measures. However," he raised his voice, "should you not honor your promise, I will see to it that your position is revoked and your spirit sent to Judgment for insubordinate and damaging conduct."

At the moment that sounded better than appearing to atone for her life, even though both scenarios could end with her spirit's destruction. Tess nodded. "You have my word, Deputy."

The lights reemerged from the creek, circling in a tight ball above the surface. Nakima turned to face them. "Please summon Argumas, the shadow lurker." As the lights vanished, he turned back to them. "Please excuse me. My schedule has now become more hectic."

They were at the treeline when Tess felt a hand grip her arm. Tess yanked herself free, facing Thomas.

"Where did you hear about all of that? Not from me. And certainly not from the Deputy's briefings."

Tess glared at him. "I pay attention."

"Pay attention?" Thomas asked with a scoff. He backed away, crossing his arms. "If you aren't careful, many will start to wonder if you're participating rather than just paying attention."

He turned to leave, thought better, then faced her. "That plan for Chloe? The one where she could be used for the Darkness instead?"

Tess felt her scars buzz beneath her jacket.

"Well, I'll know who to blame if the Darkness starts implementing such a well-defined strategy."

Thomas left her, disappearing past the trees. Tess wanted to scream. It had been a mistake to say so much. Even if she couldn't have convinced Nakima without it, it was a mistake. But she was smarter than they all thought. She could still figure this out. And then she'd make Thomas eat all his commendations. The thought made her smile as she left the meadow.

# Eight

Chloe rounded another corner and found a long hallway of the high school stretching before her, blue lockers blurring into one long barrier. She clutched the papers in her arms. Molly was waiting for her in the cafeteria. They were going to color together. She had spent so long finding the perfect designs, finally settling on a scene from *The Jungle Book*. Molly would like that. She had to get to Molly.

Chloe rushed through the hallway. It came to a T, leading to yet another corridor. Something didn't feel right. Chloe turned another corner. She was so lost. She had to get to Molly. Why was this taking so long? She had been at this high school for two and a half years. She should know how to get to the cafeteria by now. At the end of the hallway stood Mr. Barnes. Chloe froze. He was laughing and talking with Abby. He passed her a paper. Was that an answer key? Chloe's heart beat faster. She knew she couldn't trust Abby. The girl was only looking out for herself. She didn't care about Chloe at all.

She should go up there and call them out. She should tell them she knew they were plotting against her. They were trying to take her down. They were trying to destroy her life! She took one step and remembered. Molly. She had to get to Molly. What if this was the path to get to her? Chloe shook her head. No.

She turned, continuing the other direction. More hallways and corridors. She had to be getting closer to the main ramp. Why couldn't she get there? Finding Molly shouldn't be so hard, but she was starting to feel like she was in a maze. It shouldn't be a maze. Molly would be waiting. She'd be worried that something had happened. Chloe started to run down the hall; the wooden doors with silver handles stretched wider and wider as they rushed past her. When she reached the end, she found the back stairwell. Maroon and grey tiles lined the floor and walls of the corner. It was a two-story building, but somehow the stairs led both up and down a level. Had she been on the first floor? She thought she was on the first floor. But why did they go up *and* down? It was a two-story building. They really should only go one direction.

She heard footsteps echo. Tyler came down the stairs, clutching biology books. *Did he take biology?* That was a freshman course. Tyler smiled at her.

"Look who's the nerd now," Chloe teased. She threw her arms around him. His always felt safe. He could toss her up and catch her, always catch her.

The biology book seemed to disappear as he wrapped his arms around her. "I heard from Oklahoma State. They want me to play baseball for them next year."

Chloe backed away, her hands lingering on his shoulders. "Next year? What about senior year?"

Tyler shrugged. "I'll graduate in May. I'm going to play ball next year."

Chloe smiled widely, feeling the joy inside. She could go with him. He would take her away from all of this. He could save her from this town, from her life. How exciting! Oklahoma. "But why are you taking biology this year? Didn't you take that already?"

Chloe looked around, confused. Where were his books? Wasn't he holding books? He stared at her for a moment then grabbed her hands. "Look. We should go celebrate. We can drive to Phoenix. There's a concert. You'll love it."

"But what about school?"

"Who cares about school?" he asked, his brows furrowing.

Chloe backed away. "I have a math test tomorrow. I can't fail."

"Why do you care?"

"Because I have to pass his class. I can't fail," Chloe insisted. Why was he so cold? He didn't even care about what she wanted. It was always about him. He was always the one she needed to focus on.

"Forget about math. It's not important." He grabbed her hands again. "Come with me. Let's get away."

It sounded inviting, but fear welled inside. Chloe couldn't leave with him. What if something happened? Could he protect her? Chloe backed away. "You're trying to trick me. You want to see me in trouble. You want to see me fail."

Tyler shook his head, trying to grab her hand again.

Chloe slapped his hand away. "No. You want to hurt me." She turned, charging down the stairs. His calls echoed behind her, but she kept running. She had to get away from him. He would hurt her. They always hurt her.

Lockers rushed past, blue carpet stretching for what seemed like a mile. She had to be on the first floor now. That was the problem before. She wasn't where she was supposed to be. But what was she trying to do?

Molly. She had forgotten all about Molly! Chloe looked at her hands. Where were the drawings? Had she dropped them? When did she last have them? She was holding them, then she was hugging Tyler. She had lost them. Chloe placed her hands on her head. How could she have lost them? And Molly was waiting. She had to find them!

Chloe started opening lockers. They squeaked open and clanked shut as she looked. The silver lock on one gleamed at her. The papers were inside. She knew it. She spun the dial on the lock. 24–32–15. When she pulled, the lock resisted with a clink. That was her combo. Maybe... she spun the dial again: 32–24–15. Nothing. Chloe kicked the locker—it sounded like the crunching of metal and glass breaking. 24–15–32. Nothing!

She had to get to Molly! Why was this so hard? She pulled at the lock, but it just banged against the locker without budging. Maybe she could break it. She had to get to the papers. She threw the lock back and heard what sounded like a gunshot. Chloe froze. The locker shook for a moment before her. Then she could smell him. She was out in the open. She wasn't in a closet. She couldn't hide! The hallway stretched before her. Don't turn around! Don't turn around!

"Chloe," a familiar voice said. She had heard it once before. Where? The auditorium. He was in the auditorium. But... Chloe looked down, reaching into her pockets. They were empty. Something should be there. What should be there? Something. Something important. Something *real*.

"Chloe, I know you're confused. I don't want to scare you."

She had to face him. But there was that smell. Could it be him? Could he be the figure that haunted her dreams? No, that didn't feel right. He wasn't stall enough. Chloe took a deep breath, easing her racing heart. It was going to beat out of her body, she was sure. The pounding echoed in her ears. Slowly, one inch at a time, she turned away from the locker. She saw nothing but the tall figure... the arched beak. She squeezed her eyes shut, throwing herself against the locker. This was it! He had found her! He was going to kill her! The locker pushed against her as she slid to the floor. "Not real, not real."

A soft hand touched her shoulder. So tender. So kind. Chloe forced her eyes open. It was the man in the suit. His hair was slicked back, his eyes comforting. She had seen him before. It didn't make sense, but she knew him. But he was a stranger. This whole thing didn't make sense.

"Chloe," he said, looking into her eyes. His gaze made her heart slow its race. Her breath steadied. "Chloe, I know this is frightening. I don't want you to be frightened anymore, okay? Do you want to be frightened, Chloe?"

Chloe felt the tears warm her cheeks. "No," she coughed.

"Look at him, Chloe. I'm here. I won't let him hurt you. But look at him."

The ground shook and Chloe squeezed her eyes shut. Something was wrong. This was *wrong*.

"Chloe," the kind voice said. "My name is Thomas. I know what you are feeling. I've been there. I want to help you because no one helped me. Chloe. Look at him."

Chloe took a deep breath. She had to open her eyes, but it was so hard. Thomas' hand gripped hers. She found strength in that. She wasn't in the closet. The realization finally took hold. She was sitting in the open. And she was still alive.

Chloe opened her eyes, staring at the two pairs of shoes in front of her. She allowed her gaze to rise. Her body shook when she got to the beak. It was so sharp. Too sharp. But today was different. The mask wasn't glowing. Chloe forced herself to breathe. He stood there, slouched. He had never been slouched before. Next to him stood a petite woman with spiked hair. Her eyes were hard; her lips formed a thin line. Chloe had seen her before. She was angry. Always angry. And she stood next to the masked man. Like he was her friend. Of course he was.

"Chloe. He won't hurt you." Thomas said, nodding at them.

The man hesitated, the beak pointing at the woman next to him. Then, very slowly, he reached a wide hand up to the mask. Chloe pushed against the locker. No. No. She couldn't see his face! She couldn't see it! Chloe closed her eyes again, pushing against the cold locker. She had to get out of here! She couldn't be here! This was wrong!

"Chloe," Thomas said again. He stopped talking suddenly. His body slammed against the locker and he slid to the ground.

Chloe pulled her hand free from Thomas, pushing both hands against her ears. This was wrong. Not real. It can't be real.

"Chloe," his voice sounded much too clear through her hands. "You can't be frightened, Chloe. He won't hurt you anymore. I promise. But you have to calm down. You can hurt me, Chloe. If you don't calm down, you *will* hurt me."

He sounded scared. Chloe forced herself to breathe, her racing heart easing a little. She breathed in and out, feeling her pocket. It was missing. Something was missing. Something that she needed. Something that told her something important. It was missing. Not real. Not real.

Chloe breathed deeply, opening her eyes. This was not her school. This was not real. The hallway vibrated beneath her. A brick fell from the ceiling, crashing to the floor right beside them. But the ceiling remained intact.

The man before her tried again. Very slowly. His hands were shaking. He was scared. Why would *he* be scared? Chloe glanced at Thomas, who had sat up. He nodded, encouraging her. Chloe watched the man before her grip the mask. Without the glow, the gems looked more like something found at the dollar store. He removed the cardboard mask, revealing a featureless face. He appeared to be human, but his features were smooth and pale. His translucent eyes looked at her. She guessed those eyes could be frightening, but right now they were scared. *He* was scared of *her*.

Chloe pushed herself to stand, another brick falling from the ceiling somewhere in the hallway. She walked to him. Despite his height, he looked weak, like an injured animal stranded on the highway. This monster of her dream... this wasn't the monster of memory at all. He was a helpless being. Chloe raised her hand, gently touching his cheek. He felt cold and trembled under her touch.

"You're not him," was all she could think to say. The moment the words left her mouth, the bricks in the hallway started to melt. They slipped down the surface like mud on a wall. In only a moment, Chloe stood with the three of them in a white room. A rusty metal door stood closed against the white walls.

Thomas stood, his eyes wide. The woman, she looked smug but still glared at Thomas. The man before her sat down, covering his face with his hands. He was laughing and yet also crying into them.

"She... she... "

A corner of the woman's lips curled up, her eyes dark. "Her dream crossed the veil."

Thomas looked around at the white room. "How is this possible?"

Chloe frowned at them. They certainly were a weird bunch. She had never seen such a boring room. And what was up with the rusty door? "What's happening?"

she asked, her voice sounding muffled. Normally an empty room would echo.

"Does that mean *she* can cross?" Thomas asked of no one in particular.

"Don't be stupid," the woman snapped. She smiled at Chloe.

Her expression looked friendly enough, but something made Chloe back away.

"We are still in her subconscious," the woman continued. "Any physical penetration would have torn the veil."

"Excuse me," Chloe said again. "What's going on?"

Thomas turned back to her. He straightened, adjusting his suit. At least she had his attention again. "Chloe. You are such a strong person."

"I'm a mess." This man didn't know her at all. That was somewhat comforting.

Thomas shook his head with force. "Not in our world. Personal strengths in your world mean nothing here. It is what your world views as weak... your insecurities, disabilities, fears..."

"Okay," Chloe said, raising an index finger. "I'm not *that* messed up."

Thomas' throaty laugh was soothing. "I know. You see," he said, moving toward her, "most people are too focused on their own worlds to see outside. You are different. You can see things of my world. You can see *me*."

Well. She certainly could see him. But why was that important? Chloe turned, facing the white room. This had to be a different dimension. Or maybe she had been abducted by aliens. Don't all the movies show white, sterile rooms? Although they also had bright white lights. The light here was rather dim.

When she had turned completely around, Chloe placed her hands on her hips. Whatever this place was, if his world was as plain as this room, then it was very boring. No wonder he had invaded her dream. "So, this is your world?"

"A reflection of it," the woman said. Chloe frowned at her. She really wished the woman wasn't here. Something about her leather jacket and black clothes just sent chills up Chloe's spine. If she saw her walking the street, Chloe would cross over. She just had an air of violence radiating from her. Like her "normal" consisted of fists and weapons.

Thomas glared at her too, which comforted Chloe. At least she had someone on her side. She was sure he'd protect her.

"I don't understand what you're saying," Chloe said after a moment. "You need my *flaws*?"

Thomas smiled at her. "Your world is naturally evil. People kill people. Children can't walk home in the dark. All lives, therefore, are presented with challenges. Sometimes, those challenges ultimately define them and overpower their soul. It can take complete control of lives and destroy them." Thomas glanced at the woman in leather. She crossed her arms, eyes narrowing, but said nothing.

"Sometimes," Thomas continued, "they can enhance you."

"Enhance?"

"There exists a veil between your world and mine." When Chloe scrunched her face at this, Thomas grinned. "You see," he said with the eagerness of her tutors, "when you dream, you enter a plane that exists between my world and your own. It is a middle ground, a reflection of both worlds."

Talk about traveling the world. She could go anywhere in her dream and it would be like she was actually there. So many places she would like to visit. "So if I dream of Ireland... "

"Well, it'll be foggy unless you've actually been there, but a part of you is actually transported to that soil."

"And if I dream I'm living in a castle?"

"Oh! I like those dreams. Much like my world, the state of dream does not exist in the dimension of time. So that castle was somewhere at some point."

She could be dreaming about anywhere in the world, during any time of existence, and she chose her high school? Talk about a missed opportunity. She'd have to be more creative in the future. But then she thought of the bedroom filled with trees. The high school was better than that place. "So my imagination doesn't drive the dream?"

"It does. In fact, it can change physical characteristics, like the winding hallways of your high school—which, I should add, were pretty warped from our perspective. They twisted and bent before you as you were running down them. Kind of cool."

Chloe frowned. Hallways that twisted and bent before her? Like she was a hamster running the wrong way on a moving sidewalk. Maybe it looked better than it sounded, because the whole thing sounded pretty cruel.

"But," he continued, "the location is more real than I think you'd like it to be."

"So a nightmare where I'm being hunted in a house... ?" Chloe asked, fighting the images from her mind. Even still, she could feel her hands start to shake.

"Is disturbing," Thomas said as he shuffled his feet, "but the house is real. The bad people haunting you are either images you put there or participants—like my friend here—placed there to assist."

"So they aren't... " Chloe hesitated. Her hand reached for her pocket. Something was still missing, something silky and red. "Please say they aren't... "

"If it's a generic, faceless image, then that's not real. If it's a woman covered in scars—"

"Hey!" the woman shouted.

"—then your imagination is powerful enough to access our world's host of creatures." Thomas glanced at the man on the floor. The man's face was unnaturally smooth, even when he smiled. In the dark, with the mask, he had terrified her throughout most of her youth. But here, unmasked, he looked like some oversized sidekick.

Thomas added, "Most serve to help you deal with your inner conflicts."

"Deal with" versus "used to torment"... Chloe figured it was all a matter of perspective. How was she supposed to feel about all of this? Grateful? Because she certainly didn't feel grateful. And what was his objective in revealing all of this to her? He wasn't a creature. He was clearly human. "But you can be in my dream too?"

Thomas hesitated, glancing at the woman. Why did he do that? Was she in charge of him? The thought made Chloe uneasy.

"Well," Thomas said, "spirits don't usually have access. But creatures like my friend here, yes. They actually like it. It's like role-playing. And they are empowered by it."

Spirits. So he was a ghost. Haunting her dreams. Great. She was more messed up than she thought. And he was here with a creature who had played a hideous part in her dreams since childhood. If this wasn't a dream, then she wasn't sure how she should feel.

"So the crazy things in my dreams are real..." Chloe dug a nail into her palm. It didn't hurt the way it should. "I don't know if I can handle that."

"Well, yes, but the plot of your dream is still yours. But a powerful mind is dangerous. The fact that you let me in is significant because that means others can access your dreams. And if they can access your dream, then they can try to manipulate it."

The room suddenly felt much too cold and open. Chloe eyed him. She could suddenly feel every inch of the room against her skin. The three beings were the only ones in here. Somehow she was sure of it. "Manipulate?"

"Yes. And manipulation is the first step to possession. And possession is the first step to penetrating the veil."

The veil between his world and hers. The veil that separated reality and time from whatever existed on his side. Chloe looked at her oversized sidekick. He was scary with his mask, but it was an act. He was playing a part from her memory. What other things existed on the other side? Chloe took a shaky breath, digging a nail into her palm again. Still just a dull pain. Not strong enough. "And if they penetrate the veil?"

"If they can physically cross it, meaning they can exist in your world and change your life based on their own desires, well, that would tear and even collapse the veil separating my world and yours."

Chloe frowned. "That doesn't sound good."

"It isn't. Because, if that happens, then your world will collapse into mine. Time and space will no longer exist. And those beings living in time... they cannot survive."

"Besides the destruction," Chloe said, her head spinning, "what is the point of collapsing the veil?"

"Power," Thomas' eyes almost gleamed at the word. "The release of so much power."

Chloe looked at the woman. She stared at Thomas, her eyes distant. What was she thinking? What was she plotting? Would she like that power? All of this sounded like dialogue from the weirdest of movies. This couldn't possibly be real. Yet it felt real. "And what part do I play in this?"

"You can see things behind the veil," Thomas said with a nod, "and possibly the veil itself."

"And others can't?" Chloe finished his thought. They wanted her to partner with them. They wanted her to help them. She was starting to make sense of it... well, maybe a little more than she had understood before. But thinking about it still made the room spin. "Because they aren't screwed up?"

"Even though you should be destroyed by the circumstances in your life, you are not. There is something inside you that makes you stronger than the rest. For whatever reason, the effect of your life is clear. You can see us."

Chloe let silence fill the white, dull room. This had to be the most elaborate dream she had ever encountered. But one thing was certain: even if this was real—despite the evidence—then she still wanted no part of it. "Look," she said with a sigh. "You don't want me. I mess everything up. I have nothing to offer you."

"I know you feel that way because it is what your world has told you. And perhaps it is true you have nothing to offer within its standards and judgements. But I don't want someone who can conform. I want unique strength. You can help us. I assure you, there's no one more qualified."

He almost sounded convincing. He was pushing so hard for this though. Chloe crossed her arms. "How can I help you?"

"You can see those on the other side. You can tell us which people are under attack so we can attack them on this side. If we can find who they are affecting, then we can hopefully find and stop them."

He wanted her to say yes. She could see it clearly written on his face. And the woman. She wanted her to say yes. Without asking them, Chloe somehow knew it was for different motives. She couldn't even remember some stupid lines in a play. How was she supposed to... to... save the world?

"I'm sorry," Chloe said. "I can't." In an instant, the white room was replaced with the blue carpet, blue lockers, and long hallway. The locker behind her stood open, the cold lock resting in her grip. Chloe could see the main ramp at the end of the short hallway. She turned, retrieved the papers, then locked the door shut. Clutching the papers to her chest, she faced the three of them one more time. The poor monster from her dreams once more looked terrified, like he was certain something was going to come around the corner to kill him.

Chloe smiled at Thomas. "You're mistaken. I am not special. I am not strong. But I do need to get to Molly." Chloe walked down the hallway, finally free of the maze. She entered the ramp, eyes focused ahead.

Chloe jerked awake. The springs on her mattress squeaked under her as she examined the dark room. Her posters looked down at her from the shadows. The moonlight trickled through the curtain, reaching for her against the darkness. That dream stayed with her, unsettled her. Even her room didn't look right at all. What was right? What was imaginary? Was she still there?

Chloe pushed the sheets off her body. The carpet of her room padded her feet as she crossed the open space. The closet doors stood before her, forbidden. She looked around, expecting something to come out of the walls. Slowly, she slid the closet open. It creaked against the track. Her clothes were one dark mass, but she knew where it should be.

She reached in front of her and pushed the clothes aside. The ribbon hung loose, moonlight wrapping around the strands. Chloe found her breath. It was okay. She looked back at her dark room. Nothing was going to come after her here. She couldn't remember most of her dream already. It had been tucked away into the pockets of her mind.

But that white room. She could still clearly see that white room like she had just been standing there. And Thomas. It all felt too real. But it couldn't have been. This ribbon was real. There were no ribbons in that room. This was real. She couldn't lose her grasp on that fact. This life was real. That room was not. If she stopped believing that, they'd lock her away for sure. They had threatened when she was little. She couldn't forget herself now. Not when she had so much to lose.

# Nine

The blue hallway stretched before her, but this time Chloe could clearly see light marking the end. The hall was crowded with bodies, some walking in a stream, some standing before open lockers, and others gathered at the side, gossiping in between classes. Chloe clutched her history book as she followed the steady flow of students migrating through the packed hallway.

She felt like her life was a ball of string. Just a few weeks ago, she had it wound tight and orderly. Now the strands were slipping through her fingers. She desperately tried to wind them back together, but the more she tried, the looser the ball of string was. She had forgotten to do her vocabulary. She didn't even remember until the teacher asked for everyone to pass their papers up. Another zero. Another grade to signal something was wrong.

The hallway opened up before her. One of the lights above flickered. For a moment, she thought she saw the ceiling—or the floor to the second-story balcony depending on perspective—vibrate under the weight of students filing down the winged staircase. Chloe slowed her steps. Voices echoed all around as she shifted her textbook. She reached inside her pocket, her fingers instantly caressed by the red ribbon in her pocket. Chloe sighed, shaking her head.

Chloe continued her way toward the ramp. Everything was fine. She was coping with the situation. She didn't need anyone else. No adult could help her. Besides, she had a feeling the creature from her dream would no longer visit her. So she should sleep better. And she tested herself on the bus this morning. She knew all of her lines. Things were getting better. But then there was that vocabulary homework. No. That was even okay. It was just one grade. She could recover. She just had to focus.

As blue carpet ended and tan tile began, someone bumped into Chloe, forcing her into the blue rail. As her hip glided along the hard surface, something caught her attention. A group stood next to one of the exits under the left staircase. It was a nice cubbyhole out of the sight of traffic. The current group of boys in hoods and black clothing seemed to have marked it as their territory for the year. They stood there at every opportunity.

One boy in particular caught her eye. He was tall, over six feet, she imagined. His blond hair hung loose, brushing the tops of his shoulders. He wore black cargo pants. A black shirt peeked out from a grey hoodie. His disheveled appearance made him look like he had slept outside last night. His eyes were dark, but Chloe couldn't tell if he had on eyeliner or if it was a natural ring under his eye. Dylan Mitchell. Chloe shook her head, continuing down the ramp and into the bright opening of the vaulted ceilings.

Dylan used to swim in the same summer class the city put on for elementary kids. They had learned about the different strokes, practiced for a bit, and then played in the pool's wave machine. He had shorter hair back then. And his face had glowed with the light of uncorrupted youth. When had he changed? She lost track of him in middle school. That was right about the time she finally started winning her personal struggles and making some friends. Hannah was the first to notice her.

Chloe turned right at the tall clock, blue hands marking the end of school. She had seen Dylan freshman year, come to think of it. He had been waiting to try out for the swim team. How does someone go from the swim team to shady-people-under-staircases in a few years? Maybe something happened at home. A divorce. A death. Maybe he didn't make the team and didn't know what to do with his life.

Or maybe someone was corrupting his dreams. Chloe frowned at herself, nearing the auditorium's side door. *Really*? Was she really going to rationalize how he looked now with a *dream* she had? Was she ready to state Thomas was real? How could he be real?

The glass display case to her left highlighted student achievements. She stopped before the third and last one. Someone had decorated it with ships and royal sashes. Posters advertising the play called out beyond the glass, promising splendor. Opening night was this Friday... two days. That's all she had left. They were supposed to go through the entire play this afternoon. Then dress rehearsal tomorrow. Would she be able to live up to the spectacular promises of the poster? Who would be there? Her aunt? Molly? Tyler? It was her chance to prove to everyone she had a grip on her life—that the strings weren't falling to the floor.

She was strong. She was the master of her own mind. There was no Thomas. There was no war on reality. The events of the last few days could all be traced back to a car crash that had brought back old memories. She could get through this. She could master her life. Chloe nodded to herself, then marched to the blue door and yanked it open. She practically skipped inside the dim room. That is, until she saw Jessica standing in full dress on stage reciting her lines—*her* lines! The parasite took Advanced Theater during the last hour of the day. Had she been plotting against her this whole time?

Chloe froze at the top of the aisle, watching her. She wished she were wrong, but the girl was good. A natural talent. She had to be. She got into Advanced Drama her freshman year. No one does that. But Chloe had earned that role! She put in the time and dedication. Who was this girl to swing in at the last minute and take her spot?

Hannah stood next to her, pushing up her glasses. "With all our tech crew problems, they wanted to get a head start on the lighting in Act 2."

*Yeah, right.* That's why she's in full dress! Chloe adjusted the strap of her backpack, which suddenly felt incredibly heavy. "Kind of hard to do without the full cast."

Hannah shrugged. "Jessica was here. We're waiting for the rest."

*The rest of the cast.* Right. Chloe wanted to smack the smile off Hannah's face.

"Besides, Jessica hasn't had too many opportunities to practice on stage. It's good for her."

"Good for her," Chloe echoed. Hannah was her supposed friend. But she shouldn't be surprised. She couldn't rely on anyone. It was her against the world. It always had been. This was just more proof that no one else would defend her. They always dropped her. Every time. "Why would she need to practice?"

Hannah backed up slightly when Chloe turned on her. Chloe felt herself lean in. Hannah certainly had the shocked-look down. Like she wasn't behind this whole thing.

"What?" Hannah asked.

"Why does she need to practice her lines? This close to show time? It's not like everyone thinks I can't do my part."

"Well," Hannah faltered, glancing at the stage.

Chloe leaned back. Her stammering cut deeper than if Hannah had just come out and said the words. "They don't think I can do my part."

Hannah blinked at her. There was actual sweat building at her hairline. The girl was struggling to keep up this ridiculous story. But Chloe knew the truth now.

"I forgot my lines a little, but I'm good now. I proved myself!"

Hannah frowned. "You forgot them all last week," she corrected.

*Did she seriously just say that?* Chloe felt her jaw slacken as Hannah's eyes went wide.

"I didn't mean—"

Mrs. Duncan strolled up to them, resting on her cane. "Chloe! I've got great news."

Chloe turned on her. "Yes, I heard. I've been replaced!"

Mrs. Duncan's eyes followed Chloe's accusatory finger pointing at the stage. She frowned, glancing at Hannah. The girl was currently examining some speck on the floor, refusing to look up. Guilt. She must feel so guilty right now!

Mrs. Duncan cleared her throat. "Chloe. I know you've had some difficulty—"

She said something after that, but Chloe didn't hear it. The world spun as heat flushed her face. How was this happening? How was this *actually* happening? Chloe reached in her pocket. The ribbon felt rough against her fingers. This was real. This was really happening.

Chloe jerked her shoulders back, shoving her chin in the air. "Mrs. Duncan. My math grade has been suffering for some time now. I just can't see how I can continue with the play."

Mrs. Duncan's mouth gaped.

"I hope you understand." Chloe whipped around and marched away without looking back. There. She was in control. She wouldn't let them have the satisfaction of betraying her. She'd take charge of it for them. Chloe shoved the blue door open. The loud bang of the bar hit her ears hard. Chloe squeezed her eyes shut, pushing the sound aside.

She walked faster, back up the ramp. She chose the hallway to the right of middle. She had to catch Abby for a ride. Tyler appeared out of the adjacent hall and smiled at her.

"Hey! I thought you had rehearsal?"

Chloe fought back her tears. "Where's Abby? I need a ride."

Tyler caught her arm as she passed him. "Whoa. Hold on." He turned her to face him, but Chloe didn't want to meet his gaze. She continued to glance around the narrow hall.

"Chloe," his voice soothed. "What happened?"

Chloe narrowed her gaze on him. "Like you don't know."

He tilted his head. "No. I really don't."

"Go ask Hannah," Chloe's voice echoed against the lockers as she pointed her arm back toward the auditorium. "She's the one who plotted to have me replaced!"

"Replaced?" Tyler said, taking a step back. "Why?"

Chloe turned around and continued her march down the hallway. Abby's locker was the last one on the left. She could already see Abby wasn't there, but she walked anyway. "My life is crashing. That stupid BMW is ruining everything!"

She felt Tyler's firm grip stop her, guiding her back to facing him.

"Babe, chill out for a second and talk to me."

Chloe knocked his hand away. "Chill out?" she yelled. "I'm one point away from failing Algebra Two, and I just lost the lead role in the play. Chill out? That's the best advice you can give me?"

She continued to march down the hallway, stopping in front of Abby's locker. 5134. Yup. This was hers and she clearly wasn't here. What's next? Sam. Sam's locker was in the middle hallway. And she had to come from the art wing on the other side. She might still be there. Chloe continued, turning down the corridor running along the back of the school. With the back stairwell behind her, Chloe migrated past teacher bathrooms and work rooms.

Tyler trotted up beside her. "I'm sorry. This is all just kind of shocking."

Chloe frowned at him. "Don't you have practice?"

Tyler looked as if she had slapped him. His eyes narrowed. "Hey, I'm trying to support you here."

Chloe laughed. That was rich. Like he ever supported her. Like he ever thought of anything she wanted. Everything was about him and his popularity. She had once thought it could take her places, but now? Now she just wanted everything to stop. "I don't need your support, okay."

"Okay," Tyler said, throwing up his hands.

Chloe turned down the middle hallway. "Just go to Oklahoma. Be successful and leave me like everyone else." She shouted over her shoulder.

"Oklahoma?" she heard him inquire from behind her. But, to her relief, he didn't follow.

Sam stood in a summer dress that came right above her wide knees. She had two French braids running along the side of her head and meeting at one mass of curls at the nape of her neck. She hadn't left yet. At least something was going well today.

Sam turned to face her, smiling. "Hey, girl! Don't you have rehearsals?"

*Did everyone know her schedule?* Chloe shook her head. "Change of plans. I need a ride home, if that's okay."

Sam shrugged, closing her locker. Chloe closed her eyes against the bang. The lock clanked in place, grating against her like sand paper. Sam adjusted her backpack. She had colored in the white checker print with various pastels. It must have taken her hours. "Sure. When is your aunt going to let you drive again?"

Chloe shrugged, falling in step with her. "I don't know. She's all paranoid now. And my stupid math grade isn't helping."

"Well," Sam said with a wink. "We've gotten that taken care of."

Chloe strolled down the ramp, casting a glance at the auditorium door. She stuffed down the lump forming in the back of her throat and continued past the clock. The auditorium's main doors were next on her right. The glass doors stood big and haunting, but Chloe gripped her book, forcing her feet to continue. She was right. They were going to replace her anyway. It was better this way. The situation she created made more sense than the alternative. Her aunt would be pleased that she put academics first.

Whistles echoed from the doors of the gym on her left. She descended the few steps and continued past the ROTC wing and then the art wing. Finally, after what seemed like a mile, she pushed through the exit doors to the student parking lot. Chloe ignored the lights at the back of the parking lot marking the baseball fields.

She focused instead on the coolness of the spring air. The wind had picked up as it did this time of the year. Soon, summer would be here and she wouldn't have to worry about school or plays or dreams or anything. It would all be better. She just had to wait.

# Ten

Desert stretched before them. Puffs of weeds—or maybe they were miniature plants—and short mesquites were the only green against the yellow grass and reddish dirt. Tess turned in a circle. The valley continued for many miles. Blue mountains pushed against the pink and purple sky on all sides. Tucked in them, she could make out the twinkling lights of Tombstone. Distance was deceptive out here. That had to be at least eighty miles away in reality.

Behind her, a small mountain range rolled up against the empty stretch of Highway 90, its vegetation and crevices more defined because it was so close. Ocotillos clustered along the ridge. The mountain range looked basic, but Tess knew the vast cavity of a cave still lived beneath the surface.

The sun was setting off to the side, turning the sky brilliant shades of red and orange that slowly turned to purple and pink on the other side of the valley. A spring breeze pushed against her back, bringing with it the sweetness of mesquite bark and wild flowers. The sun hadn't moved in over an hour, marking this as a dream. In reality, it would have touched the horizon and disappeared within the half hour, darkening the color in one last dramatic splendor before darkness. Here, reality got all twisted in time and space. The highway that stretched the thirty miles to the interstate shifted between the newer four-lane version separated by a median and the older two-lane road.

A skinny coyote trotted across the pavement, predator eyes still scanning. Many over the years found their end on this highway. The dream world was well populated with their presence. The Department of Spirit should get on it before there was an epidemic. Tess stood, hands on her hips. She couldn't be early. But she had been all around the state park and found nothing. She certainly didn't want to go inside the cave. On reality's side, the mountain's cavity was beautiful and captivating. Stalagmites and stalactites shimmered in corners; with the calcium formations, they drew worldwide attention. But, she didn't want to see what a "living" cave looked like on the dream side of the veil.

Tess' shoes crunched on dirt as she neared the pavement. A strong wind pushed her onto the asphalt. Warmth from the black road radiated against her shoes. The colors of the sky shifted. They darkened by at least two shades, but the glow of distant lights grew more pronounced against the shadows of the mountains. "Took you long enough," she said, stopping on the center line before she turned her back to the grassy median.

Marcus eased out of the shadows of mesquites. The bones of his body protruded against his leathery skin. His knees bent sideways, giving him a bowlegged appearance. He walked in almost a seated position, bouncing slightly against the gravity of each step. His arms hung well past his waist, fingertips stained black like a mechanic's. In all her time dealing with him, Tess couldn't decide whether or not Marcus was human. If he was human, then the lack of muscle on his bony face would mark someone with serious health issues—serious enough to cross over with him into the afterlife.

He neared, accompanied by the usual scent of oil and rock. The circles around his eyes matched the darkness of his fingertips. He would look like a raccoon if it weren't for the pronounced cheekbones that fought for attention. When he spoke, he revealed stained teeth and a blackened tongue. "We have to be careful. You've created quite a stir."

Tess really hoped he wasn't human. If he was, his death must have been gruesome. His haunted eyes suggested this might be true. She waited until he reached the pavement before saying, "Yes. It is regrettable, but necessary."

Marcus shuffled his feet to a stop. She wished he wore shoes. His toenails stretched further than they should. A few nails had jagged edges as if broken, probably on the many rocks covering this high desert. His feet lacked the black stain on his fingers, but they were cracked and darkened by dirt. "They say you are working with the other chief guardian."

Tess frowned. "Yes. That is also regrettable."

Headlights illuminated them for a moment. Tess turned to face the station wagon rushing toward her on what looked like the two-lane version of the highway. Her parents had driven a similar car; it had been popular at that time. The lights and car faded about a yard in front of them, the sound of the engine whooshing past. This side of the veil had so many reflections of reality at various points of time. She never got used to it, yet strongly wanted to see a flying car one of these days. So many 80s movies had promised them, but she had yet to see them reflected here.

When she focused back on Marcus, she was met with a judgmental stare. Tess sighed. "Look. It's all under control. We have access to the girl. She proved my theory and is in prime position."

"I heard she rejected Thomas' offer to assist the Order."

Was there anything he didn't hear? Although the fact he was so in tune to what was happening made him valuable to her. "That's because Thomas doesn't know what we do. I'm telling you. This will work. You just have to trust me."

Marcus made a noise that sounded like a cross between a scoff and a stifled sneeze. Headlights coming in the other direction highlighted them. This time, the road lined up more with the current four-lane version. A silver Ford sedan with a bike rack on the roof charged toward them, bike wheels turning in the air current. The car swerved into the second lane, brakes squealing as it passed them, and disappeared.

The red and orange colors tinting the sky behind Marcus turned closer to black. She was running out of time. "Look. If you didn't trust me, then why did you agree to help me? Why did you tell me all that stuff about the Darkness and the dream possessions? If you didn't think I could help you, why even bother?"

Marcus looked down his stick-like nose at her. "You did more when you were an Associate. Then, Mathias lost command and you've done nothing."

"Nothing?" Tess threw her hands in the air, turning away from him. He had to be human. People were the most ungrateful, unappreciative of species. They never truly saw her. She used that to her advantage most of the time, but nevertheless, it grew old after so many decades. But she needed him. If he turned her in to his supervisors, Tess would have more to worry about than deputies and the Governess. This could turn south. Walking the line between both sides didn't come without its risks, but she didn't have to be stupid about her choices either.

When she had gained her composure, Tess faced him once more. "I could do more if you gave me *something*."

A rabbit rushed across the road in front of them. Marcus hesitated. "I can't bring you to a meeting. They don't trust you."

*Of course.* Why should dream creatures be any different than people? They were all untrustworthy and manipulative. The afterlife was no different from reality. "How am I supposed to advance our agenda if I can't meet with the top officials?" Tess rubbed her brow. Could spirits get headaches? Because she was certain one was coming. And tension gripped her neck. She was sure of that, too.

Finally, Tess sighed. "Okay." She crossed her arms, her leather jacket creaking. "Then give me something that will make them pay attention. Give me something that will show my worth to them."

An eighteen-wheel truck honked at the top of the hill. The red beast charged down the old two-lane highway. The paint shone bright with a coating of water, wipers whipping back and forth over the window. Headlights on the other side appeared: a Jeep Wrangler with cloth cover. By the look of the water illuminated in the light, it was pouring rain. The semi drifted across the center line for just a moment, but that was enough. The vehicles disappeared with squealing breaks and crunching metal. These images were starting to get more violent. That wasn't a good sign.

Marcus stared at the scene of the apparent accident. Crickets chirped with the approaching night as the sky grew closer to black and stars began poking through. "With the girl's rejection, you need an arrest to keep the mission at the center of the Order's attention."

"That'd be nice, yes," Tess said with a nod.

Marcus frowned at her, still hesitant. Finally, he said, "Then you should make your way to Whetstone. The RV place there. Might be interesting." He was already heading back toward the cave as Tess glanced south. In reality, that was a fifteen-minute drive. Good thing this wasn't reality. Tess took two steps in that direction before she felt a pull at her waist. The world rushed past her for a second before she saw the RV dealership on her right. The two-story building was massive against the edge of the small city. One light marked the crossroads of the city. On the southeast side stretched a cluster of houses hidden in the mesquites and natural brush.

On that same side, two gas stations battled for attention. One flickered on the north between a functioning gas station with a mustang painted on the front and an abandoned building with that same faded image, flaking paint. On the south was a Shell station. The station reflected brighter. It was probably still operational.

The RV lot had been around for a while. The building itself changed from small to large each time she looked at it. The RVs on display ranged from pop-ups to trailers to enormous mobile campers. All had prices painted on the windshield along with words of encouragement for buyers. In reality, there was probably an arrangement and order to the RV display. The reflection of past and present battled, making the space look more like a junkyard of one vehicle crammed against another.

"There you are." Tess jumped at Thomas' voice behind her.

She whipped around. What was he doing here? How could he possibly know the most inconvenient times to show? It must be a talent.

Thomas stood next to her, facing the RV lot with a frown. "What are you doing here, Tess?"

His face was shadowed against the approaching night sky. With the sun gone, various stages of the moon streaked across the sky. There were about seven moons out tonight. Some crescent, some looking more like cookies with the ends bitten off, and one nice and full. All glowed white against the black sky. Without streetlights though, she strained to see his features. She couldn't read if his statement was an accusation or an innocent question. He could have been innocently searching for her... *Yeah. Right.* Just like she could be the next Governess of the Northern Hemisphere.

"I'm following a lead. What are *you* doing here?"

Thomas turned to face her, shadowing his face even further. "I told you. I've been looking for you."

"I don't need a babysitter," Tess insisted, turning back to the lot. Why had Marcus sent her here? The place looked completely vacant.

"You are so defensive. I've done nothing against you."

Tess rolled her eyes, knowing the darkness would shield her. She was about ready to give up when she saw it. There was a group of five of them clustered on the dirt road running next to the lot. They were circled, hands pressed against each other at their sides. Tess could see their mouths moving in a chant, but didn't hear anything. In fact, they were so far back that she would have never seen them in the darkness if she hadn't been looking. Marcus had come through for her.

His sigh reminded Tess of his presence. She glared at Thomas. He couldn't have known she'd be anywhere close to this location. So he was here for another purpose. If she was correct, that purpose was not to assist the Order. Maybe she could tie him up. Blindfold and gag him. The picture in her mind made her smile. Thomas must have sensed her thoughts because he leaned back. No. She couldn't explain *that* away. She just had to force him to participate in this.

She removed her jacket, the scars under her tank top crackling against her skin. Their glow against the night illuminated Thomas' wide eyes.

"Seriously," he said. "What are we doing here?"

"*You* are here to spy on me," Tess said, linking her fingers. She stretched her arms in front of her, turning her hands to crack her knuckles. "*I* am here to take down a member of the Darkness."

Thomas raised a brow as she turned to face the group. The group shifted and she found a young man kneeling in the center. His eyes were white globes, his mouth gaping. So this is what it took to intercept a dream without traveling through the highly guarded doors. Thomas made a small noise when he finally noticed the group.

"You better get your weapons ready, Choirboy." Tess rolled her shoulders, pushing against the emotion in her gut. Her scars crackled, the electricity vibrating just under her skin. *Here goes nothing*. She crouched low, charging down the berm and onto the dirt road in front of the RV lot.

She flexed her fingers, priming her scars. They might have ripped her apart in real life, but these scars were her best asset here in the afterlife. Thomas was right about that. Some souls let their circumstances defeat them. But not her. Tess hesitated at the edge of the property fence.

Thomas breathed heavily next to her, shuffling his gun in his hands. "Kamahalan is tracking me. We should wait for backup," he whispered. Tess jabbed him in the side. *Such an idiot*! She poked him in the chest and pointed to the right, down the side road. She pointed to herself and then at the road's entrance to the highway. Thomas clenched his jaw, but nodded. He didn't have to say it. This was going in his report.

Tess grinned. Still crouched, she eased her way to the center of the dirt road, blocking the group's path to the highway. She didn't have time to encircle them in an electric fence. She'd have to settle for stunning them instead. She flexed her fingers once more, breathing in. The scars glowed strong against her. One of the members caught sight of her. She smiled as he jerked, hands falling limp to his side.

Her skin sizzled as Tess reached her arms to the sides. Before he could move, a tree of lightning shot from her chest. Tess screamed against the energy as the bolt branched across the night. It struck the ground where three of them had stood, catching the edge of their shoes as they ran. Where was Thomas?

She charged ahead, the lightning continuing to emanate from her chest. Another bolt shot from her, splitting once more. The group scattered into the field. Thomas finally showed with gun drawn. He fired, the net springing from inside the barrel. It started the size of a marble but ended up big enough to capture two of them. Not that it did. All it captured was a mesquite bush as the suspects ran past.

Tess rolled her eyes. If he wasn't in on the whole thing, then he was a horrible Chief Guardian of Order. The boy at the center of the collapsed circle was just now regaining consciousness. She'd get at least one of them. Tess spread her arms like she was going to hug a big tree. The lightning shifted from her chest and traveled through her arms. It shot through each of her fingers, wrapping around the boy like a fence. He turned around in a circle, but knew he couldn't go anywhere. Tess pushed more emotion into it before letting the strands break from her fingers. The electricity would last for a few more minutes. Enough time to capture him.

Tess smiled broadly as she strolled to the electric fence buzzing around him. Thomas came gasping next to her from wherever he had pretended to run from. He certainly looked disheveled. "Are you purposely useless, or is that just your natural state?"

Thomas lowered his weapon, frowning. "We should have waited for backup."

Tess nodded. "Sure. And let them finish whatever task they were in the middle of. Brilliant plan." She turned her attention on the cowering figure before her. He looked human except for the slits for pupils, the pointed ears and chin, and the reflective scales covering his body. The scales of his species could mimic the color of most backgrounds. And, looking at the creature currently casting her a hateful glance, she knew she had finally made progress.

"That's okay. We have one of them." Neither Kamahalan or the Governess could deny her now. This boy was going to bring the Darkness to the center of attention and attack. And, if the Darkness was attacked, then its members would have no other choice than to seek her out. She was going to do this. She just had to be smart and patient.

## Eleven

Chloe's phone vibrated in her back pocket. She passed a student mural at the entrance of the art wing. The short hallway only had three doors. She was headed for the last door on the left. Chloe paused by the second door—graphic design. She retrieved her phone and swiped the screen to open the display to a text from "Tyler Boyfriend." In the grey bubble was written *So, what? u not talking 2 me now?*

Chloe closed the phone screen and stuffed her phone in a back pocket. The play was tonight. She should be a ball of nerves, but she was not. They won. Her aunt had taken the news with silence. Chloe wasn't sure whether or not that was a good sign. She was already meeting with the psychologist once a week. She wouldn't be surprised if the doctors recommended twice a week.

Chloe didn't know what the psychologist wanted from her. She had already shared about the car crash. She shared how the man in the BMW resembled him. What more did they want? Wasn't that the perfect explanation of her current emotional state? Dr. Lewis had seemed pleased with the *breakthrough*. But the restrictions continued. She had to come straight home from school. Of course, the official story was she had to look after Molly. Why she had to tell the truth and adults didn't, Chloe wasn't sure. It didn't seem fair.

A boy with blond-tipped hair strolled past her, pulling open the second door. She sighed, her phone buzzing against her skin once more. Chloe took out the phone again, swiping it open. The Tyler Boyfriend bubble was back. *Tell me what I did.*

She had been dodging his texts for the past two days. She didn't know what she wanted. She liked Tyler. She wanted to be with him, missed his arms around her. If she closed her eyes, she could feel his strong arms wrapping around her, protecting her. But why should she continue? It was fake. All of this was fake. He would let her down, just like the rest of them. *I'm no good for you. Let's just leave it at that.* Her thumbs typed the words almost as fast as she could say them. But they reached out to her as her thumb hovered over the send button. She should do it. She should just end this. It's what he really wanted. He wouldn't want someone to tie him down. And that's all she was capable of doing. She ruined people's lives and caused them to worry.

The warning bell buzzed above her. Chloe's heartbeat quickened, but she shifted her thumb and deleted the words. Quickly, she typed *I just need to think. Please let me.* She hit send, her yellow bubble stretching across the technology universe. She shoved her phone in her pocket, walked the last few steps to class, and yanked open the door. She was seated on one of the many stools around the wide table before the tardy bell chimed.

She didn't know how she had made it to art class with time to spare. Hannah had tried to catch her at the ramp, looking up and down the crowd. Chloe had exited the side doors then re-entered in the cafeteria to avoid her. It was at least a good half-minute detour out of the six allotted. But she didn't have to fight the mass of students hanging out at the top of the ramp. Maybe her detour was actually faster.

Chloe stood at the conclusion of attendance and made her way to the side counter. She spotted her figure standing in the corner. It was a hunched man with smooth features and hollow eyes. He was green from the sculpting clay. Supposedly they could mold their figures and cast many versions at a later date. Chloe doubted they actually would. It was just an excuse to have them practice in a different medium. The thought of many versions of him made her both want to laugh and shiver.

Chloe picked up the figure. He was so light. Nothing like real life. In real life, he had to be two hundred pounds. She looked at his vacant eyes. His terrified face was as clear as if it had just happened. He had looked so scared. Like she could hurt him. But, if she could hurt him, could he hurt her? The way he cowered, she suspected not.

Chloe walked to her desk and sat down. She was supposed to be making a figure in motion. That was the assignment. He had started as a wire stick body attached to a podium. She hadn't planned it, but he just kind of formed on his own and she couldn't bring herself to destroy him. Now what? He had to be in motion. Running? Cowering? She certainly couldn't make him stand with a beaked mask. That would probably land her in the school counseling office, which would then lead to Dr. Lewis.

"Have you seen one?" a high-pitched voice asked from the side.

Chloe swiveled in her stool. Becca was a petite sophomore. Freckles dotted her round nose. Her straight, red hair was cut just below the chin. She had transferred here in January. Some sort of foster kid, from what Chloe had heard. No one really talked to her. She could have quite the ups and downs. More so than even Chloe.

"Excuse me?" Chloe asked.

Becca was currently working on defining the muscles of her running man. Well, Chloe assumed it was a man. It lacked any gender-defining characteristics—as was the requirement for anything "school appropriate." But those thighs resembled Olympians leaping over hurdles. Becca nodded toward Chloe's figure. "You must have seen one. What was yours called? Mine called himself Mathias. I know," she added when Chloe must have looked at her like she was crazy. "I told him it was a silly name."

She hadn't even asked his name. Chloe rubbed her eyes. This was stupid. Why would she? It was a dream. And this girl was clearly crazy. Chloe went about manipulating the arms. Jumping-jacks. She'll have him do jumping-jacks. The green clay smelled too oily with a stench of something else. Not quite the dirt of clay, but almost like burnt rubber.

"They're called shadow lurkers, you know." Becca said, moving on to the trailing leg.

Chloe sighed. "What are?"

Becca nodded at the figure again. "Those things. That's what they are. Shadow lurkers. You really captured their likeness." Becca hesitated, tilting her head in thought. "I wouldn't have the nerve to display it." She chuckled to herself, continuing down the leg to define the calf muscle. "If you aren't careful, they'll drag you to the office and label you with all kinds of nasty classifications."

Chloe coughed a laugh. "Add them to the list."

Becca's metal sculpting tool hovered. "Really? What are you?"

Chloe hesitated. She didn't know this girl, even though she had sat next to her for practically a full semester. But, without knowing why, she answered, "PTSD-now forty percent. Eating disorder. Reactive attachment."

"Ooo! That's a good one. Which way? Inhibited or disinhibited?"

Such a strange child. "I don't know."

"Do you push people away or love everyone?"

Chloe just shrugged. Although a part of her was now curious. Which one? Probably the first. "What about you?" She asked the question before she thought it.

Becca smiled. "Mood disorder. Borderline schizophrenic."

"Schizophrenic?" She knew it. The girl was nuts.

Becca shrugged. She pinched her fingers, defining the running man's Achilles tendon. "I'm not—schizophrenic, that is. They just think it because I saw things that supposedly weren't there."

"Isn't that the definition?"

"Yeah," Becca said dramatically. Chloe looked around the room, but no one else seemed to notice. The teacher, Mrs. Hobbs, was currently across the room working with some boy whose sculpture looked rather more like a rock-man.

"It's only schizophrenic if they aren't really there," Becca continued. "But I know they are. You've seen them too, right?" she asked, pointing at Chloe's sculpture.

Chloe had the overwhelming urge to crush her figure and start again. She could redo one quickly and still get a good grade. Better than rock-man, that was for sure. But she still couldn't bring herself to do it. She thought of Thomas. He said the creature was real. And she could still remember him like he was real. Although that wasn't saying much. When she was six, her nightmares often followed her during the day. The stability of her life always rested on the assumption that the things she saw were manifestations of trauma.

Chloe frowned at this thought. "What caused your labels?"

Becca sat back. "Dad and I were doing good when Mom got locked up for heroin. But two years ago, he never came home. Cops came to the door the next morning. Motorcycle accident on the way home. Been in foster care ever since. They blame previous parental neglect and trauma of his death." Becca shook her head, her back arching as she focused on her sculpture. "Adults are stupid."

"I'm sorry about your dad," Chloe said softly.

Becca just glanced at her. "Thanks." She pushed back a strand of hair before leaning in toward her figure.

Chloe returned to the creature of her dream, moving his legs into his jumping-jack stance.

"What about you?"

Chloe froze at this.

"What got you labeled?"

Why was she talking to this girl? They didn't hang out in the same circles. There was nothing to gain here. But something caused Chloe to say, "My dad shot my mom and then himself when I was four. I hid in the closet."

"Loud noises must suck."

Chloe laughed at that. "Yes. They do."

"I normally can't stand people in general. They annoy me." Becca swiveled in her stool. "But I think you're all right. Not all drama like the rest of them."

"I don't know about that," Chloe mumbled, thinking about the string of text messages on her phone.

Becca shrugged. "Well, at least you mind your own business." After a moment, she added, "I'm sorry about your parents."

Chloe's finger rested on the creature's biceps, or what should be biceps. She thought for a moment before letting her hand fall to the table. "You know what?"

Becca raised a brow.

"No one's ever said that. I mean, the funeral was full of *you poor thing*... but still."

Becca picked up a pointed metal tool and pointed it at her. "I told you. People suck."

Chloe nodded at her creature. "Yes. They do."

Right at that moment, the door opened. Dylan strolled in with a pink pass in hand. Chloe eyed him as he crossed the room to Mrs. Hobbs. The middle-aged woman—her brown hair in a messy bun—reached for the pass. She read it for a moment, then frowned at Dylan. Handing the pass back, she said, "Ricky. Get your stuff. Ms. Carter is requesting your presence."

Since when did they not use the PA system for that? And since when was Dylan an office aide? Ricky smiled too sweetly as he shoved his stuff into his black backpack. He returned a half-finished sculpture to the corner before strutting to the door with Dylan. Mrs. Hobbs raised a brow at the spectacle, but said nothing.

"That guy gives me the creeps," Becca mumbled.

Chloe watched the door hiss shut before she acknowledged the girl. She couldn't say she didn't agree, but she had no idea why. "Why do you say that?"

Becca's tool hovered in the frown mark she was currently carving. She looked around them before she said in a hushed voice, "You can't see it?"

Chloe hesitated. "See what?"

"The shadows. They're different than the other creatures. I can't see them clearly. They don't interact with me. They just hover around him. He had just one a year ago. Now there's five."

Chloe looked back at the closed door. The clean-cut image of the boy trying out for the swim team came to mind. Then what Thomas said. The Darkness. It was trying to corrupt. So they could cross the veil. Was she ready to believe in that sort of thing?

"Are there any other shadows?"

Becca placed her tool on the table with a click. "Sure. Most of his group has at least one. Although each shadow just focuses on one person."

What did Thomas say? He wanted someone on this side looking out for them. He wanted her to let them know who the people were so they could attack whatever was causing it on their side. That's what he said, right? Could this be what he meant? Shadows hovering around people, marking them as possessed? Was she seriously entertaining this thought?

For some reason, she found herself asking, "Does Ricky have shadows?"

Becca hesitated, staring at the door. "They aren't always present. But no, I don't think so. But he's been hanging out with Dylan and his druggies for a while now. I wouldn't be surprised if I see one soon."

"Druggies?"

Becca nodded, returning to her running man. "Dylan's friend, Richard. He was suspended for having an e-cigarette. But they all share one. I think it was Dylan's. But they can put anything in that thing. Pot, LSD, heroin. You name it."

How far had Dylan fallen? She liked to believe it was just harmless cigarettes. But if he had shadows—listen to her! *Shadows? Really?* She was going to listen to a schizophrenic foster kid? Why? There was no gain in this conversation. She would become an outcast from the life she had built. But was that a life she wanted? Why did she even hang out with the friends she had? On some levels, Chloe wondered if she even liked them, let alone considered them friends. Would she cry if they were gone? She doubted it.

"Hey, Becca?"

"Yeah?"

"Do you think the things you see can actually become reality?"

Becca frowned at her. "What do you mean?"

Chloe hesitated. What *did* she mean? "I mean, you've talked with them, but do you think they can cause things to happen here?"

Becca shook her head, her red hair swishing back and forth. "No. They have some sort of barrier between us and them. They can just walk around and talk across the divide."

Barrier... or veil. *Same thing, right?* Chloe faced Becca. "Sometimes my dreams are so intense, I can't tell if they're real or not."

She should be judging Chloe right now. She should be shutting down the conversation and asking for a seating change. Instead, Becca nodded. Like she knew. Like she could relate. "They are more real than most people could know, huh?"

Chloe breathed with relief. "Yeah. Well, in one of them, I talked to this spirit named Thomas. Cute guy, dressed in a suit."

Becca just nodded. She was listening to her. She was actually listening to her and not judging her. Chloe didn't know if that had ever happened before.

The excitement made her continue. "He said there were beings on his side who were trying to intercept dreams. They wanted to possess people so they could cross over."

"Wouldn't that disrupt everything?" Becca asked.

How was Becca following this conversation? This was pure crazy, the deepest of deepest of crazy that Chloe kept hidden from everyone. Because she didn't want to be locked away in some institution. Yet, the more she believed it... the more she followed it, the more Chloe wanted to think it was all real. What was she doing?

But she continued. "According to him, it would kill everything that existed within the dimension of time."

Becca blinked at this. "That's us, right?"

Chloe nodded.

Becca propped her head up with a hand to her chin. "Wow. That's heavy."

"Do you believe him?"

"Sure," Becca said like there was no reason not to. "He sounds like one of the spirits that guard the other side. I've talked to a couple, although most of them are standoffish. Not like the creatures. The creatures love to talk. If he reached out to you, it must be real important."

"Do you think these shadows... " Chloe hesitated, biting at her lower lip. She straightened in her chair, gaining the courage to say her thought. "Do you think they could be this Darkness? Do you think it's the creatures trying to possess and cross?"

Becca scrunched her face for a moment, her eyes distant. Finally, she shrugged. "I don't know. But I think we have a responsibility to follow them."

Chloe sat back at this. Talking about it and doing something about it were two very different things. "Follow them?"

"Sure. Chloe, we can see things others can't. We can see the danger. And you've been *told*. Don't we have an obligation to act?"

"Time to pack up," Mrs. Hobbs said.

Becca turned to gather her tools. "Besides. I'm tired of being useless, you know?"

Chloe just nodded. She knew that feeling exactly.

"This is our opportunity to actually be useful." Once all of her tools were neatly packed, Becca grinned at her. "I'm in if you are."

She had been ignoring this whole thing for weeks. And what had that gotten her? She lost the play. She was cheating in math to maintain a borderline D. She had to meet with Dr. Lewis once a week. And her boyfriend was on the verge of breaking up with her. Pretending to be normal was obviously not working. Maybe this was what she should be doing.

Even as she wanted to say yes, Chloe thought harder. Okay. So she followed this guy around. What happened if she was wrong and they got caught? She couldn't tell people Becca saw shadows and she talked to a spirit. She'd never see freedom again. She would have completely lost her opportunity at a normal life—if she ever had a shot at one.

What if she was right? That didn't seem too pleasant either. If there were shadows hovering around Dylan and his friends, they wouldn't want her interfering. And Thomas had said she was susceptible to people—no, things—accessing her dreams. What if she opened herself up to being next? What if her "strengths," as Thomas put it, were just what this

Darkness needed to achieve their objective? What if she caused it all to collapse because she interfered?

But Thomas had sought her help. He must know something more than she did. He must know how to keep her safe and still get the bad guy. Was she going to trust that? Was she going to trust him when she had a hard time trusting her boyfriend or aunt?

*I'm tired of being useless, you know.* Becca's words echoed in Chloe's mind. She was tired of being useless too. She was tired of being the object of worry and destruction. This was her opportunity to do something. And now, she had found someone else who knew these things existed. Maybe the adults were wrong. Maybe the world was wrong. Maybe Thomas was right. Maybe she could be useful, but just not in this world.

Finally, Chloe returned the smile. "I'm in." They took their sculptures to the corner. "But," Chloe said, staring at the creature locked in a jumping-jack, "I have something I need to do first." The bell rang, releasing the mass of students into the hallway.

## Twelve

The boy's scales had turned a soft grey as he sat behind bars. Tess sat in a chair before him, unable to hold back her smirk. No one could take this away from her. She had captured one of the Darkness.

Tess leaned forward, resting her elbows on her knees. "All this time I wondered how you could get past the security of the subconscious doors. But you don't need their doors, do you? You've found another way."

The boy's snake tongue flickered past his lips in a blur. His eyes narrowed, but he maintained his refusal to speak. Tess nodded. The chair scooted across the cement floor when she stood.

"You guys are hard to catch, I'll give you that. Why would you do that in the open? Necessity?" The bars were cold against her grasp. "Or just stupid?"

"Stupid enough to fool you!" The boy's voice sounded like an old man's. If his outside matched, he would sound too human for her liking.

Tess clicked her tongue. "But I did catch you." Tess let her fingers trail against the bars as she walked along the edge. "You. One of the Darkness." She tapped her fingernail against one bar, the sound clanking against the silence. "And now you're caged. So maybe not fooled enough."

His snake tongue flicked out in front of him. Was he trying to taste freedom? She certainly hoped he was. She hoped he missed it already.

"You call me dark," he said, "but I am no darker than you."

Tess arched a brow. "Oh, yeah?"

"Yes," he spat. "I know who you really are. I know what you've done."

Tess scratched a nail against the bar. "And what have I done?"

"Go ask Mathias."

Well, that was enough about her. This direction would end nowhere but with a dead chameleon boy and a disintegrated chief guardian. "Why the middle of the desert? Tell me."

The boy crossed his arms, his grey scales glistening in the limited cell light.

Tess smiled at him. She almost felt sorry for him. He was so loyal and didn't know how expendable he really was. "How long before they know you've been captured... or do they already know?"

The slits of his eyes glanced at the door to the room.

"How long before they see you as a liability? See, someone like me... " Tess motioned to herself as she paced back toward him. "... a spirit that is. I've already died. I've crossed the veil and am just existing on this side. It takes a lot of energy to snuff me out. But *you*... you can always die *here*. Cross the veil. What would you come back as on the other side? A rattler? Something for a hawk to eat. Seems fitting."

Another split-tongue blur with a nervous glance at the door. His scales turned a shade darker. "What do you want?"

Tess kneeled so she could be eye level with the boy, her shoes creaking. It was way too silent in this room. "I want to know more. You answer my questions and I'll protect you. Make you my sidekick, even."

The boy jerked at this. Tess smiled at him.

"Apprentice of Order. Sounds good, huh? You'd have greater access than you do right now. What do you think of that?"

The boy's clothes scuffed against concrete as he shifted. His eyes darted between her and the door. This was too easy.

"Did you know associates of Order have access to the doors of subconscious?"

He ran his fingers along the concrete, biting at his lower lip.

"Much better than chanting in the desert."

The boy's eyes narrowed at that. "I thought you were Chief Guardian of Order. Why would you promise me this?"

Tess stood suddenly, turning her back to him. "You know what? If you have to ask, then maybe you aren't the right person for me." Tess took only two steps toward the door when she heard him scramble.

"Wait! Wait, wait!"

Tess turned slowly, trying to look disinterested. He was gripping at the bars, pushing his face against the gap. His eyes bulged as panic made him pant.

"Please. You can't leave me here. They'll kill me."

Tess wagged a finger at him. "You know what? That is the smartest thing you've said all day." Tess strolled back toward him.

He backed away from the bars, his hands hanging limply at his side. "What do you want to know?"

This boy wasn't the smartest one she could have captured. She was starting to wonder how much he actually knew. "Why the desert?"

"Both parties have to be inconspicuous."

Tess frowned at this. "Both parties?"

From this distance, she could smell dirt mixed with some sort of slime. The last time she had smelled that, she had been fishing. After tossing her catch into the cooler, she had smelled her hands. This boy had more dirt mixed in with his smell. It took all she had not to wrinkle her nose or cough the smell out.

"We have to be in the same spot. Just the veil separating us. Otherwise, it won't work."

That would mean they were cooperating with people on the other side. The Darkness had advanced more than she had originally thought. No wonder Marcus didn't think she could make it into a meeting. Here she thought she had the whole thing figured out. In actuality, she knew very little about their plan, not to mention how far they'd actually gotten! "How do you do that with the veil?"

"At first? It was special people. Homeless who were desperate and had drugs to help them see through. Ones who would shout about demons and the end of the world. But now—"

The click of the door opening sounded like a shotgun against the silence. Tess turned to find

Thomas strutting inside, Kamahalan at his side. *Great.* She turned to find the boy sitting back on the floor on the other side of the cell. *Double great.*

"When Thomas told me you were here," Kamahalan said, "I told him you couldn't be. Because I distinctly remember a conversation where I told you he was in charge."

She should have gagged the choirboy and left him tied up in the desert when she'd had her chance. The repercussions would have been easier than trying to deal with him. "He wanted to write up his report. I figured why waste time we don't have waiting for him when I could get a head start." Tess hesitated. She folded her arms behind her back, standing at attention. "I apologize if I overstepped."

Kamahalan frowned at her, but said nothing. That was progress at least.

Thomas frowned at their suspect. "Has he said anything?"

Tess glanced at the boy, who was trying really hard to literally blend in with the wall, but his eyes were too bulgy. He almost had the perfect Cheshire-Cat-imitation happening. She frowned at Thomas. "Not a thing."

Thomas eyed her, but simply clasped his hands behind his back. Fitting. Both of them standing with their hands hidden behind them while their boss seemed oblivious to any conflict.

Kamahalan approached the cell. Her yellow eyes narrowed as she regarded the boy. "Well. This can wait." She turned her back on him and his tongue used that moment to reach out. What kind of wondrous scents could he pick up with that thing? Could he read people based on the aroma they emitted?

"You are needed at the doors."

Tess frowned. "At the doors?" She hadn't been back there since Chloe turned them down and Argumas practically had an emotional meltdown.

"Nakima sent his chief guardian."

For some reason, a picture of his chief guardian bunny rushing to see Kamahalan made Tess want to laugh.

"Apparently someone is banging on Chloe's door." Tess could practically hear the dramatic music playing when Kamahalan finished her statement.

Tess glanced from Kamahalan to Thomas and back. "I don't understand. Don't we have guardians of Order there to take care of any intruders?"

The smile that stretched across Kamahalan's face made Tess want to retreat against the wall with the boy. "The banging is not on our side."

Not on our side? What did she mean by—Not on our side! Which meant Chloe was banging on the door from her side! Tess' sneakers squeaked against the floor as she fled the jail.

Grey gravel flew behind her as Tess ran down the path. Doors blurred past her. "Why didn't you tell me?" she shouted at Thomas.

Thomas ran next to her. He looked so uninterested. Of course. He wasn't invested in this. "I don't see why we're running. We don't exist in the scope of time, Tess!"

Tess skidded to a stop in front of the rusty metal door. Sure enough, a hollow echo of someone pounding against the other side filled the space. A few times, the hinges shook against the vibration. Her subconscious was strong. So strong. If they waited, she might break the door. What would happen then? No living spirit had ever crossed over. Part of Tess wanted to wait and see.

Thomas frowned at her, gripping the handle. "For someone who was in such a rush to get here, you certainly are taking your time."

They stepped through the door into a white room. "Hey!" Chloe was standing in the middle of the room in shorts and a night shirt shouting to the ceiling. "I'm here!"

Something in the air must have changed, because she turned around. When she saw Tess, she frowned. She actually frowned! What had Tess ever done to this girl? Helped her see the truth, that's what! She looked past Tess and smiled at Thomas.

Thomas eased in front, bumping against Tess' shoulder ever so slightly as he did. She wanted to body-slam him to the ground. Everyone thought he was so special: Kamahalan, the Governess, and now Chloe.

"Chloe," Thomas said, stretching out his arms. They clasped hands, smiling at each other. Tess ground her teeth.

"I want to help," Chloe said. "I want to finally do something that matters."

Thomas smiled at her. "I'm so glad to hear that."

"I have this friend, Becca. She can see things, too."

Thomas backed up at this. "She what?"

Of course there were more people who could see past the veil. Her guess was Thomas must have had a mostly struggle-free life. His soul had not been scarred by hateful words. He didn't know how tragedies could change people—make them see things that "weren't there." He didn't know. That's why Chloe was never on his radar. Not before Tess opened her mouth.

"She can see things," Chloe restated. "I believe you, Thomas. I know you are real."

Tess could see Thomas fighting through the onslaught of strategies that currently overwhelmed him. He really was ignorant of the possibility. How could he be so ignorant? Maybe he wasn't as important as she thought. How could he be an integral part of the Darkness and not know? Or was the Darkness not as advanced as she had thought? She should have fought harder to do this alone. His participation risked the revelation of too much information. But what did they say about hindsight?

"I'm glad," he said with his nicest smile. But Tess knew him too well. He was struggling with the act. He was bothered. Very bothered. He even stole a glance her way. *How much does she know?* That had to be what he was asking himself. How far had she figured this out?

*Enough of this.* Tess took a step forward. "That's not everything, is it?"

Chloe glanced at her, her eyes narrowing.

"What did you find out?" Tess said, ignoring the insult in her stare.

Chloe hesitated, stepping back from Thomas. She looked like she was wishing Tess wasn't around. Oh well. She was here to stay so the girl better get used to it.

"My friend," Chloe said after a moment, "Becca, she can see shadows. There's a group of kids. We think something from your side," she said this to Thomas, "is following them."

Thomas stood back at this, shock on his face. If he wasn't part of the Darkness, then he was a horrible Chief Guardian of Order. Either case, he didn't deserve his station.

"We need a name," Tess continued.

Chloe hesitated, glancing back at Thomas. He just nodded, still unable to find words. "Dylan Mitchell."

That wasn't a name she recognized from her research. He was not someone with a history of trauma that caused them to see the veil. She supposed not everyone needed catastrophe to heighten their attention. Tess smiled at the girl. "Thank you. That is very helpful."

"Becca and I," Chloe continued to tell Thomas, "we can follow them."

Thomas started to nod, but Tess cut him off, "No!"

Chloe jerked. Maybe she was a little too abrupt. But the poor girl had just accepted they were real and that her dreams were not as innocent as she once thought. She was not ready to confront whatever people the Darkness was recruiting.

Tess stepped closer, trying to get in front of Thomas without shoving him away. "In your town, I need you to find Paul King and Cameron Mays." Now Thomas was staring at her with mouth agape. There was judgement mixed with shock though. Tess tried to focus on Chloe. "We work in teams. That's the only way we stay strong. You need a team to help keep you safe."

"You want these people to be my team?" Chloe said, shuffling her feet.

Tess nodded. "I can't stress this enough. Don't approach the group. Let us take care of it from our side. I don't want you to get hurt or draw attention to yourself."

Chloe studied her for a moment, but nodded. "Okay."

At least they were making progress on the trust factor. "Gather your team. We'll check back with you soon. Let you know what we discover."

Chloe hesitated, looking at Thomas for confirmation. Thomas stared at her for a long time. As the seconds ticked by, Tess gripped her hands. She wanted to smack him against the back of the head. She wanted to shake some sense into him. *Do your job*, she wanted to shout. At this point, she didn't care if it ended in a fistfight. In fact, that's what she wanted. She needed him to retaliate against her. She wanted her chance to finally go up against him and defeat him.

The only thing that stopped her was Chloe. The girl already didn't trust her. If she started a supernatural fight, she not only would lose the girl's trust, but she'd also lose her edge on this case. She had to keep herself together. She had to keep her emotions tied tight into a ball in her gut. She couldn't release them until she did it with lighting at the appropriate moments. So she waited. Although it killed her, she waited.

And Thomas finally cleared his throat. "Yes. You are too valuable to lose in a dangerous situation. Get your team together. We'll be in touch."

Chloe smiled at him. It was a smile that lit her face. The poor girl. Did she really think she didn't serve a purpose in life beyond this crazy ability? Who had robbed her of that self-worth? The world hadn't changed in the years Tess had been gone, that was for certain. It was still the same rotting place that fought to steal people's souls.

When Chloe had disappeared, Thomas turned on her. "What are you doing?" he practically shouted.

Tess blinked at him. "Whatever do you mean?"

"Don't play games with me. You had *names*? Who are those people? What are you planning to do? You obviously knew more about Chloe's situation than you shared."

"Funny coming from you," Tess said, crossing her arms. Now. Now would be a good time to fight him. All he had to do was start it.

"What is that supposed to mean?"

"You know," Tess said, tilting her head to the side. "Maybe if you would do your *actual* job, you would know more."

The muscles in Thomas' jaw flexed. She had seen that look before. It came right before a fist to the face. Back then, she had been too weak to do anything but accept the blow. Not now. She would fight to nonexistence if she had to.

"I'm starting to think you might have an inside look into what we're fighting," Thomas said, his voice much too low for someone in full control of his emotions.

His words cut into her. He couldn't know about her sources. He merely suspected. She could stay on top of this. She just had to find a better way of maneuvering without revealing anything. "Maybe I'm just good at what I do."

"Maybe you're ready to follow Mathias."

Tess leapt toward him, but Thomas stepped out of the way. She clenched her fists, electricity buzzing up and down her arms. It took all she had to hold the energy inside. She couldn't start the fight. That's what he wanted. She couldn't give this to him. She couldn't let him win. Not this time.

Thomas nodded, a smug smile pulling at his face. "You wanted things to move so quickly before. Now you slow it down. You're trying to hinder progress. That's the only way to see it."

Thomas turned, walking back toward the rusty door.

"Why don't you put that in your report?" Tess shouted. She felt herself gasping for breath against the strain of the electricity now crackling against her skin.

Thomas laughed. "Don't worry. I will."

The moment he was gone, Tess screamed. Lightning shot from her fingers, neck, even her toes. It bounced around the room like some laser field. When the light faded, the room looked unharmed aside from the smoke drifting through the air. With Chloe's cooperation, she now needed a plan. She needed a plan for reality, a plan for dream, and a plan for Thomas.

She had to get ahead of this. Otherwise, all the rotten accusations cast her way both in life and in the after may as well be true.

# Thirteen

The apples stacked in front of her glimmered under florescent lights, offering riches in every bite. Or maybe Chloe was just hungry, which seemed to happen every time she walked into a grocery store. Stores all smelled the same: dry cereal, sweet fruit, and a hint of refrigeration coolant. She swore all stores also had some sort of food-scented freshener they blew through the vents. Chloe reached for an apple, her stomach insisting it was necessary. She selected a glimmering red one that was nice and firm. The color was a beautiful, even red. No dent. No blemish. Perfect.

"You can't eat that." Molly's small voice came from her side.

Chloe glared at her cousin. The girl's hair was in a high ponytail. Her jean Bermuda shorts hugged her thighs and her current T-shirt had some sort of trolls printed on the front. Then there were those green eyes, shielded from the harshness of the world and yet much too judgmental for a ten-year-old. "I'm hungry," Chloe said.

Molly's frown was a mirror image of her mother's. One corner even hung lower than the other. Chloe didn't think Molly had quite mastered the motherly glare, but she was off to a good start. Chloe sighed dramatically. "Fine." She wanted to slam the apple back in place, but figured the whole tower would tumble. Instead, she settled on a flip of her hand when she was done. "Satisfied?"

Molly gave a stern nod.

"What's going on here?" Becca skipped over to them, munching on the half-mutilated banana in her hand.

Chloe raised her brows at Molly, motioning toward her new friend.

Molly just shrugged. "She's not *my* cousin."

"We were just looking for Paul King," Chloe answered Becca. It took a little digging (and Chloe didn't want to know what "contacts" Becca had used) but they finally discovered that Paul worked stocking shelves at the local Safeway. Since Chloe was under orders to come straight home from school to "watch Molly", she had no choice but to bring her cousin along.

Standing here now in the middle of the grocery store, Chloe wasn't sure what would likely cause more trouble: bringing her cousin to meet a strange 22-year-old man, or just leaving the girl home alone. These days, it certainly was a toss-up. She couldn't seem to do or say anything right. And her reason for meeting Paul was definitely *not* going to be a part of her now bi-weekly meetings with Dr. Lewis, which now also included meetings with her psychiatrist, Dr. Roth. She hadn't even mentioned seeing dead people in her dreams, and they were already discussing an increase in medication. Dr. Lewis, Dr. Roth, and her aunt had started their secret meetings behind closed doors to discuss a plan of action. Team *how-do-we-help-Chloe* was reunited for a second season.

When Becca had finished chomping on the banana, she eased the peel onto the ledge of the apple stand. "Well," she said through the mush in her mouth. "I saw some dude in the cereal aisle."

"Are you just going to leave that there?" Molly asked, clearly appalled as Becca turned to leave.

Becca didn't even acknowledge the girl as she marched toward the front of the store. Molly hastily grabbed the peel before taking off after them. As they passed the flower aisle, sweet roses and carnations perfuming the air, Molly tugged on Chloe's shirt and waved the banana peel. "She's going to pay for this, right?"

Chloe shrugged. "Kind of hard if they have to weigh it, don't you think?"

Molly frowned. "That's stealing!"

"Shh!" Chloe glanced around to see if someone heard. The store was filling up with the afternoon rush of people buying dinner ingredients, but all were too focused on the displays at the front of the store, or trying to find the quickest checkout line to notice. The air chilled as the girls passed the frozen food aisle. "Don't go shouting that word around. You'll get us into trouble. Do you want to do that?"

"Jesus is watching, you know." Molly said with a determined nod.

"Learned that in Sunday school, huh?"

Molly's lower lip continued to puff out at her. The girl was clearly not happy and about to rat them out to the entire store if Chloe didn't do something.

She sighed, taking Molly's hand to guide her around the checkout lines forming. They really should open another lane. Things were getting backed up. "Yes," Chloe conceded for the sake of peace. "But haven't you ever heard of a sample?"

Molly's brow scrunched at this. "Sample?"

Chloe nodded as they made their way past an aisle of canned goods. They were still four aisles away, but she could begin to smell the freshly roasted chickens ready and waiting for hungry shoppers. "Yes. Grocery stores, they allow you to sample. But just a little, so you can see if you want the product."

By the wrinkled nose, Chloe could tell Molly wasn't quite buying this story. But then her face finally relaxed. "Then we're going to buy bananas, right?"

"What?" Chloe asked, her steps slowing.

"Well. She sampled it. That means we should buy some."

She was so determined in her statement, so assured that this was the way the world worked. Chloe knew they weren't getting out of here without making a purchase. At least it would explain their need to go to the grocery store. She'd be saved if Molly could keep the secret meeting with a strange man to herself. Somehow Chloe thought it would take more than just some bananas.

A few aisles before they reached the deli and bakery, the three turned. Smells of sugar and grain greeted their noses. Creepy eyes bulged at them from cardboard boxes. Elves and animals and other creatures smiled downward, begging children to accept them, each proclaiming to be the healthiest choice. At the middle of the aisle, a thin man stood in black jeans and a tan shirt. He reached up with a scanner toward the highest shelf which held boxes of some sort of actually healthy, whole-wheat cereal no child would want.

The three of them gathered a few feet from him. Chloe grabbed a box of Frosted Flakes, pretending to examine the label like she'd seen her aunt do on countless visits. The man's face certainly looked young enough. Smooth, aside from the leftover acne scars. His wired glasses rested on a narrow nose, his brown hair cut short and spiked at the front. His tan shirt had the red label of the store embroidered below the left shoulder.

After a beep, the man turned slightly to examine the small screen on the scanner. When he did, Chloe could clearly see his nametag. Paul. She just hoped there weren't a lot of Pauls who worked here.

"Excuse me?" Chloe said before she could think. When he turned to face her, his brown eyes magnified by his glasses, Chloe froze. *Now what?* "Are you Paul King?" she stammered.

He held her gaze for a fraction of a second before looking back at his screen. "Yes." He turned to face the shelves once more. Beep.

Chloe exchanged a look with Becca. "My name's Chloe."

He nodded at her, but Chloe knew he wasn't really listening.

"Hey," Becca said a little too loudly. "You're being rude."

Paul hesitated, taking in the group before him. He stared at his shoes when he said, "I have to finish. Cereal aisle and then canned goods. I have to finish."

Becca placed hands on her hips. "Don't you have secret shoppers who come in here?"

Paul's eyes met Becca's for only a second. "Yes."

"Well," she said with a tilt of her head. "How do you know we aren't one of those?"

Paul rubbed an eyebrow with a knuckle. "You're too young. Most of them are housewives. And they don't come on Friday nights. Only Saturday or mid-week."

This wasn't going anywhere. How were they supposed to recruit him anyway? Tess hadn't been as helpful as Thomas. Chloe started to question why she was even following this plan. They lived on the other side, right? So why would Tess know anything about Paul King and how he could help them? Then again, she seemed to know a lot about Chloe. Plus, she genuinely seemed concerned about Chloe's well-being. But that didn't solve the current problem at hand.

"Is this any good?" she heard Molly ask from the side. Somehow the girl had wandered off and grabbed herself a big purple box with two bunnies on the front. The bunnies looked high on something.

Paul grabbed the box from her, glancing at the label. "200 grams of sugar." He shook his head. "That's too much."

"But is it *good*?" Molly asked as if he hadn't answered her question.

Paul glanced at her before rubbing his eyebrow again with a knuckle. "Well, I don't know. I don't eat anything like that. It's not healthy. Studies show a link between cancer and food, you know."

Molly frowned at the drugged bunnies. Finally, she shrugged and headed back toward the whole herd of drugged bunnies down the aisle.

Chloe rubbed her eyes. There had to be an easier way to build her team.

Beep. Paul had traveled a third of the way down the aisle. Chloe followed after him. He was not the easiest person to talk to. How was she supposed to bring up the topic of shadows and the Darkness and creatures trying to possess people? *Hey, seen any dead people or shadows lately?*

"I have to finish. I get off at five. I have to finish," Paul insisted, another beep of his machine confirming his story.

"Look. I was told to find you." That seemed like the best way to open. "I was told you could help me."

Paul frowned at her. Well, he frowned at her nose before punching some buttons on his machine. "I don't train people."

"What?"

Paul continued scanning. "I don't train people. That's not what I do. Talk to Tom. He said I don't train people. I just stock shelves and take inventory."

"You don't understand," Chloe said, following him.

"It's not my job," Paul said, more insistently. The force of his words caused Chloe to take a step back.

Yeah. This was not going well at all. Why was this guy important to her? How could he possibly help them? But then Chloe remembered the stares from her childhood. She had never been normal. She had never been someone people felt comfortable around. Maybe that was the point. Maybe normal couldn't see more than normal. Maybe it took something else... something altered to see beyond what was expected.

"What about this?" Molly asked, holding up a new box. This one had a picture of the latest X-Men characters displayed on the front. They promised heart-healthy eating and real berries inside. Chloe doubted those berries looked anything like the ones in produce.

"Molly," she chastised.

Paul tucked his scanner under an arm and took the box. "Still a lot of sugar," he mumbled. He flipped the box. If eyes could smile, his would be the full-teeth kind. Even though his smile didn't reach his lips, not in the traditional sense, Chloe could tell he was happy.

"Although," he added, "the picture is a lot better."

He handed the box back to Molly, who frowned at the characters. "I didn't like the last movie."

Paul looked at her like she had said she tortured animals for fun. "That movie was pivotal to the development of the franchise."

Molly shrugged. "It was boring. I like Storm. She should be in it more."

Paul stumbled over his words. Finally, he just shook his head. "You're too young to understand. But that movie was *not* boring."

Chloe marveled at the scanner still stuck under his arm. He had somehow abandoned his mission to talk about fictional superheroes with a ten-year-old.

"They just talked and talked," Molly insisted.

"They talked about the future of the mutants, who were being hunted because they were different."

"Yeah," Molly said like he agreed with her. "Talk."

"You don't get it," Paul said, finally remembering his scanner. He turned his back to her. "People hate them because they are different. They don't care about any contribution they make. They just hate."

"People suck," Becca agreed.

"Do people treat you badly?" Chloe asked.

Paul scowled at her. "I'm not in the movie."

Chloe wasn't sure who should feel stupid with that statement. Yet she felt her shoulders sag as if it should be her. One thing was certain. She was no good at this.

"I like it better," Molly said, still examining the box, "when they battle evil forces. They use their mutation and pow-pow!" Molly wiggled the fingers of her free hand, posing in a fighting stance. "They defeat them all!" Molly giggled at herself.

"You know," Chloe said, "I bet there are really people like that out there."

This statement elicited judgmental looks from all three of them. The tall sides of the narrow aisle somehow leaned closer to her.

Well, she had already started down this road. She might as well continue. "Not like with super powers, I mean." The judgmental looks eased, but clearly they still doubted her sanity. "You know. People who can see things that are different. Things that others can't."

Paul hesitated, glancing her way before another beep from his scanner. But she had his attention. He wasn't arguing with her. He wasn't telling her how silly she was being. Just silence. And that silence validated her.

"For instance," Chloe continued, "Becca can see creatures that look human but really aren't."

Paul frowned at her. Then he turned and started to make his way out of the aisle. Becca glared at Chloe. She didn't care. She knocked the box out of Molly's hand. As it thudded against the tile, Chloe grabbed the protesting girl's hand and pursued him.

He turned two aisles down and started examining the canned vegetables. He punched buttons on his screen, each one clicking at him.

When Chloe caught up to him, she said, "She also sees shadows around people."

Paul shook his head. Ignoring her, he held his scanner in front and beeped on the creamed corn tag.

"You're sounding crazy," Molly said, yanking her hand free.

"I'm not crazy," Chloe shot back a little too harshly. Molly's eyes glimmered, but she didn't cry. She just crossed her arms high on her chest and looked away. Becca strolled around the corner.

"He's not going to help us," she said as she neared.

But, as she said it, Chloe noticed Paul staring at her... well, at her chin. He was silent for a long moment.

"I think you would really like the X-Men movies."

"I'm done filling my time with fiction," Chloe said, failure creeping against her skin. She had found Paul, but she didn't have a plan. What did she think was going to happen? That he was just going to believe her? That he would know exactly what she was talking about? That he'd agree to go along with her just like that? Of course not. This was not a dream she had created and could control.

Paul clicked his tongue. "Maybe. But a lot of truth can be revealed in fantasy." Then he turned his back to her. The beep, beep of his machine stabbed at Chloe.

"Come on," Becca said softly. "We can always come back."

Chloe took a shaky breath. Molly was still pouting next to her. She had to fix this before she created more drama at the house. There was only one thing Chloe could think of to try to rectify the trip. "We have to get bananas first."

Molly was hugging a bunch of yellow bananas in the backseat as they pulled out of the parking lot onto a side street.

"It's okay," Becca said from the driver's side of her beat-up Subaru. They went over a pothole, metal jarring against metal, while the car rang a bell somewhere deep inside. "I don't think he could really help us anyway."

The day had turned hotter than anticipated. It was always like that. In the 70s one day, back to the 50s the next as the indecisive desert chose between winter and summer. Becca hadn't turned on any type of air-conditioning, and Chloe wondered if she even had any in this car. If not, she'd have to find another ride in the summertime.

Chloe thought about Paul. If Becca was right, then why had they even bothered looking for him? "But why would she tell me to find him? Why go through all that trouble?" Chloe asked. "Just to keep me busy? Because I'm not ready?"

Becca's brakes squeaked as she stopped at the stop sign. Traffic was lighter on this street, although a steady stream exiting the college filed past them. The college extension had taken over the old hospital building for their nursing program. Not the same amount of traffic as when the hospital was there, but not the abandoned road it was when the building was vacant. Her blinker ticked at them. "Maybe he's not like us, you know? Maybe that's not his talent." Becca hesitated. "But you should really ask for more details next time."

Chloe tried not to glare at her. She was just trying to help. Taking on the Darkness shouldn't be easy. Not if the situation was as serious as Thomas had said.

Chloe's head hit the passenger seat as the Subaru shot across the road. "What are you doing?" Chloe asked, glancing back at Molly. The girl was chewing on a piece of candy Chloe had purchased to buy her silence. She seemed satisfied enough not to notice Becca's driving.

"I saw him," Becca said, glancing in her review as they punched through a gap in traffic and headed down the road.

"Saw who?"

"Dylan." Becca said. She slowed as they passed apartment buildings on the corner of the road. A neighborhood of houses stretched before them, and abandoned doctors' offices stood on the left.

It took a moment for Chloe to see him. He was skateboarding down the road on the south side of the apartment complex. Becca slowed her car on a bend in the road, wooden posts separating the apartment parking lot from the residential street forming in front of them.

When Dylan was about halfway down the stretch of brown complexes, he put his foot down and kicked the skateboard into his hands. He turned, heading up the black metal stairs.

"Does he live here?" Chloe asked. She didn't know if it was because the apartment looked old or if it was the location, but she suddenly had the creeps.

"His mom's single. Works two jobs. She probably can't afford much else." Becca said, her gaze drifting toward the roof. She visibly shivered in her seat. "There are so many shadows sitting up there." Dylan unlocked the second-story door and disappeared inside.

The roof looked empty in the orange glow of the fading sun, but Chloe could feel an energy hit her. She wanted out of here. She glanced at the backseat. Molly was currently playing some game on her phone, still obliviously sucking on her candy.

Becca gasped, her tires squealing as the car launched into motion.

Chloe grabbed at the dashboard. "You have got to chill out."

"They're coming for us!" Becca said in a hushed voice, glancing in her rearview mirror.

Chloe looked behind them, her heartbeat rising. "The shadows?"

"Yes!"

Chloe swore she saw a raven soar overhead. It had to be a raven. It couldn't be anything more. "Well, slow down," Chloe said as they barreled past the houses on the side street. "You could hit someone."

Becca gripped the steering wheel, her knuckles white.

"Shadows can't hurt us," Chloe said soothingly.

Becca screeched to a stop at the stop sign at the end of the street. She looked around them, manually winding down her window to peer outside. "They stopped. They're just staring at us from the end of the street."

Chloe wound down her window and peeked her head outside. The street was about a quarter of a mile long. Most of it was empty aside from the neighborhood dogs barking at the fences. And yet, just a few yards from the apartment complex, Chloe could see the image of a man standing there. His eyes glowed red under his brimmed hat. He was shadowed, but she could make out a long coat covering most of his body.

"Let's get out of here," Chloe said as she wound her window back up, like the glass could protect her.

Becca turned right and they passed a small house with a large antenna marking the local radio station. They continued past the new light, then past the rehabilitation center and apartments. No matter how many miles they traveled, Chloe could still feel those red eyes staring at her. Maybe that woman was right. Maybe she needed a team to deal with Dylan. Maybe she wasn't ready.

## Fourteen

Fire crackled all around them. It climbed up trees, puffs of black smoke swirling toward the sky. The boy's scales had turned a deep shade of red, his eyes wide. Tess' boots crunched against the dead leaves and brush that hadn't yet burned. "This fire happened years ago. But its reflection is still pretty dominant, huh?"

The boy turned around in a circle. He looked ready to flee, but she knew he wouldn't. Not here. Not when he believed the fire could harm him. That was the thing with creatures on this side. They believed they were destructible. They hadn't yet realized what true destruction meant.

Tess watched as a wide-eyed deer ran down the hill to her right. The poor thing. It would be running for eternity. It crunched down the mountainside and along a dry creek bed in its flight. An ash tree ignited next to the mesquites surrounding her. The smoke was heavy in her nose, but still reminded her of her father smoking meat in the backyard. A lot of people paid good money for mesquite-smoked food.

The reflection of history lacked reality's heat—at least so far—which made it more like the best 3D-movie experience ever.

A tree bark popped against the heat, sending the boy to his knees. "Why am I here?"

"I thought it was appropriate. This fire was human-caused and threatened so many lives."

"How does that apply to me?" he asked, eyes still scanning for an exit.

"Well," Tess said, strolling toward the burning ash tree. "Let's see. You and your buddies are currently starting a fire in our world." The ash tree flicked sparks at her. One touched her skin and actually felt warm. So many years later and the reflection was still strong. "But no one ever plans for such a catastrophic fire."

She turned to find the boy's wide eyes staring at her. From the look on his face, he must be certain she had brought him here to torture him beyond recognition.

Tess frowned. "You're no good at metaphors, are you?" As she stepped toward him, the boy scurried to his feet.

"Would you stop messing with the kid," Marcus said. He was leaning against a boulder, arms crossed.

Tess smiled at him. "I'll stop messing with him when he starts telling me what I want to know." She leaned down and picked up a burning stick. The boy's scales turned black as she neared.

Tess watched the flames reaching up from her stick. It crackled against the wood, darkening everything to black. "Fire is so destructive. It levels everything, leaving behind stumps and ash." Her movement was quicker than he could react. She swung her stick, knocking him off his feet. The stick broke, landing on the ground and igniting grass.

The boy grabbed at his legs, grimacing. Being a spirit certainly had its advantages. It took much more than a reflection to harm her. Tess crouched in front of the boy. She made sure his slit pupils met her gaze before she said, "Tell me how they breach security to the doors. That's all I want to know... today."

His snake tongue flickered out of his thin lips. "You're pathetic."

Tess stood straight, hands on her hips. She looked up at Marcus, who still looked unamused. "Why do boys always go for the insults?"

Marcus shrugged. "Only the weak resort to name calling."

Tess pretended to ponder this. "The weak can still leave heavy marks." When she turned, she caught the boy staring at her neck. Tess smiled at him, kneeling once more. "Do you like the marks he left on *me*?"

She tilted her head, revealing the scar stretching up her neck. "This one. This was his first attempt at my life. But he did it with words too, you know." She clasped her hands in front of her. "So many words."

Tess removed her jacket, her pale scars illuminated in the orange light. She pointed to a small sliver of one running along her arm. "This one. This one grew every time he called me pathetic." She pointed to a branch next to it. "And this one grew every time I believed him." She pointed to another branch. "And this one? Every time I let it hold me back."

Tess smiled at him, her boots grinding against dirt as she shifted. She pointed back at the long, deep cut along her throat. "This one you admire? This one came after he hit me with a frying pan and I told the emergency room I had tripped and fallen in the kitchen."

The boy crouched away from her, ready for her strike. She might as well have a frying pan of her own with the way he was looking at her. She should feel power from it. But she didn't. Seeing the reflection of what she must have looked like… it sickened her.

"You see," she continued, "it's reaching for my head because he was in my mind by then. He had me believing in his lies and his words." Tess picked up a charcoaled piece of wood. It darkened her hand. "He had me believing that was my worth." Tess tossed the wood aside.

The boy watched the charcoal soar next to them, anticipating something evil to happen. When nothing did, his eye-slits focused back on her. His tongue escaped his lips for only a moment before retreating.

"I stopped believing him," Tess said. "And when I finally could see his lies, I knew I had to escape." Tess tilted her head. "Just like you."

The leaves on the ground crunched as Marcus moved closer to them, arms still crossed. The smoke was starting to grow thicker, fogging the area.

"You are caught in this lie of a better life," Tess continued. "They've belittled you and promised you greatness in the same breath. And you've believed them. But I'm your only friend here."

Air whistled in and out of the boy's nostrils, his eyes narrowing. A thundering snap echoed down the canyon as a tall ash tree crumbled to the earth. He looked toward the sound, but his body remained just as tense as it had been when she retrieved him from the jail cell.

Finally, after a long moment, he said, "They have people in high places. They will kill me if I help you."

Tess sighed. She stood straight, easing her arms back into her jacket. "He just doesn't get it, does he?"

Marcus shook his head. "You can't expect someone at his level to understand."

The boy examined both of them. "What?" he demanded.

Tess crossed her arms, smiling down at him. "You think you know who is in charge. Their lies hold you down." Tess took a step closer to him, causing the boy to prepare for a firm kick to his side. "No one has come for you," Tess continued. "No one has contacted me about you. They don't care that you are captured. You are expendable. Because you are loyal. I decided a long time ago, before coming here, that no one else would control me. No one else would decide my importance. What about you?"

The boy sat back at this. Tess uncrossed her arms, flexing her fingers. She almost couldn't hear the electricity crackle over the fire. "So. You're going to tell me how they get past the doors without being discovered. Because that's my next move."

The boy hesitated. But another tree fell, this time closer. The heat was also starting to rise. If they didn't get out of here soon, refection was going to mimic reality much too closely for him to survive. "Okay," he said. "When the guards change shifts, they always stop to confer about orders. It's a short window, but easy enough to bypass."

"How do they get out?"

The boy grinned, showing fanged teeth. "They don't."

Tess stood back. They don't leave the doors. That must be the first step to possession. Infiltrate a door and squat. It couldn't be that easy. "How do they stop the subconscious from killing them?"

The boy shrugged. "Planting the first one, that's the hardest. But, once established, we can plan a meeting."

Tess nodded. That's what she stumbled upon when she picked up this low-life. It was a three-party attack. The first two groups met in the same area on both sides of the veil with their intended target. The last group used the opportunity to infiltrate the doors and corrupt the subconscious.

She used to think there had been only four attempts over an Earth year, but those had been four *failed* attempts. She'd bet anything these attempts led to the death of creatures in all three groups. No wonder the boy was scared. He wasn't a low-level worker at all. He was instrumental in the possession.

"How many?" she asked after a moment.

The boy frowned at her.

"How many are possessed?"

When he didn't answer her, Tess let electricity crackle between her fingers. She shot a bolt at him, letting it just graze his side. It barely touched him, but the boy screamed.

He gripped at his side.

"How many?" she shouted, growing a nice electric ball between her fingers. She had to make a decision. How far was she going to take this? When did this stop being an act? Where was that line? And more importantly, how far would she go to avenge Mathias?

The boy didn't make her decide those answers today. "Five," he gasped. "You disrupted the sixth."

Tess let the electricity fade. If she was lucky, the subconscious had attacked the intruder within the door before he could harm the victim. She hadn't heard of any soul's crossing over before their time. The scarier option was the intruder successfully remained within the door.

"You can't just jump into these people," Tess thought aloud. When he was silent, she only had to crackle her fingers.

The boy slid across the dirt, hand in the air. "No. We prep them. We follow and harass them."

"More desert chanting?"

The boy nodded. "It was harder with the first. Took a lot more. But he helps us on the other side."

Smoke filled the air. She could taste the ash on her tongue. They couldn't stay here much longer. "Helps you how?"

The boy's lower lip trembled, sparks falling from the tree above him.

"Helps you how?" Tess shouted, letting electricity bounce between her fingers.

The boy whimpered. "I don't know!"

Tess backed away. How could someone so instrumental in the possession know so little? But she believed him. Maybe a soldier at any level was just a soldier. Or maybe those who could die in the process were unimportant. Putting those who were expendable in harm's way, making them believe they were important, while the actual leaders remained in safety... that strategy made sense.

Marcus stood by her side. He glanced up at the smoke-engulfed sky above them. "We need to get out of here."

Tess nodded, but continued to examine the boy before her. So they had succeeded in possession. They had succeeded, but they hadn't attempted to cross the veil yet. Maybe they needed more than that. Maybe they couldn't just approach the veil and cross through. It was too strong. She was still missing something. But if she was lucky, they also were missing that key. She had some time to catch up. It'd be so much easier if she could have gotten invited to a meeting. Yet even after capturing him, they still hadn't contacted her. She had to find another way.

"How does this serve you exactly?" Marcus asked after a moment.

"I can't take down their operation if I don't know how it works, now can I?" Tess said. He had a point. She couldn't bring this back to Kamahalan. She had a hard enough time convincing them of its importance in the first place. How was she supposed to make them believe in five possessions? And what purpose would that serve? It wouldn't make her any closer to taking out the leadership of the Darkness.

And she couldn't tell Thomas. If he wasn't part of the Darkness, then he truly was a policy-toting choirboy. Either way, he'd see to it her attempts ended in removal. Her position as Chief Guardian was the only power she had. It granted her access to so many places others could only talk about. She couldn't lose that access. Not now. Not when she needed to infiltrate a door behind Kamahalan's and Nakima's backs.

"Are you sure this is what you want to do?" Marcus asked. By the look on his face, Tess could have sworn he was in her thoughts. Or maybe he just knew what the next logical step would be.

Tess nodded. "Yes. We have to take this up a level."

"*We?*" Marcus asked with an arched brow.

"Hey. You were in this the moment you led me to that RV lot."

Marcus frowned. "I should have pushed for more."

Tess smiled at him. "You're my second. How much more do you want?"

Marcus scoffed.

No one asked about the boy's mental state when she checked him back into his cell. And no one asked why she had been gone so long with him. And obviously no one had checked in the interrogation room to see they weren't there. She was starting to see how infiltrating the doors was so easy. With trust comes weakness.

She was just out the door, walking down the hall, when Thomas rounded a corner, manila envelope in hand.

"Where have you been?" he asked, glancing at the door behind her.

"He's still not saying anything," Tess said with a shrug.

"With Chloe, I didn't think we needed him anymore." Thomas frowned at her.

Tess continued down the hall, making him follow. "Couldn't hurt. But he's content with rotting in there before he'll share anything."

Thomas pondered this a moment, but finally handed the manila envelope to her. Tess took it, flipping it open as they rounded the corner and headed back toward her office. The face of a bear stared at her from a picture clipped to the right corner.

"I have a lead on a meeting."

A lead? What was his lead? More than likely, he had inside information because he was working on the inside. Before Mathias died, he said the Darkness had infiltrated the Order. He suspected someone of higher rank to be the mole. Thomas sounded good to her. This was just another example. But she had no concrete evidence. Tess studied Thomas, but nothing in his face revealed anything more than he always displayed. "A lead, you say?"

"Yeah. When Chloe told me about that Dylan kid, I decided to ask around. The bear was assigned to him five years ago. I guess his dad was a big man. Walked out on them around that time."

Tess shook her head. "No such thing as a family unit anymore."

"Anyway, Yogi—"

"Seriously?" she cut him off.

Thomas shrugged. "That's what he wanted people to call him. Anyway, Yogi stopped dreaming two years ago."

There were only two reasons why most creatures of dream stopped participating. They no longer served a purpose or they were attacked by the subconscious. Tess suspected it had to be the latter. "Okay."

"So, apparently Yogi has been hanging out with Lexis."

"The tree?"

"Yeah. And roommate of our dear friend in lockup." Thomas motioned back where they had just come.

A boy chameleon and a tree rooming together; there had to be a joke in that somewhere. Tess shook her head, studying the papers again. "How can one be a roommate with a tree?"

"Things of dreams," Thomas mused, rocking on his toes.

Tess ran a thumb across Yogi's last known location. Presidio Santa Cruz de Terrenate. It was an abandoned fort in the middle of the desert just outside of Whetstone. Tess frowned. Members of the Darkness met out there on several occasions. At least a century before Tess walked the other side of the veil, many Spanish armies had tried to establish and reestablish the fort but were eventually slaughtered by the local natives. That kind of bloodshed buzzed with power on this side of the veil.

She discovered the location on a hunch. Shortly after Mathias died, she had confronted Marcus to confirm its use. He had reacted so strongly against the idea of her going and made her promise never to go out there alone. Knowing she'd never bring a unit of Order with her—even as Chief Guardian—his promise ensured she'd leave the fort alone. Marcus was normally such a mellow creature. The fact he had reacted so dramatically and took extra measures to ensure she wouldn't go had convinced Tess that maybe the place was truly more dangerous than she could handle. Instead, she tried to access his connections for a meeting invitation. He dodged her requests every time until eventually leading her down the path she currently traveled.

How could that place be coming back up? And from Thomas' hand. Still. Marcus had never failed her. "Take a big unit with you," she said, handing the folder back.

Thomas stared at her. "You aren't going with me?" He actually looked shocked. Had she disrupted his plans or was he truly ignorant? Either way, she had to avoid working with him.

Tess shook her head. "You did all the work. You should take the credit." She figured he would like that ego boost. "Besides, we need Nakima's help if we're going to investigate Dylan's door."

Thomas frowned at that. "Don't you think meeting with Nakima alone would be more detrimental than visiting the fort?"

Tess laughed at his boldness. She continued down the hallway, puffing out her chest. "I'm the one who got him to agree to Argumas, remember?" She flashed her best smile at him. "No. You go see what's happening at this fort. I'll make sure we comply with proper protocol before going to Dylan's door." Tess hesitated, placing her hands on her hips. "Unless you don't want us to go to his door?"

Thomas stumbled over his words before saying, "Of course I do. I just don't understand why you wouldn't want to take the opportunity to advance on this confirmed location of the Darkness. It's like you don't want us to take them down."

Tess locked her jaw. He had a lot of nerve. But his pushing so hard to go only convinced her she didn't want to oblige. If he was part of the Darkness and leading her toward a known location of the Darkness, then she could confirm they didn't want to reach out for her. They'd rather she die just like Mathias. So she had to watch for the knife aimed at her back at the first opportunity. "If you need a babysitter, then I'll go."

Thomas straightened at this.

"But I figured you could handle it while I took care of this other matter. That way, we are making good use of our resources and not doubling up where it's not needed."

Thomas pointed his folder at her. "Fine. We'll do it your way." As he walked away, he said, "I tried to work with you, but it's impossible."

Before Tess could think of a snazzy comeback, he rounded the corner and disappeared. It was dangerous to antagonize him, but she couldn't help it. Marcus owed her big time for this. She finally had her opportunity to see that stupid fort. His word of caution better be right. She couldn't take being played by him, too.

Still. All logic pointed toward following the lead on these possessions. That was the only way she could gain access to the leadership. Without identifying the leadership, she couldn't know what their plan was. She'd be just as effective as a little girl chasing fireflies while a nuclear explosion took out the world behind her.

## Fifteen

White clouds streaked across the heavens like natural brushstrokes against a pure-blue desert sky. Birds sang their various tunes high above in tall trees scattered around the park, welcoming the spring migration. The air was warm, lacking the winter chill still lingering in the morning. Chloe sat on the ledge of the bandstand. Tan walls rose well above her, lights positioned and eager for use. White letters identifying it as the Centennial Pavilion were mounted on the front. A large, silver gate blocked access to backstage.

Chloe gripped the edge, staring at the concrete area in front of her. When the city hosted events here, the concrete would be lined with people in their lawn chairs. Now it was empty. From this distance, she could still hear children playing in the nearby playground. Across the way, a young man was playing an impressive game of Frisbee with his black Lab. Another couple lay under the shade of one of the pine trees. Many people were taking advantage of the nice weather to get outside.

She hadn't messaged Tyler in almost a week. It's not like she meant to blow him off. She was busy with the whole monsters-are-real mess. Not that she could tell him that. Then she had seen him walking around with Missy in between classes. At one point, he was carrying her books. So that was that. She had been declared the crazy ex and everyone moved on. She should have confronted him. She should have screamed at him in the middle of the school. Told him how stupid he was and how much of a whore Missy was. That she'd leave him the second someone more prestigious came around—maybe someone with a Corvette.

Yet when Chloe saw him, she felt too suffocated to yell at him. She couldn't blame him. She had pushed him away, and for what? To serve a "better" purpose—like that was going to save her. She might have value in Thomas' world. Was she crazy for wanting to find value in this world where others could actually see it?

So she sat here alone like some social reject. Her aunt was starting to notice the change of friends. She was starting to notice the lack of a boyfriend. Without a plausible explanation, the view from the outside looked like she was self-destructive. She had half a mind to agree. And again, how could she explain to everyone it was all okay? *Yes, I left my friends for a new, slightly weird group, but it's okay because we're saving the world.* First the accident, then her math grade, then the play, and now changing friends and boyfriends: she was certainly painting quite the disturbed-child picture. One who needed medication to numb her, and restrictions that made her feel younger than Molly. She wasn't even supposed to leave the house, but she had to get out of there.

"Funny to find you here," she heard a familiar voice say.

Chloe smiled as Becca practically skipped over. A young brunette accompanied her. The girl looked a few years older than Molly, maybe thirteen. Right about the age where one felt the need to dabble with appearances. The girl's brown hair was a mess of ironed curls, her foundation a little too heavy, and her eye shadow a little too pronounced. But the girl was very pretty. Her shirt was tucked in the front to reveal a large, silver buckle that caught the sunlight. Chloe half-expected to see cowboy boots on her feet, but found black, worn-out Vans instead.

"This is Addie," Becca said, motioning to the girl. "She lives on my current block."

"And you felt the need to bring her here?" Chloe asked. Maybe including Becca in her group wasn't a good idea. The girl could see shadows. So what? Did that really contribute to Chloe's task... whatever it was?

Becca shrugged. "Addie was bucked off a horse four years ago during a junior rodeo competition."

Chloe looked at the girl, who was currently examining a chip in her white nail polish. "So? She's like us?"

"No," Becca said with a laugh. Like it was the most ridiculous statement Chloe could have expressed. "I mean, she's definitely labeled, but she just knows a lot of people who know things."

"That kid is ugly," Addie spoke suddenly. Her eyes were focused on a mother and her toddler walking along the concrete sidewalk winding around the park. The kid had too many rolls of fat, which might have been cute on a baby, but not at any other age. Chloe watched to see if the mother heard Addie, who didn't seem to think it necessary to whisper such comments.

"Is one of those labels 'heartless'?" Chloe asked, hopping down from the stage.

Addie shot her a look, but Becca was the one to speak. "Nah. Traumatic brain injury. It causes her to speak her mind out loud more than other people." Becca smiled at Addie, who had rolled her eyes and was again scanning the area. "I find her truth refreshing."

Chloe conceded that point. Someone who always spoke their mind—no matter how offensive—at least could never be accused of being two-faced. However, it would certainly lead to hurt feelings and fists the older she got. "We are supposed to be looking for Cameron Mays." Chloe still didn't know how she felt after her last attempt at building this crazy team. And when Addie started clearly laughing at her, Chloe began to question her entire decision to do this in the first place.

"You both don't know a thing," Addie said in between laughs.

Becca smiled at Chloe like this proved something. Chloe didn't know what, besides proving she'd be willing to slug a middle-school girl.

"She did the same thing to me when I saw her in the driveway."

Chloe raised her brows in her best *so?* exclamation. She seriously had to reevaluate her choice of friends. First she had picked snobs who cared only about appearance. And now she picked someone who probably should care a little more.

Becca tapped an elbow into Addie's side. "Enough. Tell her what you told me."

Addie gathered her composure. "Cameron can't see squat. What's he going to do at a park? Admire the scenery?"

He *can't see squat*? What did that mean exactly? How was he supposed to help them if he couldn't see anything? Chloe knew she shouldn't have trusted Tess. She was trying to slow her down. But why? Did she not want Chloe to get close to Dylan? She claimed she wanted to keep Chloe safe. Maybe it wasn't about being safe, but buying time. Time to achieve her own plans behind the scenes. Did Thomas know?

"If we can't find him at the park, then where *can* we find him?" Chloe asked with a sigh.

"Work, the skate park, the library."

"Because a blind kid can read?" Chloe asked. Maybe she should just do this on her own. None of these people had any brains at all.

"He's not blind," Addie insisted. "He just can't see. But the boy likes to read. His face is practically on the book, but he makes it work."

Chloe studied this girl before her. She looked like a rejected country rodeo princess with the mouth of a well-developed brat. Yet she was certain in her words. Most middle-school kids were certain about a lot of things, so that didn't necessarily prove much. "How do you know?"

Addie shrugged. "He's the older brother of a guy I dated."

Chloe stifled her laugh. "Dated? What? You went to the movies and held hands once?"

Addie placed her hands on her hips, her belt buckle trying to blind Chloe in its glimmer. "No! And I don't see you here with anyone!"

What did this girl know? She had probably just stopped playing with Barbies last summer. Or maybe she still played, but in secret, yet again caught in between childhood and high school. *Boyfriend. Ha!* Chloe rolled her eyes. "Okay. Whatever. Look. I can't be out much longer, so if we're going to plan when to go, we had better do it quick."

"You on curfew?" Addie asked, raising one brow.

Chloe pulled her lips into a smile, leaning in close. She balled her hands into fists. "Yes. You have something to say about it?" She wasn't above slapping some manners into this girl. It certainly wouldn't help her situation, but she was just about done with the entire thing anyway.

Addie cocked her head.

Before she could say anything more, Becca interrupted. "Guys. It's Dylan!"

Chloe followed Becca's finger across the grassy park. Dylan stood with his friends by a tree near the parking lot, his hood pulled up over his head. The skate park was across that lot. The Dylan she remembered was not much of a skater. She knew better than others though how people can quickly change. The spring air hadn't quite taken on the summer's heat, but the sun beat down too hard to require a sweater. He brought his hand close to his face for a fraction of a moment. When he tilted his head back, thin smoke escaped his lips. He leaned his head against the tree bark, eyes vacant.

He said something to another boy, also wearing a hood. The boy shrugged. Dylan looked around them, then shifted his body. A long, silver object slid down his sleeve and into his hand. With a movement best suited for a sleight-of-hand magician, the object disappeared behind the sleeve of his friend. They had quite the nerve to do such things in a public setting. Not only did police monitor the skate park, but there were countless parents and dog walkers. It was like they were daring anyone to notice.

"Is that Ricky?" Chloe asked.

Becca hesitated. "Yeah. And… " she lowered her voice as if the boys could hear, "he now has shadows around him."

"Shadows?" Addie said much too loudly. "You guys must be on something. Is it any good?"

Dylan and Ricky left the tree, climbing inside Ricky's souped-up blue Acura with a wing mounted to the trunk. They drove out of the park with an exaggerated rumble of the exhaust pipe. As they did, Chloe could have sworn Dylan made eye contact with her. It was only for a fraction of a second. It probably didn't even happen. She was just being paranoid. They were clear across the park.

"Ricky's one of them now?" Chloe asked, bringing her attention back to Becca.

"Of course he is." Addie was the one to answer. "Dylan's been trying to recruit him for months. Ricky comes with money."

"Why does Dylan need money?" Chloe asked.

"For the drugs. Duh."

This is why high-school people shouldn't hang out with middle-school kids. Not even a whole minute had passed and Chloe already wanted to punch the girl again. She certainly hoped Molly didn't morph into this when she became a tween.

"What drugs?"

Addie shrugged, examining her nail polish again. "I don't know. It's some sort of new stuff he's pushing. Dylan's a popular dealer in school."

Chloe looked back where the car had disappeared. He certainly had changed a lot in the past few years. Maybe Thomas was right. Some let what happened in their lives take control and others refused to let that define them. Had Dylan given up all those years ago?

"You certainly know a lot," Chloe said.

Addie smiled at her. "You hear a lot of things at rodeos and softball practice."

Becca's smile beamed. "See. Aren't you glad I brought her?"

Chloe felt the frown tug at the corners of her mouth. "I wouldn't go that far, but yes. Thank you for helping us, Addie."

The girl smiled at her. "I like you. You aren't fake like most of the girls I meet."

So she could say things that weren't rude. That was good to know. And hearing the compliment coming from her seemed to mean more than hearing it from others.

"So," Addie continued, "I'll try to get you a meeting with Cameron. And I can show you where Dylan and his crew hang out too."

The girl was full of surprises. Chloe didn't know if she should be impressed by the girl's connections or concerned that a middle-school kid knew about such dark corners of the city. "I would be grateful," she said, "but be careful around Dylan. He's dangerous."

"Please," Addie scoffed. "My brother could shoot the head off a rattlesnake from fifteen feet."

Was the girl bragging? About shooting things? What had become of Chloe's life? She could never introduce Addie to her aunt, that was for sure.

"I think Dylan's head would be an easier target," the little girl added.

Chloe caught her breath, but Addie laughed like it was the best joke ever. Becca clasped her shoulder. "Don't worry," she said softly. "She grows on you after a while."

Chloe cleared her throat. "Well. I have to get out of here. Becca, give her my number, okay?"

Becca nodded. "We're making progress, aren't we?"

Chloe nodded, but as she walked away, she felt more like a child than an active participant. Was she really in control of this situation? And why was she even participating in the first place? Oh, yeah. Because she wanted her life to matter somehow. That's right. She wondered if finding her purpose in life would even matter if she lost everything in the process.

Chloe let this thought haunt her as she caught the bus home. Just a few weeks ago, she had friends who could drive her anywhere her heart desired. Now she was catching a bus. Value. Yeah, right.

## Sixteen

The building before them flickered. The stone in the pillars and walls remained the same in every version, but the wood and name changed: woodsy elegance with an Italian name, blue and promising Greek, and bright yellow with a Mexican title. The place was cursed. That's what everyone said. Personally, Tess liked the original Italian restaurant the best. It didn't change into the bright yellow until well after she had died.

She crouched behind a blue Ford pickup truck. Thomas was examining his thin gun. Hopefully he was better aiming with an electric pulse than he was with a net. He had told her another group was conducting a possession tonight. There were three full moons hanging high above her, so the night appeared more like daytime. Unlike normal sunlight, the white glow reflected off the cars and abandoned building with such focused intensity it electrified the air.

When Thomas had asked her to come along, Nakima had just denied her access to Dylan's door. He hadn't seen the point of accessing yet another door when she could come and go from Chloe's—like the two situations were at all related. She was so angry, she forgot to ask Thomas what had happened with his plan to raid the fort. If her gut was correct, he had never wanted to go in the first place. He just wanted *her* to go.

After the quick inspection, Thomas snapped the safety back. "You ready?"

"What exactly are we going to encounter in there?" Tess asked. She hadn't taken off her jacket yet. She shouldn't be here with him. But if she had stayed behind, all Kamahalan would see was her not cooperating. How much she participated, however, was completely up to her.

"I told you. There's another meeting happening right now."

The neglected building had to be currently vacant across the veil. The most dominant image had boarded windows and doors. "Shouldn't we stay focused on Dylan's door?"

"Why don't you see this as progress?"

"We already have one of them captive. What is this going to do?"

Thomas shifted in his crouch. He certainly had mastered the judgmental stare. Tess couldn't see why he kept up the act with her. Did he not know she could see through him? She had lots of experience with his kind of man.

"You want to take them down, *right*?"

That's what everyone would think. If she stayed outside staring at the nearby Target building, everyone would assume she didn't want to capture more of the Darkness. What harm would come from assisting him? They could fill their jails with underlings and attack Dylan's door later. The question remained. Why did *Thomas* want to take down underlings?

After a long moment, Tess slowly eased out of her jacket. The light shifted suddenly, black meeting light in an explosion of burgundy on the horizon. Dawn had started. On this side of the veil, it could last only a moment or much longer. She could never predict it. But with the dramatic fire of light dancing in the sky, Tess suspected it would mimic reality and last only a moment.

"Your information," she said, once her jacket was folded on the ground, "suggests this is just like we encountered before. Nothing more." Needles pricked against her skin. Tess couldn't tell if it was her scars coming to life or her nerves. She didn't like this situation at all.

Thomas just nodded. He smiled at her before making a hunched run to the doors. The wooden panels covering the windows vanished as the building transferred images of reality. Thomas reached the door and grabbed the large iron pull, easing the door open. It scraped against the dirt on the porch. Tess took a deep breath before following him inside.

Past the hostess' desk, the restaurant was divided into four eating areas separated by partial walls made of stone. The one to her right wound around to the bar and patio area. The one in front led to an open kitchen. And the two on the left side nestled against the stone wall. While the inside decor transitioned from blue to rustic cabin (equipped with an antler chandelier and elk's head), they did not compare to the dominant transition of a bright, multicolored fiesta. She couldn't tell if the last restaurant to stand here had featured a hodgepodge of decorations, or if the flickers of history caused everything to clash. What she did know, however, was that the place was empty.

Thomas motioned for her to follow him to the left. Tess sighed. While he still carried himself with knees bent, keeping close to the ground, Tess strolled behind him. As she neared the kitchen, she felt a pulse vibrate against her skin, lighting up her scars.

"Wait. Was blood spilt here?"

Thomas made his way past booths that transformed into tables. "What?"

"In the kitchen? Someone died here?"

"How should I know?" Thomas said, looking over his shoulder. He was still scanning the room like he expected someone to pop out of the shadows.

The sun peeked through the wooden planks over the windows, lighting the room. Dawn had happened very quickly.

"Wait here," Thomas said, as he disappeared down a long hallway leading to the restrooms.

Tess rolled her eyes. She walked closer to the stone partition closest to the open kitchen. She remembered a time when the restaurant changed from Italian to Greek. Rumor back then was the Italian restaurant had gone bankrupt.

Tess placed a hand on the wall that came up to her chest. She leaned closer, eyes focused on the silver appliances. She felt the pulse again. The death of a restaurant, or the curse of a location, settled inside any vacant building in the after. She didn't think the place was cursed, per se. It was the location: tucked a block away from the main street, hidden behind another predominant restaurant on the main corner. That could explain the failures. Yet curses were not made by the supernatural. They were birthed from a thought that grows into a belief shared by many.

This pulse. It wasn't just a curse. This was something more. This indicated a cursed place that had claimed the blood of the owner. She was sure of it.

With a glance down the dark hallway, Tess left the seating area. Thomas was fine. No one was going to do a séance in the bathroom. She walked to the small path designated for service staff in front of the low counter for food pickup. The kitchen was relatively open to the restaurant. When she neared, she thought she could hear something coming from the back.

A kitchen where blood had been spilt... that was the perfect place for someone to attempt possession. Tess flexed her fingers, the buzz vibrating against her skin. At that moment, a large crash tore through the ceiling next to her.

Tess dove forward as plaster and support beams fell all around her. Dust fogged the air, sunlight glaring down the newly-formed hole. Tess propped herself up, looking behind her. The claw of a demolition tractor moved upward, leaving behind a large pile of rubble. Right where she had previously been standing. The image was so real. This must have just happened on the other side. Reflection matched reality here.

Tess scrambled to her feet as the claw drove through the ceiling once more, this time tearing a part of the wall out with its descent.

"Tess!" Thomas shouted. He appeared at the end of the hallway, eyes staring wildly at the pile of rubble. He seemed to notice the lack of a body, because he looked up quickly.

"Careful," Tess said. When Thomas saw her, she couldn't tell if he was relieved or disappointed. He had put her there. The creep had put her right there! Like he knew!

Tess tried to walk but pain ripped through her leg. When she looked down, she could see blood seeping from a cut on her leg. The silver color still unnerved her, reminding her that this blood was not the same. Destruction here was permanent. Tess ripped the bottom of her shirt as the demolition claw crashed down. That entire side of the building was collapsing in one big pile of rubble.

"We've gotta get out of here!" Thomas shouted. She couldn't see him anymore through the rubble. There was no way he could get to her... at least, that would be his story.

Tess gritted her teeth as she tied the cloth around her leg. It hurt just about as much as it would have in real life. Her entire body ached along with the pain. When Tess straightened, she saw them.

A group of creatures leapt through the opening of the kitchen. Their legs and arms looked like

implants from a frog, their torsos reptilian, and their round heads were without noses. They froze when they saw her. They certainly didn't look like creatures capable of staging a possession. Their eyes, however, cut at her like only the Darkness could. More wall crashed behind her, but Tess stood on her good leg, hands out to her sides. She refused to give them the advantage by looking away.

One clicked his tongue and gulped at another. The others nodded, understanding the language of this breed of dream creatures. Tess rubbed her index finger and thumb together, sparks crackling against her fingertips. The creatures rushed her before she had the chance to fire a single bolt. Tess screamed against the nails ripping at her arms. She threw elbows and kicks in every direction. Most of the time, she would hit something. Every now and then, she found air. Pain ripped at her arms and face.

The knee on her good leg buckled under her weight. In an instant, the floor slammed into her shoulders before it smacked the back of her head. Now the aching from her body was accompanied by stars swirling around her. She tried to gather lightning in her hands, but was too busy swatting away their attack. She couldn't electrocute them like this. Not while she was on the defense.

This was just like before, in life. She had fought against him so many times only to find herself helpless. He'd always taken advantage of the cheap shot, always caught her distracted. Then he'd hit her, and she'd had to play defense. After a moment, it had all become about surviving each blow. He had taken everything from her. Her life. Her love. Everything! Not now. Not here. She wouldn't just lie down and take it. Not anymore. She couldn't let them destroy her.

Tess forced her eyes open, her heart to calm. When she knew all five were near, she screamed. Her body shook with energy. The creatures backed away, staring down at her. Her torn shirt had revealed the intricate spiderweb scar circling her bellybutton. It pulsed white. They turned to run, but it was too late. All the fear, anger, and sadness she had been holding in this whole time shot out of her abdomen in an electric surge, releasing a bluish-white blast that exploded like a bomb.

It fried their bodies upon impact, continuing past them and up the walls. The entire room glowed white. Tess gasped for breath, smiling at the five charred bodies surrounding her. When the white light dissipated, she was left bathing in the sunlight beating down on her. She wasn't safe. Not yet.

The floor shook beneath her. Reflection and reality were battling. Destruction in reality always devastated the space in dream. But destruction was necessary before something could be reborn. Tess wondered what would stand in this place. Would it stay forgotten and dead? Or would something wonderful break the curse of the location?

Tess sighed, her head falling to the side. She'd probably never see it. Her body was too weak to move, and this place wasn't going to stand much longer. At least they didn't use dynamite to take the building down. Dynamite on the dream side looked and felt more like an atomic weapon. But claws ripping through walls weren't much better. In the end, either eradicated existence. Thomas was a smart guy. She had to give him that. She didn't know how he could have learned about the building, but he was certainly good.

Muffled words met her ears. It took too much strength for Tess to rotate her head to the side facing the door. A bent, shadowy figure bounced toward her.

"Tess!"

*What now*? She had spent the last amount of energy she had annihilating those creatures. She doubted she could even send an electric shock at this point.

"Tess!"

As the image neared, dodging a falling piece of ceiling, she squinted against the glare of the sun. He looked familiar. Yes. That bent walk and bony frame. She'd know it anywhere.

"Marcus," she breathed. Her voice sounded too much like a whisper.

Marcus placed a hand on her shoulder, kneeling beside her. "You can't stay here." Marcus looked at her stomach and then at the charred bodies around her.

"I should have controlled it better," Tess said. She dragged her arms closer to her body, the dirt on the ground scraping against her skin. "I don't have anything left."

Marcus looked back at the charred bodies and then at the cloth tied around her leg. He swore. "Come on," he said, reaching for her. Marcus slipped an arm around her torso and another under her knees.

"I'll break you," Tess said. Defying all physics, he lifted Tess into the air. She wrapped an arm around his neck, finally feeling life pulse through her once more.

She rose and fell with his jaunt toward the door just as another brick fell where her head had been. "What are you doing here?" she asked as they neared the door.

"I heard the chief guardians of Order were here."

"One of these days, you'll have to tell me who *your* informant is."

The desert air rushed over her skin as they continued into the parking lot, the desert sun glaring down at them in full force. Marcus put her down where the Ford truck used to be, although now the lot was vacant. Tess sat, resting her arms on her knees. She rubbed her eyes. Energy slowly seeped back into her.

"Who were those creatures, Marcus?" Tess asked, squinting against the glare of the day.

In the full sun, Marcus appeared paler than she thought he was. She could actually see blue veins lining his hands and legs.

"Servants of the Darkness."

Tess sighed. "I know. But why were they there?"

Marcus frowned at her. "They were there to kill the Chief Guardian of Order."

The building before her shook. The demolition equipment was missing from the scene, but the whole thing looked like some giant had stepped on its side. The remaining walls vibrated, each one crumbling all at once. The ceiling crashed down in a thunderous roar of metal and concrete. One moment, the building stood shimmering between its different forms. In the next, it was a pile of rubble. She could have been in there.

A loud roar erupted as the land opened. The rocks rumbled together, grinding and falling. When all was finished, the only thing that remained from the past was a clear dirt patch. Tess finally noticed the construction fence surrounding the area. It must have appeared shortly before the destruction began.

"Only one guardian?"

"Only one was known to be here." Marcus hesitated. "Why *were* you here?"

Tess rubbed the side of her head. Pieces of concrete flaked from her hair. Why was she here? She came with Thomas. And Thomas was following a lead. Had he set this whole thing up? Had he tried to kill her?

The ache in Tess' body was settling in her joints. She felt like she had just come down with the worst bout of flu. "Thomas said there was a meeting like at the RV lot." Was Thomas the target? He said he had information regarding a meeting that obviously didn't happen here. Was *he* set up? On that thought, Tess asked, "How did you know it was me and not him there?"

Marcus shuffled his feet, staring at the cleared dirt lot. "I don't know. I thought maybe that kid said something."

"You thought the kid set me up?" Tess asked. She flexed her fingers. They tingled with the rejuvenation of life.

Marcus shrugged. "Wouldn't be the first time an informant set up a chief guardian, now would it?"

She still didn't know why Mathias had trusted her with this case. For that matter, she didn't know what caused him to transfer her from the Deputy of Spirit. She was a broken spirit with scars that held the potential of consuming her. He had saved her. He had taught her how to control her emotional scars, to let them serve a greater purpose.

She had never asked how he went from a basic shadow lurker of Dream to the Chief Guardian of

Order. But she knew he could recognize the true nature of anything he saw. He knew the Darkness existed before any other. And he had worked his way inside to high-level informants.

He had been excited that day. She remembered the glow in his voice when he announced they were close. How could he have ever been so fooled? How could a man who could see the true nature of those around him not have predicted the betrayal? Maybe he didn't believe they could actually go through with it.

Tess wondered if her death today would have been treated as nonchalantly as his. A tragic accident. That's what people who were too scared to face the truth proclaimed. Such a tragic accident, but everyone must move on. Like his existence hadn't mattered. Like he had been expendable... just as she was.

"You never told me," Tess said after a moment.

"Told you what?"

"Was Thomas his informant? Is Thomas the high-level informant who went back to the Darkness?"

Marcus' dark eyes studied her. The sun was already hanging high in the sky, pounding heat down at them. The asphalt below baked against her skin like a pan in the oven. "Why do you think that?"

Tess smiled up at him. "You didn't answer my question."

"And what answer would you like me to say? Yes, so you can kill him? No, so you can look for another creature to kill?"

Tess grunted as she stood, body shaking. Her injured leg complained and the ache in her bones vibrated against her nerves, but she refused to sit back down. Standing as straight as she could, Tess said, "You promised to help me. Mathias was your friend. You promised to help and yet you refuse to answer me."

Marcus frowned at her for a long moment before his eyes drifted toward her middle. Of all the scars on her body, it was the most beautiful. And of all the scars on her body, it was the only one she never wanted to show. When he met her gaze once more, he didn't have to ask.

"I had left him," Tess said, voice flat. "It took every ounce of strength I had, but I left him. Started from nothing. Went back to school, met another man, got remarried. I thought I was safe. I knew he was still watching me, even after three years. I could still pick out his car in the parking lot of the college or driving past our street. But I thought I had gotten away with it. That I had achieved the new life I wanted. It had been so long since I left. Then he met me in the parking lot of the college on the last day of school. Drove a knife through the baby growing inside."

Marcus grimaced. She hadn't told anyone that story in a long time. Retelling it, she felt numb, as if the story belonged to someone else. Mathias helped her achieve that. Yet she knew if she thought too much on the memory, the numbness would fade into a crushing sadness. That memory could make ghost hauntings and raging spirits. That's what Deputy of Spirit Lisa Crowe had said when she saw her.

Tess had crossed over screaming, electricity shooting from the scars on her body. His emotional scars had followed her. They were engrained in her soul. She had refused to follow the guardians of Spirit. She refused to cooperate with any being she encountered. So they locked her up, afraid she'd go back to the veil. They were afraid she'd haunt the college for eternity. Mathias had come to save her—and he did save her. She had trusted no one else.

But she owed Marcus an explanation. She owed him her loyalty. He had risked a lot coming to save her in the daylight. He could be seen here. He could have just shown the Darkness he was her informant.

Tess limped closer, dragging her injured leg with each step. "So now you know how I died. And you probably know that Mathias was the only one who believed in me—on either side of the veil." She got close enough to smell the oil mixed with dirt on Marcus' skin. "Now. Will you please tell me something? Or were your promises of retribution more lies to my face?"

Marcus' eyes turned cold. "I don't know whether Thomas is part of the Darkness or not. I know there are two key agents in positions of power, but I do not know who they are."

Finally. She was getting somewhere. Two people in power. Mathias had only told her one.

"As far as the informant is concerned," Marcus continued, "maybe if you spent more time thinking about rectifying his death and less about revenge, you would not only know who had killed him but you would stop following blindly toward his fate."

Tess could feel the tears well up inside, blurring her vision.

Marcus shook his head, turning to leave.

"That's it?" Tess shouted after him.

Marcus hesitated, his back to her. Finally, he shuffled his feet to face her. "Your existence cannot be built proving something to creatures that do not exist here. And those scars on your body do not define you. I would have thought Mathias had taught you that." He was gone before Tess could say anything more.

She felt her lower lip tremble; tears streaked down her cheeks. She held back the gasp that closed her throat, instead forcing air through her nose. When the tears had subsided, Tess stood. She wiped her cheeks dry, turned, and started limping toward the street. If they were bold enough to attack a chief guardian, maybe they were bold enough to attack Chloe's door.

## Seventeen

"Hello?" Chloe asked. Her voice echoed in the house. No one was around. She had searched each room twice. Her aunt, uncle, Molly. They were all gone.

A cold breeze rushed through the hallway and up Chloe's neck. She turned around, facing the long corridor. No one was here, and yet someone was. She knew it. She was not alone. "Hello?" Chloe shouted, louder. Her voice echoed back to her like in a canyon.

How could she be so alone? How did she get to this point? Where did everyone go? They had all left her. They left her alone in this house. Chloe's breath sounded too loud as she eased herself down the dark hallway. She had always been alone. No one else bothered to stay.

She hesitated in front of her aunt's door, across from her bedroom door. But that didn't seem right. Her aunt's house had a split design. Chloe touched the brown door with a hand. The warmth emanated from inside. Her aunt's door was white. All the doors were white. But not these doors. Both were a dark wood color—hollow on the inside.

Chloe gripped the bronze doorknob. It squeaked when she turned it. The door opened with a swoosh, stale air rushing against her face. A queen bed with a fluffy floral comforter stood before a window with white cotton curtains. Off to the side stood a two-mirror vanity. A blue candle burned in a crystal pillar on the vanity, saturating the room with lavender. Next to the bed, crammed in the corner, was a rocking chair. It rocked despite being empty. The yellow baby blanket neatly folded over the back swayed forward and backward with the movement.

Across the room, a large dresser stood. Chloe's gaze drifted to the impressionist painting hanging above. It reflected the yellow fields and blue mountain range of the city. Her grandfather had painted it before his death. The painting stole Chloe's breath. This was her mother's room.

Chloe reached for her pocket, only to find her yoga paints. She had worn the crop pants and a white t-shirt to bed. Was she awake? Or was this all part of a dream? It had to be a dream. There was no doubt she had been in her aunt's living room just a moment ago.

Chloe saw movement against the window, a shadow outside. She backed up, looking down the empty hallway. She quickly shut the door to her mom's room, stepping back. When she bumped the knob across the hall, Chloe slowly turned around. She knew what she'd find. She knew it, and yet her hand reached out anyway and opened the door. Baby powder and sugar perfumed the air. Against the adjacent wall stood a twin bed with pink sheets. A miniature Barbie doll house was crammed into the corner of the room across from the closet, a mountain of stuffed animals displayed next to the house. The room was much cleaner than she had ever seen it. Her mother would organize it this way only to have the tornado effect appear within minutes of Chloe's return.

A door slam echoed down the hallway. Chloe jumped inside the room, pushing the door to a crack. She peered down the hall. She was alone. She had been alone. She had checked. Footsteps echoed against the tile floor of her aunt's living room. Chloe shut the door. She pushed and turned the knob, locking it into place.

Backing away, Chloe listened. A gunshot sounded. Chloe jerked, diving to the floor. She crawled to the closet, easing herself inside. But when she pulled the sliding doors, they refused to shut. Chloe whimpered and pulled until she thought the doors would break from the track. Still no movement. Her heart beat against her chest as the footsteps neared her bedroom door.

This can't be happening. Not like this. Not like this. She had to close the door. Someone pounded on the locked bedroom door. This wasn't right. Chloe looked at the window. The night outside was dark. No full moon. No light seeping through. This wasn't right. This wasn't her dream.

Chloe scurried out of the closet, searching around the room. She dove for the bed, pushing herself against the floor. The frame of the bed dug into her shoulders, refusing to let her under. Chloe pounded the floor, but froze when the door rocked against its hinges. She couldn't hide. What was she going to do?

Chloe sat up, eyes scanning the room. Movement outside her window made the hairs stand on her arms. Someone was here. They were here. Chloe placed her hands against her ears and rocked back and forth. She had to stop them. What was she going to do? Why were they here? This was wrong. It was all wrong.

The door to her room erupted into a blast of splinters with a bang that echoed in her brain. Chloe's body shook as she watched the figure panting in the doorway. He looked like a cross between an antelope and a human, his antlers touching the top of the frame above his head. He would be perfectly cast for *The Lion King* musical on Broadway if it weren't for the red glowing in his eyes. This was not right. This was not right. Chloe rubbed her hands against her thighs, searching desperately for a pocket. "Not real—"

He came up to her in two strides, his sharp claws digging at her as he gripped her arm and forced her to stand.

The entire room shook, rattling the furniture like in the doll house.

"Hi, Chloe," the antelope man said in a gravelly bass voice.

Chloe pulled against her arm, but he gripped her tighter. Pain shot through her. It felt too real. More shadows passed outside her window. She could feel them in the dining room. Chloe tried to stomp on the man's foot, only to find a hoof that felt more like a rock. Chloe gasped against the pain.

Down the hall, dishes crashed and someone screamed. The antelope man smiled. "You are strong. You killed three of my men before we could get in the house."

Chloe felt her teeth chatter. What was he talking about? Killed people? Who did she kill? Chloe pulled against him.

"But you have a weakness." The antlers shifted in the air, pointing toward the closet. "Your fear controls you more than it can defend you."

The room shook once more, tipping the nightstand and spilling its trinkets across the floor. Chloe closed her eyes against the scene. "Not real, not real," she chanted, trying to ease her racing heart.

Wind rushed through her hair right before her back slammed against the wall, knocking the air out of her lungs. Chloe opened her eyes, the long snout of the antelope man inches from her face.

"Does that feel fake to you?"

Chloe struggled to find her breath again. The room shook and she could feel her mind trying to escape. If this was a dream, she should be able to wake up. Chloe screamed as he slammed her against the wall again. The shadows filled her living room, making their way down the hall. She could feel them.

She had to fight back. She had to get out of here. But all Chloe could do was push against him and wish for the closet. She wanted to hide. She had to get away.

A bolt of lightning shot through the door, striking the man in his back. He cried out in pain, finally releasing her. Chloe fell to the floor, but took the opportunity to scramble away from the wall. But where could she go? They were everywhere.

A figure moved into the doorway. It took a moment for Chloe to recognize Tess. Her entire body was lined with scars that pulsed with white light. She was without her leather jacket, and her shirt was torn to reveal a wicked spiderweb wrapping her bellybutton. Angry red scratches ripped against her face and arms.

She looked like she had dived through a pool of concrete dust, flakes standing predominantly in her spiked hair. Apparently, she was having quite the night as well.

The antelope man growled at her, much more of a predatory sound than it should be. Tess pushed her hands in front of her, electricity shooting from her wrists. The man dove to the side as the electric blast shot into the window. Glass exploded, showering both sides of the room. Tess chased the antelope man toward the window as Chloe crawled toward the door.

Her hand hit something hard, stopping her pursuit. The ground shook as the energy of the trinket pushed against her hand. Before she could look down, someone had grabbed her shoulders. Chloe pushed against the hands as her body turned around and she sat down. Tess was in her face, her eyes focused.

"You can't do it, Chloe. You can't bring them to the veil. You can't show them you have that power. They'll cross over, Chloe. It'll all be over."

Chloe shook her head, the words rolling around in her brain. What was she talking about? "Is this a dream?"

Tess hesitated, but nodded.

"Then why can't I wake up?"

Tess's touch on her shoulder soothed her nerves. "You can. You just don't believe you can. But you're strong. They were already starting to retreat when I got here. I only had to kill two of them. Your subconscious killed a lot of the others."

Chloe sat back, the mattress of the bed cushioning her head. She could feel it, but asked anyway. "Are they gone?"

Tess nodded. "Yes. And I hurt their leader. I think I can find him on the other side."

This whole thing was so strange. It made her long for the man in the beaked mask. Those dreams terrified her, but at least they were predictable. Chloe rubbed at her arms. If she didn't know any better, she would swear she'd have a bruise when she woke up.

"How did they get here?"

Tess sat down next to her, grimacing. It was then that Chloe noticed a wrap around one of her legs. "They gained access to your door. I'm still trying to figure it out. But they knew they could, which can only mean they have someone telling them inside the Order."

Chloe shook her head. "I know you *think* you answered my question... "

Tess smiled at her. For the first time, she looked soft... almost kind. She leaned her head against the mattress, and for a moment, Chloe thought about how dirty she was making the fabric.

"Most creatures or spirits who enter your dream go through a door—that's literally how we access your dreams. Anyway, most creatures who try are not acknowledged by the subconscious. If creatures try to make themselves seen, they face almost immediate attack."

"But I didn't attack them?" Chloe asked.

Tess shook her head. "Not all of them."

"So," Chloe looked at where she had been pinned against the wall. "You're telling me I *let* that happen to me?"

When Tess didn't answer, Chloe felt the tears come to her eyes. What was wrong with her? She would let someone hurt her like that?

"It might not be that simple. I think they are using some sort of power to infiltrate the doors. With a normal person, this could be a drug or something. But you... your reality borders on dream so closely. That makes you strong, but it also makes you vulnerable." Tess hesitated. "You are correct in saying you let it happen. You are in more control of your mind than you think. You just have to believe in yourself and take control."

Chloe laughed. "You sound like a school presenter."

Tess scoffed. She shifted her weight, gripping at her leg as she did so. "I probably do. But it doesn't make it any less true." Tess groaned, closing her eyes. She looked like she was ready to pass out. Could spirits pass out? Was that even possible? Although up until just now, Chloe would have thought spirits couldn't get injured.

"What happened to you?"

Tess opened her eyes. She dusted her hair, flakes of concrete falling to the floor. "I assume you're talking about today?" When Chloe nodded, she said, "We intercepted a creature on our side. He was in the middle of staging a possession."

"Staging a possession?"

"In most cases, a possession takes a group on your side, a group on my side, and an attack on the door.

There's a lot of chanting, but the goal is to implant someone in the subconscious."

Chloe frowned at that. She thought about Dylan. How much he had changed over the years. Was he even himself anymore? Or was he one of these creatures? "Like if you stayed here with me?"

Tess met her gaze, her face growing serious. "More like if that creature had stayed and you were locked in the closet."

Chloe shivered. If that's what happened to Dylan, she felt sorry for him. He was not his own person right now. He was locked away somewhere in his mind. He may even believe the dream he walked was actually reality. He might not even know he had lost control. The thought made her sick.

"My friends and I," Chloe said after a moment, "we've noticed shadows following Dylan and his friends. What does that mean?"

"I think the creatures shadow their mark. I told you before. We all walk on the same surface, separated by a veil. Sometimes, we can approach that veil, approach your reality. They would need to shadow so they knew where to meet."

"I still don't think I understand."

"That's because you're thinking about it in terms of space and time. Remember, I no longer live in a place like that. Take this house." Tess motioned around them. "We are currently in your bedroom as it was years ago. In my world, it is just one of many reflections. But it is the one you accessed. The front of the house though, belongs to your current living space. You meshed the two reflections together. So when we sit here, we are in a reflection of your past. When we stand in the living room, we are in a reflection of your present."

"Even though they are in two different places?"

"Space and time don't exist here. You can put whatever you'd like together and move between them as if they were all in the same location. But me, I no longer have that kind of control. I can just observe. I can no longer participate. Only someone on your side of the veil can do that."

"And these doors?"

"They grant me access to seeing my world the way you—and only you—do."

A door to view the world through the lenses of a person... it seemed like that kind of access would solve a lot of the conflict in the world. Or it would add to disputes because nothing was hidden. Either way, Chloe felt violated.

"So," Chloe began, "these creatures are gaining access to our doors so they can lock us inside our own dreams. For what purpose?"

"Let's say I approached the veil. If I had enough power, I could see your side as it is. I could even see you and your friends. But you couldn't see me. And even if you could, I can't affect your life at all. I can't interact or change anything. I'm just an aberration to you."

"Like the ghost hauntings of old buildings?"

Tess nodded. "Spirits have more access, yes. They can flicker lights or brush a touch against your skin. But they can't alter your reality. They can't burn the house down or stab you with a knife. They also can't maintain a constant presence, which is why an event happens every now and again."

"That's good to know."

"Possession is another form of accessing the veil. They interact in your world through their host's body. They can change things through that person. But they cannot physically be present. Only their host."

"If their task is to cross, how does possession help?"

Tess shrugged. "Do you remember the dream where you saw the Tinkerbell trinket?"

Chloe shivered against the thought. Her father had given it to her as a birthday present. Then, a month later, he came home with a gun. She nodded.

"In that dream, you brought us to the veil of reality. Closer than I have ever been before." Tess paused. "Just imagine what we could have done if you were possessed. Imagine the connection we could have established."

"The ones possessing don't cross over? They just enable a connection so someone else can?"

"You can't tell anyone that," Tess said, more insistently. "No one else knows what you did. They all think it was a typical night terror. They don't know you had the ability to physically move us close to the veil. If they did ..."

She didn't have to complete the thought. This little nightmare would become something much worse if they knew. She could help stop these creatures because she could see and sense them. But because she saw and sensed them, she was open to manipulation. Great. No strength came without a weakness.

"You need to be careful." Tess continued. "I think

you caught their attention. I can have someone guard your door, but I think they sense you might be the possession they are looking for."

Well. She always wanted to be special. She just didn't want to be special in this way. Chloe nodded her agreement. "I swear."

"Not even Thomas."

Chloe frowned at that. What was going on between them? They were supposed to be on the same side.

"Please."

There was a sadness in her eyes. She wasn't demanding. She wasn't even acting superior like she normally did. She seemed broken as she sat in disheveled clothing and a dusting of concrete. All of that combined caused Chloe to nod. "I promise."

Tess eased. Her head swayed to the side slightly.

"Are you okay?" Chloe asked, touching her shoulder. She felt cold to the touch. Chloe didn't know if that was the way she was supposed to feel. But Thomas' hands on hers had never felt cold. They were always warm. "Tess?"

She blinked then shook her head. "Yes. I'm fine. I just need to have my leg looked at."

"You never said what happened to you."

Tess hesitated, her eyes distant. "We're getting close. I just have to be more careful. We both just have to be more careful."

The thought of antelope man in her bedroom made the hairs on her arms stand once more. She could still feel his grip on her arm. And she hadn't even made contact with Dylan yet. Yes. It was good advice for the both of them.

# Eighteen

Water dripped, the hollow sound echoing against the brick walls. Everything in the room was white, except for the potted rubber tree in the corner and the vines growing up the painted brick. The small bed felt more like the floor to Tess. Although spirits did not have to sleep much, even when injured, they needed energy. A bag filled with silver-blue liquid hung on an IV drip above her head. The doctors—two oversized owls—had shoved a needle in her vein the moment they saw her. It must have been working because the insistent ache in her joints had subsided.

She lay flat on her back, her hands resting palm down at her sides. Her leg still felt like it was on fire, but that was progress from the skin-ripping pain she had been feeling before. The steady drip soothed her, but she must be losing her mind. She couldn't remember the last time she had thought about the creatures in the restaurant building, and she really couldn't care less about the Darkness right now. This was the most relaxed she had felt in a long while. Maybe there was more than just energy in the life drip. She wouldn't put it past the owls to add a sedative of some sort as well. Would it be made up of the same chemicals as in reality?

The sound of feet slapping against tile saved her from her thoughts. Tess didn't bother to move her head. The way she felt, if they wanted to take her out, they could do so. She wasn't going to stop them. Although, the idea of Thomas approaching made her want to prime her scars.

The featureless face of a shadow lurker that hovered above her certainly wasn't Thomas. When she saw his unique marking, Tess smiled at Argumas. "Have you come to destroy me at my weakest moment?"

Argumas rolled his eyes. "I should. But no." Argumas backed out of her immediate view. "Can you sit up, please?"

Trying to explain to him how much discomfort that would inflict was a lost cause. Tess grumbled, pushing her palms against the bed. She slowly pushed herself to a seated position, resting her back against the wall. The IV pulled at her arm and her leg screamed at her, but she managed to find a comfortable position.

Argumas stood with crossed arms. "I think you have something to say to me."

There were moments when the lack of time was a benefit, and there were moments when it was torture. This day of one event after another was just never going to end. She longed to become lost in the drip of the water once more. To breathe in the fresh, moist air and pretend the action would somehow matter to her lungs.

"I've been through a lot since we last saw each other. Can you refresh my memory on what it is I'm supposed to say?"

"You set me up."

Tess rubbed her eyes. "Which time?"

Argumas stood back at this. How could he be so shocked? Did he not live through the experience?

"At Chloe's door," Tess offered, "with the Governess, or when I forced you to remove your mask?"

Considering the assault he took in that whole dream, Argumas looked good. After the initial dream, he had looked like he had lost about twenty pounds. Now he was back to his full stature. His personality was just as rock hard, too.

"I used to think you were my friend," Argumas said, his pinpoint eyes somehow pulling off the puppy-dog pout.

"You brought me before the Governess with the intent of sending me to Judgment!" Her voice echoed off the walls. She must have gained back more strength than she had thought.

"Only after you betrayed me by interfering with my assignment!" The high-pitched whine in his voice hurt her ears each time it echoed.

Tess pounded the bed with a fist. "What do you want from me? I was doing my job."

Argumas nodded, turning away. "You're always doing your job. That's all that matters. Who cares if anything or anyone gets hurt along the way?" His shoulders slouched lower.

He was really upset by this. It wasn't like he was irritated at her exertion of authority. This was different. He really looked hurt. She tried to pretend their interactions didn't mean anything. She had tried to ignore his compliments to her. He had an oversized ego, sure. But so did all shadow lurkers. But at Mathias's funeral, he was the only one of them to come up to her. She was so used to working alone and ignoring the rest of the world, she never considered the connections others might have tried to make with her...

"Argumas," Tess began. What could she say? She didn't even know how he was feeling. She was so focused on proving herself and doing her job. She wasn't going to apologize for that.

The creature shook his head. "It's my own fault. I didn't know you trusted only Mathias."

The bed creaked as Tess swung her legs toward the side. Her leg complained, but it didn't hurt nearly as bad as it had. She gripped at the edge of the bed, unable to look up at him. "I never believed you were in any danger." Before he could comment, she added, "But I treated you like a pawn in my plan and for that I do apologize."

When he didn't say anything, Tess looked up. He had his back to her still, his arms hanging loose at his side.

"Do you remember when Mathias first introduced us?"

Argumas looked over his shoulder.

"It was at that ball the Governess threw. The one for the Governor of the Northwestern Hemisphere. I was there making sure all the guests kept to their promise of diplomacy."

"Like those creatures have the same class as we do," Argumas scoffed.

Tess laughed softly. "Everyone had treated me like an outcast. I was only a guardian apprentice. Not even a full-fledged guardian. But Mathias wanted me there, so I shadowed him."

"I knew he was mentoring you. He must have seen something in you."

"I know. And you were the only one." Tess pushed the memory of that night aside. It hurt too much to think of her predecessor. He had saved her life... well, her afterlife.

Argumas turned around. "I never defended you. Whenever they criticized. Whenever they questioned how quickly you advanced."

Tess smiled at him. "I know." She couldn't blame him. Why would he put himself out there for her? She didn't expect anyone to stand up against the ridicule. She deserved it. She was a disaster in life, and a reflection of that disaster here. She should never have advanced to Chief Guardian.

"Do you know they are all wrong?" Argumas asked, cocking his head.

"That's a matter of opinion," Tess said. The bed groaned when she sat straight. "But you didn't come here to compliment me."

Argumas neared the bed, his large hand resting on the small post. He looked like he could crush it by simply closing his fingers. "I went to the doors today. It was my first time back since..."

Tess nodded. He didn't have to finish the sentence. Since she had exposed him to the wrath of Chloe's subconscious.

Argumas cleared his throat. "That's how I heard you were in here. I heard what happened. That they attacked her door and you saved her."

Tess shrugged. "She's a strong girl. I think she could have survived without me."

"Well, at any rate I knew I owed you. She is not my assignment anymore, but I did grow fond of her—in my own way."

The relationship between a shadow lurker and their assignment must be a strange one. He came into her dreams and caused fear, which fed his energy. But that fear was being repressed. Without acknowledging it, Chloe could never move on. In a way, they helped each other. And yet in another way, one fed off the other's torment. Tess supposed it was true for any creature of dream. Not all dreams could be filled with fluffy bunnies and flowers. Some had to address the darker aspects of life. Confronting that was the only way for people to overcome their demons.

"While I was there," Argumas continued, "I spoke with the guardians of Order. They were changing shifts."

His comment reminded Tess about what the boy had said. That was the time when the doors were at their most vulnerable. She would need to address that issue with Kamahalan, given the attack on Chloe.

"They were surprised because Thomas was starting an investigation against you."

Tess jerked at this. He'd been busy while she'd been laying here like it was a spa day. "An investigation?"

"Into your connection with Mathias."

That didn't sound right to her ears either. "As one of his six associates?" That reminded her. She had six associates now. She could place two of them on Chloe's door. But which ones did she trust?

"Thomas claims Mathias had connections to the Darkness. That they took him out as a power play."

Tess ripped the IV out of her skin. This was the most ridiculous conversation she had ever heard. Was he serious? "Mathias was taking down the Darkness. His connections were informants helping him!" All of which were probably dead now. That's what Tess would have done if she was the leadership of the Darkness. Take out those who betrayed them.

"Did you talk to Mathias before he left that day?"

The world slowed around her. Tess pushed herself off the bed, her legs holding steady. "Yes. Why?"

"Thomas is saying a source heard you telling him about the location. He's saying you are the one who set Mathias up. Because you are part of the Darkness."

Tess was shaking her head half way through his statement. "They can't be buying that!" When Argumas met her with a steady gaze, she said, "Can they?"

"Not trusting anyone makes you look guilty."

Well. That was just perfect. She didn't know whether it was a statement against her or proof that she was right all along. They were all sheep happily following the shepherd toward a cliff.

"There's more."

Tess pinched the bridge of her nose. Of course there was.

"Thomas said he identified your connection with the Darkness. He said you communicated your plans to a cave dweller named Marcus."

Tess stood up straight at the name. They had found out about him. Tess ripped off her torn shirt and reached for another one folded neatly on a chair next to the bed. If they found him, then she couldn't stay here relaxing on holiday. She had to warn him. He shouldn't have come to save her. Tess looked around, but didn't see it.

Not until the leather hung in front of her. Argumas held it out, saying, "They found it at Chloe's door. I brought it with me."

Tess nodded her thanks, grabbing the jacket and pushing her arms through the holes.

"Who is Marcus?"

"He's my informant," Tess said, adjusting her clothes.

"Don't you guys register them?"

He really was such a simpleton. "Mathias never did. Why would we? When we believe the Order is compromised?"

Argumas stood back at this. "Compromised? Who?"

Tess attempted to walk. Her legs were steady. Her injury burned slightly, but the leg held its strength. She rubbed her hands together, blue sparks crackling against her skin. "I don't know. I'm guessing Thomas. Maybe more."

"You should tell Kamahalan!" Argumas shouted, his eyes wide.

"She could be one, too," Tess said. She let her hands fall to her sides, satisfied she could fight. "Mathias seemed to imply it. And I can't take it to the Governess. Not until I have some sort of proof besides just hunches."

Tess rushed past him. She was halfway to the door before she turned around. She was about to make the same mistake she had before. Argumas stood there, wringing his puffy hands. "Thank you for telling me. And I hate to rush out on you, but I have to warn Marcus. He exposed himself by saving me and now they're after him."

Argumas nodded. "Of course. What can I do?"

Tess hesitated. He wasn't part of the order, but he was all she had. "Go guard Chloe's door." He didn't question her. He didn't argue that it was outside of his role as a creature of Dream. He didn't argue that the guardians of Dream would yell at him for breaking protocol. He just nodded, eyes set. It was at that moment she understood. The shadow lurker cared for his assignment.

Tess turned around and raced out of the infirmary. She had to get to Marcus. He couldn't die because of her plan. She couldn't let another one die because of her actions.

## Nineteen

The office that posed as a living room was cold. Who would turn on the AC in the spring? Dr. Lewis sat in her usual chair across from Chloe. Two nights ago, when Tess had saved her, Chloe awoke to find a broken lamp and bruises on her arms. They certainly looked like fingertip bruises. She had tried to hide them with a quarter-length sleeve. It was the stupid coffee mug's fault. A glittery Minnie Mouse cup she had gotten on a family trip to Disneyland. Her favorite. She had reached up to retrieve it when her aunt saw her arm. Chloe didn't have a good story and she couldn't tell her the truth. She wasn't even sure what the truth was. How could a bruise follow her? Unless someone was in her room—what did Tess say, chanting and stuff—but she didn't want to think too much about that possibility.

The appointment had been scheduled shortly after.

"We are here to help you, Chloe," Dr. Lewis said in her soft voice. Chloe often wondered if she was trained to talk like that. Soothing, soft, never harsh. It didn't sound normal. It sounded fake. No one talked that softly, only when they were whispering at babies or kittens. Not in normal conversation. Not unless she thought Chloe was that scared baby.

"You know that, right?" Dr. Lewis added.

Chloe shifted in the chair. It felt too stiff today. Not comforting at all. "Yeah. Sure." She nodded.

Dr. Lewis had her hair up in a clip today. It elongated her neck and chin. Between that and the glasses, she looked more like a librarian. Her eyes were the only feature that gave her away. They were much too judgmental to be a librarian.

"Your aunt tells me you were hanging out with a man in his twenties?"

Molly must have finally cracked. She could only half-blame the girl. A piece of candy could only go so far against her aunt's interrogation. But Chloe wouldn't necessarily call it "hanging out".

"I don't know where she heard that from. I was asking him a question. Is that a crime now?"

"What was the question?"

Chloe shifted in her seat. The window in the office was small. An Arizona willow tree stood outside, its purple flowers dancing in the slight breeze. It really looked more like a bush, which was typically what passed for trees in the desert. But it certainly was pretty.

"Chloe. You need to talk to me. Something is clearly bothering you. You aren't sleeping."

"Like you could sleep." Chloe thought she had mumbled it in her head, but Dr. Lewis sat back.

"Your aunt also says you aren't eating."

Chloe had always had issues with food. When she was little, she used to think her aunt was poisoning her food. It just didn't taste right. Doctors had explained that was a result of her attachment condition. Now she just couldn't find her appetite. For the first time, she felt like she was involved in something important. And she couldn't tell anyone. Not that they'd listen. They saw her as having problems. They were looking for something wrong.

"Chloe."

"Why do you want something to be wrong with me?"

Dr. Lewis adjusted her glasses, leaning against the armrest. "Why would you say that?"

"Because you do," Chloe said, her voice rising. "People change friends all the time. It's called high school. My friend Sam, she had three boyfriends freshman year. Why isn't she in here talking about what underlying issue caused it?"

Dr. Lewis had folded her hands on the armrest. She held eye contact the entire time, insisting she was listening. But she wasn't. Not really. Chloe knew she was strategizing and planning against her. Just like every other time. Dr. Lewis let the silence linger for a fraction longer than any normal conversation. "Do you want to be like Sam? Because that's normal?"

Chloe tried really hard not to roll her eyes, but she failed. "I'm not trying to be anything. I just want everyone to back off."

"Back off how? What do you feel you need, Chloe?"

Before Chloe could answer, she felt a presence prick against her skin. She drifted her gaze to the window. He stood there with his antlers towering above his head and his antelope snout just outside the window. His red eyes fixed on her just like they had that night. Chloe jerked, sitting up straight. "Leave me alone."

"Chloe? What's wrong?"

Ignoring her, Chloe reached for her pocket. When she felt the ribbon inside, her whole world felt like it crashed against her. This was real. How could this be real?

"Chloe? Talk to me. What are you thinking about?"

Chloe looked at Dr. Lewis. Surely she could see it? Couldn't she see it? But she sat there calmly, leaning forward. Becca had said she could see things across the veil when others couldn't. Becca had even talked with them. But Tess said they couldn't interact with Chloe. That's why he was still outside. He could see but not affect her. He couldn't hurt her here. Because this was real.

Chloe shifted in her seat. "I'm—" she began to say. But she felt the ribbon fall from her fingers. It gracefully glided toward the carpet. Chloe froze. It was out in the open. It was right there for all to see. She met Dr. Lewis' confused look. But she was too slow. When her hand reached for the ribbon, Dr. Lewis already gripped it between manicured fingers.

She lifted it in front of her face, sitting back in the chair. "Chloe? What is this?" she asked. Chloe just met her gaze, gripping the couch. This could *not* be happening. With the silence, Dr. Lewis sighed. She knew. How could she not know? She dealt with people who couldn't distinguish reality from fantasy every day.

Chloe could almost hear her thoughts. If she had to mark reality, then she was seeing things. And if she was seeing things, then she must have relapsed a lot further than they had thought. Before she knew it, she was sitting just outside the office door. The muffled voices inside sounded serious. Her uncle was even here on this visit. What were they saying? That Chloe was paranoid? That she was losing touch with reality and the traumatic memories from her childhood?

It all sounded logical. The car accident had come on Chloe's first time out as a driver. The heightened emotion of the event mixed with the anxiety about the crash and the man's features reminding her of her father... it all created a wonderful foundation for a relapse. Memories were plaguing her, they would say. She was struggling against the intense memories and reality around her. She was becoming immersed in her memories, unable to distinguish where she was and what was really happening.

Chloe tapped a finger against the armrest. The phone blared through the silence. The receptionist turned around, picking the phone up from its cradle. Someone inside the room moved closer to the door. From the sound of the voice, it had to be her aunt.

"I just don't know what to do," the muffled voice said. "I feel like admitting her is a betrayal."

The soothing muffle of Dr. Lewis commented back, but Chloe couldn't hear her. Her heartbeat increased. Admitting? They're talking about hospitalizing her. They must think she was a danger to herself, completely out of control. This was bad. This was really, really bad. The receptionist swiveled in her chair, punching the computer keys.

If she was admitted, no one could help Dylan. Not to mention she'd be admitted into a hospital! How would her social life ever recover from that? Although, knowing Becca, she'd think it was a badge of honor.

And it wasn't like she had to worry about keeping a boyfriend through all of this, so that was going for her.

She had to get out of here. The voices neared the door. They were finishing their meeting. The receptionist swiveled further in the chair, reaching for a filing cabinet. It was now or never. Chloe pushed herself out the chair. She was through the lobby and out the glass door before she heard anything.

Chloe took off through the parking lot. She had once run a nine-minute mile. She had to be running faster than that now. She ran down the street before jaywalking across Wilcox Drive. When she reached the bus transfer station, she jumped on the first blue bus she could find. The door swished shut as she sat down, the air brakes sighing as the bus rolled away. She had her phone to her ear, watching as the bus traveled along Coronado. No one was outside the office yet. They must not have noticed her absence yet.

"Y'ello," Becca said.

"Hey. You need to come get me."

"Okay. What's wrong?"

Chloe bit her lower lip. "I think I just ran away. Look, I'll tell you about it later. Will you get me?"

"Sure. Where are you?"

"I'm on a bus. I'll text you when we stop."

The bus stopped at the park. It wasn't the best location. Despite the surrounding trees, it felt too open. She settled on hanging out on the pool side of the bandstand. She was visible to those parking at the pool and kids playing in the playground, but at least she couldn't be seen from the main street on the other side. Becca would be here soon. She just had to avoid getting caught until then. If they weren't going to lock her up before, they certainly would now.

She didn't see him coming, only felt his hand grip her arm. She wanted to scream, but what good would that do? He pulled her around the back of the pavilion, blocking her view to the parking lot. When Chloe looked up, she saw Dylan leading her up the stairs to the back wall of the bandstand. She had never realized how much taller he was until he had her pinned against the brick wall. She looked up at him.

"Why are you following me?" he asked.

Good to see someone else was paranoid. "I'm not!" She whimpered when he gripped her harder. She was going to have bruises on top of bruises.

"Don't lie to me. I know you're watching me. What do you know?"

His eyes were darker than someone his age should have been. He had either seen a lot of harshness in his life over the past few years, or those were someone else's experiences reflected behind his eyes. She couldn't tell if he was possessed from this distance. But when she turned her head to the side, antelope man was standing in the back parking lot with arms crossed.

Chloe stifled her scream, pulling against Dylan. Possessed. Definitely possessed. Or somehow cooperating with them. In either case, she didn't want to be here.

Dylan glanced over his shoulder. He locked eyes with the antelope man. Antlers bobbed in a nod and Dylan turned back to her. "You can see him?"

"See who?" Chloe forced out, pulling against him. Why wasn't anyone coming by? Did they not see her with him? They were kind of hidden back here, but still. No one saw him take her? A second ago she didn't want to be seen. Now that was all she longed for. Someone had to notice her. Or did they just not care?

Dylan pushed her against the wall, brick digging into her back. "What do you know about what we're doing?"

"I'm messed up, okay. I don't know anything. I can just see things that aren't there. I swear. I don't know anything."

Dylan eyed her and she couldn't tell if she had gotten away with it. Surely she looked messed up. He had to see that. Everyone else seemed to see it.

Finally, he let her go. Chloe breathed a sigh of relief, gripping at her aching arm. Her phone buzzed against her leg and she knew it was Becca. Chloe stepped to the side and Dylan let her. She charged down the steps and around the building. She saw Becca's car circling the lot and took off after it.

When she climbed inside, her phone started ringing. A picture of her aunt was on the screen. How long had she been gone? They finally thought of calling? Chloe pressed the power button, shutting down her phone.

"What happened?"

Chloe shook her head, leaning against the seat as they took off out of the parking lot and onto the side street. "It's been such a crazy day. Where do I start?"

"Well, you can crash at my friend Alex's house. Her mom works two jobs, so she won't notice."

Chloe nodded. What had happened to her life? She had gone from having the lead in a play and a stable social life to running away and being assaulted in the park. Maybe they were right. Maybe she was just messed up and this was all made up. Chloe didn't feel like she even knew anymore.

"You look like you need good news," Becca announced. She turned right at a light leading onto the highway and main road of the city.

Chloe felt tears burning her eyes. "Yes, I do."

"Addie called me. She set up a meeting with Cameron. He's working at the movie theater tomorrow. Thankfully, you picked a weekend to run away."

Chloe wasn't sure if that was good news or not. But she had already set off on this path. She might as well follow it to her destruction.

# Twenty

Tess walked up the hill with her arms stretched to the side, electricity buzzing against her skin. Grass rose to her calf as she climbed the path leading up the mountain. The shade of ash trees cooled the air on the back of the mountain range that would otherwise be in full sun. Marcus had three caves that he frequented in the area, but this one was the one he called home. The dirt path leading up to the mouth crunched beneath her shoes in the silence of the afternoon. She hesitated when she reached the opening. The mouth was pretty small. She'd have to crouch to get through. And the drop on the other side looked pretty steep. This wasn't good. When would she learn to bring backup with her? Was that still an option in this investigation? Maybe this wasn't her best idea ever, but she had to try to help him.

Tess kneeled. She sat down, sliding down over a few rocks for about eight feet until she reached the bottom. The room opened into a giant space that was probably wider than her old house. The air must have dropped another ten degrees in here.

"Marcus?" her voice echoed against the darkness. The cave smelled musty, of wet dirt and rock. The floor didn't look wet, but covered in a nice layer of dust.

Tess moved forward, darkness slowly shutting out the light from the opening. Tess shook her hand, electricity running through the scars. The resulting glow didn't provide the best light, but at least she could see two feet in front of her. "Marcus, are you here?"

The cavity of the cave closed altogether as she reached a passageway. She could see scratches dug into the rock. Tess put her fingers against the crevices. It looked like someone had dug them while being dragged deeper into the cave. Her scars pulsed light in front of her, their buzz echoing all around. "Marcus?"

She was careful with her steps as she continued down the path. A few more feet and she had to choose from two options. Tess held her hand against the walls in both directions. Both appeared as just tunnels of black. As she leaned closer, she saw more scratches on the left path. *Guess that's the way to go.* She eased her feet forward, careful of the stones along the way. Her shoes crunched against the rocky walls. Anyone could hear her coming.

Tess squinted at the wall. There was something along with the scratches. She leaned closer, bringing her hand just above the surface. Something had spattered against the wall. She hadn't much experience, but it looked like a blood-spray pattern. Although the patches appeared black in this light, they could be anything. Then again, Marcus probably wasn't human. Did he even bleed red?

"Marcus!" she could hear the panic in her echo. The silence of the cave weighed against her, raising the hairs on her neck. She anticipated a sound, any sound.

She needed it, craved it. Any sound to fight off the void of darkness. How could Marcus live here?

Tess continued forward, the smell of iron mixing with the moist earth. She shuffled her feet along, dirt scraping against the stone floor. She hadn't made it much further when her toe hit something soft. Tess stumbled forward, scraping her hands against the dirt floor in her fall. She flipped onto her back, shooting electricity into the air from both hands. The bolt bounced against the ceiling, landing back onto the ground a few feet from his body.

Tess electrified her hand once more. Marcus lay on his back, arms covering his face. His mouth was locked in a scream, his legs frozen in a running position. Black liquid leaking from gashes had soaked his body. The liquid had hardened. He must have been here for a while... the entire time she lay relaxing in the infirmary.

Tess crawled closer to him. She touched his shoulder, hoping he would move. It would scare her, but she wanted him to gasp and reach for her. Anything to mark life. But he felt stiff to the touch. The nails on his fingers were all broken, black liquid settling around each tip. He had been dragged back here. He had died fighting against whatever attacked him. He had been helpless against it.

Tess sat down, placing hands on her temples. Squeezed her eyes shut, rocking back and forth. Two of them. She had lost two of them. Mathias had suspected the Darkness. But she was the one who told him about a conversation she had heard between the associates of the Chief Guardian of Dream. Creatures had complained about shadows intercepting their dreams. The bunny had dismissed their concerns. No one could do that. It was impossible. After all, it was the guardians of Order's job to prohibit such action.

She had set Mathias on the path that eventually got him killed. When he'd said he was going to spy on a meeting with the highest leaders, she had wanted to go with him. She had begged him. But he had told her no. It was too dangerous to sneak two people in. He was just going to identify the leaders, record their meeting. Then she could help him. It was her fault he died. She should have gone with him.

And now this. Marcus had sought her out when Mathias died. He had wanted to help her. He had wanted to honor Mathias's memory. And what did she do with his desire? She had wasted it. She had failed to get any valuable information out of him because she was so focused on her own agenda. And then she got herself trapped in a decaying building so Marcus had to come and save her. She got him killed.

The sound of a rock falling down the path behind her made Tess sit up straight. She electrified her hands, the light revealing three forms approaching her. When they saw her, they charged forward. Tess shot lightning at them, scrambling to her feet. She stepped over the body, said one last goodbye to Marcus, then charged down the path she had just traveled. Footsteps echoed behind her. Tess shot blindly over her shoulder. She didn't expect to hit anything but hoped she could hold them off until she reached the light at the opening.

Her feet pounded against the stone surface. She was sure she'd fall at some point. But she kept moving. She reached the split in the path and rushed back the way she had come. Cool air rushed at her as she reached the grand opening of the cave. She'd have to climb the boulder leading up to the mouth if she wanted to get out.

Tess turned around, her hands crackling at her sides. From deeper inside the cave, the three figures burst forward, skidding to a stop when they got to her. One was a spirit, a fifty-year old man with a grey goatee and bald head. The other looked like a cross between a human and a dragon. Green scales from his head right down to his webbed toes shimmered against the darkness. Two small horns protruded from his block head next to his small, pointed ears. When he gasped for breath, he revealed a row of pointed teeth. Both were associates of Thomas. The third made Tess shake. It was a jackrabbit standing on hind legs. She stood at the same height of the other two and ears that normally hung to mid back stood straight in the air. Lilija was one of her top associates. In fact, she was the one everyone thought would become Chief Guardian when Mathias passed. Lilija couldn't be part of the Darkness. But if Lilija wasn't, then they were not here for Marcus. They were here for her.

"Tess," Lilija said, extending her front paws. "We know you didn't kill Marcus."

It was eight feet up to the opening of the cave. Could she climb that before they got to her? Maybe if she shocked them first. Nothing to kill them. Just something to slow them down.

"Tess," Lilija continued. "We need you to come with us."

Tess scoffed. "Why? So you can help Thomas accuse me of a bunch of nonsense and send me to Judgement?"

Lilija exchanged looks with the other associates. She turned an ear sideways. Tess listened, but the associate could pick out the sound of a bug at the bottom of the cave with those ears. Tess backed up a step while they were distracted.

"I don't know how involved you are, but I know Marcus must have been your friend. You came here to save him."

Like she knew anything about Tess or the Darkness. She didn't become Chief Guardian for a good reason. The girl was good, but she didn't know what was going on. Tess did. Kamahalan must have known that. And if Kamahalan wasn't in on the whole thing, then she should have been the first person Tess went to when things went south.

"Please. Come and help us. Help us before they all turn on you."

"Oh, shut up," Tess said, causing Lilija to stand back. "I know I am not the most likeable person, but you can't possibly be gullible enough to believe everything Thomas says."

A rock clicked next to her. Tess turned to find a fourth associate—a life-sized beaver and another one of her best—within arm's reach, silver cuffs in his hand. Without thinking, Tess pushed him. When she did, she felt the blow of electricity surge from her arms. The shock jerked the beaver's body rigid, shooting him five feet away. He landed hard on the rock, smoke twisting up from his fur. Oops.

When she turned back to the other three, she knew negotiations were over. She had just assaulted the associate of a chief guardian of Order. It didn't matter that he reported to her. Her action erased her title instantly. She had solidified her guilt.

When they charged, Tess hesitated. She didn't have a choice. She shot a bolt of lightning from her wrist, maintaining the current. Using it like a whip, she swept the spirit's feet out from under him. She dodged a fireball, landing hard on the ground. She was on her feet within a second, lassoing Lilija around the waist with the current. She held her only long enough to stun the rabbit before dissipating the bolt. Lilija slumped to the ground, her ears lying across her head.

Dragon Boy's chest puffed out with a large inhale. Tess planted her feet, placing both hands in front of her. She sent a ball of electricity to collide with his fireball. They exploded on impact, sending both flying through the air. Tess' back slapped against the boulder. If she had been human still, she would have struggled to breathe with the air knocked out of her. Instead, she just felt a sharp pain resonate down her spine. Tess looked up at the patch of sunlight calling to her.

Taking this as her opportunity, Tess climbed the boulder. A hand grabbed her foot as she climbed over the top. Tess sent a small bolt down an ankle scar and she was free to scurry down the mountainside.

In only a few steps, she ran down the mountain. She jumped and her whole body vibrated. In a moment, she landed in the long hallway of the jail. She had to be quick. She eased along the wall, listening for anyone. This had to be the stupidest rescue she had ever conceived. But she needed his help. The halls were vacant leading up to the jail door. When she eased her way inside the room, she relaxed.

Tess ran to his cell, slamming her hands against the door. The electric charge blew the door off its hinges, iron barely missing the boy as it flew against the back wall. He scrambled to his feet, eyes wide.

"I guess I better know your name if I'm going to break you out of here." She didn't know why, but Marcus had led her to this kid. It was about time she started focusing on his guidance and not her own plans.

The boy shivered in his corner. "Arbor."

Tess scrunched her nose. "Really?" When the boy shrugged, she just shook her head. Motioning for him to come, she said, "Well, we haven't got all day."

She must have looked like a psycho, but the boy stood anyway. Apparently crazy was just what he needed to cooperate. Tess clasped a hand on his shoulder, guiding him toward the door. "Well, Arbor. What can you tell me about Dylan Mitchell's door?"

Arbor froze, his scales turning a sickly green. "Why?"

She smiled at him. "Because. We are going to break into it together. You and me."

When he hesitated, Tess sent an electric pulse through his shoulder. Arbor cringed, then nodded. "Okay. Yes. I can get you there. But are you crazy? His door is filled with like five creatures."

Tess opened the jail door, peering down the hall. They would think about the jail cell—it was only a matter of time. But at least she wasn't as predictable as people proclaimed. "Five creatures sounds pretty crowded for one subconscious, don't you think? Come on. You're going to help me. Because Thomas killed Marcus and tried to kill me. What makes you think he's not coming for you next?" Tess arched a brow at him, but the boy was already shivering.

"Okay."

She smiled, leading him into the hallway. "Okay. Let's go break into a door."

## Twenty-one

The mall was relatively empty for a Saturday night. Only a few people strolled through the hall while the voices of a few families eating dinner echoed up the high ceilings. The moment Chloe stepped inside the mall, she could smell old frying oil and cold-cut sandwiches from the chain restaurants in the food court. Every other breath was accented by buttered popcorn, the scent drifting through the open doors of the theater.

Even with the small crowd, Chloe could feel eyes on her. "I don't like this," she said, turning to face Becca. Addie was standing next to her, a silver belt buckle trying to blind Chloe with reflected florescent light. Her hair was pulled up in a ponytail with curls that somehow elevated it beyond the mundane hairstyle.

"You want to meet Cameron, right?" Becca asked.

"What if I'm spotted?"

Becca smiled, slapping a hand on her shoulder. "You worry too much for someone who can see things that aren't really there."

Chloe rolled her eyes as they made their way to the ticket counter. A man probably five years older than Chloe sat behind the glass. The craters on his face marked a zit-riddled past, but it was probably his thick glasses that had doomed him to social isolation.

"Can I help you?" The window muffled his deep voice while it crackled through the speaker.

"I was hoping to speak with Cameron."

The man's magnified eyes blinked at her. "What movie do you wish to see, miss?"

Wait? Movie. This was not part of the plan. Chloe turned on Becca. "I have to buy tickets?"

Becca shrugged. "I doubt they'll believe us if we promise not to sneak into a movie we didn't pay for."

Chloe grumbled, reaching into her back pocket. "What movie is showing next?"

After a few button clicks, the man said, *The Muppets Take on New York*.

Chloe turned her wide eyes on Becca. It's not like she was going to watch the film, but this man could tell people she knew. What would she say when people found out? The first place she goes after running away is to a Muppet movie?

Becca took the money dangling from her hand and shoved it through the slot in the window. "We'll take three tickets please."

"It's eighteen with the matinee price," the voice crackled.

A chair scooted across the floor from the food court behind them, reminding Chloe about the presence of other people. Becca reached into her pocket and pulled out three more dollars. "That should do it."

The printer buzzed as the tickets emerged from a slot on the counter. The man ripped them off the roll and slid them under the window. "Enjoy your show."

Becca grabbed the tickets and skipped through the glass doors.

"He's judging us," Chloe said to the back of her head.

"Why? Going to the movies is about the only thing kids can do in this town... well, unless you want to be a little more rebellious."

"She already ran away," Addie stated. "How much more rebellious do you want?"

A bing sounded from the adjacent arcade, muffling Addie's last sentence just slightly. Yet Chloe felt like Addie had just yelled into a megaphone. "Can we not announce that to the entire city?"

Addie smiled as they turned to head up the ramp. Becca handed the tickets to the girl standing by a podium at the top of the ramp. Chloe thought she recognized her from theater class: a sophomore who never missed the opportunity to present a Shakespearean monologue in class. As the girl routinely folded and ripped the tickets along the perforated edges, Becca asked, "Is Cameron working today?"

The girl nodded, handing their half of the tickets back. "He's cleaning theater five." She smiled at them. "Your movie is the second door on the left."

The flicker of an image caught Chloe's attention. When she looked toward the bathrooms, she could see a shadow standing off to the side. Her heart beat faster until another flicker showed Thomas standing there.

"Hey," Chloe said. "I'll catch up to you."

She turned to go toward the bathrooms.

"Really? Now?" Addie said.

"I'll only be a minute," Chloe said. The dimly lit hallway was short on this side. It didn't take her long to get to the bathrooms. She tried to catch Thomas' eye as she pushed open the bathroom door. She made her way to the very last stall, closing the door. Great. Now she was meeting with ghosts in the bathroom. Maybe they *should* lock her up.

She jumped when Thomas appeared beside her. She bumped into the toilet, her hand flushing it in a loud swoosh. Chloe glared at him. "What are you doing here? I thought you couldn't approach the veil?"

Thomas frowned. "I'm sorry." His voice was so muffled, she could barely make out the words. Somewhere within the room, the hand dryer turned on. "It... an emergency."

"I'm meeting with one of the people Tess told me about. It's not a good time."

"You need... stop. Tess... to be... both sides. She... injured our men... broke him out of jail... on the run. She's wanted... treason... conspiracy... working... Darkness."

"Wait," Chloe said, cringing when her voice echoed off the walls. She peeked outside the stall, but it looked empty. At least one thing was going for her. She turned back to Thomas. "What are you saying? That Tess is a criminal?"

"She's dangerous," Thomas said with a nod. "Who knows... has been up to. We're looking... to arrest her." He hesitated then added. "Be careful."

Chloe shook her head. She couldn't believe this. "She saved my life."

"It was all a lie."

The door to the bathroom squeaked open. "Chloe! Come on. I saw him!"

Chloe rubbed her eyes. "I have to go." She heard muffled words, but pulled the stall door open and hurried out of the bathroom.

When Becca saw her face, she hesitated. "What happened?"

"I think one of the ghosts I was working with is a fugitive. But it doesn't make sense. None of this does."

"What are you saying?" Becca asked. "Do you want to stop?"

Chloe hesitated. She didn't know exactly what Thomas had been trying to tell her, but he had been pretty clear she should stop pursuing this plan. If she did, then she was saying she believed him. She believed Tess was a criminal and setting her up. Then why would she save her? Tess had been obviously injured and yet came to her rescue anyway. Why would she do that if she was sending Chloe down a destructive path? It didn't make sense. But Thomas had always been the one Chloe trusted. Thomas had always been the one that Chloe listened to. Why was this time different?

It just didn't feel right. None of it did. Maybe Thomas had been fooled. Maybe he was afraid because he didn't know what was going on. No. She had a purpose. If she stopped now, then it was all for nothing. She would deserve the confined room awaiting her return. She deserved all of the loss of friendships and weird glances. No. She wasn't going to let this be for nothing.

"No," she said finally. "Let's talk with Cameron."

"Good," Becca said, smiling. "Because I know where he is."

They strolled down the carpeted hallway, soft lights glowing on the walls. When they got to the last theater on the left, they pulled the doors open. The theater was brightly lit with white fluorescents, unlike the dark atmosphere of most theaters. Two boys swept away popcorn and spilt candies from between the folded leather seats.

Addie strolled across the room to one in particular. He wore the maroon uniform shirt. His brown hair hung in his face, partially blocking his eyes. He was cocking his head to the side as he swept, making him look a little odd. Somehow that made Chloe feel confident they had found the right person.

"Cameron?" Addie said.

Cameron looked up at her and smiled. "Hi, Addie." While his voice was loud enough, he somehow seemed also to mumble.

When he stood, he noticed Becca and Chloe approaching. His smile faded.

"Addie, you should be more careful who you hang out with."

Chloe frowned at Becca. Why would he say that? Did he know her? She hadn't thought her reputation had diminished enough to warrant such a response.

Addie shrugged. "You're one to talk. You hang out with all the head bangers and screamo music."

"What did we ever do to you?" Becca asked, hands on her hips.

Cameron's eyes looked at her, but they somehow seemed to be pointing in separate directions. He even leaned in a little, which might not have been meant as intimidation, but definitely encroached upon personal space. "I can just tell."

"Look," Chloe said, as the second cleaner made his way toward the lower section of the theater. "I was told to find you."

The disjointed eyes focused on her. "Was told?"

Subtlety hadn't worked before. Chloe decided to go with the blunt approach. "There are creatures trying to possess people. They want to break the veil between dream and reality, which will end all life."

"Wow," Addie said, taking a step back.

"Subtle much?" Becca asked.

Cameron, however, didn't budge. He pushed a strand of hair from his eyes and stood up.

"I was told you could help me, but I don't know how," Chloe added, feeling breathless.

"I can't see much of this world," Cameron said. "What I do see is blurry without my magnifying glass. But," Cameron said, pointing toward Becca, "I see three creatures standing beside your friend here. I can mainly see their glowing yellow eyes. Their faces only become clear as they take hold." He turned his attention back at Chloe. "And you. You have one, but he's pretty well defined. I would say you are close to possession."

Silence hung heavy in the theater, pulling Chloe toward the floor. What was she supposed to say to that? She and Becca could see shadows, but they didn't see this? Did the shadows only come after possession? Then Cameron could see those who were not possessed yet but somehow under attack. Her dream. They had tried to attack her in the dream. They had wanted to possess her. And Tess had saved her. She didn't know what the truth was, but she was certain Tess had nothing to do with the possessions.

"So," Cameron continued, "you must be involved with something bad to invite that. Why would I want Addie to be around you?"

"What does it look like?"

Cameron frowned. "What?"

"The creature next to me. What does it look like?"

Cameron squinted, looking to what she thought might be over her right shoulder. After a moment, he said, "Pale skin. Featureless. Kind of like that thing from Big Hero Six but more human." Cameron leaned forward. "Actually, he looks like he's on guard."

Chloe breathed a sigh of relief. Only a month ago, she had feared him in his mask. Ever since he took his mask off, he had lost that power over her life. She could feel it. She didn't have to fear him anymore. Thomas had ordered him to remove his mask. Or had he? Could that have been Tess, too? If he was now guarding her from possession, then Tess must have put him there as a result of the dream. She didn't know who to trust anymore... not that she ever made the correct choices in her past. "He used to participate in my dreams. But now... I think he is kind of my guardian angel... except he's not an angel."

Cameron leaned back, but seemed to accept that.

"What about me?" Becca shouted. "I'm under attack?"

"Not if we stop this," Chloe said. "What do you know about Dylan Mitchell?"

Cameron watched as his partner left the theater. "He's already possessed. Has been for a year now. But his following is growing. Four of his friends are also possessed. Creatures are circling ten others."

That was a lot of people. "Wait," Chloe said, shaking her head. "Dylan's dad left and the trauma opened him up for possession. Becca... " Chloe trailed off when Becca gave her a look that suggested imminent death. "Well, she has her own attractions for them. But there can't be that many messed-up people in town. Ricky, for instance. Nothing's wrong with him. How are they accessing so many people?"

"Those people smoke a lot of e-cigarettes," Addie offered. "You know those things can hold more than just nicotine?"

"Like what?" Becca and Chloe asked in unison.

"I don't know. Lots of stuff. LSD? It's not hard."

Becca raised a brow. "And he thinks *we* corrupt *her*."

Addie shrugged. "I'm not saying it's a real drug. Maybe they have something new. Maybe Dylan is like their drug dealer and it somehow opens them up for attack."

"She doesn't sound wrong," Chloe said. In fact, she sounded much more right than Chloe would like. The Darkness would need access to more people. Teachers always said drugs were bad. They never said it was a gateway to possession. A month ago, she would have laughed at the thought. Now it was more than plausible.

"I don't want you going near Dylan," Cameron said to Addie. "He's dangerous."

"We have to stop him," Chloe said.

"Cameron," a voice shouted from the doors. "You ready, man? We need to open this up."

"Yeah," Cameron yelled back. "Go ahead."

The fluorescents turned off, leaving behind the soft yellow glow of the lights on the wall.

Cameron picked up his broom. She had gotten so close. This couldn't end with the same result as Paul. She had to make some sort of contribution. She couldn't fail again.

"Please, you're the only one who can help us," Chloe said. "We can't see what you see. We can stop them with your help."

Cameron sighed. "You find Dylan and stop him. Then I'll help you identify the rest. But she," he pointed at Addie, "doesn't go with you. Or I'm out."

Chloe nodded. "Deal."

As Cameron left them and the first of the guests started to enter, Becca turned to face her. "And how the hell are we supposed to stop Dylan?"

Chloe shrugged. "I don't know. But it starts by finding him." Chloe started heading for a door near the screen with a glowing exit sign. "But first you've got to get me out of this town. Otherwise, I'll get locked up and be no good to anyone."

## Twenty-two

Slime dripped from the door and rolled down Tess' back. She cringed. "What are we doing, Arbor?"

The boy had his eyes closed. All she could make out was a slight distortion where the oak door stood. If she hadn't known the chameleon stood there, she would never be able to spot him. Thin red lips appeared long enough for him to say, "Shh."

He had brought her to what he called the edge of the doors. In reality, it was in the realm of expansion. The grey pebbles dropped off into a line of nothing that very much resembled the edge of the universe. This must be what the sailors of the 17$^{th}$ century thought they'd encounter if they drifted too far out to sea. Multicolored galaxies swirled around her in greater density than she had seen before. She didn't know how far she could see from here, but it felt like she was staring at the true definition of eternity.

They were here for a moment before he lifted a sheet of moss from this wretched, rotting door and shoved her underneath. It felt as if the smell of rotting fish was saturating her pores. She'd forever be remembered as the guardian of Order who smelled like a fishing ship. Water seeped from the hinges, soaking her pants. More sludge drifted over her shoulder and Tess cringed. She had never been a beauty queen, but she had her limits of disgust. Fugitive or not, she didn't know how much longer she could stay here.

The ground shook suddenly. Pebbles jumped up and down through the vibration. Crunching mixed with a mechanical grind flooded her ears. Slowly, the edge of the land expanded eight feet into the vast space. A blue plastic door that looked stolen from a child's playhouse shimmered out of nothing. Once it settled in its frame, the pebbles stopped dancing and the land stopped vibrating. She had never seen the creation of a door. She wondered if they all started that small. Did they grow along with their subconscious dwellers? If that was the case, how did one turn into the rotting mess she currently stood against?

Footsteps crunched nearby and Tess stood straight. She held her breath. This was it. Suddenly, she wished the moss was thicker. The guardians of Order walked past her in their usual blue uniforms with gold stripes around their sleeves. The constellation Scorpio glimmered below their right shoulder. They joked about something as they passed. Tess sighed as they rounded the corner, the sound of their footsteps diminishing.

As the moss ripped away, Tess held back her scream. Arbor still looked very much like an oak door, although he no longer stood against it. The whites of his eyes appeared as he backed away and let his color fade to green. She heard the crackle electrifying her shoulders. He had a right to be frightened of her. "You should be more careful with sources of electricity, you know."

"Come," Arbor said in a small voice. "We don't have much time."

Tess adjusted her jacket, only to feel something seep between her shoulder blades. She didn't even want to know what she looked like.

They charged down the path, following the edge of existence until they reached a golden door with leaves carved into the surface. Arbor turned, running even faster. Doors blurred past her as she ran. The chameleon boy was fast. She kicked her legs harder, trying to keep up. They made another left around a bright red door with a golden handle. So many doors: some normal sized, some elfish, others towering above her. If they weren't so scattered, she would have thought this was a cemetery of eccentric antiques.

Finally, Arbor skidded to a stop, a layer of grey pebbles piling beside his foot. Tess rested her hands on her knees for a moment. She didn't have to catch her breath, but she could feel her energy pulsing. When she felt stable, she straightened. The white door in front of them looked strong as steel. Four even panels protruded from the front, making it appear more elegant than she would have anticipated. The frame of the handle was narrow with decorative etchings around the side. The knob itself was a long handle that formed a feather. A small key slot sat just below. The whole thing looked like the front door of some house belonging to a multimillionaire in LA. Not the access to a possessed subconscious.

A second look made Tess lean closer. She put her hand to the door. Energy pulsed against her. There was something against the keyhole. She leaned even closer.

The inside was shadowed. Placing a finger against the opening, she felt something sticky. She rubbed the black tar between her fingers, pulling away. Another drop oozed from the slot.

"The doors do that," Arbor said from her side. "When the person is possessed. They do that. We spent a lot of time limiting the impact to not be as noticeable. But it still seeps through."

Tess straightened. That would be helpful to know if she ever made it out of this thing.

"Since we aren't members of Dream," Arbor said, "the handle might shock you."

"I thought there were five people inside."

Arbor nodded. His eyes were so wide and his scales so pale, he looked ready to bolt. "It killed two members before they could get inside."

That was unnerving to say the least. She had never tried to open the door without Nakima's permission. It was a written statement filed for recording. She hadn't thought about the consequences of not filing that paperwork. Actually, she always thought it was nothing but mindless protocol once again. Good to know it actually had importance.

Tess rubbed her hands together, electricity pulsing against her skin. "Let's try it with a shock of my own."

She reached for the handle, but felt cold fingers on her arm. Tess turned to find Arbor next to her, much too close for her liking.

"Even if you get past the door. There are five of them in there. They will kill you."

Tess smiled at him. "Two against five is not bad."

Arbor backed up, rocks grinding beneath his feet. "I... what?"

"I broke you out. While the order might think that confirms my alliance with the Darkness, I think we both know how the Darkness will see it."

Arbor licked his lower lip, eyes darting from side to side. "I told you I'd show you to the door. Why should I help you any further?"

"Because," Tess said, turning back to the door, "both sides now want to kill you. Helping me is the only chance you have at freedom." She cast him one last glance, adding, "You were done with them the moment I caught you."

Arbor straightened at that but said nothing. He was a lot smarter than she had first thought. He must know she was right. Loyalty isn't an expectation when one dances with the devil. Everyone's expendable. He must finally be realizing that.

Tess reached for the handle. "Here goes nothing." Tess hesitated, closed her eyes, and then reached the rest of the way. The cold metal chilled her for only a moment before it blew her backward. Rocks scraped her back as Tess slid across the path before slamming into the corner of a doorframe.

Tess lay on the pebbles, all the doors swaying before her. Arbor's face circled in front of her eyes, black spots blocking her vision.

"You dead?" he asked.

Tess groaned at him. The ground felt like it tilted below her as her world spun on a wobbly merry-go-round driven by a sadistic child. She pushed herself up to her elbows, closing her eyes against the movement.

When she opened them again, she could still see spots speckling her vision, but the ground was stable. "Well," she said, pushing herself to a sitting position. "Maybe we need to open it a different way." She wondered if Argumas would have better luck since he was a creature of Dream. Or did he need permission, too?

Arbor smiled at her. Was he laughing at her? But something about his face looked proud. Tess stood and stared at the wide open door before her. The space within the frame was as dark as the cave she had just survived.

"You moved the handle. The blast took it the rest of the way open." He smiled even wider. "You should have seen the color of that spark."

Tess shook her head. "That's okay. I felt it." Cold air rushed through the open door. What now? Was she going to just barge inside? She slipped out of her jacket. Her scars pulsed white. "If there are already five creatures inside, will the subconscious attack us?"

Arbor's brows went up like he had never thought of the possibility. Maybe he wasn't so smart after all.

Tess rolled her eyes, grabbing onto his arm. She led him to the door, but then hesitated. *Here goes nothing.* She took a step through and immediately began falling. She heard Arbor scream for only a few seconds before water engulfed her. She struggled against some sort of current, flailing her arms in the water. Which way was up? She kicked and stretched out her arms. She could feel her lungs burning as she tried to hold her breath. Panic swept through her. She was going to drown!

She flailed for a moment before she finally remembered: she was already dead. She didn't have to breathe. Tess lay still, letting the water roll around her. The murky water was dark, a small ray of white light flickering every now and then. She saw the chameleon boy struggling in front of her. Arbor, on the other hand, could certainly drown in here.

Tess tried for a perfect breast stroke, making her way to the boy. Arbor had managed to flip himself upside down, his legs and arms flailing. Tess swam behind him, hooked an arm around his chest and kicked her way toward the flashing light above them. Arbor broke the surface with a gasp and was immediately slammed back under with a rolling wave.

Tess held on, pulling him back above the surface. He came up choking, water leaking from his nose. As they bobbed along the surface, Tess looked around her. Water rolled from horizon to horizon. Lightning bolted from the sky, hitting the water at what looked like miles away. The weird part was the sky. Stars speckled against the clear, black sky. A full moon hung high, casting the water in a bright white light. Yet rain sprinkled against her face as she looked up and the waves rolled with an unseen storm.

She would have thought this belonged to the algae door she had hid behind, not Dylan's elegant red one. It just went to show the outside never quite revealed the battle going on within a person's soul. Arbor's gag brought her attention back to the boy. He gripped her arm like it was a life jacket.

"I can't swim!"

Tess sighed. "This is a dream. You can't die in his dream unless the subconscious attacks you."

"It's not attacking me?"

"No." Tess didn't know what she had been expecting. That was a lie. She was expecting to walk into a room filled with creatures and single-handedly zap them all to dust. Arbor would have been a great help in that situation. She did not expect to fall into a dream. It's not like she had ever been in a possessed mind before, but Arbor's presence only complicated this particular situation.

They rolled high in the air with a wave. When they did, she saw Dylan. He was about a hundred yards away, splashing in a developed free-style stroke. He was making unnatural progress through the waves.

"You want out of this, then we've got to get over there," Tess said, pointing in his direction.

"I can't swim!" Arbor shouted back.

This day was just getting better and better. "Well, I can't drag you and catch up to him. So, you have to at least try kicking your feet."

She felt Arbor nod. Finally. Something was going her way. Tess rolled onto her side, still clutching the boy, and they both began to kick together. Keeping one arm around him, she started using her other arm to help. Remembering she was in a dream, she focused on her energy. Each kick propelled them further through the water. First it was a few inches... then a few feet. Before she knew it, they were moving like a sailboat through the waves.

"When we get close, I'm going to have to let you go." Tess felt Arbor tense at this. "Don't worry. You won't drown if you don't believe you'll drown. You can do anything in a dream." Tess kicked again, judging her distance and angle of interception. "If you believe your kicks will keep you above water, then they will."

There was a hesitation, but then she felt Arbor nod once more. As much as she didn't want to admit it, she was starting to like this chameleon boy. The fact she could trust a boy who had proven himself part of the Darkness, and she could never trust a colleague she had no proof against, probably spoke more about her judgment than anything else.

Tess pushed her arm against the water once more. She had the angle just right. They should collide with the swimmer in just a few strokes. "Okay!" Tess shouted at Arbor. She gave him only a moment before she let go. She let Arbor sink below the surface for a moment. He came propelling back out, eyes wide. When his doggy paddle held him above the rolling surface, he grinned at her.

Tess kicked her legs one last time, eyes focused ahead. She reached out, grabbing the swimmer's torso as they collided. His bones smacked against hers, making her wonder if they could snap in a dream. The boy screamed. She felt a strong foot jab her in the gut. He used that motion to propel himself away from her as Arbor doggy paddled over in a very non-intimidating way.

Tess groaned, but maintained her stroke against the rolling waves. "Dylan."

The boy eyed her. "How do you know my name?"

"I'm here to help you. You must be tired of swimming."

Again, a wave lifted them high into the air. There was truly nothing around them, just a wall of water rolling against itself for as a far as the eye could see.

"I have to finish," he said, looking like he was about to start swimming again.

"I'm sorry about your dad," Tess blurted.

The boy hesitated. His eyes grew dark as he stared at her. "What do you know about him?"

"I know he left you." Lightning struck the water much closer than she would have liked, thunder cracking and rumbling against the clear sky. "I know he walked out on you."

Dylan rolled onto his stomach. "You don't know anything."

"That's true," she shouted.

Dylan hesitated, treading water like he had been doing it his whole life.

"But I know it haunts you."

He stared at her. If he wasn't swimming, then maybe she was on the right track here. She didn't know how to help him, but it had to begin with him believing in the reality. He was not in control of his own mind. He was locked here. If he could believe that, she might find her way to those who possessed him after all.

"And I know you do not want to be here. I know you are not swimming toward something. You are swimming away from something."

Lightning struck even closer. She could be imagining it, but she thought she felt a tingle against her skin. It would be fitting for her to be attacked by electricity. She had certainly done it enough to other creatures.

"I have to swim," Dylan said with the roll of another wave. "It's the only way out."

"Out of what?"

"Out of this." He looked around them. "That's what they said. They told me if I swam, I would be free. They told me it would make everything better."

Tess looked at Arbor. The chameleon just shrugged. That's how they possessed people. They locked them in a constant state of dream. If that's how they took over, then she should be able to fix it the same way. "They were wrong," Tess said. "You can't run from your regrets and fears, Dylan."

"I don't want to keep living like this," Dylan said.

"Like what?"

"Knowing I'm a failure. That's why he left. I'm a disappointment."

Lightning branched horizontally across the sky above them. The thunder vibrated against her skin.

"I don't know why he left," Tess said. "But I know it is never that simple."

Tess jumped when Arbor said, "Did you ever talk to your mom?"

The boy shook his head.

"Maybe that's what this is about," Arbor said. He looked so helpless in his dog paddle, but his voice was steady. "All your life, you swam. You focused on something else. But you never talked to her. You never asked her why he left. You just assumed."

Dylan treaded water, looking between the two of them. "I was not a kid when he left. I knew more than they thought."

"Sure," Arbor agreed. "But you don't know it all."

"Let me ask you this," Tess added. "How far has this swim gotten you?"

Dylan frowned. For the first time, he looked like he finally saw the scene around them. There was nothing but water. He was swimming toward nothing. "I'm not sure."

Tess let his words linger for a moment. "Maybe that's the point. You can't swim your way to answers. You need to take back control. Because right now, you are letting someone else control your actions."

Lightning struck so close, Arbor yelped. Tess felt the electricity burn against her skin. She couldn't tell if this was Dylan or the result of the possession. In either case, she was starting to wonder if her belief in her own safety was unfounded.

"I didn't want to be there anymore," Dylan said.

Tess nodded. "I know. I didn't either. But," Tess hesitated. She could feel the ball of emotion inside start to shift. She had to hold it together. "Dylan, my life was stolen from me. I don't have the option of going back. You do. You can go back. You are in charge of your own life. Take it back. This is no way to live. Go back, take control. Live your life. Don't you want that? To move on?"

They rolled with a wave as lightning streaked across the sky. Tess tried to focus only on him and not look around for the next bolt that could electrocute them. Dreams had power only if she believed they did. She had to believe she'd be safe. She had to hold on to that. But as another grumble of thunder sounded, she felt herself tremble against the chill in the water. She was starting to believe this storm had power. If she believed in its reality too much, she would be lost here.

Dylan looked above him and sighed. The rain stopped falling and the sea settled. "I'm scared," he said, looking back at them. "What if it was me?"

The stillness unsettled her more than the rolling waves. Tess shook her head. "I promise. It's never that simple."

Dylan stood. When he did, Tess felt the concrete bottom. They were in the shallow end of an indoor pool. The smell of chlorine was more welcoming than anything she had ever smelled before. She stood with Arbor, who looked ready to pee in the pool.

"I don't know how to take back control," Dylan said, staring at the ceiling. If he could feel them, then he might have a chance at making this work.

Tess smiled when he looked at her. "You already did. This is your mind, Dylan. Nothing can exist here without your permission."

When the ground shook, Tess braced herself. Water sloshed and the glass front door shattered. When the shaking stopped, five figures fell from the roof. They fell into the deep end, disappearing under the surface for only a moment before they came up with a splash.

There wasn't much time. "Kick us out," Tess said as the figures pulled themselves over the edge of the pool. The room shook again. "This is your mind. We don't belong." Arbor yelped, pointing toward the deep end. The figures moved toward her, but Tess remained focused on him. "It's okay. You are in control of your own actions. Kick us out, Dylan. Now!"

A figure leaped through the air toward her. Tess turned, raising her crackling hands. She didn't have a chance to shoot electricity at them before the whole place exploded. Concrete and water blasted around them, the energy hitting against her body like a truck.

Tess flew through the air in a rush of energy. The grey pebbles slammed against her, scratching her back until the familiar door frame slammed against her back for the second time today. Given the circumstances, she preferred the electric shock that sent her propelling from Dylan's door the first time. Tess tried to stand, not sure what else she'd find. However, this time it wasn't just a matter of the world turning. Her knees buckled, slamming her back onto the harsh surface.

She pushed herself to her hands and knees. "Arbor?" she shouted. At least she thought she shouted. An overpowering ring chimed in her ears, muffling everything aside. Was her vision affected? She blinked at her scratched hands, but they flickered before her. Manicured nails like the kind she used to get after her divorce. It was a present to herself. Idiot. In a moment, the nails were gone and scratched, harsh hands replaced them. "Arbor?" She wished the ringing would stop.

Her arms shook and she could no longer stay up. She collapsed onto her chest, the dust from the pebbles settling around her face. There was movement around her. And voices. Did she hear voices over the ringing? Surely the guardians of Order heard the blast.

The guardians of Order. She was a fugitive. Tess rolled onto her back. She had to get out of here. She had to get it together. She couldn't be found here. Five bodies lay scattered to her side. They looked in just about as good a shape as she did. Maybe worse. They probably got the brunt of the subconscious.

She turned her head the other way. She couldn't see Arbor anywhere. He could be blending in with the pebbles. Could he do that if he was injured? She didn't know a lot about his kind. More voices and movement. Tess pushed herself up, gasping at the pain that shot through her arms. The guardians of Dream weren't kidding. Invading a dream had horrible consequences. But she had to get out.

Before she could move, a firm hand dug into her arm. It pulled her to her feet. When her knees threatened to give again, another hand gripped her other arm. She should electrocute them. She could get away. But she couldn't. She could barely see.

"Secure the door!" Was that Thomas? It sounded like him. After a moment, Choirboy came before her. She had the overwhelming urge to spit on him, but the best she could do was keep her head upright.

"By the Deputy of Order, I am placing you under arrest. Your time with the Darkness is over, Tess."

Tess couldn't help but laugh. She shouldn't be surprised. She had let him take control of this whole thing. But she stole Dylan back. How did he like that?

Thomas leaned in. "You think this is funny?"

"You and me. We'll have our time. Don't worry."

Thomas scoffed at her. "Take care of these prisoners."

As the guards dragged her away, Tess searched around. Still no Arbor. He couldn't have stayed in the subconscious with a blast like that. He was out here somewhere. She couldn't decide if she cared that he escaped. He served his purpose. He helped her when he didn't have to. Yet, she was still hoping he'd continue to help her. How stupid was that? To trust a member of the Darkness. Maybe everyone was right. There was something seriously wrong with her.

A large silhouette stopped their travel. "What's going on here?" She'd recognize Argumas' voice anywhere.

"She's under arrest for the attempted possession of a door."

"He was already possessed," Tess mumbled. "A thank-you for freeing him would be nice."

"You can't do this," Argumas said.

"Take it up with the Governess." They continued dragging Tess.

"Argumas," she shouted over her shoulder. "You stay with that door! Don't you leave it!"

She might have done some things wrong, but guarding Chloe's door was not one of them. She needed him there. She didn't know how she was going to get out of this thing, but she had to know she had done one thing right. "Promise me!"

The ringing made it hard, but she swore she heard his harsh voice. "I won't leave her."

With that, the guards dragged her out of the realm of doors.

## TWENTY-THREE

Benson was a bigger city than the I-10 junction made it appear. While it looked like nothing more than a one-traffic-light town with a gas station and McDonalds, the city continued down the hill, spreading across the valley. This particular slump block house had three small bedrooms, and it sat on a lot at the end of a long dirt road. The front yard was cleaned up with brown rock and a couple of barrel cacti, but the backyard was a vast spread of high desert grass and wild, unkempt mesquites. The best part was the neighbors had to be at least two hundred yards away. That's all Chloe cared about.

She wasn't sure how thoroughly her aunt was looking for her or if she even cared. If the roles were reversed, Chloe would feel relief. No more drama that came with a damaged child. But if her aunt *was* looking for her, then they'd never look for her in Benson. And even if they did, this place was pretty secluded. She had to hand it to Addie. The girl had connections. One of the girls renting this house was a recent graduate attending Cochise College. Apparently they had met in some sort of junior rodeo network. Even better, everyone in the house was working to put themselves through school. They didn't care about the runaway staying with them, especially while they smoked pot and drank their nights away.

As Chloe strolled through the narrow hallway into the small kitchen, she wondered how Molly was doing. She had only been out of the city for a night. She couldn't be homesick already. What was there to miss? She had lost all of her friends. Her aunt was looking to lock her up. But Molly hadn't done anything. She'd actually been nice... most of the time.

Gravel crunched outside as an engine grumbled up the driveway. Chloe's heart beat quickly. They found her. She didn't know how, but they must have. She wandered into the living room, ready to bolt into her small bedroom. When she saw Becca's beat-up Subaru park in front of the cacti, Chloe sighed. Who was she kidding? She was not built for the runaway life. She didn't know how she was going to fix this. It had all gotten so out of control. But she had to fix it.

Addie bounced up the walkway next to Becca. Chloe greeted them at the door with a smile. "What brings you around?"

"These are *my* friends," Addie said with a grin.

"Then you should know they're all at work. On a Sunday, which kind of sucks."

"We came to take you away," Becca said.

"Oh?"

"Yeah. I stalked Ricky, which was way creepier than I thought it would be." Becca eased past Chloe and into the coolness of the house. The day was promising to be a hot one, a reflection of what was to come this summer. "But it paid off," Becca said, turning once she was inside. "I heard him say Dylan was going with his mom to the University of Arizona. There's some sort of book festival there."

Chloe blinked. "A *book* festival? ... with his mom? Doesn't that seem... I don't know... a little weird to you?"

Becca shrugged. "I'm having a hard time judging what is weird right now."

Chloe couldn't argue the point, but something still felt off. But she couldn't stay here for too long. "Okay. Let me get my stuff."

The sun beat down from a clear blue sky as they drove I-10, casting everything in a bright yellow light that made the grasses look browner and the plants drier. The interstate was relatively clear of traffic and construction, adding to the peculiarity of the day. But, in what seemed like record-breaking time, the land flattened before them, revealing the big city spread against two small mountain ranges. The interstate opened to multiple lanes as the cluster of downtown skyscrapers became more predominant.

Just about the time traffic began to build, Becca exited onto Kino Parkway. After a few blocks and what seemed like hours fighting for parking, the three of them walked through the university campus. Tents spread over a large field of grass much too green for the low desert. It was a Sunday afternoon and yet there were thousands of people walking up and down the aisles. Tents devoted to books or publishers or people claiming to be related to literature spread before her. There were places for children to play, stations promoting local news stations, and bookstores with lines of people waiting for author signatures. People walked amongst the tents, but then headed in and out of the college buildings, holding pamphlets and searching for their next speaker on the list of presentations. Chloe squinted against the sunlight, wishing she had remembered to grab her sunglasses before running away.

"How are we supposed to find him here?" Chloe marveled as they passed by a large tent filled with people listening to someone talking about literature.

As they neared the halfway point in the field—which had to be a quarter of a mile from the beginning—Chloe could smell spiced meats, bread, and sugary creations. They must be nearing the designated food court. That's when she caught sight of something. Chloe stopped, causing the group behind her to grumble and pass around. A large building marked science and engineering stood just off to the side. He sat under a tree, almost blocked by the tents on that side of the walkway. She almost didn't recognize him with his hair cut so short. He was still dressed in all black, but he somehow looked different.

Ignoring the voices behind her, Chloe sifted through the flow of traffic and made her way to his tree. The shade relieved her skin from the beating of the sun's rays. In a few months, no one would want to walk the pathway this time of day. Dylan looked up at her as she approached, but he didn't try to move.

Chloe sat down cross-legged in front of him, the grass cool against her jeans. "Do you know me?"

Dylan hesitated, watching closely as Becca and Addie walked closer. They remained standing, probably looking ready to attack him if he tried anything. But even if he was still possessed, what could he do? They were surrounded by such a large crowd and police officers. Nothing. He could do nothing to her.

Finally, he focused back on Chloe. "I've done a lot of things this past year I'm not proud of. Most of it is fuzzy, but I do remember. I'm sorry about the park."

For a moment, a chill ran through Chloe. He remembered. Could he remember if he was possessed? But he looked so different. His eyes were not haunted. Chloe took a moment to look behind her at Becca. She looked confused as well, relaxing her crossed arms. Chloe shot her a questioning look, to which Becca shook her head.

No more shadows. Chloe frowned. Something must have happened. She turned back to face Dylan, who was watching them with interest. His eyes were filled with concern, his lips pressed together. He was a foreigner thrown into a world he no longer understood.

"I heard you ran away," Dylan said after a moment. "Is that why you're here? Did I make you do that?"

Why was she here? They were looking for Dylan, but for what purpose? To save him? It looked like he was already saved. She could just walk away, but then what? A cool breeze brushed past the trees, bringing with it a reminder of the winter they had just left. Even if she wasn't here to confront him—perhaps naively thinking she'd save him from himself—he could still remember what happened. Maybe he was more useful than she thought.

"No. You were involved in the situation, but I can take responsibility for my own decisions." Chloe hesitated. She didn't even know what to ask. Finally, she said, "You said you remember what happened."

"It's a little fuzzy, but yeah."

"How much? Like... do you know what they're planning?"

"*They?*" Dylan pulled his brows together. Maybe he didn't remember as much as she had hoped. But she was certainly used to people judging her as a weirdo. What did she have to lose?

"Dylan... " Chloe hesitated, glancing behind her. The girls were staring at her like lost dogs. They were just following her lead. She had become a leader. When did *that* happen? This was all on her now. Chloe sighed, looking back at Dylan. "Look. This is going to sound crazy, okay. But there are creatures trying to possess people. They want to somehow break the veil between reality and dream. But I don't know how and I was hoping you could help me."

Dylan jerked, rising quickly to his feet. That's it. She had lost him. Chloe followed, ready to plead with him, but she noticed he wasn't running. He was looking at someone.

"Hi, Mom."

Chloe froze, turning slowly to a plump woman with cropped blond hair. She had round, purple sunglasses that covered part of her cheeks. She smiled at the girls, waving at them with fake nails bought at a store. "The session just ended. I was going over to the University of Arizona pavilion. J.A. Jance is going to be signing her books there and I want to go before the line gets too big."

"Oh," Dylan said, fidgeting.

"Who is this?" his mom said. Even through her sunglasses, Chloe could feel the suspicion. This woman must have endured the change in her son and then seen the change back to the boy she once knew. Of course she would be suspicious.

Dylan rubbed the back of his neck, fumbling. Chloe finally broke out of her fear and waved. "Hi. I'm Chloe Parker. We knew each other in swim class. We were just catching up."

Dylan's mom relaxed her shoulders and visibly sighed. "Oh, how lovely. You must be a pretty good writer."

Chloe frowned. "Excuse me?"

"All that stuff you were saying about dreams and reality. It'd make a pretty good story. I'm afraid my Dylan here has never been much with the imagination though," she said with a chuckle.

Chloe tried to laugh with her, but it sounded much too tortured to her ears. She stopped, adjusting her shirt. "Well, I do get kind of carried away with my imagination sometimes."

She caught a glimpse of Becca pinching the bridge of her nose. She tried not to pay too much attention to it so his mom wouldn't notice. Who would have thought? The way to not sound quite so psychotic was to stand in a place filled with books and imagination. Hers was probably not even the craziest conversation currently taking place.

"Hey, Mom, can I stay here? Talk with my friends for a while? I know where to find you if we finish before you do."

Chloe endured the scrutinizing gaze for a moment before Dylan's mom nodded. She shifted her purse to her shoulder, clutching the overstuffed bag close to her side. "Yes. I think that would be good for you to connect with someone from your past."

Chloe tensed as his mom approached, placing a warm gentle hand on her shoulder.

"He needs some good influences in his life, you know."

Chloe felt a wave of guilt as Dylan's mom smiled softly before turning around. "You kids don't get into too much trouble now," she said with a lightness of a mother who no longer has to be serious with such a statement.

Another wave of guilt crushed against Chloe. What was she doing? Was she sucking him back into a life from which he had finally been freed? Chloe ran a hand through her hair. "I'm sorry," she said, turning back to face Dylan. He frowned at her. "I shouldn't bring this back on you."

Dylan shook his head. "No. I've done a lot this past year. I want to make it right." He paused before adding, "Please."

Chloe nodded, sitting back down on the grass with him. This time, Becca and Addie joined them. "So you don't think I'm crazy about the possession stuff?"

Dylan picked at the grass by his feet. "You're forgetting something." When his soft gaze met hers,

Chloe didn't need him to say anything more. He had been possessed. He above all people should know.

"Right." Chloe folded her hands in her lap. "Do you remember anything about the plan?"

"Some stuff. Not a lot. I remember I needed to get a group of at least ten, but that it still wasn't enough. We talked a lot about the strength it would take to merge the two sides. I don't know what that means, but it seemed to be an issue."

"They want to break the veil between reality and dream. That must be the two sides."

"Yeah," Dylan said. "I guess. I know we had to meet with people on each side. And there was some kind of ritual. And someone had to cross through, I remember that. Cross through, that's all they talked about. If someone could do that, then it would work. But they had to pick the right person because it failed last time. They also needed a place with... blood power? That sounds stupid."

Chloe shook her head. "My guardian angel is a man with a featureless face. Nothing sounds stupid to me anymore." She nodded. "Please, go on."

"That's really all I remember. People on both sides, somewhere with blood power, and a special person strong enough to walk through. And you, they were very interested in you."

"What if you are the one to walk through?" Becca asked.

Chloe frowned at her. "I'd have to do it voluntarily. But why would I do that?"

Dylan shrugged. "I don't know. They were talking about your door. It was blocked. But they were very interested in Village Meadows Elementary. They knew they could get you there."

Chloe shook her head. "That makes no sense. I don't even go there... " Chloe felt her body shake. She shot to her feet, searching the place for an exit. But how? She couldn't go back there without being caught.

Becca caught her shoulder, forcing her to make eye contact. "What's going on? What's at Village Meadows?"

"That's Molly's school. They're going after my cousin to get to me."

"That'll make you cross the veil," Addie said with a nod.

"We have to go back," Chloe said, pulling away.

"We *can't* go back," Becca said. "You are wanted, remember? There are legal consequences for running away."

Addie grinned, "She should know. She ran away shortly after entering foster care."

"Shut up," Becca shot at her. "Look. We'll figure something out."

"I'll help," Dylan said.

"No, I don't want to bring you back into all of this."

"I'm not asking," Dylan said sternly, "I want to help you fix this whole thing. I started it, I can fix it."

Chloe nodded. "Okay. Give your number to Becca. But go back to your mom. I don't want you to worry her any more than necessary."

Dylan nodded.

As the girls took off toward the car, Chloe knew this wouldn't be as simple as going back into town. She had to stay hidden if she was going to stop this thing. But she had to save her cousin too. It was Sunday. Molly didn't go back to school until tomorrow. She had tonight. Chloe just needed a nice little visit with her nightmare friend to clear this all up. She needed guidance. She needed a plan. And then tomorrow, she needed to add kidnapping to her list of charges.

## Twenty-four

The world had stopped spinning a while ago, but Tess still felt like a brick was hitting her repeatedly in the face. She lay in her cell, eyes closed, pressing palms against her eye sockets like she had in her old life. Nothing she did stopped the pounding. That'll teach her to mess with the power of someone's subconscious. Now she knew why Argumas was so frightened to take his mask off in front of Chloe. She had a feeling he could have endured far much worse than an explosive exit. In fact, he probably *did* endure more, considering how long he was in the infirmary afterward. If this was reality, she would owe the man a gift card or something. What was the equivalent amongst the Dream creatures?

"Psst!"

Tess groaned against the sound. She was in no mood to talk with others trapped in cells. The world was spinning so much when she arrived, she didn't even know who else was in here. At least the ringing had stopped. Otherwise, she probably couldn't hear anyone.

"Wake up!" The whisper was certainly harsh.

Then again, there were pros to not being able to hear. Tess didn't even know if she had the strength to push herself into a seated position. Instead, she settled for dropping her hands to her sides, staring at the concrete ceiling, and stating, "Go away."

The silence that lingered made her believe she had been successful. That happy thought was short-lived. "You can't give up. What am I going to do? You've ruined me."

Who the hell was this person? And what right did he have coming in here and yelling at *her*? She should be in the infirmary right now. In fact, she should have seen a doctor at some point. Of course, she was dead and all they could have said was the blast diminished her essence slightly, but still. One would think she had earned the courtesy. Although she *was* charged with being a traitor to all creatures on this side of the veil so... maybe she should be happy she sat in a cell rather than subjected to more subconscious torture.

"What about the girl? You going to abandon her, too?"

Tess grumbled. It took too much effort to roll her body onto its side—like rolling a log across the ground at summer camp. When she looked toward the front of the cell, she didn't see anything. Tess frowned. Maybe this was worse than she thought. She pulled a hand in front of her face. She still looked solid, not translucent. But was she hearing voices?

Someone slapped the cell bars with a vibrating ping. Tess pulled energy from her core and sat up. She looked closer at the gate. Everything looked fine, except for the small distorted section, like how a picture looks when a camera moved while snapping. "Arbor," she stated. Guess the chameleon boy wasn't dead after all. And, even more surprising, he had come for her.

The distorted brick shifted and eyes blinked open, seeming to hover in space. He certainly had a talent.

"How were you not captured?"

The eyes bobbed in what she could only guess was an invisible shrug. "One of those men had grabbed me when the blast happened. His body shielded the energy. When he landed on top of me, I just blended into the ground. No one saw me."

Most people don't look closely at their surroundings. It was easy for creatures to blend into the background, chameleons or not. "Well, I don't know why you're here."

A red mouth opened and yellow bile projected through the space onto the floor. It was the most disgusting thing Tess had ever witnessed, and she had been spit up on by friends' babies. There were a thousand reprimands she wanted to say, but all she could do was sit with an open mouth and cringe.

Finger indentations streamed through the liquid until a metal key lifted into the air. Arbor inserted the key into her cell and the lock clicked. The door swung open and Arbor finally changed to his typical green. He had his hands on his hips, chest puffed like the proud chameleon boy he was. When Tess didn't jump up and praise him, his chest slowly deflated and his faced creased with worry.

"I just got blasted through a door, expelled like a cannonball. You think I can just skip out of here?"

Arbor held up his index finger. "Wait, I have something for that."

Tess held up a hand, giving him the sternest look she could possibly perform. "I swear if you vomit another thing up, I will die electrocuting you."

Arbor looked down at the mess on the floor and grinned. "Oh, not that." As he scurried down the hallway, Tess decided she might as well try to stand.

Her legs wobbled like she had just run a marathon, but they held her weight. In what felt like an eternity, she was stable enough to let go of the bed and face the gate. That's when something Arbor said finally registered. "Hey," she said much too loudly, "what did you mean when you said I would be abandoning the girl?"

Arbor ran back to her, clasping a bottle in his hands. It was much too big to fit down an esophagus, so Tess felt safe it had not been retrieved the same way as the key. "Oh," Arbor said. "Her door's under attack."

"What?" Tess shouted. She took a step, but her knees buckled. Tess grabbed the bed as the pounding in her head intensified. He had said it so nonchalantly, like he was stating they were out of milk. As Arbor rushed toward her, she said, "What do you mean under attack?"

"Well, it will be. Cici, one of the members of the possession party, the one you caught me from, well, I heard her saying that's where they were headed." Arbor handed her the bottle. "Here. Drink. It'll help."

Tess wanted to argue, but obeyed. She squirted a rush of liquid into her mouth. It tasted like electrified water tingling down her throat. She had three big gulps, and she could feel the surge of energy surface from deep inside. It rushed across her body, prickling against her skin. Tess gasped, standing up. "What was that?"

"Electrolytes and ground lotus seed." The voice that answered was not the harsh voice of Arbor. It was deeper. A voice she barely trusted. Thomas emerged around the corner, taking his place beside Arbor. "All processed by creatures of healing, of course."

Tess crackled with electricity. She might be well enough to walk, but she didn't know how well this water would help her kill him.

Thomas raised a hand. "Easy. I'm here to help you."

"Help me? You *arrested* me!"

"I went to him on your behalf," Arbor said, taking a step back. "I told him how you had saved Dylan. I told him you were close to taking down the Darkness." Arbor took the bottle from her. "He gave me this for you."

Tess eyed the bottle with new skepticism. There had to be a catch. He was a member of the Darkness. He had her right where he wanted her. Why would he help her now?

"Look," Thomas said with a sigh. "I think we somehow got off on the wrong foot. Mathias said a member of the order was involved."

"Don't talk about him," Tess said, clenching her fists.

"I figured it was you, but obviously he told you the same thing, and you think it's me." Thomas crossed his arms. "But why would he tell me about the Darkness if that was the case?"

She couldn't buy into his lies. But his coming here didn't seem to match the Darkness. He was after something. "Told you what?"

"He said the Darkness was led by one of the deputies."

That narrowed it down to three. She already didn't trust Kamahalan. What information did he really have to offer her?

"He also told me about the meeting. He didn't want me to go with him, said it wasn't safe."

That rang a little more true.

"But he said the deputy was meeting with the top leaders. He wanted to gain insight from their meeting before taking them down. He said he was really close to gaining evidence against the whole group. He just needed proof, and he thought the meeting was the proof he needed. He never intended to be discovered."

"But he was," Tess said, feeling numb. "And if he told you all of this, how am I to believe you didn't betray him?"

"Because, while he was dying, I was fighting at the door of Frederick Anderson."

"The spirit killed by possession?" Tess asked. She had heard about the fight. Members of the order had intercepted creatures approaching Frederick's door. A fight broke out, but Frederick was possessed. The fighting ultimately killed the host when the creature in control unexpectedly made Frederick walk in front of a bus. The death of the door took with it the creatures nearby and two guardians of Order. Tess had tried to intercept Frederick's spirit, but the Department of Spirit had moved him along in record-breaking speed due to Thomas' new proposal on spiritual protocol. She hadn't known Thomas had been at the fight.

"Frederick was already possessed when Mathias sent me there. They were trying to cross the veil. But Frederick's body wasn't strong enough."

Tess steadied herself against the bed. It wasn't an attempted possession, but an attempted crossing? They were further behind than she had thought. But why wouldn't Mathias have told her that? Why wouldn't he have sounded the alarms? Because a deputy was in charge of the whole thing? Did he not trust anyone to assist him? But he had told her some things already. He had trusted her when they first joined. Why would he wait to tell her this part?

"Now," Thomas continued, "why would I go to intervene on his behalf if I was part of the Darkness?"

She hated that he had a point. He seemed to do a lot of things that went against the Darkness. Yet wasn't that part of playing both sides? "But it was *your* protocol that accelerated Frederick's departure from the realm of Dream."

Thomas nodded. "Yeah, and I regret bringing that legislation up. I didn't see its implication until Frederick. It wasn't even my idea. Diane Wood brought the idea to me. Persuaded me to submit it."

"She's a guardian of Spirit. Why wouldn't she bring it up herself?"

Thomas shrugged. "At the time she said it was because her low position would invalidate her ideas. I was so egotistical I bought into it." Thomas hung his head, unfolding his arms. "Now I know she just didn't want to be associated with it."

Tess frowned. "So, you're saying Diane is part of the Darkness?"

"I think so, yes. It would make sense. They need guardians of Spirit to cover up their mistakes with hosts."

Tess nodded. "And members of Dream to access the doors."

Thomas frowned. "What are you saying?"

"I'm saying I think the Darkness would need all three divisions to pull this off for so long. They need creatures of Spirit to clean up, creatures of Dream to infiltrate, and creatures of Order to divert."

"And you still think I am the connection to the order?"

Tess hesitated. He made compelling arguments. She found it a lot harder to suspect him after what he had said. But her gut still told her he couldn't be trusted. Yet this was the same gut that trusted Arbor to the point of drinking out of a bottle he had offered. And Arbor was a *proven* member of the Darkness. On the other hand, Arbor never pretended to be anything different. He owned what he was and appeared to be making strides to fix it. That, or he was just in it for his own survival. Either way, Tess had never learned how to trust again. Not after all she had endured in life. Maybe it was time to start. There was only one question that remained: who?

Tess sighed. "Do I think you're the connection? I don't know, but we can't waste any more time here. Come help me save Chloe and maybe I'll start to believe you."

Thomas nodded.

"And Thomas," she waited until she locked his gaze. "Don't tell Kamahalan."

"You think she's the corrupted deputy?"

"This kind of organization… it makes more sense than any of the others."

Thomas nodded. "I think you're right."

Tess looked at her chameleon friend and smiled. "Are you ready to join the winning side?"

Arbor smiled back at her. "Let's go save someone."

The three of them left the jail. She certainly was spending a lot of time in the realm of doors. She only hoped they were not too late.

## Twenty-five

White, puffy clouds floated across a bright, blue sky. A soft breeze rushed past, pushing through her hair. Chloe sat in the grass, watching people walk their dogs toward the dog park, play volleyball in the nearby sandpit, and walk around the exercise loop. The happy giggles and shouts from kids climbing in the play area drifted with the breeze. Chloe closed her eyes and she could almost feel him here with her.

They used to come here a lot when she was young. Her dad would push her on the swings. She'd giggle as she soared closer toward the sky. She had felt like she could fly back then, her little body soaring above his head. She knew he'd be there to catch her if she fell. She knew he'd protect her. How did it all fall apart?

"I see you have found peace here." Chloe opened her eyes and smiled at Argumas. His voice was not something she could get used to. It sounded like some sort of computerized voice, making him seem less real. But as he slowly eased his large body into a seated position, she felt connected to him. It seemed fitting: someone she thought would protect her had taken everything from her, and someone she thought would hurt her had now become her guardian.

"I need to talk with Thomas."

Argumas nodded. "I can tell him whatever you need."

Chloe shook her head. "No. I need to talk to him. My cousin... she's in trouble. I don't know how to help her."

Dogs barked in the park behind her, echoing against the silence. Argumas' face was hard to read, but she thought he frowned at her. "I sense this cannot wait."

"It can't. I need to see him now."

Argumas shifted. "Well, then let's get you to the door." He looked regretful as he rolled himself onto his knees. With much effort, he rose to his feet.

Chloe waited until he was finished before she stood. She looked back at the park. Half of her wanted to stay here, in this time where everything made sense and the world was not quite so harsh.

"What is this place?"

Chloe watched a girl on the swing being pushed by her father. "Tompkin's Park. My dad used to take me here all the time after work." Cars buzzed along the adjacent highway. "It didn't matter how stressful work was or how mad my mom was. He'd always take me here to swing." Chloe shook her head. "I was clueless."

Argumas hesitated. "I have to ask you something. It's been bothering me."

A slight breeze brushed her hair behind her. The park was filled with such peace. She didn't remember a time when she had felt calmer and at the most inappropriate time.

"Chief Guardian Tess. She gave you a trinket that day. The day she met you. It upset you."

The breeze picked up into a steady wind, turning cold against her skin. Tinkerbell. Every time she thought of it, her heart raced. "Yes."

"Why does it have power over you?"

Chloe closed her eyes; the barks behind her sounded more vicious. They were going after something. "My father gave it to me. We went to the park and he gave it to me. When he got home, they started fighting and she kicked him out."

"Do you still have it?" Argumas asked.

Chloe didn't want to see it, but when she opened her eyes, the park was gone. They stood in the middle of the cold room of her childhood. She could clearly see her father in the room, searching for her. The trinket was on the nightstand where she had left it. "No," Chloe's voice was hollow.

His silhouette bumped into the table when he entered, the trinket shimmering as it fell to the ground. It crunched under his foot as he exited, leaving behind a silence that smothered her. Argumas jumped at the gunshot that followed shortly after. The room slowly faded, revealing the white room.

Chloe pushed back her tears. "Can we talk with Thomas now?"

Argumas looked around him. His shoulders sagged, his eyes regretful. "Yes. Of course." The creature moved toward the door, then hesitated. He turned back to face her. His pupils were the same pinpoints as always, but he somehow reflected compassion. "We don't know the history, you know."

Chloe frowned at him. History? What was he talking about?

"When we are assigned doors. We are not told why. Our costume just appears and we are asked to play a part. I'm sorry. I did not understand."

He had been such a strong presence in her childhood. There were so many nights she'd wake up screaming after his visit. She'd run through the hallway, trying to get away from him. One night, she even slapped her aunt for trying to stop her. That was the night they started locking the bedroom door. That was the night Chloe started to hang red ribbons in her closet to mark reality. Chloe sighed. "I think I gave you that mask. You said it was just there. I gave you everything you needed. You were just playing a part I had created. You couldn't have understood. It was my demon to confront."

Argumas studied her for a moment. She realized he was a creature who had never thought of humans before. He had likely never thought of a world outside of his own existence. She couldn't really fault him for it. That was probably true of most humans, too. But he was seeking to learn more about his world than what was presented to him, and she had to respect him for it.

Finally, Argumas settled on some unseen decision. He nodded at her, then turned toward the door. "Wait here. I'll go get Thomas."

Chloe looked around the drab room. Maybe she could conjure up a tablet to play on while she waited in this blank space. Her door squeaked on its hinges. And then there was shouting, lots of shouting. Chloe whipped around just as a mob flooded in, pushing Argumas backward. When Chloe shouted, the white walls vibrated, throwing two of the dark creatures back out.

Their presence crept along her skin like oil. She wanted to drive them from her space. She wanted to wash them off. Lightning blasted from the ceiling, striking another. The scaly creature erupted into flames, turning to dust in a matter of seconds. She knew she was killing them, but Chloe cringed against the sensation creeping up her arm.

They were wrong. They were so wrong. They did not belong here, but they were like honey sticking to her fingers. Another lightning bolt struck, sending sparks flying from each corner of the room. It took out two more as three entered. The two piles of ash lay next to Argumas. She couldn't kill them all without killing him too.

In the moment's hesitation, she felt cold metal encompass her wrist. She looked down to see an iron bracelet attached to a spiked chain. Chloe screamed, but the lightning didn't come. Only a flicker of a light on the ceiling. Argumas fought against three of them, yelling as he swung his big, solid arms. Chloe screamed as one of them raised something that looked like a crystal knife.

Blue lightning penetrated the space, branching into spears that hit five of them. Tess stepped through the door and the creeping feeling eased slightly. With her help, Argumas regained momentum against the attack. Chloe smiled at Tess until she shot a bolt of lightning at her. Maybe Thomas was right. The girl was a fugitive!

Chloe braced herself against the impact. Metal screeched and then collapsed to the ground. When Chloe opened her eyes, smoke rose from her iron bracelet where the chain used to attach. "Are you crazy?" Chloe shouted.

"A little help would be nice," Tess said. Her shirt was torn and her hair pointed in every direction. The woman looked like she had survived a hurricane.

She couldn't do anything too dramatic without killing Argumas and Tess. Finally, Chloe knew what she could do. She took a deep breath before letting out a scream. Water burst from the walls, sweeping their feet out from under. Everyone in the room washed across the floor and out the door. The moment they left, the door slammed shut.

Chloe shivered. The creeping feeling was gone, but she was alone. So very much alone. The door vibrated on its frame like someone had taken a hammer to it. The light in the room flickered when the door vibrated again. This time thunder sounded above her. If she listened closely, she could hear shouting from behind the door… and shadows moving against the threshold. The fight was still happening outside.

Chloe hugged herself. She wanted to hide. She wanted to crawl into a corner and hide. She backed up until her back rested on the wall. She slid down, staring at the shadows and listening to the shouting. She rocked back and forth, placing her hands on her ears. She couldn't do this. She couldn't do this. Not again. Not again.

Then she saw it just as clear as if it had happened yesterday. The glittering of glass in the moonlight.

Tinkerbell, mangled on the carpeted floor. A childhood broken along with the trinket. He hadn't even noticed it. He had given it to her out of love, and then broke it like it meant nothing. She meant nothing. She was done. She didn't want to cower anymore. She would not hide behind another door. Not now.

Chloe's teeth chattered as she forced herself to rise to her feet. She was no longer a scared five-year-old. She would no longer let this moment define her. Chloe forced her steps forward, approaching the vibrating door. Blue light pushed through the hinges. They were out there fighting for her. She had to help them.

Chloe reached forward and gripped the door handle. She took a breath, then yanked the door open. Air rushed past her into the void before her. Bodies scattered along the grey pebbles while others hid behind the mass of doors before her. They were all sizes and colors. Chloe looked at the black sky above her, glowing with galaxies she had only seen in pictures from the Hubble Space Telescope. This place was not as mundane as her white room.

Buzzing sounded and a figure to her right went rigid. The body fell to the ground, bringing Chloe's attention back to the present. Tess was hiding behind a big red door, with Thomas next to her shouting something in her ear. They seemed to be motioning around them. They didn't have much backup and the creatures were overpowering them. Chloe had to do something.

She took a breath. This had to be against some rule of nature, but she had to try. Chloe eased one foot through the threshold. Her shoes settled in the gravel before she pulled her other foot through, crossing from the white room into a land of doors. When she had stepped over the threshold, she felt a surge of energy pass through her body. Her skin glowed yellow against the black space.

When she turned, she found creatures frozen in terror. She was right. This was not supposed to have happened. In the front stood a large jackrabbit, as tall as any human. Chloe smiled at her, then bent down and pressed a hand against the pebbles. Like a defibrillator, energy shot through her, rippling through the pebbles. When the energy reached the creatures in front of her, they burst into an orange light as bright as the sun. Then just smoke remained.

Chloe turned to face the rest of them only to find the entire group of creatures fleeing the area. Chloe smiled at herself. She did it. She didn't hide and she actually accomplished something!

"Chloe!" she heard Tess shout. The woman charged over to her, skidding to a stop. "What are you doing out here? How…?"

Thomas stayed where he was, frozen. Maybe they didn't think this was as cool as she did. But she had just vaporized a group of creatures. The whole thing felt like the best dream ever. How could this be bad?

Tess went to touch her shoulder, then stopped. "You need to go back inside. Now."

Chloe frowned. "I thought you were a fugitive."

Tess cast a glance behind her. Thomas was slowly talking himself into standing, eyes still glued on Chloe. "A misunderstanding. Please, back inside the door. I don't know how long you can last out here."

Last? The way she said that didn't sound good.

"Chloe. Only the dead can enter the realm of Dream."

Oh. That wasn't good at all. Chloe quickly backed up, the threshold practically embracing her as she stepped back through. The glowing immediately disappeared as Tess followed her inside.

"Dead?" Chloe asked, touching her arms to check. "I'm not dead, am I?"

Tess hesitated, studying her. "No. You aren't."

Chloe backed up again. "So I shouldn't have been able to do that?"

Her silence spoke more about the situation than any words ever could. What did this all mean?

Thomas stepped through and closed the door behind him. "I ordered Argumas to keep guard. I think we need to let a few of our associates in to help him."

Tess rubbed her temples. "Yes. I guess we can say for certain Chloe is part of their plans."

"Yes, I am!" Chloe shouted. She had almost forgotten. "They're after my cousin."

Tess frowned at this. "Your cousin? Why?"

"To get to me." When she was met with confused looks, Chloe realized she had yet to share her news about Dylan. "We spoke to Dylan. He's not possessed anymore."

"Yes," Tess said dryly. "I did that."

"Well, he remembers some stuff. He said they needed beings on both sides. He said they needed somewhere that holds the power of blood. And they needed someone to walk through. I don't know how or why, but I think they want me to walk through the veil, and they'll use Molly to make that happen."

Tess was already shaking her head before Chloe had finished her sentence. Chloe forgot how frustrating this woman could be.

"Trust me, if they want you to walk through, they don't need Molly. She serves no purpose but to lure you closer to them."

"People on both sides," Thomas said. "That means they have to be in the same place on both sides of the veil."

Tess adjusted her jacket. "Just like the possession parties. Breaking the veil wouldn't be that much different. They'd have to get close enough to the veil to pierce it. That has to take power from both sides."

"Dylan said he was supposed to get ten people, but they didn't think that was enough."

"That would barely be enough in the Dream realm," Tess said.

"This is much bigger than we thought," Thomas added.

"If they're coming after Chloe, then they are close to implementation." Tess turned back to face Chloe. "You can't go to sleep for a day or so. Can you do that?"

Had this woman completely lost her mind? What did one thing have to do with the other? Chloe was supposed to be a part of this whole thing, and yet felt like she had no idea what was going on. "Not sleep?"

"If you don't sleep, there is nothing for them to attack," Tess said with impatience.

Chloe shook her head. Like that was an answer to her question. But Chloe gave up trying to get anything out of her. "Fine. I've done 24 hours before. What's another few after that?" She'd have to get Becca to buy some energy drinks. She could do this. Prove to them that she was part of the team.

Tess nodded. "Good. In the meantime, we need to find the meeting ground."

"What about Presidio?" Thomas suggested.

Tess practically rolled her eyes. She rubbed her temple, but sighed. "Okay. But go get the guards first. We need to bring a team with us."

Thomas nodded, opening the door. He waved over a few figures on the other side. Tess faced Chloe. "You need to let them in. They are friendly."

Four figures entered alongside Argumas. The creeping feeling returned with their presence. "I don't like this," Chloe said without thinking.

Tess nodded. "It's normal." She motioned toward a beaver who stood as tall as any human. "This is Max—he's one of my associates." She motioned toward a man who looked more like a dragon with arms and legs. "And this is Masat. They will help protect you along with these two guardians of Order."

Chloe shivered against their presence. Maybe Tess was right. After what she had just endured, of course she wouldn't want someone to enter. "But Argumas will be here too, right?"

Argumas stepped forward. "I will not leave for anything."

Chloe nodded. There was only slight comfort in that statement. This small white room was starting to feel very crowded. If Tess said they were safe, then Chloe had to believe her. She didn't want another attack. That last one was too close. "What about Molly?"

Tess shrugged. "Do what you want when you are awake, but I'm telling you she's safe. It's you they're after. Just don't go to sleep for as long as possible, okay?"

Chloe nodded. "Okay, but what are you going to do?"

"You know that jackrabbit, the one you vaporized?"

Chloe nodded.

"Well, her name was Lilija. She was one of the best associates of Order."

"So?"

"So," Thomas added. "There's only one way someone of such a high rank could be part of this. Our boss must have organized it."

"You asked what we're going to do," Tess said. The smile Tess gave Chloe made her shiver. "We're going to take down the head of the organization."

# Twenty-six

The Deputy of Order had the best office. Sure, Nakima had a meadow and a creek, but this room always took Tess' breath away. The ceiling stood two stories high. Leaves and swirled designs were etched in the gold plates lining the ceiling. But that wasn't the best part. Books filled mahogany shelves that towered to the ceiling. Two sweeping iron staircases led from the tile floor to the highest platform. More bookshelves protruded from the walls, creating a narrow pathway in the middle along with cozy cubbyholes throughout the room.

Cement statues of some of history's best minds stood guard over glass tables along the pathway. The sight of such knowledge in one room was not only intimidating, but also inspiring. The books had offered her access to things she never knew, and to a better world than the one she currently occupied. Not to mention, one of the cubbyholes had the most comfortable blue love seat on which she had ever sat on.

"We have some time," Tess said, turning to face Thomas. He was standing with his arms clasped behind his back, leaning slightly as he stared up at a top shelf. He almost looked like he was staring at something in particular. "Kamahalan just left for a deputy meeting with the Governess."

Thomas nodded, meeting her eyes. "Those always take forever."

Tess still couldn't believe they were organizing an attack on the Darkness without Kamahalan. She still didn't want to believe her boss was part of such evil. Mathias had told her the Darkness had infiltrated someone in a superior position. Tess had always suspected Kamahalan. Yet, given the fact she typically went around not trusting anyone, she didn't give her suspicions much value—and neither did anyone else for that matter. Now Thomas and Tess had now made the decision to go against Kamahalan. Their action would be viewed as nothing short of open defiance should the Deputy of Order actually be innocent.

But she couldn't be. The logic was sound. No one else could have organized such a large group. No one else could have kept it from the deputies of Order for so long. Kamahalan not only knew the movements of the guardians of Order, she orchestrated them. She could easily keep them away from any important meetings and possessions. That would also explain how the creatures knew how to bypass the guards at the doors. She controlled the whole thing.

Everything pointed to her and when Lilija attacked them at Chloe's door, that solidified Kamahalan's guilt. Now it made sense. Lilija didn't get recruited to Chief Guardian because the Darkness didn't need anyone in that position. They had already captured the highest level of leadership. Lilija could go unnoticed better as an Associate Guardian. That's how Tess got promoted instead. Her promotion had never made sense to Tess until now. Kamahalan wanted to keep her close so she could monitor the investigation. She wanted to keep Tess within striking distance if she got too close, just like Mathias.

"Did you contact the guardians?" Tess asked after a moment.

"They should be here shortly," Thomas replied. He still stood with his arms behind his back as usual. He didn't seem to look much like a choirboy right now.

"And you know they are not part of the Darkness?"

"I personally looked at each file. They've been on the job less than an earth year. They're too new to hold much value to the Darkness."

"But are they too new to be of much value in a fight?" Tess could just see a handful of rookies fighting up against some of the strongest Darkness forces. Maybe it was better to go alone. Even if the alone strategy hadn't been working so far. She had to have faith someone else could do their job just as well.

"They might be inexperienced, but they were trained in the academy just like everyone else. It shouldn't be a problem."

Tess sighed. "Okay. Well, let's get the map out and make this look official."

The two of them split up. Tess wandered down the stacks of books until she got to a section with a red straight-backed chair. She climbed a small ladder to reach the seventh shelf. She pulled down an atlas and marveled. In the day and age of Google, the realm of Dream still used atlases. When she reached one of the glass tables, Tess put the book down and opened it.

The brown pages were marked with black ink. They looked like something that had come from the scrolls of the first century. The pages scratched as she flipped through the book, looking for the Spanish expeditions into southern Arizona.

As Thomas made his way to her, Tess took out the pages devoted to Presidio Santa Cruz de Terrenate and laid them on the glass table. The table glass moved like resin around the pages, sucking them beneath the surface before hardening once again. Once the pages were accepted as part of the table, the black ink began to shift, projecting upright into a 3D-ink model of the different stages of the fort.

Thomas stepped by her side. In front of the table stood fifteen of the most scared-looking set of guardians of Order Tess had ever seen. There were bears, squirrels, foxes, and deer along with fairies, a Satyr, and a Minotaur standing just as tall as the human spirits dispersed among them. The group itself looked too much like misfits to represent an effective army. And their saucer eyes confirmed her analysis.

*We're all going to die*, Tess thought with a frown. If he were still alive, Mathias would be castigating her for her stupidity, forcibly removing her from the case. But he wasn't here. And this was their only option.

"Thank you for coming, " Tess began. Start with pleasantries. That's what they always had to do. "You have been called upon to engage in a mission of utmost importance."

"We have all been betrayed," Thomas said, "by creatures calling themselves the Darkness. Their whole purpose is to break the veil between this world and life on Earth."

"Such an action will destroy all life on Earth," Tess continued. "Our world and that of Earth will merge, flooding us with the spirits of those destroyed."

"More importantly," Thomas said, "it will flood our world with a significant source of power. If harnessed, that power can create a being so strong, they can dominate our realm. Our world structure will forever be changed, and a supreme power will emerge. Those who support that person will be enhanced as well. Together, they will take over and dominate our world."

Tess stared at Thomas for a moment. Was he conducting an informational meeting or a sales pitch? She cleared her throat, then said, "They will destroy us and the lives we have worked hard to create. You all are members of the order. It is our job to stop this. And this is where we will do so."

Tess motioned toward the images of the fort reflecting over the table. Some of the images showed an installation city, some a well-defined fort, and one of ruins. Each image turned in a synchronized dance. "We do not know what form Presidio Santa Cruz de Terrenate will take. Whatever the form, it will be powerful. There has been a lot of blood spilt on its grounds. And, with the San Pedro River nearby, the power will be greater."

"Remember, even though the earthquake of 1887 sent the San Pedro River underground," Thomas added, "it still holds a lifeline of water. No matter the time period, it will enhance the blood spilt there. So be careful."

Tess said, "We will come from the hills. This should give us some cover as we approach the ruins. We need a group approaching from the north, south, and river sides. They are harnessing power somewhere on site, probably the chapel. Our mission is to destroy that power and capture as many members of the Darkness as possible."

"That sounds like a complicated plan." Tess froze at Kamahalan's voice. The panther stepped around a stack of books. She had blended so easily into the shadows.

The guardians of Order stood at attention, looking even more uneasy. Kamahalan approached the table, yellow eyes examining the ruins of Presidio circling before her. Tess didn't know what to do. Were they busted before they even began? But Kamahalan couldn't do anything in front of these guardians of Order.

Kamahalan wiped her hand through the projection, closing the image. The glass pushed the maps back to the surface, papers ruffling as it hardened once again underneath. "Thomas?" she said.

Thomas stood at attention.

"Please take these guardians outside and prep them for their journey."

There went all of her witnesses. But she said prep them for their journey. Did that mean they were going to Presidio after all? And if they were going, what did that mean about what awaited them there? As Thomas left her, Tess seriously started to question their entire mission.

When they were alone, Kamahalan turned to face her. "You have made significant progress in your investigation if you're planning an attack. I just wonder, of all the guardians, why did you pick the newest recruits?"

"This is a delicate mission," Tess said. "They are the best available option."

Kamahalan nodded, pursing her lips. "I see." Her yellow eyes focused on the papers before her. "Mathias went to Presidio and died."

Tess felt her body chill. That's not what he told her. Why would he go there after specifically telling her not to? And why would he go alone? That was not like him. No. This couldn't be true. She was trying to trick her.

"I always wondered about the power there. But Thomas argued against sending a mission." Kamahalan tapped a nail on the glass surface, each click cutting across Tess' skin. "I see you are working with him, as I suggested."

Tess was so confused by the entire conversation. She didn't know what to make of it, but she did know how to recognize a distrustful person when she saw one. "Yes, ma'am."

"That's good. He had made an accusation against you."

"It was a misunderstanding."

"I see." Kamahalan stacked the papers from the table and laid them on top of the atlas. "The trouble with accusations, they always reveal something about both parties."

"And what is that?"

Kamahalan shrugged. "I'm not sure yet. But I know if you both are going to Presidio with a group of new recruits, then you are going to need a lot more help. I'm not sure why you both kept this from me, but I will not allow you to move without my presence."

*This can't be good.* "You are much too valuable to endanger," Tess said quickly.

Kamahalan shook her head. "You forget. I started as a fighter just like you. If you are ready to make a move against this organization, then I want to be there."

What could Tess say to that? She couldn't order the woman to stay. But why would she want to go? Why wouldn't she have heard their plan and left without being seen? She could have told the Darkness everything. She could have set up a trap... unless this was the trap.

Kamahalan was a few feet away when she turned back around. "I hear Lilija was part of the Darkness."

Tess nodded, still unsure of the angle.

"Guess you never can tell." Kamahalan thought a moment, then added, "I can now see why you wanted to work alone. It is really a strength in these circumstances."

Outside the room, Kamahalan led the group of guardians down the white hall. Thomas took a step next to Tess at the back.

"What'd she say?"

"Besides the fact she's coming along, I'm not sure." Tess frowned.

"You think she's going to sabotage us?"

Tess nodded. "Yes, but I'm hoping that's all it is. Look. Can you stop her while I attack the chapel?"

Thomas nodded. "Of course. And if she does anything, we don't have to worry about proof."

Tess tried not to roll her eyes. Leave it to Choirboy to find the silver lining. She was heading into a blood-fueled fort with a group of inexperienced guardians and the head of the Darkness with nothing more than her power and an alliance with a man whose integrity she still questioned. If he hadn't been dead already, this would have killed Mathias. But she had no choice. This was it. They had to do this before Chloe fell asleep or lose to the Darkness. And she really hated losing.

## Twenty-seven

Children scurried everywhere. Some chased each other around the large field while others bounced balls and guarded on the basketball court. They were like little ants enclosed within a chain-linked fence surrounding the school, their shouts and giggles echoing in the neighborhood. Teachers stood in skirts and pant suits with badges and whistles hanging from turquoise lanyards around their neck.

Chloe watched them from a nearby park. Nancy Hakes Park was small with a single piece of equipment that boasted three yellow slides, a monkey bar, and a set of swings. A wooden "bridge" to the far side of the park led into the neighborhood running up against the back of the school. From this distance, she couldn't see her sister, but it was mid-morning. Molly could be amongst the children running around the playground, or her recess could be in the afternoon. The school itself was a series of rectangular buildings lined up for an entire block, and the playground stretched across the back side. Her presence here was stupid, Chloe thought. Even if Molly was on the playground playing tetherball or on the swings, it would take forever for Chloe to find her.

Maybe she should try to check Molly out of school. Could she even do that? What if the school knew she had run away? No. that was too risky. Chloe sat on an old metal bench behind a large mesquite tree, looking like a creeper staring at children playing. She should just trust Tess. Molly wasn't at risk. The only person at risk here was her. She shouldn't be back in town. She needed to get out of here. But how could she leave Molly until she was sure? She had done so much to frighten that girl. Molly didn't deserve any of it. She deserved a childhood without drama. As a toddler, Molly shouldn't have had to deal with Chloe's night terrors or the screams coming from the next room.

Molly should be with her father. They should all be together in one nice family. No one spoke about it, but they didn't have to. Her aunt had separated from him because he wanted her to get rid of Chloe. He had wanted to protect his daughter from the fits of a growing child who thought all men were going to kill her. Chloe had wanted to trust him, but how could she? He was tall. He was the image of protection, just as her father had been. Then he had started to fight with her aunt. They tried to hide it, but voices could be heard through the walls at night. Cloe knew the tone of those voices. She had lived through it once before. She had lived with the fear of angry voices at night between the two people she loved the most. She had lived with the uncertainty of what those voices meant. And she had lived to see what came after: an emptier house that would be invaded one night by a loud bang.

This time the fighting had been about her. She was troubled. She barely talked. And she cried every time he came too close. One night, at one of her lowest years, she had even stolen a prized possession. It was some stupid baseball with a signature from some stupid player. She was a little older than Molly, who was just a baby. She didn't know why. She just went into his office. She wasn't supposed to; it was forbidden. She had wanted to know why it was so forbidden, so she went in there. She went in and saw it sitting on display on the desk. She could tell he had taken such care of it. Before she knew what was happening, she took it.

She had felt so alive at that moment. In some small way, she had been taking back control. She would get back at him. For what, she wasn't sure. The neighbor's dog was huge, one of those dogs left outside all year long to bark at anything and everything that came by the house. She had giggled when she tossed the baseball over the side of the fence to the dog. The ball had lasted for a day or two before the beast broke the seams. That must have been the last straw. They had stopped arguing... stopped talking really... and he moved out a month later. She had done all of that.

Things had gotten better. It took years, but Dr. Lewis helped the nightmares go away. She helped the anger go away. She helped the anxiety and fear go away. Things were normal by the time she got to high school. Things were on the up side. But she had never apologized. She had never acknowledged her part in the chaos. And now she'd run away.

Chloe rubbed her eyes. Molly didn't deserve any of this. And yet Chloe couldn't envision a future where she wasn't messed up. She had hidden behind closet doors and watched her life change. It was a defining moment. She had chosen a path, not really knowing what that meant. And like most defining moments in life, someone else had a hand in the outcome. Chloe pulled out the phone she had borrowed from Abby. She still had hers turned off so they couldn't track her. Watching all those cop shows with her aunt was finally paying off. She quickly typed a message to Becca: *Forget it. Come get me.*

Chloe stood. She should wait somewhere else. She needed to get out of the school's line of sight. When she turned, she noticed a flash of something out of the corner of her eye. The dried grass crunched beneath her shoes as she stepped closer to the chain-link fence. It was that stupid Oregon Ducks t-shirt Molly's dad had given her last Christmas. Practically glow-in-the-dark yellow. Chloe swore he did it so Molly wouldn't get lost in the Tucson malls anymore. That, or he was color-blind. She had never loved that shirt until today. Molly charged from the open doors of the closest building, and flew down the slight hill leading toward the basketball courts. She wasn't into playing basketball, so Chloe couldn't figure why that was her destination. But this was her shot.

Chloe looked around her. There were so many teachers, but also so many kids on the playground. Being dressed in all black was about to pay off. Chloe followed the chain-link fence until she got to the alley that ran between the back of the neighborhood and the school. The trees lining the back of the school didn't start on this side of the alley. She'd have to get further down before they could block her. She was completely in the open, crouching down the mowed pathway. Chloe stopped just past the wall of some person's yard.

She hesitated, stealing a glance at the teachers. They were at the top of the hill by the doors in some sort of deep conversation. Years ago, she and Molly had gotten into *The Hunger Games*. Chloe whistled the slow three notes from the movie: low, high, low. Molly hesitated, standing out even more against the blue backdrop of mountains towering in the distance. She looked around, eyes focused. Chloe did the call again, feeling like both a dork and an idiot for drawing attention to herself with something from a movie.

But it worked. Molly caught sight of her and practically jumped vertically into the air. She looked over her shoulder at the teachers before calmly walking toward the fence, but Chloe could tell she really wanted to run over. Smart girl.

Molly gripped her fingers through the fence, feeling warm to the touch. "Where have you been? Mom's been crying ever since you left."

Guilt panged at her heart. They all didn't deserve this. "I know. I'm sorry. I have to help a friend out. I'll be back, I swear. How are you?"

Molly tugged at the fence. "Forget your friend. You need to come home. It's not the same without you."

Some kid cried foul on the basketball court as the chain net rattled with a score. "I can't."

"Were you bad? Are you mad at Mom about something? Because I know she's sorry for whatever it is. She'll forgive you."

A cool breeze rushed down the alley. Tears were forming in her cousin's eyes.

"I know. I will. I promise. I just have to do something first. But soon," Chloe told her.

A group of kids yelled at each other next to the metal soccer post without a net. One had a soccer ball tucked under his arm while a group shouted about something. For the moment, the teachers were still distracted, but if the group drew their attention, they were bound to see her standing here. She had to make this quick.

"Look. Molly. I need you to listen to me, okay?"

Molly frowned at her, but nodded.

"I need you to fake a stomachache. Your mom will check you out of school, thinking you're just upset about me. But I need you to be convincing."

"We take our Accelerated Reader test today. If I get twenty more points, I will be in the lead for the iPod drawing."

This kid. She was definitely choosing a path foreign to Chloe. "I know. But this is important. I need you to stay with your mom. Until I get back. You can't leave her, okay?"

Molly's face wrinkled. "Why?" she asked slowly.

The group's shouting got louder as a boy went to take the ball out of another's hands. "Look. I'm helping a friend, okay. But that friend is in serious trouble. And I don't want that trouble coming back on you."

Now Molly really looked like she was going to cry. "Am I in trouble?"

Chloe shook her head as a whistle blew and teachers shouted from their perch. She crouched closer to the dirt. "No. But this is important to me. I want you to be with your mom. Can you do that for me?"

"Hey!" she heard a voice say from the front of the alley.

Chloe's heart pounded in her temples. "Please, Molly. Please do this for me. I'll do anything you want."

"You'll come home."

"Tomorrow," Chloe promised, hoping it was true.

Molly pursed her lips, but nodded. She looked so much like her mother in that look: a miniature adult judging a misguided teenager. She was so much younger, and yet still made Chloe feel inferior.

"You're not supposed to be back there!" the voice shouted again right as a whistle screeched.

"Molly?" a concerned voice hollered from the perch.

She was done here. She had to leave. Now. "I love you, okay?" Chloe said as she backed away.

Molly nodded but said nothing.

Chloe turned and ran down the alley. When she reached the edge, she almost didn't recognize Paul King standing there out of his Safeway uniform. His harsh eyes stared at her through his wire glasses. "What are you doing? You are not allowed back here."

He had some mutt on a red leash pulling at him to continue their interrupted walk. When the dog saw her, its fluffy tail whipped back and forth and it rushed over. "Whoa," Paul said, tugging on the leash.

"I just had to talk with my cousin," Chloe said, sidestepping the chaotic scene. "You know, they have puppy classes at the park every week."

"He's five," Paul said like that meant something.

"Okay."

"We have to go on our walk so I can get to work. But you shouldn't be back there."

One-track mind. "Well," Chloe said. "I'm not back there anymore." She hurried past him and along the road passing the park. She had to get into the neighborhood. She passed beside the wooden bridge over nothing and stopped at the stop sign. Becca had gone to Culver's. She should be back by now.

She heard her phone collide with the street as a pillowcase smothered her face. Chloe screamed, pushing against the arms locking her into their grip. She tried to kick behind her, vaguely hearing a dog bark. Her head hit something hard as she heard the door to a van slide shut. Wheels squealed as Chloe ripped the pillowcase off her head. She banged on the window at Paul, who stood shouting at the back of the van. "Paul! Help me!"

Then something slammed against the back of her head and everything went black.

## Twenty-eight

The land rolled in front of them. Small mesquites scattered all over the area, green bushes painted against the yellow desert grass. The valley spread before them, a different mountain range stretched on each horizon. On the reality side, this area could look very bright and dry in the full sun of midday. But this was the dream side of the veil. And this place held the power of blood soaking the earth.

Tess felt the ground pulse against her shoes as she crouched low to the ground. The mountains surrounding her remained a constant shade of blue up against a purple sky. Directly above the fort, the sky twinkled with the stars of twilight. But when the ground pulsed beneath her feet, red streaks vibrated against the sky. She could see why Mathias hadn't wanted her to come here. From what she could tell, this place hadn't seen much death in a long time. Yet past violence still affected the stones of the ruins glowing before her.

At this particular moment, the fort remained a shell of bricks up against the ground. The biggest wall belonged to what was once a church. It was the typical ghost town, just hinting at the greatness that once lived and now was gone. Tess frowned. Most places would still flicker between the current state and the standing fort. Yet this place remained still, as if the past had been erased, forgotten even in the scope of the dream's remembrance. Or maybe the evil practiced here was too much for the glory of history to overcome.

She was satisfied with their hiding spot. Between the rolling hills, mesquites, and twilight shadows, no one could spot her approach. Tess crept forward for a better view of the fort. She could see a group of five creatures standing two hundred yards away. Two were bony creatures with broken noses, their green skin stretched like overused leather. Two were fluffy brown rabbits with prized antlers any hunter would be proud to mount on a wall. The last was a fox with large white wings protruding from its shoulders. She had no doubt they were all creatures of Dream.

The ground crunched beneath her shoe as Tess turned to face Thomas, who was crouching beside her. "That can't be all of them."

Thomas shook his head. "Not if they are going to tear the veil."

"Exactly how are they supposed to tear the veil?" Kamahalan asked. Tess jerked a little. The woman's skill for hiding spoke clearly of a predator nature. She had almost forgotten her boss was there. But how could she forget? Her presence was the biggest reason their plan was doomed. How could she possibly take down the Darkness with its leader crouching right next to her? For all she knew, they were currently surrounded and would soon be dead.

"I'm not sure," Tess said. "It would take a lot of effort on both sides of the veil. They'd need more than five."

"Maybe more are coming," Thomas said. He seemed too calm. The ground pulsed below her.

"Whatever they're doing," Tess said, "they must have established a connection to the fort somewhere. To access such ancient blood, they must have been building it for quite a while now. If we can find their source, we can destroy their connection. Arrest everyone here and worry about the rest later."

"I think we should wait," Kamahalan said.

*Of course she does*, Tess thought, throwing a look Thomas' way. Again, he looked unconcerned. He may not be part of the Darkness, but that didn't make him any less annoying.

"If we want to take down the Darkness," Kamahalan continued, "we need to know who is at the head. Otherwise, we'll be constantly chasing them."

The plan actually sounded like a good defense. Under any other circumstance, Tess would agree without hesitation. But now she wondered about Kamahalan's angle. She'd be stupid not to feel a trap coming. Then again… what if they were wrong? They couldn't be wrong. Kamahalan was in charge. It was the only thing that made sense.

"If they had something," Thomas said, "My bet would be on the old church."

Kamahalan nodded.

"Not the river?" Tess said.

All three looked at the string of trees cutting through the hills. Thomas frowned. "The creek bed is dry. Even with water underground, it would only support the ancient blood. The church is a better source for the connection."

"I agree with Thomas," Kamahalan said. Good to know being part of the Darkness didn't change anything. The mere fact she agreed with Thomas made Tess want to run toward the creek bed. The ground pulsed beneath her and the horizon turned from purple to a deep magenta.

"Well," Tess said. "Then maybe we should make our way in that direction while we wait for the others to arrive. That is, if this is even the place."

Kamahalan frowned. "Why do you suspect it isn't?"

Tess shook her head. "Think about it. They're supposed to tear the veil between two realms. That takes a lot of power. This place. It should be electric. It should hurt to stand this close. It should be... I don't know.... More."

Kamahalan studied the group before them, her eyes sharp. "You think the blood is too old?"

"I'm starting to," Tess said.

The air shifted, bringing with it the stench of something rotting. Another group of creatures emerged down a path leading toward the fort. There had to be fifteen creatures belonging to all three divisions. There were spirits, different-sized creatures, and guardians of Order. Amongst them was one of the chief guardians of Dream—a green fairy whose blue hair glittered along with her skin—and the dragon boy who had come for her at Marcus' cave—one of Thomas' associates. Tess looked at Thomas for a reaction, but he still remained much too calm. Her trust issues might go deeper than she had originally thought, but she still didn't want to think of him as on her side. He might not be on the side of the Darkness, but he knew more than he was telling her.

The stench grew. It was a cross between a skunk and lettuce left rotting in the fridge. It hung in the air, threatening to sour even the sweetest of flowers forever. The group joined the five at what looked like the center of the ruins. They all nodded at each other before forming a circle. They touched hands, palms pressing against open hands. The ground pulsed once more, this time sending a flash of white light from beneath their skin. They chanted, eyes closed. The pulse happened again, this time light erupted from their eyes as well.

"I don't think they're trying to break the veil," Tess said, watching the way they continued to chant. "This is the backstage where they prepare for it."

Kamahalan frowned. "What do you mean?"

"This makes sense now. They haven't been coming here to establish a place to break the veil. That's too risky. What if they're found out? No, this is where they come to pump up their own power. This is the staging ground, but the main event is somewhere else."

Thomas' eyes narrowed on her. He went to say something, but the snap of a nearby twig stopped him.

Tess shot to her feet as a centaur charged, hoofs pounding the ground and bolder-sized arms outstretched. She shot him in the human chest with a bolt of lightning just as Kamahalan ripped open his skin at the flanks. The creature screamed, faltering. It was enough. The ground vibrated as the group below charged them.

Whether they were ready for a battle or not, one was here. And the creatures they were fighting were amped up with blood power. Electricity crackled between her fingers. This should be fun. Tess thought of Mathias and the electricity pulsed along with the power in the ground. If they used the blood energy, so could she.

The centaur picked up a large branch to swing at her, but Tess was quicker. The power of Mother Nature's heaviest bolt shot from her arm. He went rigid as the smell of burnt flesh filled the air. The centaur fell to the ground and she wasn't sure he'd ever get back up.

Thomas pulled out his net-gun while gripping a gold trench knife in the other hand. He slashed the throat of an overgrown ferret before shooting a net over a group of elfish creatures. Tess heard battle cries coming from the river. Arbor emerged with the small collection of new guardians of Order. Better late than never.

Tess dodged a fireball, watching it crash into a mesquite behind her. The ground pulsed and the flame erupted into an explosion toward the sky. It knocked everyone to the ground, but only for a moment. Tess pushed back to her feet, throwing a bolt that branched into five strands. Each strand struck members of the Darkness, sending them falling.

As Kamahalan roared next to her, Tess caught sight of movement. She leaned to the side, a large rock grazing her head. Her skin stung even after it landed behind her and her head threatened to pound. Tess clenched her teeth and fried the crocodile who threw it. There were so many of them. No matter how many Thomas netted, Kamahalan slashed, and Tess burned, there were just too many of them.

Tess found her feet flailing from under her as a blue tail swirled around her. The dirt and rocks pounded against her ribs, threatening to crack them. Tess gasped, trying to flip over before the creature could turn on her. He was a blue turtle with the tail of a snake. His face might look friendly, but he looked like something from the worst of her nightmares. What imaginations had created such creatures?

On her belly, Tess flicked a bolt at him. He dodged it, but she at least had enough time to stand. She shot a better bolt at him, but he turned his shell, blocking the electricity. It bounced off and singed Kamahalan's back before driving a wicked hole into the skull of a moth-man. He fell to the ground with steam coming from his head. Kamahalan slashed the elf she was fighting as Tess turned back to the blue turtle. She jumped in the air as the tail came swooping around again.

Tess swore. She was sick of this thing. She leapt forward, arms outstretched. Grabbing hold of the tail, she sent all her emotions through her fingers. The turtle fell shaking onto its back, feet shrinking into the shell. She didn't let go until she was sure it wouldn't get back up.

When she turned, she saw a blade swinging through the air at Kamahalan's back. Before she could think, Tess screamed, two bolts shooting from the scars at her chest at the bony figure holding the blade. Kamahalan slashed the neck of its companion as the blade dropped to the ground. Her boss turned suddenly to watch the creature erupt in flames from the blast and fall limp to the ground.

They both stared at each other. Either Kamahalan had just lost her power in the Darkness or she was never the lead. Whatever the scenario, Tess had just saved her life.

They hesitated only a moment before Tess pushed back to her feet and continued shooting bolts all around her. The fighting lasted for only a minute or two, although it felt like a lot longer. In the end, the three of them stood around a group of five creatures in nets and the carcasses of the rest. Blood seeped from cuts on Kamahalan's face and arms while Tess' skin burned around her back and legs. Thomas looked a little dirty, but remained otherwise unharmed.

Arbor came up to her side. "Wow. That was crazy."

Tess tried not to roll her eyes. She limped over toward Kamahalan. "If this isn't the targeted place, we need to find it. And soon. Chloe has been under attack. I don't know how much longer she can last."

Kamahalan approached the green fairy. She pushed against the netting and bared her teeth. "Chief Guardian of Dream. How nice to see you again," she said flatly.

The fairy flapped her wings, only to have them tangle even more in the netting. She sighed, lying flat on the ground. "You can torture me, but I'm not saying a thing."

Fire erupted into the air along with a frustrated shout. The two of them turned on Thomas' associate. His square face pushed against the netting to no avail.

Apparently he thought he could burn the net with his dragon's breath. Creatures of Dream should be more aware. They walked over to him. Tess crossed her arms.

"Why did you kill Marcus?"

The dragon dug his nails at the net. "You'd have to ask Lilija. Personally, I thought Marcus wasn't worth the bother."

Tess looked up at Kamahalan, who gave a nod. She knelt, placing her hands on the net and pushed a surge through her skin. The net glowed white for a moment, the perfect anchor for her shot of electricity. The dragon went rigid, his clothes singed. The dragon screamed and then relaxed when the moment passed.

"She has a lot of anger," Kamahalan said. "I suggest you cooperate. Who knows? I might decide to be lenient with you."

"It's not over yet," the dragon said with a hiss behind his words.

Tess let her fingers linger over the netting. The dragon went rigid, but said nothing. "How does one break the veil?" she asked. "It has to go beyond just the blood."

"You are too insignificant. You couldn't do it."

Tess looked up at her boss. "Doesn't that sound like a challenge?"

Kamahalan shrugged. "Yeah, but there's the whole ending life in reality. The influx of spirits alone would be catastrophic."

Tess smiled, placing her hands on the net once more. Light flashed below her, followed by a scream. "True. But he's not stupid. The flood of spirits would be no trouble for someone looking for the surge of power promised to anyone who helps." Tess finally looked down at the dragon, whose eyes showed she had his full attention. "That's what they promised, isn't it? Power beyond anything you could obtain from any dream. Enough to sustain you without ever having to step foot into another door."

"That's good," Kamahalan said. "because the doors would lead nowhere after they're done. But," she said taking a step closer, "here's the dilemma."

The sky shifted from pink to red to almost black as more stars erupted against the sky. The dark sky hid Kamahalan, her yellow eyes practically glowing against the night. She knelt on the other side of the dragon boy. "No one told you what would truly happen when the veil is torn. It's dangerous, you know? It'll kill everything near the spot of the collapse. It'll blast everything in a thousand-mile proximity like an atomic weapon."

"Not if you match time on both sides," the dragon boy argued.

Kamahalan met Tess' gaze. They had to make time match in dream along with reality. Unless they were ready to accuse the Governess of trying to take down a structure she had helped create, there was one creature on this side that had the power to do that. With the guardian of Dream thrashing next to them, it wasn't hard to think of Nakima as the head of the Darkness. He had corrupted those around him first. His greatest feat was corrupting the Department of Order. He had needed them to access the doors. But penetrating the order was also what brought on Mathias's investigation.

"That's interesting," Kamahalan mused. "Yes. If time matched, the blast would be localized. It would still kill all around the tear. Tell me, where were you supposed to be stationed?"

The dragon boy growled, but remained otherwise silent.

Kamahalan nodded. "That's what I thought. But even if you survived the blast, the power wouldn't evenly disperse. It would be attracted to the strongest among you."

"The person controlling time, for instance," Tess offered.

"Exactly," Kamahalan said. "It would feed into him. Sure, other charged beings would obtain some residual leakage, but he would become the Supreme Being."

"Greater than any Governess," Tess said, flexing her fingers. She followed Kamahalan's lead, rising to their feet.

"So," her boss said, "you see it is very fortunate you were captured."

"You could be dead," Tess agreed. They took a few steps away before Tess turned back to dragon boy. "Hey. You wouldn't be willing to tell us where the best source of new-blood power is around here, would you? You know. Seeing how we saved your life and all."

The dragon thrashed under the net, his tail stretching against the edge before he tired. Well. At least they knew one thing. Nakima was leading the Darkness. And they needed a place with a lot of new blood to force time to match on both sides. What role

Chloe played in all of this, she didn't know. But something told her they were running out of time.

## Twenty-nine

The car engine rumbled as the Mustang sped down the highway. The way it took the corners of the winding road, Chloe thought they were going to flip over. The car raced out of Tombstone, traveling through the desert in pitch darkness. The hills rolled before them as the car traced the turns in the road.

It was a miracle no one else was out here right now. The tires drifted over the center line as they wound through another corner. Ricky sat on the driver's side, but he did not look like the same Ricky she knew. His eyes were dark. Just like Dylan's had been. This was not Ricky. The tires squealed as they took another forty-five-mile-per-hour turn at fifty-five. The engine growled when Ricky accelerated on the straightaway.

"What are we doing?" Chloe asked, looking around her. At least they had a seatbelt on her. They hadn't bothered to tie her down any further. The speed alone kept her from jumping out of the car. Her body slammed against the door as they took another turn. She thought she could feel the wheels lean much too far. The road cut through large hills. The full moon outside dimmed the stars, but she could see the Huachuca Mountain range in black, marking the horizon in front of them.

"Deadliest road in Cochise County," Ricky said. His voice was steady, as if they were on an easy Sunday drive around town. She tensed when he took his eyes off the road for a moment. "Did you know that?"

They charged up a hill, and for a moment, she could see the twinkling lights of the city spread out against the blackness of the mountain range. "What do you want with me?"

The tires squealed around another turn in the road. The tires drifted over the center line as they moved up another hill, blocking any vision of oncoming traffic. "You're special. We need you."

Molly. She had to be safe. She was on the playground when Chloe had been taken. She had to be safe. "What did you do with Molly?" Chloe asked.

The confused look Ricky gave her was comforting. "That girl you were talking to? She was bait. You're the one we wanted."

Tess had been right. Chloe should have just listened to her. But Dylan had told her about the school. "Where's Dylan?"

Ricky grinned at her. "You know where he is." The car jumped over the top of a hill, fishtailed, then continued down the road. "Your friend Tess stole him from us. But I'm here now."

So Dylan had just relayed information without remembering what it meant. That made sense given his overall haziness about the events. A light reflected in her eyes against the rearview mirror. Chloe looked behind her to find a beat-up Subaru speeding behind them. Even in the dark, she recognized Becca's car. She didn't know how they found her, but they found her!

Chloe giggled. "Well, I don't care what you're planning. My friends will save me."

Ricky looked in the rearview mirror before accelerating through another turn. "They can't stop this."

"And what is *this*?" If they weren't already drifting and squealing down the road, Chloe would have grabbed the wheel. Something told her she'd rather crash here than arrive at wherever they were going. When he didn't answer, she continued, "What do you want with me? I'm nothing."

Ricky shook his head. "I am convinced human childhoods ruin you all. You are nothing? You really don't know your value, do you?"

The car leaned around another turn. He really needed to slow down. They would flip over. While the possibility seemed tempting, she didn't want to die today. And in this darkness, anyone could just drive by without ever noticing. Chloe glanced behind her. The Subaru was starting to fall behind. She was kind of glad. She didn't want to see them crash either.

"This world might see a broken child," Ricky continued. "But I assure you, you are meant for much more."

"Oh, yeah? Like what?"

"You can see your own door."

Chloe tried not to look at him, but he wasn't asking her. He already knew. How could he know that? Tess seemed to think it meant something special too. What was the big deal? It was a white room with a stupid door. "So what?"

"And I hear you stepped through that door and survived."

Chloe could still see the fear in Tess' eyes when she had told her to get back inside. "I'm sure a lot of people could do that." She had to find a way out of this car. But they were going too fast to jump. She really wished she had paid more attention in physics. Maybe the solutions to all those velocity problems would have been helpful right now.

"People can't even see their door, let alone survive going through it. And if you can go through the door, then you can break the veil."

Break the veil. Tess seemed to think the same thing. She could break the veil. "How?"

"We've always known how to tear the veil. But breaking it... " The car jumped over another hill. "That's baffled us for a long time. It takes something unnatural, something that goes against all rules." As they made a turn, Chloe could see a line of trees cutting across the land. They were approaching the San Pedro River. From the river, she could make out a large orange glow. It was unnatural. Not a campfire, not a spotlight, but something else. Something stronger.

Ricky continued, "You see, not just anyone can step through the tear. It has to be someone special. It has to be you."

She wanted to reject his hypothesis just because he had called her special. There was nothing special about her. She knew that. She was damaged. She had no value. But he said it with such confidence... and believed in it enough to kidnap her. "Why me?"

"Because nature dictates when anyone leaves their body—whether through coma, near-death experiences, etcetera—that person is trapped inside the door to the subconscious. All that's theory, mind you—no one has been able to even attempt it. BUT if you cross through the door and survive, your body should stay in a coma. How long it can survive without you... who knows? If it survives long enough for you to cross back through the tear in the veil, to return to your body without using your door—in the most unnatural way that breaks all rules dominating our existence... well, that will break the entire veil apart."

Tess had always been guarded around her. Did she know? She must have suspected it. She suspected it to the point where she didn't even trust her own partner to keep Chloe safe. Chloe was starting to understand why. "You were never going to make me cross the veil from my side of reality." Chloe's body started to shake. "You were going to make me cross from your side of dream."

Ricky nodded. "Absolutely. Two unnatural events coming together for a catastrophic conclusion."

The car passed mile marker nine and the city lights glowed brighter before her. She saw the twinkling stars and white moon above and the blackness of the mountains that separated the two worlds. He wasn't a crappy driver. He was trying to crash the car.

Chloe reached for the wheel just as the road took a sharp turn to the left. She scratched Ricky's arm as he let go of the wheel. The car continued straight, leaving the road behind. She couldn't register much more after that. Just the crunching of metal against the scraping of dirt as the car jostled her inside. Then there was deafening silence and darkness.

Chloe screamed, pushing herself to her feet. She stood in the white room. Argumas rushed to her side.

"What happened?"

Chloe scrambled to her feet just as the large beaver approached. "Look out!"

Argumas turned just as Max threw a crystal dagger at him. Argumas turned again, taking the dagger in one of his large arms. The dragon-man leapt toward Max as Argumas cried out in pain.

The entire room shook as the door rattled on its hinges. "You can't let them take me," Chloe shouted. This stupid room! She needed something to fight them off.

Argumas took the dagger out of his arm. Masat had Max trapped in his arms as Argumas approached. He slit the beaver's throat in one clean movement. "Don't worry," he said, turning back to face her as the beaver slid gurgling to the floor. "It's all under control."

A blast rung her ears and threw her against the far wall. She tried to orient herself as a crowd of shadows entered. Her skin crawled with the feeling of dirt and slime. She clenched her hands. They were all invaders. They had to go!

She screamed and sparks burst from the ceiling. Two figures fell as Argumas and Masat took out two more. Chloe pounded the ground. It exploded with energy that knocked everyone to their backs. She looked up, finding Argumas and Masat on their backs, gasping for breath. How could she save herself without killing them?

The feeling of dirt rubbed against her skin once more. She cringed and screamed. The walls burst, throwing bricks at the onrushing assault. There were too many of them. She couldn't throw them all out. She killed twelve before one finally found their way to her. The crystal cuffs that dug into her wrists stopped the shaking in the room.

Chloe slammed her hands against the ground, but nothing happened. She was defenseless. They lifted her as Argumas and Masat battled. They threw punches, slashed open scaly skin, but there were too many of them.

"Stop!" Chloe screamed as she fought against the large creature holding her.

As they approached the door, Argumas shouted, "No! Chloe!" Then his face contorted, a large sword plunging out of his chest. They carried her through the threshold as his eyes dimmed and he fell to the ground. Masat blasted a few with fire, but they were closing in on him as they stepped through. The space outside her door looked like a battlefield with vacant-eyed creatures scattered everywhere. Then her door slammed shut against the frame. When it did, the entire thing burst off its hinges as if blasted by dynamite. Unnatural occurrence number one complete. Chloe tried to kick against her captor. She had to stop this before they brought about the second one.

# Thirty

The grey pebbles crunched beneath her shoes as Tess charged past the doors. Even before she saw the first body, she knew. The place did not feel right. It was cold. Electricity filled the air with static. One spark. That's all it would take to destroy the entire place. That's the feeling she had. Just one spark.

When she saw the first guardian of Order bloodied on the ground, she pushed harder against the pebbles. Electricity bounced between her fingers as she neared. The bodies mounted. Some guardians of Dream. Some guardians of Order. In death, she couldn't tell for which side they fought. Death, yet again, was the great equalizer.

Not long ago, she had walked this path. She had come looking for Argumas then, too. This time, as she dodged the onslaught of bodies, she somehow knew she would no longer find him. She skidded to a stop when she rounded the corner. Just a few days ago, she had seen him there with his mask, ready to continue in a routine set for many millenniums. Now he was nowhere to be seen, and the door hung in splinters, partially off its hinges.

Thomas moved next to her, the site holding him back as well. "Be ready," he said, bringing out his trench knife.

Tess shook her head, feeling the weight of the door. She let the electricity in her hands subside. "No. They aren't here." The pebbles sounded much too loud against the silence as she approached the door. She stepped through the threshold. The energy of an occupied door was missing, leaving behind the draft of an empty cave. Chloe had done a great job. She could see at least fifteen dead inside, all contorted in the way of beings destroyed by a subconscious. Others were bloodied or charred.

She hesitated in front of the large figure lying flat on the ground. His translucent eyes were foggy and hard. She had spent most of her time here pushing him away, but somehow he had been one of the only creatures she could truly call a friend. Tess sniffed back her tears, kneeling before him. She touched his stone cold arm. Her chest constricted. If she had to breathe, she'd be gasping right about now. In spirit though, the pain seemed just as strong.

Masat lay on his side only a few feet away. They had taken out quite a few, but they had been up against an army. Thomas was right. This was bigger than anyone had suspected. This went beyond just one department. This was a full-blown civil war, and no one had seen it coming.

"What are we doing?" Thomas said from behind her. "We need to go after them."

Tess bit into her cheek, pushing herself to stand. "And where is that?" she said, whipping around. "Where have they gone? Presidio?" The last word echoed in the empty void.

Thomas jerked back at that. "What are you implying?"

She didn't know what she was implying. They had gone to Presidio to stop this, a place far from access to the doors. Not only did they not stop it, but all they discovered was they had suspected the wrong person as the leader—someone who was almost assassinated. That would have been catastrophic. And she couldn't even remember whose idea any of it was anymore. Who was she mad at? Thomas? Herself? Her rotten existence that left her without any army of her own? She had thought she could do this alone. She had thought she could take on the entire universe by herself. And now she stood in carnage alongside the one man she had never liked or even trusted.

"I don't know," Tess said after a moment. She rubbed her temple. "We are at a dead end at the most inconvenient time. And they are winning."

Kamahalan entered the doors, her eyes hard. "We just have to think smarter. We did not rise to our positions without learning something along the way. They have to be somewhere."

"I say," Thomas urged them as Arbor entered, "that we go back to the cells. We have the Chief Guardian of Dream. We make her talk."

"Tell you what," Tess said, stepping closer. "You go and do that. Go waste time. And while you're at it, go ahead and build a bunker for when this whole world blows apart!"

"Easy," Kamahalan said.

"No!" Tess shouted. "I'm tired of this! This entire time, I've been told to step back. Let Thomas take the lead. Don't do what I want to do because it is not proper or protocol. It's too edgy. Well, look where that's gotten us! He's dead! They're all dead!"

Arbor whistled. "Wow. They really didn't tell me anything."

Tess could feel the tension shaking her shoulders as she turned to face him. "What?"

Arbor pointed to the charred corpse of a man with a squared foxlike head. "That's Enid. He is associate to the Governess."

Tess frowned at him. "What does that mean?"

"Don't you see? No one knew who all was involved. No one knew the other members because that would reveal too much."

Tess tried not to shoot electricity at him. He had a point. He just wasn't getting to it. "We don't have a lot of time, Arbor. Why do I care about this guy?"

"Think about it. The Deputy of Dream organized the whole thing, right?"

They nod.

"He increases the Darkness by promising all of us the same: eternal power. He promised everyone in servant positions a world where they were the master. But he promised everyone that. Because no one was going to get it."

Thomas went to say something, but thought better of it.

"Arbor," Tess said, "Focus. Why do I care one of these buffoons was the associate to the Governess?"

"Not just any associate," Arbor said with a smile. "The one who oversees mass casualties."

Tess hesitated. When she was in reality, she thought of mass casualties as those events that made headlines. Some crazy person took out innocent people for some ridiculously glorified cause. Nothing like that existed in Sierra Vista, at least nothing recent enough for fresh blood. But dream didn't exist in time. Mass casualties did not relate only to a one-time event. Mass casualties referred to multiple deaths, even if they happened over time. A continuously deadly event even if just one person died at a time. "Mass casualties. Old blood amplifying new blood. It has to be a deadly spot, one that is still taking life in the current time period to maintain its power. And they need a water source to amplify it. I think I know where to go."

Thomas scoffed. "How can you possibly know where to go?"

"There are only a few places here known to kill a lot of people over the course of time." For once, Tess felt in control. She could stop this. But she needed a team to do it. She was no longer alone. "Arbor. You're coming with me. Kamahalan, can you organize an army of guardians that you trust? We're going to need everyone we know on our side. Maybe even ask the Deputy of Spirit to lend a few guardians?"

Kamahalan nodded. "Gladly."

"And Thomas," she said. "Go interview the green fairy. See what you can get from her." Thomas glared at her. Apparently her suggestion revealed her true intention to dismiss him more than she had wanted. She barely cared at the moment.

She marched past them, making sure Arbor followed. Within seconds, they stood at the foot of a rocky cliff. The waterfall only ran this time of year if they had had a large amount of snow. It ran the most during the monsoons. She wasn't sure what time of year Chloe currently lived. It would have to be running if they were going to use the power of water.

Tess eased past the bushes at the base of the falls and touched a hand to the dry rock. Arbor stood on the dirt road twisting up toward Carr Peak.

"What is this place?" he asked.

"It's a waterfall... well, a seasonal one."

"And why is it important?"

Tess looked up the side of the mountain. The moon shone full above her, its light bouncing off the jagged edges of the rocks supporting the waterfall. She couldn't see the top from here. Unlike most falls, it was made of three disjointed parts that ended in one long drop at the bottom. That was part of its deadly allure. It looked innocent until it was not. "There are warning signs, but people still fall much too often. It's taken a lot of lives over the years."

Arbor frowned. "Sounds like a good place to tear the veil. But where is everyone?"

Tess shook her head. "No. They aren't here. This isn't the place." She pushed against the rock, moving back toward the dirt road. "We're missing something. There has to be someplace worse."

Arbor frowned, leaning to look up the dry bed of the falls. "Worse than falling to your death?"

"Worse in number."

Tess stood with hands on her hips, looking up and down the road. She had to think. "Did they tell you how they planned to tear the veil?"

Arbor shook his head. "All I knew about were the possessions. I thought that was enough."

"To take possession, you had to have a group on each side chanting, yes?"

Arbor nodded. "Yeah. The chanting breaks the power of the door to the subconscious. But then they got some sort of drug on the reality side that served the same purpose. At that point, we weren't as important. Minor possessions and pulsing energy. That was all."

Tess had to think. There had to be a connection. Only spirits could walk up to the veil. Most creatures didn't even see it. They couldn't get close. They had to do something to get closer. "Explain the process to me. What did it entail?"

Arbor thought for a moment. "Well. We had to stand with hands touching. We'd cut our hands, drop our blood at the center of the circle, and then join hands."

Why did all satanic rituals have to be so unsanitary? "That's because you didn't have the blood already. They didn't have to do that at Presidio. And there was a light that formed from their joined hands."

Arbor nodded. "Just imagine what that would look like if the same connection was established on a grander scale."

"With new blood to charge it? It wouldn't take much effort." Tess looked up. She scurried up the road. "I have an idea."

They bounced up rocks along the side of the mountain until she was standing on Miller Peak. Over 9,400 feet high, it was the highest peak in the Huachuca Mountains. The summit was a large rock platform. From here, she could turn in any direction and see nothing but horizon. The stars looked close enough to touch. The city twinkled below her, stretching from the mountain edge like scattered diamonds over the land. It didn't take her long to find what she was looking for.

On the other side of the city, in the middle of blackness, she could see a large orange light. It was twice as big as any other light shining at her. She pointed. "There. Where is that?"

Arbor frowned. "Isn't that the river?"

Tess jumped. "I'm such an idiot. Of course. Charleston Road. Kills multiple people almost every year."

"There's a ghost town right by the river, you know," Arbor said. "Charleston. That's how the road got its name."

"What are you, a history buff?"

"Didn't tell you the best part. They have a marking for the battle of the bulls."

"A battle took place there," Tess shouldn't get so excited at the mention of a battle.

"No. It was literally a stampede of bulls, but it caused a lot of injury. Nine bulls and other livestock died."

Tess rubbed her eyes. Nine bulls in over a century? That's it. He was about as much help as Thomas. "Look. We've got to get over there. It looks like they've already begun." She had to get back to tell Kamahalan. She might just beat this thing after all. Or be just a moment too late.

## Thirty-One

Stars twinkled above her head. Chloe pulled against the crystal chains, but they held strong. Every time they rubbed against her skin, a searing burn radiated up her arm. Chloe kicked at the chain staked into the ground, only to have a spark burst against her shoe. She couldn't just sit here and do nothing. Chloe focused on her hands because she didn't want to look up. As with anything forbidden, the urge tugged at her until she could no longer resist.

The car's tires were still moving even though they were sticking straight up in the air. Smoke rose from the car along with the dust kicked up with the car's roll from the road. The car had landed about a quarter of a mile from the river. It was so far away from the road, no one would have found her. But her friends had been following behind and their headlights showed they had stopped on the road. Even from the dream side of the veil, she could hear their shouts on reality's side.

The headlights of Ricky's car shone through the grass. Ricky's body was gone, the windows all blown out and bloody. There was still a passenger though. Her black hair covered most of her face, the seatbelt hugging her tightly to the car. Chloe didn't have to see the face. She knew who it was. Talk about an out-of-body experience. She averted her eyes, not wanting to look. That was, by all definitions, her own corpse.

She turned away from the scene. Just down the hill, she could see the two groups. They both appeared to stand in the same place, the images of their bodies flickering between the two sides. In one image, an orange glow radiated from the group's touching hands. It radiated out of the mouth and eyes of the one creature standing at the center. It flickered again to a group in the same pose. Besides the white eyes, there was no other light. The air pulsed between the two sides, forcing the images to become one.

Even the road flickered—dark and dry to pulsing red and shining. Chloe turned to find the river stretched before her. That was the only constant. A fog of purple rose from the river toward the moon high in the air. An electric field crackled where the purple fog met the pulsing red road. Chloe cringed as the land shook. The group chanted louder. Energy filled the air, prickling against her skin. The images around her vibrated, the dream side merging with reality. She could feel it. They were getting close.

"Chloe!" her friends' voices drifted toward her. She seemed to be the only one who could see reality's side. The dream creatures surrounding her couldn't even see the car. They had guessed its location when they staked her to the ground. She didn't feel inclined to tell them the car was another thirty yards over.

"There!" someone shouted. She couldn't tell if it was Becca. Chloe forced herself to turn back toward the car. The group charged down from the road, led by Dylan. How did they even find her?

Then she saw Paul King following behind, wringing his hands. Paul King. He had been walking his dog when she was taken. She had called her friends right before seeing Molly. He must have told them when they arrived at the elementary school. And now here he was. She was sure how they found her was quite the story. She really wanted to hear that story, if for no other reason than she would still be alive.

They rushed the car.

"She's here!" Addie. That sounded like Addie.

"Someone call an ambulance!" Dylan said as he knelt to the ground near the passenger door. "I think she's still breathing!"

Chloe looked down at her hands clasped in chains. Breathing. That was good to know. She wasn't a corpse just yet. Would she feel different when she died? Would these chains no longer hurt her?

"I'm so sorry, Chloe," Dylan said with tears in his eyes. "I didn't know."

The world shook, or at least the world on her side did. Dylan didn't seem to notice. She had participated in a play at school about two girls who walked the halls of their old high school without knowing they were dead. The girls finally figured it out when their classmates couldn't see them. It was creepy back then. It was even creepier now.

The chanting got louder and a red fog burst from the road. She could no longer see her friend's car. Brakes squealed. Metal crunched. Screams. They all echoed in the fog. Headlights passed through. Some swerved as they did so. The sound became louder, the road glowing brighter. It stretched all the way to the bridge over the San Pedro River. The river's energy zapped against the red fog like a fly in a trap. It consistently buzzed and crackled against the night, until the purple fog was tainted by the red. The color drifted upstream toward the ghost town. One minute, there were buildings standing tall in a prosperous river town. The next, the buildings were gone and ruins remained, ruins she had walked Sam's dog through on countless bored weekends. Sam. Wow. It seemed like so long ago that Sam was helping her cheat on a math test.

Now the township remained in ruins. Everything looked exactly as she had left it. Had she left it? Everything was so confusing. Chloe pulled against her chains once more and yelped.

"Oh... my... God... "

Chloe looked up to see Cameron staring at her. Wait. He was staring at her! "Can you see me?" Her voice sounded loud to her ears. Chloe glanced over her shoulder, but everyone was still focused on the chanting.

Cameron looked over his shoulder at the car. "You guys? You sure she's alive?"

Dylan reached inside the car, his hand disappearing behind a curtain of hair. "I think I can feel a pulse. I don't know. Should we move her?"

The group started talking, converging on the car. Addie stood by the road, her cell phone raised toward the air. She paused long enough to dial before jumping up and down.

"Cameron," Chloe whispered.

Cameron didn't respond. Maybe she was wrong. Maybe he hadn't been looking at her. And yet... he had that expression on his face. Like he was fighting the pull of an image he didn't want to actually see.

She was so stupid. He couldn't hear her. He wasn't psychic. But he could see faces through the veil. He could *see* her. And if he could see her, then she could try to fix this. They had to know about the group chanting on their side. They had to stop this whole thing.

Chloe pulled against her chains, once more cringing against the shock radiating to her bone. She must be alive if she could still feel bone. Chloe continued to move, flailing her arms until Cameron turned to face her.

Chloe smiled at him and waved.

He froze. "Guys?"

Paul paced past him, rubbing a hand to his head. "We can't be here. I can't be here." He continued to mumble as he walked away.

Chloe waved at Cameron. She pointed very sternly at him, then motioned him to come closer. Cameron's eyes grew wide. "You're dead, aren't you? Oh, my God. I can see dead people."

Chloe rolled her eyes, shaking her head. She motioned him closer. He hesitated, looked over his shoulder, then approached. Chloe giggled. This was working. This was actually working. She pointed behind her.

When he frowned, she tried again. She pointed very dramatically at him, then very dramatically pointed at where the group stood. She pounded her fist to her hand. *Please let him understand.* She felt like the worst mime ever.

Cameron turned and walked away. Chloe covered her eyes with her hands, feeling the wave hit. She was going to fail. She was going to die. And these psychos were going to do whatever they were trying to do. Headlights illuminated her. Chloe ducked to the ground as a car soared above her head before vanishing into the sky. She breathed against the dust and grass. The road glowed red now. Headlights were shining through from every direction. Metal crashing. So much death pulsing against the road.

Then there was Addie, standing by the roadside, frantically shouting into her phone. She had a hand on her head, her face crippled with worry. This couldn't be how it ended. For the first time, Chloe had a purpose. She was special. Tess said so. She had power here. She had to do something.

Chloe kicked at the stake, a spark stinging against her leg. She clenched her teeth and kicked again and again. On the fourth kick, the spark pushed her backward in a blue blast. Her entire body went rigid and the ringing in her ears deafened her. When she looked down, she could see the ground through her translucent hands. Chloe breathed against the pain as her hands came back into full focus. Okay. So maybe she couldn't kick her way out of this. But she had to do something.

Then she saw it. Cameron was talking with Dylan. Pretty emphatically. He pointed in her direction, to which Dylan just frowned. He pointed at the body in the car. Cameron pushed Dylan, then pointed at Chloe. Dylan looked about ready to hit him when Becca came over.

When the ringing in her ears subsided, she could hear Becca say, "Stop this! What's going on?"

"I'm telling you, I saw Chloe."

"Like, she's dead?" Becca asked, her voice cracking.

Cameron shrugged. "I don't know. She was all hunched over and I don't know why. But she wanted us to go fight something over there." Cameron pointed in the direction of the group.

Chloe clapped her hands. It worked! Her stupid plan actually worked! How's that for her first time with a ghost haunting? Oh, she had never felt happier. Not even when her aunt had surprised her with concert tickets and they skipped school freshman year. Chloe stopped clapping. Her Aunt. Molly. She had to get back to them. She couldn't stay here. She had to get back to them. She wanted her life back. Even with all the crazy dreams and messed-up social life. She wanted it all back.

"Stay here with her," Dylan said to Becca. "Don't move her unless the car is about to explode."

Paul paced beside the car. "We have to leave. We can't stay. It's not right." He rubbed violently at his hairline, walking away.

Becca nodded. "I won't leave." She knelt next to the car. "Chloe? Can you hear me? Addie called the cops. They're sending an ambulance. Everything will be okay."

Cops. It was bound to end with the cops. She had a lot of questions to answer. But she had to get back to her door if she was ever going to answer them.

Dylan and Cameron took off in the direction of the group. Just as they did, the world glowed in front of her like the reflection of the outside through newly-cleaned glass. The screams from the road grew louder, the chanting merging with the sound. Chloe covered her ears against the noise as her friends neared the group. Then the glass in front of her cracked in a spiderweb of destruction. The damp night air rushed her through the opening. Chunks of the barrier fell in front of her and Chloe pushed away. The veil. They tore the veil. Becca looked up. By the freaked-out look on her face, Chloe knew she could see it too. If the veil was torn...

"They're going to hurt me! You have to stop them!"

Dylan and Cameron whipped around as Becca shot to her feet. "Chloe?" They all said in unison.

"By the river. Stop them! Please."

When Chloe turned around, a group of overgrown wolves approached with a man in a trench coat. This was it. They were ready for her to cross the veil.

## THIRTY-TWO

"We're late," Tess said as they approached the bridge. Electricity crackled against air where the road met the river. Red fog hovered along the road and drifted up the river. She could feel the blood power vibrate against the soles of her shoes.

"There's still time," Kamahalan said, clenching a crystal blade.

The ground shook. Even from here, she could see the barrier splinter and burst. "They tore the veil," Tess said, "We need to stop this. Now."

Kamahalan pointed her blade and the fifty guardians of Order charged down the road. When they crossed the bridge, the team split. Ten ran toward the river while the rest ran toward the group of chanting creatures. Tess charged toward the crack in the veil. If she was going to find Chloe, that's where she'd be.

Shouts from the guardians drew her attention. The chanting group had guards, maybe fifty of them. It was like they had been warned. Tess continued down the grass. She could see a pack of wolves circling the girl, along with a guardian of Spirit. They grabbed Chloe right as something slammed against Tess' side. Tess shot a bolt from her arm, setting the creature's fur on fire. He screamed and rolled away before she could get a clear look at what had attacked her.

She didn't have much time to respond before another creature leapt toward her. Tess threw dirt into his eyes before rolling on her back. The creature approached, a cross between a knight and a bird. His beak protruded from a mechanical face and eyes. She kicked at his hip, a bolt of lightning flying from her ankle to between the sockets of his hip. The light bounced inside his armor, lighting him up as his body went rigid. She covered her head when the bolt finally reached his heart, exploding inside like a tank of fuel in a fire.

Metal struck her pants, burning upon impact. Tess scrambled to her feet, continuing her pursuit. The guardian of Spirit had Chloe by the shoulders, but the girl was putting up a good fight for a new spirit. She screamed and bit his hand while kneeing him in the groin. This, of course, only served to aggravate the guardian of Spirit, but Tess was impressed by her basic survival skills.

On the other side, Kamahalan was making progress against the guards near the river. That's where they would likely find Nakima. Out of blast range, but powered by the energy of the river. Guardians of Order struggled against the chanting group in the middle. They had taken out most of the guards, but the energy surrounding the chanting group seemed overpowering.

Tess had to get to Chloe. She only made it five more feet before she had to dodge a flying dagger. Tess turned to find a team of ten creatures surrounding her. "I'm flattered," she said as they closed in. "Although it's pretty silly to think only ten can stop me."

Tess ripped off her jacket as they neared. She focused her energy on all the times he had ever hit her. All the times he had ever called her a name. Then she focused on the new life she had been creating for herself. She could still see him in the parking lot. That look of pleasure when he jabbed the knife inside her. The crippling pain seared through her body, but she smiled. The group paused at the glow from her abdomen. She reached above her head and screamed. Her body rocked until the blast surged from her spiderwebbed scar. When she opened her eyes, the group of ten were frying on the ground.

Tess' knees buckled and she fell to the ground. That probably hadn't been the smartest thing to do. Her hands shimmered between solid flesh and translucent image. If she wasn't careful, she would expel all of her energy. Then again, at least she wouldn't exist to see what happened when Chloe crossed the veil.

Tess spat at the dirt, pushing herself up. She clutched at her stomach, her shoulders pulling her downward. She was almost there. She could make it.

"That's a nice little weapon you have," Thomas said from behind her.

Tess turned to face him. He stood in front of her with a calmness about him. "What are you doing? Help me get to Chloe."

Thomas shook his head and Tess finally had the proof to justify her suspicions. Thomas raised what looked like a revolver. But she knew better. He wouldn't shoot her with bullets. He would shoot her with a black dart. The dart would travel into the core of her soul. It would pull her in until she was just an empty space. It was the only thing that could kill a spirit on this side of the veil. And it was illegal to carry outside of the realm of Judgment.

Tess raised her arms in the air. That seemed to be the natural response when someone had a gun pointed at you. "So. I see you know someone in the Judgment realm too."

Thomas shook his head. "No. Nakima took this from them yesterday."

"Going out in a blaze of glory then."

Thomas laughed. "It's not like they'll need it. But it does simplify things a little."

Tess looked over her shoulder. Chloe had jabbed the guardian of Spirit in the eyes. She must have surged some power through her chains because he was bent over, grasping at his face. She, on the other hand, was also writhing in pain on the ground from the blast the chains must have sent through her. If she expelled too much energy against those things, she might end up on this side permanently. Tess wondered if that would make this entire endeavor useless.

"Tell me something," Tess said, turning back to Thomas, who had taken a step closer. "Why did you save me from prison? You are the one who gave Arbor the medicine to get me back to fighting, yes?"

"Doesn't sound like a good conspirator, does it?" Thomas said with a nod. "You see, Nakima was pretty upset when we lost Dylan. I assured him we could use Ricky. But he said Dylan was stronger. I had failed. Not only that, but I had proven I couldn't keep you down. That was my one job. To keep you away from the Darkness. I had failed on both accounts."

"They kicked you out," Tess said. She had to find a way out of this. She couldn't make a move for the weapon. It was too risky.

A blast sounded. Guardians of Order flew through the air. The surge from the chanting group was too much for them. They couldn't break through.

"I was lucky. They were going to kill me. But then I promised them Kamahalan. She was getting too close. We needed her gone. I'd let her die in the same place as Mathias, and it would be all your idea."

"Presidio. Of course," Tess said. "But that didn't turn out for you either."

"No," Thomas said. "but you showed me the last piece of the puzzle. You showed me the only thing we hadn't figured out."

Tess looked back over at Chloe. The girl was kicking at her attacker and shouting at the tear in the veil. "Chloe left her door."

Thomas nodded. "Chloe left her door and *survived*."

"And if she crosses back through to her body without the door..."

Thomas flicked his fingers to mimic an explosion. "With that information, I was back in. I just had to ensure you would all fail."

Tess looked toward the river. She couldn't see Kamahalan. She couldn't see anything. "Where's Nakima?" When Thomas grinned at her, she knew the answer. He wasn't at the river. No. They had a trap at the river. Kamahalan was either dead or fighting in the battle of her life. And Nakima was tucked away safely, able to manipulate time.

Chloe was about to be thrown through the veil. And Thomas was officially part of the Darkness. And she had seen it coming. She wasn't a completely flawed, untrusting spirit. She had been right. Sure, she had thought Kamahalan was part of the Darkness. But she had been right about Thomas. She had never liked him. She had always thought he was just like her ex: a reflection of one thing in public and something completely different in private. And she had been right.

Tess couldn't help it. She started to laugh. Thomas at first frowned at her, then he grew angry. "What is wrong with you?"

The laughter wouldn't stop coming. It actually started to hurt her still throbbing stomach. "I'm sorry," she managed to say. "It's just that I finally realized something."

"And what's that?" Thomas said as he cocked the gun.

The laughter subsided, but Tess still smiled at him. "That for once in my existence, I am not the victim."

The world shook, sending them both to the ground. Thomas scrambled to his feet, immediately looking upriver at the ghost town. By the look on his face, Tess had guessed right. A fireball blasted from the site, mushrooming into the sky. The sky flickered between the moonlight present, and a bright and shining daylight. The ghost town was a nice safe distance away, but still close enough to the river. And Thomas had conveniently left it out of every conversation. While Nakima must currently be scrambling, he still maintained a grip on time because the moonlight persisted. He was a lot stronger than she had thought.

But she really was better than she gave herself credit for.

"What was that?" Thomas asked.

"That?" Tess said, motioning toward the hill. "That's the second wave of attack. See, I told Arbor to take our rookie guardians of Order up to the ghost town just in case something was there."

"Second wave?" Thomas asked, still confused.

"Did I forget to tell you that?" Tess said with a frown. "So sorry, partner. But you see, I have trust issues."

And with that, he shot the dart at her head at the exact same moment she shot lightning from both arms. The two met in between them. The dart sucked the energy into a black hole hovering in front of her face, but then exploded into the air. For the second time in much too soon a period, a blast sent Tess flying through the air.

## Thirty-three

Chloe kicked against the man in the trench coat as he took another step toward the veil.

"Don't you want to go back to your body?" the man said. "Go back to your body."

Chloe kicked against him again, pushing away. On the one hand, she desperately wanted to be back in that car. But on the other, she knew this was wrong. It just felt wrong. The closer she got, the more she felt it. Like a kid searching through her mother's purse. Not that Chloe had ever had the best moral compass. She cheated on math exams after all. But she could still remember the first time she had ever crossed that boundary. It pricked against her skin and made the air around her feel heavy. This was the same feeling, only worse. It did not prick against her skin but stuck there like slime.

She couldn't let him do this to her. But she didn't have the energy to fight anymore. That last blast from the chain still buzzed in her ears. They were only ten feet away from the veil when the blast at the top of the hill sounded. Her assailant hesitated, looking up. She took that opportunity to push against him. She shot her energy at him, which was nothing. But the blast from the chains knocked him to the ground.

He had ripped the stake from the ground to get her close enough to the veil. Chloe picked it up, and while screaming, drove the stake through his chest. Her whole body shook—partly from fatigue and partly from the surge of energy that made the whole world swerve. She didn't know what she had been expecting. She figured he wouldn't bleed. But she thought maybe he'd seep black goo or his insides would burn like they always do on television shows. Nothing happened though. He just looked up at her, irritated.

He cried out as he ripped the stake from his chest and tossed it aside. Chloe screamed, running in the opposite direction. A hand caught her ankle and Chloe flew toward the ground. She slammed into it with too much physical impact, considering she was outside her body at the moment.

Chloe scrambled to her feet. As the man grabbed her once more, she could finally see her friends. They were by the group at the river, but there was a team of six guards. Dylan and Cameron were throwing fists, but it didn't look good. The chanting was deafening as she was pushed closer to the tear in the veil.

When they reached the tear once more, another blast sounded. This time, something hard hit them and Chloe found her face planted into the ground once more. When she looked up, she found Tess lying flat on top of the man in the trench coat. She blinked, looking as disoriented as a boxer who had just endured a blow to the head.

"Tess!" Chloe shouted.

Tess groaned and pushed herself up. "We've got to get you back to your door."

"Agreed!"

The man rose to his feet, turning on Tess. She looked like she was in no shape to fight him off. Chloe could have sworn a pistol sounded. Tess jerked, shoving the man in the trench coat in front of her. He stumbled forward and a black dart hit his shoulder, disappearing beneath flesh. Chloe turned in the direction of the shot. Thomas stood with a gun raised, smoke rising from the barrel.

The man in the trench coat jerked rigid, screaming. His entire body vibrated as he fell back to the ground. He kicked against the dirt, body shimmering. As his image slowly faded, Tess grabbed Chloe's hand and pulled her down the field and further from the road.

"What was that?" Chloe screamed.

"Don't worry. He only has one more shot left!"

Chloe continued to run. It was like the woman thrived on not making any sense. "One shot left justifies worrying!"

Tess laughed. She actually laughed. Like she was enjoying this. Who knew? Maybe she was.

Chloe pulled back, stopping. "Wait. Was that Thomas?"

"Yeah," Tess said, pulling her forward once more. "Isn't that great?"

"Great?"

"He's part of the Darkness."

*What's so great about that?* In fact, that seemed the opposite of great. Here she was betting her life on this woman to protect her, when Tess had clearly lost her mind.

The two of them ducked behind a boulder, the darkness of night making it hard to see Tess. "That's what he said about you."

Tess looked down at her torn shirt. "I don't have enough energy for another large blast. We'll have to figure out another way to hurt him."

Chloe looked over the rock, but all she could see was Paul. He was kicking and screaming at the car and at Becca. "I don't like it here! Make them stop!"

Becca raised her hands, palms out. Chloe couldn't hear what she was trying to say over Paul's shouts. Paul continued to pace. She thought she heard a siren. When she looked at the road, she could barely see Addie. She was jumping up and down on the road, trying to flag them down.

What would happen with Dylan and Cameron when the cops arrived? What would happen to her if the paramedics tried to revive her and she wasn't in her door?

"We're running out of time," Chloe said to Tess.

Tess nodded. "I know. But I'm out of ideas."

"My group is trying to fight on their side, but it's not working."

Tess jerked. "Wait. You have people on your side?"

Chloe frowned. "Yes. You can't see them?"

"They aren't on this side." Tess looked back over the rock. Thomas was searching only a few feet away, gun pointed. "Can they hear you?"

"Only after the veil tore."

Tess nodded. "I need you back at the veil."

"What?" Chloe said too loudly. Thomas turned on them, his steps crunching against the grass.

Tess grabbed her hand. They took off back toward the rip in the veil. It must have shocked Thomas, because he stopped for a moment before taking pursuit.

"They have to disrupt the connection between the two worlds. It's too strong on this side. But if they can break the connection, then everything shuts down."

The two of them skidded to a stop in front of the veil. Tess turned her back to Chloe, electricity crackling along her body. She shot a few bolts toward Thomas. "Now, Chloe!"

Chloe turned to face the tear. The dew of the night drifted through, bringing with it a chill. "Becca!"

Becca turned, her whole body shaking.

"Becca! Tell Paul to help Dylan. You guys need to stop them. It's the only way!"

Becca nodded. She got in Paul's path, but he just pushed her away.

"This isn't right, this isn't right, this isn't right," Paul said in his own little chant.

Tess shot lightning bolts from her side once more. Chloe couldn't see the attack, but figured they were getting much too close. "Paul, the group! Go to the river!"

Paul pounded a clenched fist against his head. Chloe shook her head. "Tess, it's not working!"

"Just step through," Thomas said from behind her. "It's the only way to stop this!"

When Chloe turned from the tear, she could see him approaching with two other beings. One was a tiger with red and black fur, and the other was an elf with disheveled hair, pointed teeth, and dark eyes just like those in a horror movie.

"Tess," she said.

"Run," Tess said as she swung her hands in front of her, sending bolts as she did. Chloe took off toward the road. Headlights and screams and crunching metal pounded against her ears as she neared.

Something caught her ankle and she fell to the ground once more. When she flipped over, she found the tiger circling. It growled at her. Just then, a scream made the ground shake.

When Chloe looked up, she found Paul charging down by the river. He was pelting rocks at the chanting group. Dylan and Cameron dove to avoid the onslaught of rocks. Paul screamed again and the whole dream world shook. He had such energy in his outburst. It even caused the creatures of Dream to stop their fighting, they were looking around with dazed expressions.

Thomas grabbed Chloe by the arm, and pulled her screaming toward the veil. Turning from the smoldering elf, Tess took off after them. Out of nowhere, a tiger shot out from behind, long claws striking at Tess. She tried to turn a shoulder on him, but he had sliced through her shirt, allowing white light to shine through the rips in her skin.

"You're fading, my friend," Thomas said to her as he pushed Chloe closer.

Tess tried to come forward, but the tiger pounced again. She blocked him with lightning, but the bolts seemed dimmer. Thomas was right. She truly was fading. Her image flickered the more she fought, the light in her arm seeping out her energy with every second.

Chloe fought against Thomas, but she no longer had the energy. She wanted to lie down and go to sleep. She wanted to just close her eyes and let this be enough. Chloe threw an elbow at him, knowing she couldn't let him win. At the same time, she realized there was very little they could do. Even with all the fighting across the valley, this was it. This was where the battle was won or lost.

Chloe dug her feet into the ground as the tear neared. She cried out, pushing and pushing. The world shook again with Paul's scream. Her foot crossed the threshold as Paul threw a rock, pelting one of the chanters in the head at close range. The chanter's body went limp and he fell to the ground as Dylan and Cameron fought with the rest. And just like that, an orange blast blew the circle on the dream side apart. The entire world shook with the force of an earthquake this land hadn't felt since the eighteen-hundreds. Everyone fell as the blast rushed over them. It crashed against the veil in a fireball.

Chloe felt her body surge up into the air and slam back onto the ground. The world spun in front of her. But when it stopped spinning, she rolled onto her back and watched the sky. Swirls of twilight, darkness, and bright blue sky circled above her. Stars appeared and disappeared along with the sun and many stages of the moon. The sky finally settled into a twilight pink. Cicadas sang and the grasses swayed in an easy breeze.

When Chloe pushed herself to a seat, she started to cry. The car and her friends were no longer there. More importantly, neither was the tear in the veil.

## Thirty-four

Screams and shouts pushed past the ringing in her ears. Tess pressed her hand to her temple. What had happened? Where was she? She squeezed her eyes shut before the image of her attacker came to mind. Tess forced herself onto shaky legs. With sheer determination, she primed her arms for any attack, but the world swayed beneath her. The fatigue welled up inside her once more, but she tried her hardest to fight it back.

The tiger that had been attacking her remained limp on the ground. The blood rushing from his head wound made Tess suspect he'd never get up. A large rock glistened with fresh blood and fur, confirming his head trauma. It was an unfortunate place for him to land after that blast, but fortunate for her.

Tess turned around. The imperfections of the tear were completely gone. All she could see were the rolling desert fields of the dream world, tinted in pink light that was quickly changing to the crystal blue skies of summer. Seasons didn't typically change so quickly, even without the presence of time. Nakima must have really affected the natural sway on this side. Nakima. Thomas.

Tess looked around her. Chloe was missing, and so was Thomas. A large blast sounded from the direction of the ghost town. With it came the shouts of a war party. Nakima must have escaped because Arbor came charging down the hill with his band of amateur guardians of Order. The group collided with members of the Darkness who had once been guarding the chanting circle. There was nothing to guard anymore. Only the mangled body parts of the creatures who once stood in the circle. The blast must have torn them apart. She could only hope Nakima had earned the same fate.

Tess scanned the field. This wasn't over until Chloe was back behind her door. But she had to find Chloe before that could happen. What was Thomas up to now? Then she saw them. They were passing a group fighting near the blasted circle, heading toward the river.

Tess took a deep breath. She had the energy for one more fight. She could do this. She forced her feet to push her into a run, charging down the hill. The road still pulsed red, but the mist of the river had returned to its typical purple. Out of the corner of her eye, Tess could see Nakima flying down into the cottonwoods lining the river. This must be a backup plan of some sort. She had to get there.

Tess had to zap creatures of the Darkness before reaching the banks of the river. In all worlds, this was an Arizona river. Most people elsewhere called it a creek. The water trickled northward, barely able to cover the rocks lining the bed. The grasses grew thicker near the edges and leaves crunched under her shoes as Tess came to a stop.

Purple fog made it hard to see across the bank. From this distance, she could feel the energy surge from the fog into her body. It brought an unnatural new life surging through her body. She had to be careful. The fog was like a drug. It might make her feel invincible, but it only masked her fatigue. It didn't replenish her energy supply.

"No!" she heard Chloe shout from her right. Tess turned, running up river. Kamahalan was over here somewhere. She was not alone, even though it certainly felt that way.

Thomas' silhouette emerged from the purple fog. The skies changed into a bright blue, the unobstructed sun hovering high above them. The rays of the light pierced into the fog, highlighting the images of ten creatures. The only figure she could make out was Nakima, his wings stretched out above his head. Tess pushed forward, ducking behind a cottonwood.

Thomas shoved Chloe to her knees in front of Nakima.

"We're done," Thomas said. "The veil is whole once more and we've lost half our men."

Nakima shook his head, his mane shuffling. "No. We still have her. We need to regroup. She cannot survive long outside her door. She's already weakening."

Chloe whimpered, still on her hands and knees. She certainly looked ready to curl into a fetal position.

Tess eased herself closer, staying on the outskirts. She didn't see any other members of the Darkness lurking nearby. Most probably were fighting the battle on the field. A frog croaked downstream along with a bird chirping high above them in just another example of the crazy warp in time and season trying to right itself.

"What's the plan?" Thomas asked, looking around him.

Tess thought she saw movement behind him, but the purple fog made it hard to know for sure. She had to be smart about this. She couldn't just plow her way to them. She had to conserve her energy, plan the best ways to use whatever she had left. But if the water could help the Darkness, maybe it could help her too. Tess looked down at her fading hands. Upon command, her hands glowed with blue electricity. Even if she perished saving Chloe, at least it would be for the right reasons.

"Bring her to me," Nakima said.

Chloe cried out as a creatures of the Darkness pulled her to her feet. They held her steady in front of Nakima. He stood with his head tall, his wings spread high above him. The fog swirled around them, electricity making the hairs on her arm stand on end.

The sky above them rushed from blue to pink to black and back to blue in a cycle that looked like a time-lapse video. The cloudless skies rumbled around them.

"Gather everyone into the water. We'll use its power to tear the veil right here."

"I thought you said—" Thomas began. The thickness of the fog did not diminish the lethal look that cut him off. Apparently they were moving on to the inferior plan B. Tess did not want to see what that entailed.

Right before she pushed outside of the protection of the cottonwood, Tess saw movement behind Thomas. She was sure of it. Kamahalan moved on the other side of the riverbank. Tess could only hope she had a group of guardians with her.

Tess nodded. Now or never. She moved out from the cottonwood and charged down the bank. The water levels of the river rose and fell in rapid succession as the sky above them continued its psychedelic change from night to day.

Thomas turned just as she neared. She didn't have a shot at him though. Her feet were knocked out from under her, and the damp earth pounded against her face with the impact of a perfect right hook. Tess rolled just in time to miss the jab of a spike. She grumbled. The spike was connected to a long, scaled tail. *Great.* She jumped to her feet as the scorpion repositioned its tail above its head. She had hated scorpions in real life. The ones as big as a Labrador in the dream world were even more disturbing.

Before the scorpion could attack once more, a gunshot echoed across the valley. It took only a split second for Tess to remember Thomas' last shot and dive to the side. Her arm burst into fiery pain as she fell into the riverbed. Instead of landing on rock, Tess found herself submerged in a vast body of water. The current kicked her body around as Tess flailed.

She couldn't decide what to focus on first: the pain eating at her arm, or the current sweeping her toward the rocky bottom. The bullet must have just grazed her, or else she suspected she'd be in more pain. The water rushed around her, turning her over and over.

The pain in her arm radiated throughout her body as the water muffled her screams.

As clear as yesterday she could see it. The parking lot had been dim in the twilight. Her footsteps echoed in her head. That economics test was a lot easier than she had thought. After today, she was one step closer to graduation. One step closer to a new life.

Her phone buzzed in her pocket. She pulled it out, stepping over the curb and onto the asphalt. She didn't bother looking at her surroundings. Most students were still inside. *Outback tonight to celebrate???* Triple question mark. His way of asking how her test went. She had lucked out. How could she have found such greatness after such darkness?

Tess passed the first parked car, her fingers quickly typing. The burning pain in her gut was quickly followed by a punch. Her phone clicked against the asphalt as Tess gasped for breath. That's when she saw him. His face was twisted with such hate, but his eyes were already dead. The reason, in the version of the story he always told, was it was her fault. It always was.

*The baby*, she thought just in time for another jab to her chest. She thought she had screamed. She couldn't remember the sound. All she remembered was the unnatural gurgling. Someone behind her screamed. Then there was darkness. Always darkness. He took everything from her. At first, he had taken her confidence. Then he took her friends and her connection to anything outside of himself. He had taken her soul. She thought she had regained that, but in one instant, he took it back. Then, he took her life.

She had been defined by him. Her scars were his. But in this moment in the river, with the images flashing in front of her, Tess wanted the chance she'd never had. She wanted the chance to fight back. She wanted the chance to not let him take anything else from her. She wanted the chance to finally rise above him.

Tess clenched her fists, screaming in the water. It boiled around her, building. In a rush, it pushed her skyward. It held her as tall as the cottonwood branches. She held out her arms, electricity shooting from them. These were no longer his. This body, this life, these scars… they were no longer a product of him. The cottonwoods burst into flames, embers raining down on members of the Darkness cowering below.

Thomas stared at her with mouth agape. He thought she was weak. That's why he used her. That's why he thought he could destroy her. Tess screamed down at him. The earth shook. Electricity shot from every scar on her body, creating a force field. The Members of the Darkness who tried to flee immediately turned to ashen corpses upon contact.

Nakima turned on her. He raised his wings, the clouds above circling dark grey. He stomped his foot and a strong wind blew against her. The water holding Tess up started tilting backward, but she held her stance. She could barely see past the bright light shooting from every scar on her body. She released his power over her in one push of energy, determined never to let him control her thoughts again. She had control. And she was not going to let herself down one more time.

Lightning shot from the skies, striking her. White light burst around her and the water dropped. The rocks of the creek jabbed at her legs as Tess fell. All around her, flesh smoked and charred. Nakima bared his teeth, coming closer. Just then, Tess heard a loud roar.

Kamahalan's eyes glowed yellow as she approached from behind him. She rushed under Nakima, slicing his underbelly with her claws. Nakima stopped, his wings drooping. The river turned red as Kamahalan came around to face him. She grabbed his dazed head, looking deep into his eyes. "Nakima, Deputy of Dream. By the power of the Governess, I relieve you of your position." With one movement, Kamahalan jerked Nakima's head. A sickening snap echoed and Nakima fell to join his insides on the ground.

Before Thomas could move, five guardians of Spirit surrounded him. Kamahalan turned on him. "Thomas, Chief Guardian of Order. By the power of the Governess, I relieve you of your position and hereby order you to the realm of Judgment."

Thomas screamed as the spirits shimmered with gold light. All six images faded from view, leaving behind Kamahalan and the carnage of the Darkness. The world swirled beneath her as Kamahalan approached.

"You know what your problem is?" Kamahalan stopped when she was just a few feet away. "You think you can do everything yourself. But sometimes," Kamahalan offered a hand to her, "you need to ask for help."

Tess took the hand and allowed Kamahalan to assist her to standing. "Where did the guardians of Spirit come from?"

"I had a chat with Deputy Lisa. Her spirits arrived shortly after your waterworks display. I've never seen anyone ascend before."

"Ascend?" Tess asked, the world swaying again.

Kamahalan smiled at her. "Another time. Get this girl back to her door. We can clean the rest of this up."

Tess nodded. "Gladly." The rocks slipped under her first few steps, but as Tess approached Chloe, she felt her steps come with more strength. Chloe looked up at her, eyes wide. "Let's get you back," Tess said, placing a hand on her shoulder.

Chloe didn't seem to notice the carnage around her as Tess rushed toward her open door. She was practically carrying Chloe by the time they reached the broken door. Before stepping through, Chloe turned. "Did we do it?"

"Tell your friends they were a big help."

Chloe smiled. "I will." Chloe moved toward the threshold then stopped. "You're not coming with me?"

Tess shook her head. "I have to stay on this side. There's a lot to answer for. But I won't leave your door until I know it's safe. I promise you."

Chloe nodded. "Thank you, Tess."

"Go," Tess said forcefully. Chloe smiled at her, then stepped through the threshold.

The door actually sighed with her return, shaking on its hinges. Tess stood off to the side as the bodies of those inside flew out. The door stretched, shifted, and rattled. Finally, with a loud bang, the door swung shut. Everything looked like it had the first day when she had arrived at this door. Well, except for the carnage outside.

Tess leaned against the closed door and rubbed her eyes. Her body ached. She slid down the door and sat on the pebbles, closing her eyes. She felt ready to die. She could go just like this: saving another soul from an unjust ending. That would be her legacy. Nothing he had defined for her. She had defined herself in spite of him. Tess sighed, leaning her head against the door. Yes. She could die just like this.

# THIRTY-FIVE

The room was dark, sunlight trickling in from the window on her right. A persistent beeping cut through the silence of her thoughts, pulling her away from the comfort of sleep. Chloe stirred, but her entire body ached. She opened her eyes.

There was about an hour's worth of chaos that followed. Her aunt immediately started shouting. Then there were nurses and doctors and people she didn't know. There was even a cop at some point. When everyone determined she was fine, they left her for a moment.

In the end, she wasn't sure exactly what had happened. Something had been said about legal repercussions of running away and having to answer questions about a car wreck, but ultimately the most important thing was she would live. They threw around words like "miracles" and "the power of seatbelts".

She was still listening to the beeping when Dylan knocked on the door. She smiled at him as he entered. "They let you in?"

He smiled at her, settling on a chair beside the bed. "Your aunt convinced them it would be good for a friend to visit."

The room had felt so small and cold before. Now with the presence of someone she didn't have to lie to—someone who knew the truth—she finally found some comfort. "A friend, you say?"

"My mom has been bringing food to your house the entire week. She's informed your family of our close friendship that saved my life from drugs and death." He paused. "She can be kind of dramatic."

Chloe shifted in the bed, each movement aching. She pushed a button on the side to get to a sitting position, the mattress shuffling. "Well, she's not entirely wrong."

Dylan eyed the IV drip. "Yeah, I guess so."

"How free are we to talk?" Chloe asked. The closed door looked heavy, but at the moment it seemed like such a small barrier.

"There's a guard at the door, but we're good."

"How did you find me?" Chloe asked.

The monitor beeped in silence for a moment as Dylan seemed to battle with where to start. "Well, we arrived to find your cousin screaming at her teachers and Paul screaming at the street. We couldn't take your cousin, so we took Paul."

"What about his dog?"

"That dog is annoying. He smells like dirt and always tries to lick your face."

Chloe giggled.

"Anyway, he pointed us in the direction you went. We followed the van through Palominas, past Bisbee, but lost them in Tombstone. I have to hand it to Paul. He can really get people moving when he's frantic. He helped us find a house where the van was. Neighbors said they saw you inside the Mustang. We just got lucky finding you on the highway coming back to Sierra Vista."

"What happened to Ricky?"

Dylan shook his head. "Thrown from the car when it crashed. He didn't make it."

Chloe closed her eyes. It was scary to think that something could control him so much it ultimately killed him. "Wait. You said all week. How long have I been here?"

"You were in a coma for a little over a week."

No wonder the chaos. Now they would have to give her some sympathy when addressing the whole issue of running away. Life always had consequences. She just hoped she could find some leniency. "What's the official story?" Chloe asked, gripping at the blanket.

Dylan looked at the closed door, then back at her. "We knew each other when we were little. You saw what I was going through and wanted to help me. You went to meet with Becca in the park, but found me there instead. You all staged an intervention and saved my life. But we knew Ricky was heading down the same path. You didn't want to go home because you thought your aunt was going to lock you away. So you ran away to help us. You went to talk with Molly and turn yourself in when Ricky came and kidnapped you."

Chloe whistled softly. "That is some story." The truth merged with such an intricate lie. She didn't know if she could have thought of it, but it held enough of the truth to make the rest of such a crazy story seem reasonable.

"You know, I think the cops were just happy to find the crew created by the creatures who possessed me. They had an SUV filled with all kinds of drugs and stuff. They really feel like we helped them take down a big drug ring preying on the county's teenagers." Dylan paused, before adding, "Addie is an interesting child. She's very good at lying."

That would be good to remember for the future. She had set out on a mission to save some people. That wasn't entirely false. And she had also helped a few people on this side as well. Maybe that was her purpose. To help people. And her purpose came as some of the best realizations in life do... unexpectedly. A light knock on the door marked the entrance of her aunt.

Chloe smiled at her.

"Dylan, Chloe needs her rest now, okay?"

Dylan nodded. "I'll see you later," he said to Chloe.

Chloe smiled. "Of course." Her new circle of friends consisted of a blunt-spoken rodeo child, an ex-possessed drug dealer, and two people who saw things not of this world. Then there was Paul. How life could change without warning. Even if they looked like misfits on the outside, Chloe knew they were better than any friends she had ever chosen for herself. Sometimes things just worked themselves out.

Her aunt settled into the chair once Dylan left. "You gave us quite a scare."

"I'm sorry I'm so much trouble," Chloe said, her voice cracking.

"No," her aunt said, reaching out a hand to pat her leg. "I'm sorry we gave up on you."

"I shouldn't have run away. That wasn't fair."

Her aunt leaned back, wringing her hands. "While I was watching you here, in this bed, I wondered if I drove you to it. I just never know how to help you."

Chloe reached out with her hand, which her aunt readily grasped. "I've put you all through so much. You should have left me on a doorstep somewhere, but you never did. Not even when I drove Molly's dad away."

Her aunt shook her head with more force as Chloe continued. "No. Her dad left for a lot of reasons. You might have been one, but you were not the only one. I am happier now. I promise."

"Until I chase him away, too."

Her aunt smiled at her. "When I wasn't here, he was sitting with you. And when you ran away, he was flooding Facebook and Twitter with messages. I even had to yell at him for posting your picture up around our neighborhood like you were some lost dog." Her aunt laughed at the thought. "He's not going anywhere." Her aunt caressed her hand. "No. You are stuck with us, my dear."

"I promise to be better."

"Don't promise to be better. Just promise to do better." Her aunt kissed her forehead. "Let me get you something to eat."

Chloe lay back on the fluffy pillow, and stared out the window. She stayed there for a moment before she heard a familiar voice.

"Man. Even in death, I hate hospitals."

Chloe smiled at Tess. She stood in her typical leather jacket. While her image swayed like a reflection on a lake, she was clearer than Thomas was the time he had tried to enter her world. Under her right shoulder sparkled a large insignia of Scorpius. "If this is a dream, it sucks," Chloe said.

Tess laughed. "I agree. No. Apparently, deputies are strong enough to approach the veil. Although most don't have a reason to."

"Deputy?"

Tess frowned. "Yeah. Apparently I ascended into power just as the Deputy of Dream retired." Tess adjusted her jacket, suddenly looking a little out of her comfort zone. Chloe could only imagine. The woman seemed more like a loner, and now she was in charge of a long list of creatures.

"Retired. Is that what they're calling it?"

"It's more politically correct than 'gutted and slayed'," Tess said. "Anyway, my boss transferred to Deputy of Dream and I was promoted to Deputy of Order."

"Congratulations."

"We'll see how long they can tolerate me," Tess said with a wink. "Especially after I made a former member of the Darkness my new Chief Guardian."

"Oh?"

"Yeah. He's this chameleon boy who helped me out a lot. A little annoying, but he kind of grew on me. Plus, he earned it with his help destroying the Darkness. And, he had a brilliant idea to help assure the Darkness doesn't get so far anymore without detection."

"A boy seeking retribution. I like it."

Tess moved closer to the bed, her image shifting. "Look. I don't have a lot of time. But I came here for something more important than just to reconnect."

*She really had to work on her people skills if she was going to be in a leadership position.* But Chloe kept the thought to herself. "Okay."

"I want to establish a new department within the Department of Order. We're calling it the Department of Earth. Since the Darkness used both sides in their plot to destroy the world, I think having a defense on both sides is needed."

"To watch for what, exactly?"

"Possessions, to start. Any abnormal activity. Just because one crisis is averted doesn't mean you are no longer needed. Your group can help us completely circumvent future attacks before they become so dangerous. Like what you did for Dylan."

"Of course," Chloe said. She shouldn't feel inclined to continue her role as leader to the misfits. She shouldn't want to continue interacting with crazy dreams and things unspoken of in this world. But she also knew she could make a difference. She could use what life dealt her to make something better of it. How could she pass that up? "Do I get a title and everything?"

Tess hesitated. "Chief Guardian of Order, Earth Division."

Chloe wrinkled her nose. "That's not very catchy."

"None of them are."

The joy in Chloe dissipated quickly. She looked toward the door and frowned. "I just wish I had some purpose here on Earth, too. You know, one that other people could see." She looked back at Tess and added, "Can't I matter in this life too?"

Tess frowned at her. "Chloe. If this has taught you anything, it is that your life is in your control. If you want purpose, then go find it and make it happen."

"That's easier said than done," Chloe complained.

Tess nodded. "Everything of value is worth the effort. Stop trying to overcome your differences. Take it from someone who knows. The key is to embrace every flaw with your strengths. Both make you complete. The trick is to use them all to make your life better."

Tess looked at the door and sighed. "I have to go. But we'll keep in touch."

Chloe nodded. Tess stepped away and was gone in an instant. If Chloe told her aunt she was seeing dead people in her room, they'd definitely take her off the medication. As her aunt re-entered, she was tempted, just so she could emerge from the medical fog. But instead she just smiled. It was time to take back control.

# Epilogue
*Eight years later*

Chloe looked at herself in the mirror hanging in the lobby. Her brown hair was cut short in the back and longer in the front. The stylist said it would make her look more professional. She wished for her long hair back. Maybe not the black and green of her youth, but she missed the length.

She turned from the mirror and looked at the lobby before her. She had gone with the pale blue with black leather chairs. Her aunt had talked her into the green plants tucked into the front corners; she had to admit it added a welcoming feel to the room. She walked through the space. Her engagement ring glistened against the light as she pushed open the glass door. The summer air hit her like an oven, but she didn't care. Traffic buzzed down Fry Boulevard as she turned to face the sign hanging above the entrance. *San Pedro Crisis Center*.

She had started a "youth in crisis" group in her final year of high school. That dream had morphed into something much bigger. She wanted to matter. And the only way she could matter was by helping others. She wanted to help them, no matter the difficulty. She satisfied her aunt's push to get a bachelor's degree in business before she opened the doors, but she had already had a business plan and was looking for investors before walking across the stage for her diploma. Now, at twenty-three, she was ready to start her own business. She was ready to take her own experiences and finally use them to matter. Tess was right. She didn't have to overcome her demons. She just had to learn how to make them work for her.

The door chimed as Paul pushed it open. "It's three. The newspaper will be here at three-fifteen. Dylan said not to let you get distracted."

Chloe smiled at him. Paul was a valuable asset to the business. He was so task-oriented; he served her well as an assistant.

"Now," he said when she didn't move.

*Well, it's not like there weren't edges to smooth out.* Chloe laughed, heading in his direction. Besides, Molly still liked debating with him about which Harry Potter character was the best, and what Star Wars movie had the most plot holes.

As Chloe moved past him, Paul added, "Dylan said you have to be done no later than four o'clock. You're meeting the florist at four o'clock."

They still had a lot of planning to do before the wedding. It was her own fault. Dylan had proposed a year ago, but she wanted to open the business first. And she had always wanted a fall wedding, but Dylan refused to listen to another year of questions by his mother. That left two major events happening in the span of a few months. But she was built for this.

Becca stood behind the front desk with her arms crossed, surveying the room. "I can't believe we open tomorrow."

Becca was halfway through her degree in child psychology, but she still worked as an office assistant for now. Chloe had promised her a job the moment she graduated. Addie appeared from down the hall, practically skipping. She was still earning her associates through Cochise College while attending rodeos. She hadn't changed much, in fact might be a little more wild than her youth, but she was a valuable asset with her community connections. A man with short, sandy-blond hair followed behind her. He was one of the main investors.

He circled around the front desk and approached Chloe with an extended hand. To say Jesse Montgomery came from wealth was an understatement. The city was all abuzz about how his family had acquired such wealth, but Chloe didn't care about rumors.

"You have done a great job here, Ms. Parker."

"Thank you, Mr. Montgomery."

He circled, still taking the place in. "I just wish I had something like this back when my nephew had his troubles," he marveled.

Charley Montgomery had been sent away during Chloe's freshman year of high school. There were two main rumors. One: that he had gotten mixed up in drugs and a teen rivalry. Two: that he was a sorcerer with an evil plot of revenge. After what Chloe had seen in her life, she wasn't going to judge the people who believed the latter.

"I think we can do a lot of good here," Chloe said with what she hoped was a businesslike nod.

"I'm sure you will."

"Where's your nephew now?"

Jesse grabbed his sunglasses from their perch on the top of his head. "He lives in Phoenix now working as a buyer's agent with some realty firm up there. He makes it down with his fiancé to visit every now and then."

"Well, give your wife my best."

Jesse smiled at her. "Of course. She said to thank you for the apple pie. Said if you wanted to start a bakery, that I should help fund that, too."

It was easy to forget the city was a small town until people really started talking. Jesse's wife had been Molly's teacher back when the whole dream invasion started. She sat with Molly for a long time, comforting her after Chloe's abduction. She had only been engaged to Jesse at that time. Most gossip revolved around the shock that Jesse could find a girl after driving his last girlfriend out of town. Most of those gossips must never have met his wife. She was the nicest lady. She even helped Molly get a part-time babysitting job in high school. Chloe was pretty sure she was the reason her cousin had declared she was going to become a teacher one night before her high-school graduation.

Molly would make a good teacher. Chloe hadn't seemed to mess her up too much with her youthful struggles. Her cousin had turned out to be such a compassionate girl. She put them all to shame. And she had turned out to be just as much of a geek as predicted, graduating top five in her class. It earned her a pretty hefty university scholarship. Between that and the other scholarships, her cousin was going to college on practically a full-ride. That would be a good thing when she realized how much teachers make in the state of Arizona.

Chloe said goodbye as Jesse pushed out of the building. It was only a few moments before Paul was back up front.

"It's three-fifteen." Paul said. "She should be here."

Chloe grinned as the sedan pulled into their parking lot. "I see her." As Chloe moved toward the door, she found Tess standing in the corner. A boy with green scales stood to her side with his hands clasped very professionally behind him. Chloe smiled at her, holding up her hands.

Tess nodded her approval before disappearing. Chloe watched the space. Tess was right. She had needed to take control. When she trusted that she could, she finally found her purpose.

"It's rude to leave her out there," Paul said from behind.

Chloe pushed out the door of her business. She extended her hand to the short woman approaching. "Welcome to the *San Pedro Crisis Center*. My name's Chloe Parker, and I'm the owner."

# About the Author

B.J. (author of the *Atlantis Series, Lord of Nightmares,* and *Challenging Fate*) currently resides in her hometown in Arizona where she enjoys instructing students in high school and college. She discovered her passion for writing while doing weekly writing assignments in the sixth grade and has been hooked on the craft of storytelling ever since. She is a member of Sisters in Crime national and Tucson chapter. She's also a graduate of two creative writing classes through the Odyssey Writing Workshops. For more information about her, speaking events, and any upcoming books, please visit her website: www.bjkurtz.com.

Made in the USA
San Bernardino, CA
10 January 2019